NO PUCKING WAY

USA TODAY BESTSELLING AUTHORS
C.R. JANE
MAY DAWSON

Devils

Join Our Readers' Group

Stay up to date with C.R. Jane by joining her Facebook readers' group, C.R.'s Fated Realm. Ask questions, get first looks at new books/series, and have fun with other book lovers!

Join C.R. Jane's Group

Join May Dawson's Wild Angels to chat directly with May and other readers about her books, enter giveaways, and generally just have fun!

Join May's Group

Sit the f*ck down and read hockey romance like a good girl....

Please Read...

Dear readers, please be aware that this is a dark romance and as such can and will contain possible triggering content. Elements of this story are purely fantasy, and should not be taken as acceptable behavior in real life. This is a reverse harem romance, which means that there is more than one love interest and the heroine will end up with all of them. Our love interests are possessive, obsessive, and do a lot of crazy shit. Red Flag Renegades rejoice. These men will do anything to get their girl.

Themes include ice hockey, stalking, a scene of dubious consent (but Kennedy loves it) manipulation, birth control tampering, dark obsessive themes, sexual scenes. There is not cheating involved.

Prepare to enter the world of the Devils...you've been warned.

No Pucking Way

I woke up in the hospital five years ago with no idea of who I am...

Every day, I walk aimlessly around the city, searching for anything that helps me remember my past.

I don't find it until I apply for a job at the local hockey arena, home of the NHL team, the Devils.

Three sexy hockey players inside look...familiar.

They all insist they don't know me.

But they watch me. Every day.

Their silence continues until a handsome, tattooed stranger dressed in a suit saunters into the arena and starts sweet talking me.

Then they jump off the ice, ready to fight him to the death.

And for some reason...he seems ready to return the favor.

Now, I'm being swept into a life of glamorous darkness...**and into a war between men I evidently used to love.**

Asheville

Devils

TEAM ROSTER

CARTER HAYES	CAPTAIN, #1, GOALIE
JACK CAMERON	ASST. CAPTAIN, #27, LEFT WING
SEBASTIAN WRIGHT	ASST. CAPTAIN, #14, DEFENSEMAN
DAVID WEISS	#42, DEFENSEMAN
JONATHAN MACHOWSKI	#18, LEFT WING
MICHAEL LOGAN	#12, DEFENSEMAN
FOX ANDREWS	#2, GOALIE,
ADAM RODRIGUES	#4, RIGHT WING
SERGEI IVANOV	#32, DEFENSEMAN
DAVID SMITH	#12, CENTER
MICHAEL WILLIAMS	#48, DEFENSEMAN
ROBERT ANDERSON	#17, FORWARD
MATTHEW BROWN	#9, RIGHT WING
PATRICK LEWIS	#3, DEFENSEMAN
JAMES TAYLOR	#41, FORWARD
ANDREW MILLER	#8, FORWARD
RICH CLARK	#88, FORWARD
BENJAMIN HALL	#6, DEFENSEMAN
AKIHIRO TANAKA	#26, FORWARD
VIKTOR HENRIKSSON	#24, FORWARD
IVAN PETROV	#16, FORWARD
DIEGO FERNANDEZ	#20, FORWARD
BILL KING	#4, FORWARD
DANIEL STUBBS	#60, WING
ALEX TURNER	#53, CENTER
PORTER MAST	#6, DEFENSEMAN
LOGAN EDWARDS	#9, DEFENSEMAN
CLARK DOBBINS	#16, WING
KYLE NETHERLAND	#20, DEFENSEMAN

COACHES

KEVIN HARRIS, HEAD COACH

MICHAEL "MIKE" SULLIVAN, ASSISTANT COACH

XAVIER MONTGOMERY, ASSISTANT COACH

TIM REED, GOALIE COACH

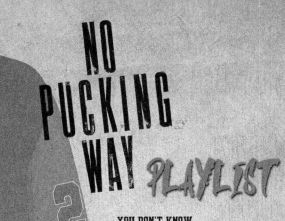

NO PUCKING WAY PLAYLIST

YOU DON'T KNOW
Inna Brandi

CLARITY
Zedd

METEORITE
Banks

ALWAYS BEEN YOU
Jessie Murph

I STILL LOVE YOU
Banks

POWER
Little Mix ft. Stormzy

NOW THAT WE DON'T TALK
Taylor Swift

BLUE JEANS
Lana Del Ray

LOVIN ON ME
Jack Harlow

ONCE UPON A DREAM
Lana Del Ray

PARTITION
Beyonce

DON'T BLAME ME
Taylor Swift

TRAITOR
Olivia Rodrigo

ANTI-HERO
Taylor Swift

LISTEN TO THE FULL PLAYLIST HERE:
HTTPS://OPEN.SPOTIFY.COM/PLAYLIST/2ZFXMG2UN2IENPQBJZSR2S?SI=A7D1ED996AB640D2

"I will personally challenge anyone who wants to get rid of fighting to a fight."
—Brian Burke

1

Kennedy

L ong before I could open my eyes, I could hear the nurse talking about her bad date.

My head swam. I kept sinking back into the darkness, no matter how much I tried to pull myself up. Sometimes it felt as if I were sinking into a fathomless black pool, the water closing over my head.

But sometimes, her voice threaded through my dreams.

"It's the absolute last time I let my sister set me up. I'm pretty sure she's pranking me now."

I couldn't hear the other voice of whoever she was talking to. Maybe they had just accepted it was best to let her go.

"I think it might be because once, when we were teenagers, we double dared each other to go streaking. And I chickened out, but she doesn't believe me. It was just in our backyard, but we had the meanest next-door-neighbor who happened to be picking her tomatoes just then. She was ringing our doorbell to talk to our mom before Chloe even got her clothes on." She let out a deep belly laugh that made me think she was still not sorry.

"Anyway, I think she's still mad, because when I called her about this date to ask why she did this to me, she said it was to help me get over my fears. Fears of what? Having a nice time?"

The darkness seemed to be pulling me back down. But I really wanted to know what this bad date was like, so I forced myself to surface, trying to open my eyes.

My lashes fluttered, but no one noticed. There was no one waiting at my bedside. I'd figured that out already. I was alone most of the time.

But not always.

There was just this nurse, moving energetically around to take care of me, chattering all the time to the friend I never heard answer.

"So she sets me up, and it's supposed to be a picnic. I usually would say a big no thank you to going anywhere less crowded than Costco on a Saturday with a first date. You never know if a guy is a creep or not. But this is my sister, right? She's looking out for me. He's not going to be a serial killer, and even if he was, he would know better than to unalive me. Because obviously, someone knows where I am. Well, unless the serial killer had low impulse control. I guess I really shouldn't have agreed to a picnic."

"But anyway, I did, and there I was. We go off into the woods and he's just got this backpack, which is a little less than I expected. I was thinking of one of those baskets like they sell at Crate & Barrel with wine and cheese...hopefully brie, I love brie. I've always wanted one of those baskets. But whatever. I'm not like high maintenance."

"Then we sit down, and he's got like... two bottles of water and a bag of chips. He tells me it's a snackwick. First of all, that's not a thing, and second of all, brie makes for a great snack. You don't take a girl on a date and feed her store brand potato chips."

"And yes, you're right. The way to my heart is through cheese. And not murdering me in the woods. At this point, I'm like, if not cheese, what's in the backpack? Is it an axe? But no! It was not an axe! It was worse!"

I'd drifted in and out of consciousness for the past few days, never quite surfacing enough to get anyone's attention. Once I'd blinked my eyes open to be greeted with bland ceiling tiles and apparently my brain had decided it could not even, and I'd fallen back to sleep.

But now when the darkness tries to claim me, I fight it.

I need to know what was worse than an axe.

"It was puppets! This crazy motherfucker pulled out two puppets. Puppets! And I'm like, oh no, I shouldn't have come out here...and he puts a puppet on each hand and they start having, like, a ventriloquist's duel. Over which one likes me more. One puppet likes my eyes a lot, but the other puppet is just all about my tits. Which is pretty fucking intense for a puppet, may I say? I'm a nurse. I can deal with gore and death, but I cannot deal with whatever that was..."

I finally managed to blink my eyes open. The light burned.

She made eye contact with me as she was fixing my blankets.

A look of complete shock crossed her face, then resolved into joy. "You're awake!"

I just wanted to ask her how she got away from the puppets.

My lips moved, but the sound that came out of my mouth didn't sound human.

It was better than facing the sterile hospital room and the fact that I had no idea how I'd gotten here.

Or what was wrong with me.

Or who I was.

Terror washed through me.

3

"I'll get the doctors," she told me, straightening, and I made another sound that made me even more terrified. I didn't want to be alone. I'd been alone so long, drifting through that darkness.

I tried to grab her wrist, and the tubes connected to my arm yanked painfully against my skin.

"It's okay," she told me, her eyes wide with concern. "You're alright."

"What?" The word didn't sound quite right either, my voice rusty from disuse.

"I don't know what happened to you, exactly," she said, sounding sympathetic. "You were hit by a car."

I tried to remember being hit by a car. I tried to remember anything. But my head ached painfully, and there was nothing in my mind but shadows, the way we half remember bits of a dream.

"Hey there." A doctor came in, tall with curly hair pulled back from a lean face. "Welcome back."

There must have been a dozen other people who followed her into the room, watching me. As if I were some kind of medical oddity. A sense of panic washed over me.

Why couldn't I remember anything?

"You've been in a coma for a month," the doctor told me gently. "It's going to take some time to get used to being back in the world with us. But you're going to be alright."

"Who's—" I frowned. "I don't remember anything."

The doctor exchanged a meaningful glance with another doctor, which made me want to scream. "You're experiencing post traumatic amnesia," she told me. "Your memories will probably come back eventually... at least, most of them."

Most of them?

"I'm fine." I tried to push myself up to sit, but my arms felt weak and boneless.

4

I felt like I had to get moving, to find out what had happened to me, to find out who I was.

"No, you're not," the doctor said gently. "But you will be."

The doctors put me through so many tests until I was exhausted. They explained that along with the loss of memory, my dreams would feel real and confusing. It was terrifying to know I was alone with no one to help me plant my feet on solid ground. No one to tell me who I really was. No one to help me sort dreams from reality, fantasy from fiction.

I fought sleep, terrified of the dreams, terrified of the dark pool. I tried to focus on the sound of the hospital outside my door, the clatter of trays being taken down the hallway, the voices outside.

But in the end, sleep swallowed me anyway.

I woke up the next morning to streaming sunlight and a familiar, cheerful voice. "But the thing is, I don't think that was even the worst date I ever went on!"

Without being prompted by her friend, she went on, "Okay, it was pretty bad. But there was the guy who took me out running, which is like the worst date. And then lunch, where I made the mistake of going to the bathroom, and he ordered for me—prune juice and kale salad. And then he started preaching to me about the benefits of prune juice, in extraordinary detail... I mean, at least I like eating chips."

My voice was so rusty when I tried to say something that I almost gave up, horrified by how weak I'd sounded.

But she rushed to me, looking delighted.

"You're awake! Sleeping Beauty!"

"How... did you find... prune man? Did your... sister strike again?" The words burned in my throat after having been intubated.

She let out a hearty, surprised laugh. "You heard all that?"

"I don't... have a choice... eavesdropping."

"You weren't eavesdropping," she told me.

I looked around for the other nurse who had also kept me company. "Where's..."

She looked around too, as if she was expecting someone else to crawl out from under the bed. "You haven't had anyone visit you, sweetie," she told me, her voice gentle.

"Who were you talking to?" I asked, because I couldn't deal with thinking anymore about how no one had come to be here for me.

"Oh," she said in surprise. "That's... you, actually. I've been talking to you a lot. You seemed like you needed a friend and... well, so do I."

She picked up my hand to shake it, since I was still weak. "Carrie."

I tried to remember my name, and a sudden headache came on, like something rupturing in my brain.

"It's alright," she told me, her usual frenetic energy ebbing away. She lay both our hands down on the bed between us. "I'll stay here with you."

And she did.

I spent the next few weeks in rehab. And the police tried to find where I'd come from.

But no one knew anything about my past, and no one came forward to claim me. Someone out there had to know me. It was so frustrating.

And humiliating.

The staff at the hospital collected the money to pay for the down payment on my first apartment. It was around the corner from the hospital—so not in the best part of town—and as I stood in the doorway a few months after I woke up, it felt like I should be somewhere else.

I should be walking into my home.

Carrie walked in with me, and somehow her usual

sparkling warmth seemed to fill the small, slightly musty-scented apartment. "Let's get these windows open. Look, we got it furnished for you. That futon came from Harley's house, but I febrezed the hell out of it—can you explain to me how a nurse can smoke?"

"We all have our vices."

"Except you," she teased me.

"Only because I don't know what they are."

My biggest vice so far was snacks from the hospital vending machine. I'd worked my way through, trying to find what I liked, hoping something would spark a memory. Had I eaten a honey bun for breakfast rushing to high school? Jelly beans out of my Easter basket when I was a kid? Pringles while watching movies with my best friend?

But nothing jogged any of my memories loose.

I did love gummy bears, though.

That was about all I knew about who I was.

"You'll find out," Carrie told me. "Your memories will almost certainly come back. You're young, you've got a healthy brain."

"Maybe." I had this weird, superstitious feeling though, like I wouldn't be able to get my memories back until I got some pieces of my life back.

Also, maybe I didn't have a healthy brain. That seemed like a pretty big assumption, looking around the world. Lots of people clearly did not have healthy brains.

I sat down on the threadbare couch and opened the plastic bag they'd given me when I left the hospital with my old clothes. Carrie had brought in clean clothes for me to wear out, but when I opened the bag, I expected something to happen. Memories to rush back. It felt like it should be a big moment.

Instead, I pulled out a black fleece hoodie, stiff with old blood, that smelled like death. There must have been so much blood. I felt suddenly sick to my stomach, and I stuffed it back into the bag.

"Do you want me to wash those for you?" Carrie asked.

"No," I said. I couldn't stand to look at the clothes anymore. I couldn't imagine who I had been when I pulled that hoodie over my head.

But as I picked up the bag to stuff into a closet until I could bear it, something gold glinted at me from inside. I knelt on the carpet to rummage through the bag and pulled out a broken necklace.

The slender gold chain had snapped. But dangling from my fingertips was a name in cursive: *Kennedy.*

A sudden surge of hope rushed through my chest. I had my name, and soon I would have the rest of my life back.

"Kennedy," I whispered. "My name is Kennedy."

Carrie stared at the necklace for a second, then her face lit up with joy as she realized what it was. She reached to hug me, and I hugged her back, clutching the name necklace so tight that it bit into my palm.

"It's nice to meet you, Kennedy," Carrie told me. "See? Everything is going to come together."

"Maybe it will," I said.

"Let's go out for a walk," Carrie said. "Maybe we'll see someplace you've been before. Someplace that jogs a memory. And at a bare minimum...I can get a Diet Coke."

I had never met anyone who loved Diet Coke the way Carrie did.

We found a 7-11 for her to get a fountain drink, which she insisted tasted better than it did from a bottle, but we didn't find any memories.

Still, as we wandered the city, a thrill ran through me.

I could turn any corner and be walking down a street I'd

walked down before, and suddenly, part of my memory would snap back into my brain like a rubber band. Any day now, any block I walked, I'd be closer to knowing who I was.

* * *

Five years later

"He took me on the worst date the other day," Carrie told me as the two of us walked down the street. "What mother of two wants to go to a hockey game? I spend my days trying to get people to stop screaming, to stop fighting–"

I raised an eyebrow. "At the hospital or with..."

I tapped the handle of the stroller she was pushing as the two of us walked. Somehow Carrie set a breakneck pace even when she was pushing a double jogging stroller and simultaneously drinking Diet Coke.

"Both!" she said.

"I'm sorry your adoring husband took you on a boring date," I teased her. "I don't know why he didn't bring the puppets I gave him."

Carrie had kindly included me in their Christmas dinner celebration every year. I had kindly gifted them a set of puppets at the last one, which had made both of us double over in laughter while her husband gave us the worried look he so often did.

"Really, the worst date he ever gave me was a trip to the hospital to give birth to twins," she muttered. "Although I'm so glad they're here!" she added loudly to her babies, even though at eighteen months, I doubted she was creating any lifelong trauma.

"We walked there too, and I wore high heels, and it was so cold—"

"Did he carry you? Piggyback? Give you his coat?"

"Yes," she admitted, and I laughed. Carrie's bad dates had all been worth it in my opinion, because she had found the best, most adoring man I could imagine. He was a little boring for my tastes, but then, I hadn't found anyone in my own dating life who wasn't.

"See, there it is." She pointed at the enormous building spreading in front of us, the city's professional hockey arena. Carrie had moved to a new neighborhood recently—and a cute little townhouse because their growing family needed more space—and I had taken to driving over there for our weekly walks because otherwise she complained endlessly about getting the stroller in and out of her Honda. "And you know how far we've walked today!"

I stopped on the sidewalk.

"I don't understand why you throw the pacifier and then scream at me; there's a more efficient path here," she told Charlie, then turned back to me. "What's up?"

Then her face lit up. "Do you see something familiar?"

"No," I said. "No, probably not."

She looked so disappointed.

I didn't want to get her hopes up—like in the great mall incident of 2023—so I let it go.

But there was something about the arena.

Something pulling me inside.

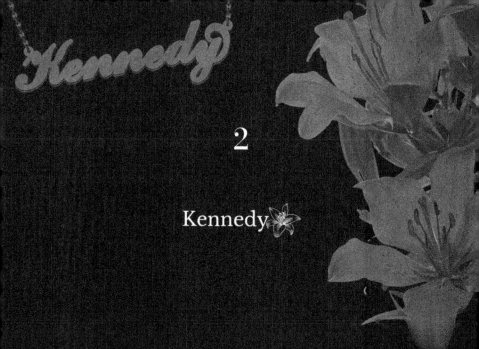

2

Kennedy

T he next day, I went back to the hockey arena.
I couldn't shake the feeling I was going to end up regretting it, feeling stupid and vulnerable the way I so often did.

But I'd found a job application online. I'd filled it out, and even though I was supposed to be headed to my actual job making smoothies, I drove to the arena instead. The application would be an excuse to go inside, wander around, and see if any memories jogged loose. I'd have the application in hand to explain why I was there if anyone stopped me, even though I was pretty sure no one hired people like that anymore.

When I stepped out of the car, I took a quick check in the mirror, trying to make sure I looked okay. I'm not sure an eleven-year-old Honda Civic with one mirror falling off offers anyone the most flattering sense of self, though.

My dark hair was loose around my thin, pale face. I looked fine. Boring, but fine. Nondescript and ordinary, and maybe it was no surprise I wasn't special enough for anyone to have recognized and claimed.

When I started along the sidewalk toward the arena, a man and woman walked toward me. As the cold breeze rushed along the sidewalk, he shucked off his coat without a second thought and wrapped it around her shoulders. She smiled up at him gratefully, the two of them moving in sync; the thoughtful act seemed effortless.

A familiar ache of longing tightened in my chest.

I wanted to be loved like that.

But I'd settle for someone stopping me in the supermarket because we were in fifth grade together.

I'd settle for someone saying my name.

I headed into the arena's lobby. It was upscale, a huge venue with several different concession stands, all of which were closed this early.

Clutching my application in one hand, I felt drawn to the big double doors that took me out into the bleachers. Right now, when the team wasn't practicing, there was an open skate, and the soft sound of blades over the ice sounded... familiar.

The ice seemed far down below. But as I breathed in the cold scent of the arena and listened to the hushed sounds of skating, it felt...comfortable. Homey.

"Can I help you?"

I turned to face the older woman who stared me down like I was about to steal the Zamboni and drive off with it down the highway.

"Oh, hi," I said.

"Are you here for open skate? You need a wristband," she snapped.

"I was just looking to apply for a job at the rink."

"You're in the wrong place," she told me. She bustled out, then threw over her shoulder, "Come on. Follow me."

Even though she wasn't exactly welcoming, for the first time in...forever...I felt as if I were in the right place.

To my shock, there was an opening at the bar attached to the arena. My brusque new friend had brought me over there, and I found myself turning in my application, feeling rather dazed.

But I didn't want to leave the arena, even when the paper was out of my hands and the older lady was back to glaring at me.

"I think I am going to get a wristband," I said.

I think I'm going to find out if I know how to skate or if I fall flat on my face.

This felt a lot riskier than finding out whether or not I liked processed foods from the vending machine.

She checked her watch and eyed me suspiciously once again. Apparently my behavior did not suggest to her that the Zamboni was safe after all. "Open skate closes in half an hour."

"I can probably get my money's worth of falling in half an hour," I promised her and hustled off. I gave the girl who worked at the ticket counter a $10 bill, and she gave me a pair of black skates with worn, knotted gray laces. And of course, that precious neon yellow wristband.

I took them down to the entrance to the rink and sat on a bench. I felt wobbly when I stood up in the skates on the black mats, but I managed to flounder my way over and onto the ice.

"Here goes nothing," I said to no one. But that wasn't unusual. I talked to myself a lot, given how many hours there were with no one to talk to.

Gripping the wall with both hands, I stepped out tentatively onto the ice, expecting my skates to fly out from under me.

But they didn't.

Instead, I found myself gliding forward on the ice, my hand still catching the wall over and over until I realized...I knew what I was doing.

I was good at this, actually.

Somewhere in my past life, I had learned how to skate.

And now I was flying across the ice. My hair flew back, the chilly breeze on my skin feeling invigorating. It felt as if I could take flight.

I let out a surprised, bubbly laugh that I couldn't hold back.

I knew something new about myself: the girl I'd been could skate.

And the girl I was now loved to skate too.

I lost myself in the feeling of flying over the ice, but then I felt someone watching me.

It startled me out of my reverie, and I looked up to realize a man was leaning against the rink windows, watching me. He'd paused against the glass, one powerful, tattooed arm braced over his head. He had dark hair, and he stared at me with eyes that felt penetrating from this distance.

Did he know me?

There was something about the way he stared at me that felt electric.

I started to skate toward him, feeling as if there was some sort of magnetic pull between the two of us. Then I realized I was being awkward. He might have been someone who worked on hiring for the bar, curious about my application.

I was so eager for someone to recognize me, maybe I was imagining things.

He turned and walked away, his t-shirt hugging his broad shoulders, big biceps, the lean taper of his waist. He must be cold, but he didn't seem to show it.

"Mom!" a kid near me called, skating past me eagerly. He stopped in disappointment and turned around, his skates sending a spray of ice into the air. "He's gone."

Who was *he*?

"You were lucky to catch a glimpse of him, honey." A

woman skated up to meet him and tousled his hair. "Maybe another time."

The affection between the two of them, so casual when she ruffled his hair, left me wondering what my own parents had been like.

Were they alive out there somewhere?

The thought felt cold and heavy, and I started to skate again. For once, the weight fell away, and I was just gliding over the ice, listening to the satisfying hushed sound of my skates.

But I couldn't stop thinking about the way he had looked at me.

3

Greyson

Fucking hell.

I'd never get over her.

I watched her from the shadowed entry across the rink, my heart pounding with a mixture of longing...and lust. It felt like I could breathe after years of fucking suffocation.

Kennedy glided gracefully across the ice, her every move a testament to the beauty that had drawn me to her years ago. She was here, right in front of me.

Finally.

Her gaze tracked Carter as he walked away. He'd also been completely unaware I was standing here.

She had no idea who he was. But Carter had stared for a little too long and she'd noticed.

I knew the feeling.

Since the moment I'd met her, that's all I'd been able to do. Stare.

And I was having the same problem since I found her.

Watching while she tried different coffees, trying to figure out which one she used to like. Not knowing that she hated coffee and had only drank chai tea.

Watching while she tried out different styles—preppy, sporty...even goth. Not knowing she'd almost always worn dresses.

Watching while she tried to find herself. Not knowing *we* knew exactly who she was.

She finished her free skate session and stepped off the ice. I remained hidden in the shadows, my eyes never leaving her. She smiled at a group of children rushing past her, lighting up the whole room.

I'd once had that sunshine all the time. I'd wrapped my life around it, my future.

And then it had been taken away.

I had been relentless in my pursuit of Kennedy. After our separation five years ago, I left no stone unturned, determined to find her. The men I'd once called my brothers had done everything in their power to protect her, to ensure she remained hidden from my reach. They had erased her from official records, making her a Jane Doe in the world's eyes...she'd become a ghost.

Maybe they would have succeeded in hiding her from most men.

But I was not most men. I was the Jackal.

And Kennedy was mine.

It took me years of painstaking detective work, a web of informants, and a few close calls, but I finally uncovered a trail that hinted at Kennedy's existence. A small piece of information led to another, and another, until I had pieced together a puzzle that revealed her new identity and location.

I'd tracked her to her shitty apartment as soon as I got the address, and I'd been watching her for a week. I was leader of the Jackals because I was always prepared. I didn't go into battles that I knew I couldn't win.

When I'd seen the medical records detailing her amnesia, I'd laid out a plan, and I'd spent the last week watching the new Kennedy.

Although I realized pretty quickly that Kennedy hadn't figured out who *the new her* was yet either.

I'd always prided myself on my control, but it had never been tested like it had this week, keeping myself away from her.

My dick was experiencing major chafing from all the jacking off I'd been doing since I found her.

I hated fucking chafing.

But it was necessary at the moment.

Her silk panties were making the experience a little easier.

But they wouldn't be necessary soon. Now that she'd run into *them*, it was time for me to stop watching...and move in.

Carter may have kept his distance today...but that wouldn't last long.

One thing none of us had ever been good at was staying away from Kennedy.

Even though the three assholes had evidently stayed away these past few years, they would have cracked.

It was only a matter of time.

I continued to watch her from the shadows, my heart pounding in my chest like it had just started beating again. Reconnecting with her wouldn't be easy. She had built a new life, surrounded by people who had no idea of her past, her true identity, or the love we had once shared. I had to tread carefully, to approach her with caution and patience. But I was willing to do whatever it took to bring her back into my life.

What I felt for her went beyond love. It was obsession. Need. I didn't have a soul. I'd only ever had Kennedy.

And that had always been enough.

I didn't know what to think about Kennedy's new life. We'd been her world before. And now she had friends, a job, even a new smile.

I didn't like seeing her give her smiles out to other people. They'd once belonged to me.

And soon, I'd have them back.

She left the rink and I followed discreetly. I kept my distance, always mindful not to be seen. Kennedy took her time, walking through the stench-filled crowded streets of the city, a small smile on her face.

She passed a small, shitty café, her eyes lighting up like it was a Michelin star restaurant.

I knew what was about to happen. It had happened every day.

She went up to the counter and stared at the menu. Hard. Her nose scrunched up in an adorable way that reminded me of a puppy.

I headed for a seat in the corner, keeping a watchful eye on her as I wound through the tables.

The barista was staring at her, a starstruck expression in his gaze that made me want to slit his throat.

She hadn't noticed, and that was the only thing saving his life.

Kennedy asked for an iced white chocolate coffee with almond milk, and I smirked to myself as I pretended to look at my phone.

Another drink she was going to hate.

I couldn't wait to see her eyes light up when I got her that first chai tea latte.

Followed by an orgasm.

A winning combination if I ever heard one.

My phone buzzed and I pulled it out. It was Sunny, my right hand man.

Shipment coming in at 11:30.

I huffed in annoyance. Because his text meant that instead of watching Kennedy sleep, I was going to have to make sure our latest shipment of guns made it to our warehouse safely.

Kennedy took a sip and grimaced immediately, just like she had all week. I wasn't sure why she hadn't tried something besides coffee, but she seemed bound and determined to find a coffee drink she liked.

There was a part of me that was comforted after seeing her skate and now this. She was the same, even if she didn't remember.

Which meant I still had a home.

Kennedy forced herself to drink the whole thing, sighing as she threw it away and then walked outside.

The barista was still staring after her, and I glared at him until he noticed and his skin paled in fear.

I left the café and continued to follow her, staying inconspicuously behind her all the way to her shitty apartment. The one I was shocked hadn't been condemned.

I hated the fact that she lived there. She deserved the mansion I had waiting for her.

I couldn't wait to make that happen.

I watched as she walked inside, wishing I could just follow her.

Maybe others would see my obsession as a weakness, maybe even a curse.

As I strode away, wishing that I could have followed her in, I wasn't sure.

I only knew that I needed Kennedy like I needed oxygen.

And despite my best attempts...that wasn't going to change.

* * *

"Please! No. Noooooo!"

Sunny snickered as I sliced through the traitor's fingers, his screams ringing through the air. We'd found out that one of our warehouse guys was trying to find a buyer for the weapons we'd just received. It was bad luck for him that one of the prospective parties who'd contacted him about his weapon supply...had been us. Once Sunny realized that the weapons on sale were ours...we made quick work of capturing Ed Tate.

I was now elbow deep in his blood as I chopped and slashed at his body.

There was an art to torture. And I was definitely an artist.

But I could admit I was not using my usual finesse.

I hated traitors. Hated them with everything in me.

My phone buzzed loudly on the table, interrupting my relentless questioning done between every slash of my knife. Ordinarily I wouldn't have stopped, but I knew the text was from the guy I'd assigned to tail Kennedy when I couldn't be there.

And she came first. Always.

Cursing under my breath, I ripped off my glove, reached for the phone, and glanced at the message.

Lucas: She's on a date.

What the fuck? The words hit me like a punch to the gut. Kennedy was not allowed to date. I didn't think about the men she could have seen...could have fucked...before I found her. It was the only way to keep myself from going insane. Dating now was obviously not an option. Jealousy and anxiety festered inside me, threatening to consume me whole.

Me: Details.

Lucas: Her friend had set up a blind date.
They just left the restaurant and they're now
at the movies.

I was going to be a man down after this screwup. Why the fuck hadn't he sent me a text when they were at dinner?

I took a deep breath.

Address, I typed out, turning my attention towards the macabre scene in front of me.

"Get what we need and then finish him," I barked at Sunny as I stabbed a blade into Ed's thighs and then strode from the room, ripping off the plastic cover over my clothes as I did so.

I was in my Rolls-Royce Wraith a few minutes later, the engine roaring to life. Every second ticking by felt like a march to a death sentence. I didn't know why I was so unreasonable when it came to her. She didn't even remember that I existed. I'd already lost her once though. No one was going to make me lose her again.

Not even her own heart.

I sped through the city streets, disregarding speed limits and red lights, my only focus on reaching the movie theater where Kennedy was on her date.

The minutes felt like hours as I weaved through traffic, my mind racing with a thousand thoughts.

Finally, I pulled up to the movie theater, my heart pounding in my chest like I was having a fucking heart attack. I scanned the area, searching for any sign of trouble out of habit more than anything.

No one was going to mess with me in this town.

I strode towards the entrance casually, not wanting to catch her attention.

I came to a halt at the entrance because there she was...

Standing in the concession line with the smile on her face that only belonged to me...her date by her side.

Hot jealousy licked through my veins and my hand twitched towards the gun hidden beneath my jacket. For a second I imagined pointing the gun at him, blood spattering everywhere, his body falling to the ground.

I took some deep inhales. Only Kennedy made me lose control like this. She was my redemption and my hell all wrapped up in one perfect package.

I can't kill him just for standing next to her...

Except he was leaning in, attempting to put his arm around her as they stood in line. Kennedy, ever graceful, smoothly slid out of his reach, her smile never faltering.

"Good girl," I murmured under my breath, ridiculously hoping she'd moved because her body knew she belonged to someone else...even if her head did not.

The idiot said something to Kennedy that made her throw her head back and laugh, in an unabashed way that was different from how she'd been when we'd first met her.

I guess one perk of amnesia was that she didn't remember all the things from her childhood that had held her back. She could laugh like that now, when she couldn't before.

She looked so happy right then, I was almost tempted to let the date continue just for the movie...but then his hand slipped to her lower back. And I couldn't take it.

The date was ending. NOW.

My phone buzzed with a message from my security team. The text contained the identity of the guy, along with his phone number. Just what I needed.

As Kennedy's group approached the theater entrance, I sent a text message from a burner phone to her date's phone.

Brian? I found your credit card near the
theater. Meet me out front to claim it.

I watched as he glanced at his phone, his eyebrows furrowing in confusion, and then quickly excused himself from Kennedy's side, heading toward the entrance of the theater.

What a fucking sheep. He hadn't even checked to see if the card was missing. Or wondered how I'd gotten his number.

Kennedy, her friend Carrie, and Carrie's husband proceeded inside, and I stepped into the shadows outside the entrance.

Minutes passed, and then I saw him, emerging from the theater doors, his expression a mix of curiosity and concern. He scanned the area, looking for the person who had supposedly found his credit card.

I'm by the movie statue, I texted, referencing an eyesore of a sculpture near the side of the building.

Without seemingly one concern, he strode towards me.

I stepped forward from behind the statue, making sure to stay in the shadows, and I grabbed him by the collar and yanked him into the alleyway before he could react.

"What the hell?" he stammered, attempting to break free from my grip.

Slamming him against the brick of the building, I pulled out my gun and pushed it against his chest.

His face drained of color and he whimpered.

Pathetic.

I tightened my hold, leaning in closer so that my words were a menacing whisper against his ear.

"Stay away from Kennedy," I warned. "You won't contact her, approach her, or even think about her. Do you understand?"

His eyes widened, and he stammered, "I...why? Who are

you?"

If he hadn't just pissed his pants...I would have almost thought he had some courage.

I leaned in closer, my words dripping with menace. "I will kill you if you ever talk to her again. Is that clear enough?"

Tears welled up in his eyes, and he nodded vigorously, his voice trembling as he replied, "I won't. I swear."

Just for good measure, I slammed his head against the brick and then reluctantly loosened my hold on him, allowing him to stumble away a few steps. Without another word, he turned and fled into the night, his footsteps echoing with desperation.

Wipe the footage, I texted my team, making sure the cameras around the theater were cleared of all evidence.

Satisfied that my message had been received, I took a step towards the theater, before remembering I still had work to do to make sure there weren't any more rats working within my organization.

Just one more look.

A reward for a job well done...

I'd just gotten inside when she came out of the theater. She stared around, probably looking for her date. When she didn't see any sign of him, her gaze took on a resigned expression...but it didn't look like she was actually upset.

Kennedy, with her dark brown hair cascading down her back and those enchanting light green eyes, had always been the most gorgeous girl I had ever seen. I'd been spellbound from the moment I laid eyes on her.

Sebastian threw his arm around me and I shrugged it off, hating affection of any kind. We were standing in the lobby of the local arena, just finished with an unofficial practice with our club team.

"I just spent two hours with you," I drawled. "Why are you hugging me?"

"We're friends," Sebastian said with a smirk.

"Are we?" I asked, knowing it drove him crazy.

"Since preschool," he sighed, tightening his hold around my shoulders.

"I guess we must be," I said, in a resigned voice, "because otherwise, you'd already be dead."

"That's Greyson," a girl's voice whispered from behind us, and I turned, wanting to know who was talking about me.

And that's when I saw her.

A goddess if I'd ever seen one.

Long, wavy black hair that I immediately wanted to tangle my fingers in as I fucked her from behind.

And those eyes, seagreen and soulful, like she'd seen darkness so she wouldn't be scared of mine.

"Dibbs," Sebastian whispered in my ear. But I didn't pay attention to him. Because that sure as fuck wasn't happening.

Sebastian flirted with her...but I'd felt tongue-tied. Not the greatest first impression, but I'd make it up to her.

That meeting had stoked an obsession inside me, a flame that burned brighter with each passing day.

"Hey there," I had said the next day at school, my voice oozing confidence as I stepped into her path.

Kennedy's light green eyes widened in surprise, and her cheeks flushed with a hint of embarrassment. "Oh...hi."

Memories, most of them painful because they meant so much, came flooding back as I watched her stand in the lobby before finally sighing and returning to the theater.

My phone buzzed, and I didn't have to look at it to know it was Sunny, wondering when I was going to be back.

"See you soon, pretty girl," I murmured, texting the new security I'd put on her to let me know everything that happened tonight.

See. You. Soon.

4

Kennedy 🌸

The arena was alive with energy as I made my way through the private suites, serving drinks and snacks to the excited fans. Dressed in a crisp black uniform with the team's logo, I shakily balanced a tray laden with drinks, maneuvering through the lively crowd. This particular suite belonged to one of the team's sponsors, and the fans in here were a little crazy.

The Devils were locked in a thrilling battle on the ice. As I weaved through the suite, I couldn't help but steal glances at the game whenever I had a moment. The fans, a mix of die-hard hockey enthusiasts and corporate guests, were all eager to catch a glimpse of their favorite players in action. The three stars of the team—Sebastian, Carter, and Jack—had become local—and national—legends, their faces adorning billboards and merchandise all over the city.

Sebastian, with his striking blond hair and piercing dark blue eyes, was a defenseman. Carter, the team's captain, had tousled brown hair and mesmerizing green eyes, and was one of the best goalies in the league. Jack, with his ash blond hair and captivating hazel eyes, was the star wing known for his incredible speed and goal-scoring prowess.

My gaze was drawn to the three of them whenever I got a chance. Carter had been the guy watching me on the ice the other day. I'd realized that when I'd come into work and seen his picture on the wall. I'd also seen Jack and Sebastian's pictures.

And I definitely had a little crush.

They were the heart and soul of the Devils, the reason why the team had such a dedicated fanbase. And to be honest, they were the most attractive men I'd ever seen.

I tried to ignore the fact that they also looked familiar, figuring my brain was just making things up...

Because why on earth would three NHL hockey stars look familiar?

"Drinks for you gentlemen," I said with a cool smile as I set them down in front of the suited men watching the game.

One of them flashed me what I'm sure he thought was a charming grin. "Thanks, sweetheart," he said, as his companion nodded appreciatively, his cold brown eyes lingering on mine for a moment longer than necessary. "Just what we needed."

Another guy leaned in closer, his eyes dull and glazed from how drunk he was already. "What's your name?"

"Kennedy," I replied stiffly, trying to give off the vibes that I was not interested.

I was especially not interested after my date the other night, which I thought had been going well. Only for the guy to ghost me by pretending he needed to meet up with someone who'd found his credit card.

Spoiler alert. He'd never come back.

"Kennedy," the guy repeated, as if savoring the name. "That's a beautiful name."

I held in my eye roll, my gaze drifting to the next suite like someone needed me.

"I'll be back to check on you guys in a bit," I told them, walking away.

"Can't wait," one of the guys called after me. The attention would have been flattering if the three jackoffs hadn't all been sporting wedding rings and dire receding hairlines.

I wondered if men had sucked this much in my old life.

As I moved on to the next suite, I couldn't resist stealing another glance at the game. The Devils were locked in a fierce battle with the L.A. Cobras. Everyone was excited for the matchup since Ari Lancaster, one of the league's star defenseman, had just joined the team. I'd gotten a glimpse of him on the jumbotron, and he was as beautiful as Carter, Sebastian, and Jack. Maybe there was something in the water that hockey players drank.

Or maybe not. John Soto, one of the L.A. Cobras popped up on the screen, and he was not in any way, shape, or form fun to look at.

The tension was palpable, and the crowd's roars and cheers echoed through the arena.

Jack had already scored a goal, and the fans were on the edge of their seats, hoping for a victory against a much flashier team. Even though I had a few games under my belt now that I worked for the arena, I couldn't help but get caught up in the excitement.

My shift continued, and I found myself stealing glances at the scoreboard whenever I had a moment. The clock was winding down, and the Devils were clinging to their lead. The arena was a roar of cheers, jeers, and nail-biting tension.

In the final minutes of the game, the Cobras launched a relentless offense, desperate to tie the score. The Devils' defense, led by Carter and Sebastian, held firm, blocking shots and preventing any last-minute heroics.

Jack gave Soto a face wash and a fight broke out—wait...face wash? How did I know what that was? Face wash was hockey slang...not soap in this case, but probably not commonly known.

A wave of unease passed over me—or was that deja vu? Everything with hockey seemed to come pretty easily to me.

Like I already knew it all, and just needed a reminder.

The crowd booed, and my dark thoughts broke as I glanced down at the ice and saw Jack skating towards the penalty box. Yikes. There were two minutes left and the team would have to finish without their best scorer.

The crowd roared with anticipation, knowing that every second counted.

Sebastian took charge. He slammed an opponent against the boards with bone-crushing force, sending a clear message that the Devils weren't going down without a fight. The crowd erupted in cheers, and the L.A. Cobras player struggled to regain his composure.

Carter was playing lights out. He faced a barrage of shots from the Cobras, each one more intense than the last. The tension in the arena was unbearable as the clock ticked down.

A deafening roar filled the arena as Carter made a miraculous save, diving across the crease to deny a surefire goal. The crowd leaped to their feet, their cheers echoing through the arena as Carter's save kept the Devils in the lead.

The final two minutes felt like an eternity, and when the clock finally ticked down to zero, the arena erupted in jubilation as the Devils secured the victory.

Jack emerged from the penalty box, joining his teammates on the ice as they celebrated their well-deserved win. He glanced up, seemingly up to where I was standing, staring down at the ice. We locked eyes for a second before he jerked his attention back to the celebration.

No, we didn't lock eyes. Especially not all the way up here.

Get your shit together, woman, I snarled at myself before I turned back to the crowd milling around in the suite and served one last round of drinks.

As I made my way back around the room, I couldn't shake the feeling of being watched. But of course, every time I glanced around, no one in particular was staring at me.

It was just a weird night apparently.

The crowd in the suite finally cleared out, and I started cleaning up, tidying tables and collecting empty glasses. The suite was in a state of complete disarray, a testament to how hard everyone had been celebrating the win.

As I worked, my gaze wandered toward the large screen TV mounted on the wall, which was broadcasting the post-game interviews with the players.

And there they were.

Sebastian, Carter, and Jack, all looking like wet dreams in their Devils jerseys. I couldn't drag my gaze away. They were literally the hottest guys I'd ever seen.

And they were charming, answering the reporter's questions with patience and hot smiles that made me want to rub my legs together. Judging by the goofy smile on the reporter's face, she agreed with me.

Other reporters and camera crews surrounded them, asking about the key moments in the game, their strategies, and how they felt securing the victory. The three of them handled the attention effortlessly, their smiles and charisma evident even through the screen.

The camera panned to the crowd of fans that had gathered around the players during the interviews. Girls of all ages approached them, some shy and starstruck, while others were more confident, boldly requesting autographs and selfies.

A twinge of jealousy stirred within me, though I couldn't quite put my finger on why. It's not like I knew any of the team. I'm sure they had their pick of puck bunnies.

It was just that something inside me wasn't crazy about the idea of that.

I shook my head, trying to dispel the irrational jealousy that had crept in. With a sigh, I continued to clean up the suite, reminding myself I was a nobody, with no past, no family, and certainly nothing that could ever catch the eye of men like that.

The world was obsessed with men like Sebastian, Jack, and Carter–gods among the rabble–while it didn't even notice girls like me.

I pushed hard at the self-doubt creeping in, the one that told me I was so worthless, I was nothing more than a Jane Doe.

There was no room in my life for thoughts like that.

As I gathered the last of the empty glasses and plates, I couldn't help but steal one last glance at the TV screen. Sebastian, Carter, and Jack were still there, still basking in the spotlight of their victory, but there was now a group of kids, all dressed in Devils jerseys, gathered around them.

I walked over to stare down at the ice, a smile on my face as I watched the three guys playing around with the kids. Their faces were all lit up with awe and excitement, and their squeals were loud enough to make it up to where I was standing.

I went back to cleaning up, but I could see what was happening on the ice on the tv.

One of the kids, a young boy with a missing front tooth and a wide grin, held out a small notebook and a pen. "Can I have your autograph, Mr. Sebastian?"

Sebastian crouched down to the boy's level, his blond hair

falling into his eyes as he gave him a wide grin. "Of course, buddy! What's your name?"

The boy proudly declared, "I'm Timmy!"

Sebastian signed his name on the notebook, and Timmy's eyes practically sparkled with joy. "Thanks, Mr. Sebastian!"

Carter knelt beside another child, a girl with pigtails and a shy demeanor. "And what about you? Would you like an autograph too?"

The girl nodded, her cheeks flushed with excitement. "Yes, please."

Carter signed her notebook with a flourish, and the girl clutched it tightly to her chest, beaming with happiness.

Meanwhile, Jack was chatting animatedly with a group of kids who were eagerly asking questions about the game. He seemed patient and engaging, making them feel like they were the most important people in the world.

They seemed so down-to-earth at the moment, paying complete attention to the kids despite the bevy of babes waiting nearby.

It was kind of...cute.

"Kennedy," my boss's voice called from behind me. I turned and saw Todd standing there in the doorway.

"Management's throwing a little reception for the team and the donors to celebrate the win. Any chance I could convince you to stay a little longer and help?"

I opened my mouth to politely say no—because I was exhausted.

"The pay would be overtime," he cajoled, and my mouth promptly closed.

I wasn't going to say no to time and a half. Not with how expensive living in this city was.

"Sure," I said, and he shot me a wide smile. I liked Todd.

He was respectful and fair, and he hadn't hit on me. A winning combination for a boss in my book.

Picking up a few more stray glasses, I followed him down to the bar kitchen and dropped off the glasses for the cleaning crew before heading to where they were holding the reception.

I entered the bustling events room, slipping through the crowd unnoticed as I wound my way towards the bar where I'd be working for at least the next hour. The room was a whirlwind of activity, a blend of excitement, and chatter that filled the air.

My eyes scanned the room. There were the donors, easy to pick out because most of them were guys in suits, with the general air that they pissed excellence. Then there were the players from the team, their mere presence commanding attention. And in the midst of it all, there were the girls, each with her own strategy to capture the players' attention. Some engaged in subtle flirting, while others took bolder approaches. Like a crotch grab.

I'd definitely just seen that.

My reverie was abruptly shattered when the air seemed to shift. The atmosphere changed, and I felt a sudden rush of warmth spreading through me.

I turned my head, and there they were—Jack, Sebastian, and Carter, freshly showered and decked out in their team gear. They looked nothing short of stunning, their chiseled physiques accentuated by the snug fit of their t-shirts...their intense gazes meeting the clamoring crowd's adulation.

My heart skipped a beat as I watched them, my body getting that slightly flushed feeling again.

It seemed like everyone in the room had the same reaction. The room crackled with excitement, and a collective gasp of appreciation swept through the crowd. Women and men alike couldn't help but turn their attention to the trio as they made their grand entrance.

I watched from behind the bar, my own thoughts swirling as I observed the frenzy that surrounded them.

I dragged my gaze away from them, working on drink orders and collecting the tips that would make sure I wasn't on a ramen diet this month.

Feeling like eyes were on me, I glanced up, only to lock gazes with Carter, who quickly jerked his head away after he'd seen me look. This happened a few more times. Enough that I wasn't sure I could completely dismiss it as pure wishful thinking.

But why were they staring so much?

One of the guys from the suite I'd been serving earlier that evening sauntered up to the bar. He oozed confidence, flashing me what he thought was another charming grin.

Newsflash, buddy: it still wasn't charming.

"Hey there, Kennnnnnedy," he drawled, drawing out my name like I should be proud of him for remembering it. "How about you take a few shots with me and my boys."

Referring to his middle-aged friends as "boys" seemed like a stretch, but he could keep trying to live that dream.

"I'm not supposed to drink on the job," I murmured, wishing that more people would come over so this guy could move on.

"Come on...one little shot won't hurt. And then you can go home with me after this."

I was momentarily stunned at his audacity, since his wedding ring was still glinting on his finger in the light.

I was trying to come up with a response when— "She's not interested."

It was said in a mild, cool voice that was familiar...but not.

Familiar to the extent that when I turned and saw Sebastian there—I wasn't surprised. But I didn't know why.

"Sebastian Wright," the douchebag said in amazement, like he'd forgotten this event was specifically for donors to mingle with the hockey gods. "Can I get you a drink?" he continued, like he'd also forgotten that drinks were free at the moment.

"I'm good. What I'd like is for you to leave," Sebastian drawled, his voice still placid, like he was discussing the weather. His eyes were at odds with his tone though, filled with a possessive protectiveness that made no sense—or maybe that was just wishful thinking.

The guy's head jerked back, his gaze darting from Sebastian to me, until he finally raised his hands in mock surrender, chuckling nervously. "Easy there, buddy. I was just having a bit of fun. She's all yours, Bas. Just keep playing like that."

With a self-assured wink, he backed away from the bar and made a hasty exit, his laughter trailing behind him. I watched him go, relief swirling within me.

I managed a shaky smile. "Thank you," I murmured, feeling shy and unsure as I spoke to him for the first time.

Sebastian nodded, his gaze caressing my skin...like he couldn't help himself. "Anytime. You're part of the team now, after all." He opened his mouth like he wanted to say something. And then he sighed and shook his head, walking away without another word.

What the fuck was that?

I watched as Jack and Carter descended on him, eyes darting towards me in a totally obvious way that said they were talking about me.

Why exactly were they talking about me? Why had Carter been watching me? I couldn't think of a reason. Because if they did know me before, why wouldn't they tell me? It didn't make sense.

Unless I was an asshole in my former life. Or maybe a groupie that had stalked them? That could explain their behavior.

Except I really didn't get the feeling I'd been an asshole or a groupie in my previous life. It didn't feel right.

But then again, nothing did, so maybe I was wrong.

The next hour was torture, with the three of them sending me surreptitious glances, and me pretending like I didn't see them as my station got busier with people ordering drinks. Girls descended on the three of them, and I pretended like the sight of it wasn't like knives embedding themselves under my fingernails.

As the night wore on, the girls got more aggressive, and then finally, how I assumed the night would end all along since they'd come in, Carter and Sebastian both left with hot blondes who had glued themselves to their sides. Jack didn't walk out with a girl, but he did give me a look as they left, like he wanted me to see them with the women, to know I wasn't part of their world.

Just another thing that didn't make sense, and made me feel like I was going crazy.

It also made me hurt, my mind filled with unbidden images of them all in bed with women much prettier than me.

I left the arena that night, flush with cash, but feeling the most out of sorts that I'd experienced since I'd left the hospital...a girl without an identity.

One thing was for sure though. I needed to stay away from the three of them.

Nothing good could come from it.

* * *

Sebastian

"Alright sweetheart, time to go home," I told Matilda—or was it Mallory...as soon as we got out of view from Kennedy.

"I was hoping you'd say that," she purred as she clawed at my arm in a way that I'm sure she thought was cute...but actually felt demented.

I sighed, hating this part. Hating myself. Girls were nothing but props, especially now that Kennedy had come back. But it didn't make it any easier, or make me any less of an asshole that I used them to create an image before sending them packing.

The look in Kennedy's gaze, like we'd betrayed her...I felt fucking sick. For a second, it was almost like she remembered us—remembered everything, but then she'd blinked and the recognition was gone, and I'd been staring into the eyes of a girl that used to be my everything. Who I was nothing to now.

"Back to your house, unfortunately," I said when she tried to swipe at my dick...my dick that had been hard the entire stupid reception just knowing Kennedy was nearby.

"Whattt?'" she whined, eliminating the guilt I'd just been feeling that I'd used her to make sure Kennedy stayed away. I stared down at her, wondering if she'd been going for Puck Bunny Barbie tonight, and if her sights had been set specifically on me—or if anyone on the team would have been fine for her.

"I'm tired," I said, feigning a yawn. "We'll have to play another night." It was best to give them hope. Girls who had hope didn't talk. They didn't want to mess up a chance of getting with me another night. It was the girls who didn't have hope that were the headaches. I'd learned that lesson early on.

"I could give you a massage," she cooed, pressing her freakishly hard tits against my arm.

Not that I liked rock tits, but for a second I wondered what it would be like to give in, to just let myself be distracted from the constant memory of *her.*

As soon as her face came into my head though, I knew it would never work. Along with the blind panic that laced my insides when I thought of her reappearance, I also would hurt.

Having something fingertips away that you wanted more than anything, but couldn't have, was absolute fucking torture.

"Another night," I told her, flashing my most charming smile. It had the effect I wanted, like usual. She blinked, a glazed look in her gaze like I'd put her in a trance. "I'll see you later," I continued, extracting myself from her grip and walking away. Slowly. Just in case sudden movements made her run at me.

"Call me," she whimpered behind me desperately, obviously not remembering I hadn't asked for her number. I waved over my shoulder, not looking back, since that would make me want to go back to Kennedy.

Which could *not* happen.

I got into my truck where Jack was already sitting in the passenger seat, his expression like someone had kicked his dog. We didn't say anything, not even when Carter slid in, having successfully extracted himself from his "prop" as well.

It wasn't until we were on the highway to the highrise penthouse we shared, that Jack broke the silence.

"This isn't good," he huffed, dragging his hands down his face.

"Fucking understatement of the century there, Captain Obvious," Carter growled from the backseat.

"What do we do? Should we get her fired? She can't be here," I spit, even though the thought of her not being there was making my heartbeat go haywire.

We'd kept our distance since she'd gone to the hospital five years ago. It personally had felt like my balls were getting ripped off right along with my soul...but it had been what was best. For her. For us.

I thought it would fade. That this pain in my chest would eventually disappear one day. I'd forced myself to stay away from her, to not look her up, to not drive by her crappy apartment...to pretend like she didn't exist.

But the ache hadn't gone away. I'd pushed it under the surface where it had festered, clawing back to life the second we'd realized she was at the arena.

"We can't do that," Jack murmured, the same resignation in his voice as was in my head. "We just have to stay away."

"Meaning tonight can't happen again," Carter snapped, locking eyes with me in the rear view mirror.

My cheek ticked and I stared at the road, turning on the exit that led to our place. I couldn't help tonight. Watching guys talk to her...flirt with her...harass her—we hadn't allowed it when she was ours.

How was I supposed to allow it now?

I was a reasonable guy, about everything but Kennedy. She unlocked my crazy, and tonight had been tame for me. What I'd really wanted to do was stab the guy in the eyeball, slice open his throat, tear out his organs until they were scattered on the floor for daring to touch what was mine.

Like I said...tame.

"Old habits die hard," I finally drawled, after I realized I'd been thinking about the guy's death for a minute too long and forgotten to answer.

Jack side-eyed me like he could read my mind.

42

And maybe he could. We'd been friends for so long, sometimes it felt like they knew everything about me.

Of course I'd once felt that way about Greyson as well...and look what had happened to that.

I took deep breaths, trying to get myself under control before I got into a road rage accident.

"I don't think I can stay away," Jack said in a pained voice, even though he'd been doing the best of the three of us, it seemed.

"What the fuck?" Carter snapped, punching the seat next to him. "You will stay away. We gave up years to keep her safe. We're not blowing it now."

Except she'd found us anyway...hadn't she?

Didn't that...mean something?

We didn't say anything else for the rest of the ride, Jack and Carter jumping out of the truck like it was on fire as soon as I pulled into the underground parking garage.

Assholes.

I stayed in the car, trying to remind myself of all the reasons we'd stayed behind in the first place—the years of missing her, of hating ourselves we'd endured.

But it wasn't as easy as it used to be.

Not by a longshot.

* * *

I stood in the shower, scalding water slicing my skin with lashes of pain as I tried to wash off this...feeling. Like my skin was on too tight, like I was going to go crazy from not touching her.

My hand went to my dick, weakness setting in. She was on her knees in front of me, her dark hair covering her chest, rosy pink nipples peeking through, her skin slick with water.

Like every fantasy come to life.

43

Which maybe was easy, because every fantasy I'd ever had since I met her was about her.

She smiled sweetly at me before her hands grasped onto my dick, her touch tentative and shy. What would she think of my piercing? Her pink tongue licked her bottom lip before darting out and licking my swollen head.

She moaned like I'd just given her ice cream, and my balls tightened at the sound.

Another slide of her tongue, lapping at my slit like a cat, her hands sliding over my shaft, my balls...

Fucccck.

My hands tangled in her hair. "That's my good girl," I breathed as she suckled on my sensitive head, whimpering at the words that drove her crazy.

She loved being my—our–good girl.

Always had.

My hands slid down, cradling her jaw as she sucked me in deeper. Just a few more minutes and then I'd fuck her against the—

I growled as I came, calling out her name, hot cum spurting against the tile...the orgasm so intense the edges of my vision darkened.

Fuck. Fuck. Fuck.

How was I supposed to live like this? Stay away. Live without my fucking heart.

I couldn't come without thinking of her.

I couldn't breathe without being near her.

It was starting to feel like I couldn't...live without her.

After all that had happened...what the fuck was I supposed to do about that?

With or without her...

I was fucked.

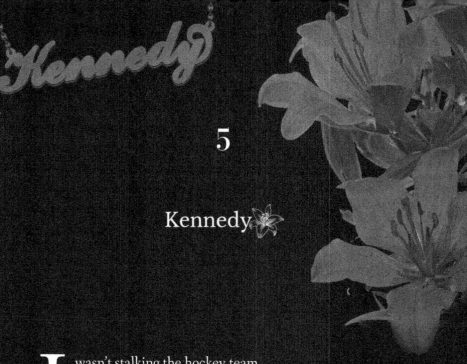

5

Kennedy

I wasn't stalking the hockey team.

Maybe I was stalking three of them...a little bit.

Ever since Carter stared me down during my skating session, I'd been curious about him. And then Sebastian had charged to defend me... because I was 'part of the team'. They seemed inseparable with Jack, so I was curious about the team's blond-haired golden boy.

And I could have sworn, all three of them watched me while I watched them. Every once in a while, when I saw them around the arena, they looked at me as if they knew me. Then they glanced away. I wanted to ask them if they knew who I was, but when I thought about doing something that would seem so crazy, my stomach tightened.

I didn't want to lose this job...my chance to be here at this arena that felt like home...or the opportunity to catch glimpses of these men who seemed to jog something inside me.

Tonight, it was driving me a little nuts knowing they were out on the ice, hearing the roar of the crowd and the distant sounds of the announcers and buzzers, while I was still stuck at work.

But eventually we came to a lull.

"Take your break, Kennedy," my manager Todd told me. "You've earned it."

It had been a busy night.

"Thank you," I said. At first I headed for the little café to try a drink, but then I heard a buzzer sound.

I found myself pulled away, diverted toward the ice.

I shouldn't be here, but there was no one manning one of the entries to check tickets this late in the game. I slipped through it and stepped through the double doors into the arena.

It was so much louder than it sounded from outside. It was overwhelming, and yet...I didn't want to leave. I hesitated on the gum-splattered concrete steps, and then I slipped into an empty plastic seat. It felt cold under my butt, even through my jeans.

The arena felt alive with the electric buzz of anticipation, the crisp scent of ice mingling with the noise of the crowd. I usually hated crowds, but this one gave me a rush of shared excitement, making my heart beat faster.

Even before I saw number 27.

Jack.

I'd looked them all up on the internet, adding more details to the faces that stared down at me from posters in the lobby and flags outside the rink. I couldn't get away from the three of them.

His number had lodged in my mind as I studied the photos of him both in his uniform and dressed up, the way the team was when they traveled. His ash blond hair was disheveled in a sexy way even when he was dressed in a suit, and he'd grinned in the photos in a way that was both rakish and boyish. He was a heartbreaker.

Now I couldn't see that handsome face, but watching the way he handled himself on the ice was even sexier.

He moved with easy grace with the stick, then suddenly lashed out, moving so fast with a hard, brutal shot. The other team skated forward to block it desperately, and the goalie was on the move, but as I watched, I already knew it wouldn't matter.

That fierce shot was going in.

The puck caught the corner of the net, going in past the outstretched arm of the opposing goalie.

I grinned. That was poetry to watch.

Down on the ice, one of the other guys threw his arm around 27's shoulders.

Sebastian.

Their helmets dipped in, close enough they probably clinked together. What were the two of them talking about? I craned forward, as if I could somehow hear from this distance.

Jack clapped Sebastian's shoulder before the two of them broke apart. They skated back to set up for another round.

I watched Sebastian, who was grinning like he'd scored that goal himself.

But of course, he didn't often get the chance to score. He was on our team's defense, and I didn't know when the hell I had started to think of them as *our team*. Just because I worked here? Why did I find myself leaning forward, watching every move like it mattered if we won?

Maybe I'd get better tips if we won.

As Jack skated forward, the puck seemed like an extension of his own will. I leaned in, whispering to myself, "Drop it back, Jack," as if he could hear me across the distance, through the barrier of glass and cacophony.

And then, as if connected by an invisible thread, he shot it back, quick and effortless, sending the puck sliding back to

Sebastian. Jack didn't telegraph at all until he was taking the shot. He had incredible speed and decision making. I found myself smiling as if I were proud.

Sebastian, with number 14 flaring on his back, already hovered in the ideal position. "Now, Sebastian, now!" I urged silently.

My heart raced as he connected with the puck, seamlessly passing it to Carter, who was poised at the net.

It was a risky move, sending the puck all the way back to our goalie. The other team's offense skated down hard, and Sebastian flew across the ice to meet one of them, blocking them from Carter.

Even from here, I could almost feel the tension in Carter's muscles, the intent that radiated from him. My hands clenched in silent support.

Carter skated forward out of the net as the other players bore down on him. Sebastian skated into one at full power, taking him out before he could get in Carter's way.

Carter slammed the puck down the ice.

And despite its speed, Jack picked it up easily, skating around an opponent, moving so impossibly fast. He passed it to another player in front of their net. His decision making was so quick and determined. The other player took a shot, lost it to the goalie.

Jack clapped the other player's shoulder as if to comfort him, then skated off with that same easy grace.

Even though they played well with the whole team, there was something about the three of them on the ice that was special.

Their cooperation was a thing of beauty, and it kept drawing my gaze. When an opponent aimed a sly elbow at Sebastian, Jack was there in a heartbeat, a protective wall of fury. Sebastian watched over Carter, falling back and playing the game safer than I thought he wanted to, judging from his body language.

Then it struck me.

Once again... I wasn't just engaged in the game.

I understood it.

When did I learn the rules of hockey?

I'd been lost in the game because I actually understood and —oh, no. I was about to be late getting back from my break. I had lost track of time. I'd been so focused on the players.

On those *three* players.

I stood up to scramble to the door. But as if I were some kind of good luck charm, when I stopped at the double doors leading out, I turned back to see one of the opposing team skating down the ice toward Carter. I slid into an empty seat near the doors, watching as Jack flew along the ice, trying to outpace them, but hanging back ready for someone to pass him the puck. Sebastian surged forward to meet one of the players.

But they were throwing the entire team forward against the defense.

They were setting up a shot, but there was no chance they could make it past Carter.

I leaned forward, my hands knitting into fists.

Because I could already tell one of them was heading straight for the goalie. But that was against the rules.

They slammed into Carter as one player passed the puck to another, who was skating up on the corner of the net. The second player slammed the puck home.

It was a major penalty.

But I wasn't sure that mattered when Carter was going down on the ice. He slammed onto his back.

I held my breath.

He didn't get up, his stick a few feet away where it had

fallen when he went down. The crowd around me murmured. Some of the opposing team cheered.

I was on my feet. I wasn't sure when I'd gotten there, and I sat down, feeling a sudden rush of embarrassment that warmed my cheeks.

Sebastian and Jack were already throwing helmets, ready for a fight. But while Sebastian did start throwing punches, Jack skated to Carter. Carter's face was etched with pain, but he shook his head at Jack, who helped him up to his feet.

I caught the look of frustration and worry written across Jack's face.

Carter said something that might've been *go kick their ass* judging from the way Jack turned and slammed into one of the players involved in that play.

The thought that Carter was hurt pulled at my heart, and I froze, feeling as if I couldn't leave now. I didn't know if he was going to be alright.

He looked up from the ice, as if he had felt the intensity of my concern.

Our eyes met across all that distance.

Then the medic was crossing the ice toward him, and Carter was distracted, shaking his head, saying he was fine.

But he wasn't fine. Watching the way he moved, I was sure of it.

But it felt as if the spell between us had been broken, at least enough for me to remember I was late coming back from my break. I hustled back to work.

After the game, I heard hubbub outside the bar. Another waitress, Jacqueline, smiled at me. "Fan club in action."

"Whose fan club?" I racked my brain for the names of other

players on the team. Three of them seemed to take up all my attention. "Weiss? Logan?"

"No, most of those guys went out the back from the locker room," she said. "But there are three of them who can't resist meeting their adoring fans."

Three.

Why did I assume that had to be *my* three?

I was not sure what the expression was like on my face, but she smiled at me. "Go, see for yourself. We're slowing down now."

"Thank you," I told her gratefully.

I ducked out into the lobby.

Jack was the first one I saw. He towered above the crowd, his blond hair wild from his helmet, but it was a sexy look on him. He smiled at everyone as he greeted them as if they were his long lost best friend, his eyes crinkling at the corners as if he were genuinely pleased to meet people. I didn't think most celebrities could manage to seem so real when they greeted people.

It was a good thing I'd spied him when I did, because he abruptly vanished from view. He had knelt down, surrounded by a bunch of little kids, who were all wearing jerseys: some hockey team for the under-tens. He talked to them seriously, giving them a little pep talk about playing as a team, then talked to each of them individually. He was one of those people who seemed to give all his attention.

I looked for Carter, hoping I would see him to know he was alright. But I couldn't see him anywhere.

I slipped around the edge of the crowd, wondering where Sebastian was. I already had the feeling the three of them always moved as a pack.

A man collided with me. "Oh, sorry, sweetheart," he said, putting his hand on my shoulder to steady us both.

"It's alright," I told him, veering away from him and into the open space of the hallway that surrounded the arena.

Only to see Carter stalking toward us, his big body barreling forward, his face set and furious.

Then he stopped abruptly as our eyes met.

The man moved off, patting my shoulder. Carter's eyes flickered after him, then returned to mine.

The two of us gazed at each other as if time had stopped. There was a scar through his eyebrow that gave him a sexy rakish look. His face was all hard angles and lines, a big jaw, sharp cheekbones. But his lips were puffy, like he was made for kissing.

He turned to go.

"Are you alright?" My voice came out too eager, and I was cursing myself as he swung back around.

"I'm fine." He said the words slowly, as if I were a little bit thick.

As if I didn't have a reason to ask. As if we all hadn't seen him go down on that ice.

But even though he sounded like a jerk, I didn't want him to leave yet.

"It looked like maybe you had an old injury," I said, touching my own right thigh. I'd noticed that he favored it, though I hadn't been sure of it until I saw him go down. "Your knee?"

He scoffed. "You don't know anything about me."

He turned, and this time when he walked away, I made myself stay. Then I turned and went back to work, my cheeks burning. Why had I talked to him as if we knew each other? I'd totally embarrassed.

It was late and the place was empty when I finally clocked out. As I walked the block to the employee parking garage, I shivered, feeling nervous,

There was something about crossing streets that sent a little thrill of terror through me. As if my body remembered the accident that had changed my life, even though my mind couldn't capture any part of it.

The parking garage was still emptying from the arena, and the streets felt packed. They'd stopped on the crosswalk. Nervously, I stepped out into the street, winding between the cars that were stopped.

A motorcycle revved, winding its way through the parked cars. I startled, realizing it was rushing up on my right side.

I had time to get out of its way, but I felt rooted to the ground, as if I couldn't move. I stared at the motorcycle.

Suddenly, a tall, dark-haired figure stepped between me and the motorcycle, holding up his hand with an imperious gesture as if he were in charge of the street.

And honestly, he had this aura of power and magnetism, as if maybe he did.

At any rate, the motorcycle braked to an abrupt stop.

"Get out of the way!" the motorcyclist yelled, then fell silent as the man glared at him.

"Are you okay?" he asked, escorting me to the sidewalk.

The light changed and traffic began to move again. His gaze flickered up to the motorcyclist, and he raised one finger, ticking it back and forth in a *no, no, no* gesture. I couldn't see the rider's expression through his helmet, but from his posture, I could've sworn the other man rushed off in fear.

"Yes," I said. "Thank you."

He turned and faced me. "You shouldn't walk alone. It's busy here on game nights, but it's still not safe."

I raised my eyebrows at him. "Next, are you going to tell me I shouldn't talk to strangers?"

He chuckled softly. The streetlights cast his face in hard shadows, but nothing could hide how handsome he was.

"I'm not a stranger," he told me. "I'm Greyson."

"Just knowing your name doesn't mean you aren't a stranger," I told him.

He shrugged. The smile that crossed his face was so charming that it made me want to keep standing here on the street, talking to him.

"Can I walk you to your car?" he asked.

"That seems like exactly the kind of thing you would suggest if you were the kind of man I shouldn't let walk me toward my car."

"It sounds like exactly the kind of thing I would suggest if I were the kind of man who had two sisters," he chided in response.

There was something about him that felt... magnetic.

The way I felt about my hockey boys.

He felt safe.

"Fine. You can protect me from any more rogue motorcycles."

His answering grin was like the sun coming out.

"My name is Kennedy," I said, sticking my hand out.

When he shook my hand, the warm, dark scent of his after-shave washed over me. There were scars on his knuckles, his palms hard. He looked polished in his suit, but his hands didn't match.

"So, big hockey fan?" he asked as we walked toward the garage.

"I don't know yet," I said with a smile and a noncommittal shrug. "Are you?"

"Yeah. I used to play." A slight smile played over his lips. I couldn't read the emotion that flashed over his face. Regret? Nostalgia? Longing? "A long time ago."

"And now you have to just root for the Devils?"

54

His answering smile was a quick flash of his teeth. "I wouldn't say I root for them. But I like to watch sometimes."

"I was way too invested in tonight's game," I said with a laugh. "I only saw a few minutes of it. But it was exciting."

"Did you see Carter go down?"

I nodded. I couldn't understand the expression on his face. Curiosity? Concern? Satisfaction? Whatever emotion it was, it was gone in a second, too fast to read.

We reached the dark parking garage. It felt too empty and cavernous, our feet echoing as we headed toward my car.

"This is me," I said, and when I pointed at the Civic, he didn't try to hide the face he pulled. "Hey! It's a perfectly fine car. It gets me from home to work, that's all I need."

"But what about what you want, Kennedy?"

"I never know what I want," I said with a laugh. I slid into the driver's seat.

He put his hand on the top of my car door to stop it from closing and dropped a business card inside. Then he closed my door for me, as if he knew I'd be nervous and he wanted to make sure I felt safe.

I popped the locks closed, giving him an apologetic smile.

"Good idea. Stay safe, Kennedy." He patted the top of the car. His deep, sexy voice was muffled through the glass, but I could still hear him. "And call me, if you choose."

"What am I going to call you for?" I asked him with faux innocence.

He grinned back at me as if he had plenty of ideas. But all he said was, "Call me for a date."

"A date?" With a strange man I met on the street?

But he was alluring.

"A date," he said with confidence. Then he stepped back from the car. "Good night, Kennedy."

I pulled out of the parking spot, my hands clumsy on the

steering wheel as if I were too conscious of his gaze. I already had questionable parking skills in a tight garage like this.

As I drove home, I couldn't help replaying the night. The memory of how I'd embarrassed myself in front of Carter rose, and I groaned out loud now that I was in the safety of my own car.

So embarrassing. Usually, I would have re-lived that moment six times on the way home and another dozen at 2 am.

But then I thought of Greyson, and I found myself smiling all the way home.

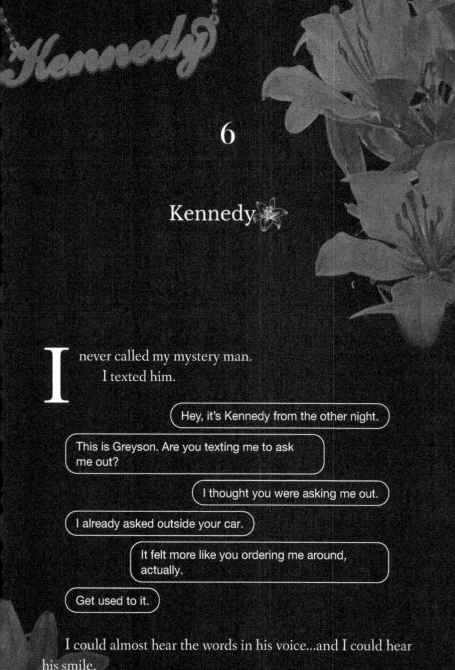

6

Kennedy

I never called my mystery man.
I texted him.

> Hey, it's Kennedy from the other night.

> This is Greyson. Are you texting me to ask me out?

> I thought you were asking me out.

> I already asked outside your car.

> It felt more like you ordering me around, actually.

> Get used to it.

I could almost hear the words in his voice...and I could hear his smile.

> Wear something casual. We're going to walk around the city.

> In public, brightly lit places?

> Of course. I want you to feel safe with me.

Carrie had prepared me for a world of terrible first dates. I'd avoided dating for the most part since I woke up. It had just felt wrong. I didn't even know who I was; how was I going to figure out who I was in a relationship?

She left for her shift an hour early to come over and help me get dressed.

She eyed me skeptically. "I think you should go sluttier. This is a guy you found on the street? He wasn't drawn to your personality."

"Carrie," I chided in exasperation.

"At least wear that lacy tank top so he can see the girls."

"Why are you here again?"

Since it was a casual date, I reluctantly flipped past the handful of dresses in my closet. I felt prettiest when I wore dresses for some reason. But I didn't own very many; I'd tried out a bunch of different styles, and I'd learned to go minimalist in my clothes purchasing. Someday, I'd figure out what exactly I loved most.

So far, the closest I'd come to identifying my style was *kindergarten teacher*.

I pulled out the black leather jacket, which was a staple item and not, as Carrie called it, evidence of a brain injury. She had been very opinionated about the goth phase.

"This is an acceptable time to wear it," she admitted as I turned around, holding it up.

I threw it on my bed as I headed for the mirror to finish my makeup. I was just wearing dark jeans and, on second thought, I doubled back to take off my sweater and replaced it with the lacy tank top. Carrie smiled at her victory, but didn't rub it in.

"It's weird that he asked me out on the street, right?" I asked as I started to line my eye, winging it up for a smoky eye.

I seemed to have a practiced hand with makeup that made it easy for me to recreate any look I found on Youtube. Another clue to who I used to be that had ultimately led me nowhere.

Carrie scoffed. "No. Girl, have you seen yourself?"

I straightened, examining the long, dark brown hair that hung around my shoulders. "I don't know."

"Then I'm assuming the answer is no, you've never *really* seen yourself. You're gorgeous."

I turned back to her, smiling. But before I could say anything, she added, "Did I ever tell you about the guy who ordered us prune juice on our date? At least he paid."

Carrie finished giving me the worst pep talk for a first date as we walked to meet Greyson.

"I'm going to bounce to work as soon as he sees that you have someone waiting for you to come home," she told me.

We walked into the little coffee shop Greyson had picked as our meeting place.

I could place him as soon as I walked in, even though he was standing with his back to me. His fine jacket clung to broad shoulders and a lean waist, and his dark hair was immaculate. Most of all, it was the aura he exuded.

"There he is," I told Carrie.

"Good. I need to memorize his face so I can tell a police sketch artist if I need to."

Then Greyson turned around, and she gasped. "I am not going to need to work to memorize that face. Oh my god, you didn't tell me he was gorgeous."

"Don't embarrass me," I begged through my smile, given the way she was openly staring at Greyson.

He gave us both a broad grin in return as he headed toward us.

"You two are going to make beautiful children!" Carrie said.

Hopefully Greyson hadn't heard that.

"You've seen him, now it's time to go," I told her, giving her a little push. "You can't be late for work."

"Yes, I can. What's going to happen? People die?"

"Yes! Go!"

She raised two fingers to point to her own eyes, then turned them on Greyson in the international signal of *I'm watching you.*

"Have so much fun," she told me cheerfully, as if she hadn't just set me up for the most awkward date anyone could have without prune juice. Then she walked off, and I followed her with my eyes until the coffee shop door closed with a tinkle of bells behind her.

"She's right, you know." Greyson loomed over me, given his height. The smile he directed my way made me feel warm all over. "We will make beautiful babies."

"Let's see how the night goes. I think you're getting ahead of yourself."

The barista called the name *Greyson.*

"I'd better order," I moved toward the counter.

"Wait." He touched my arm, holding me back, though his grip was gentle. "I ordered for you."

"You did?"

"You look like a chai girl to me," he said, then moved to the counter.

He returned carrying two to-go cups.

I raised an eyebrow at him. "Ordering for me? Is this the 1950s?"

"Just take a sip and have some faith."

I shrugged and raised it to my lips. The spicy scent of the tea wafted up along with the steam, and I took a sip.

It was the most delicious thing I'd ever tasted.

"Do you still doubt me?" His eyebrows arched in a way that was adorable.

"I trust you to order beverages for me," I conceded. "I still don't trust you not to be a murderer."

"I would never hurt you, Kennedy."

Later on, it would occur to me that he specifically never said he wasn't a murderer. He just promised that I was safe with him.

"Let's walk," he told me, offering me his arm.

I let out a laugh. I'd never walked with my hand looped through the crook of a man's arm before, at least not that I remembered.

"You are surprisingly old fashioned," I told him, tentatively taking his arm. His forearm felt hard and corded under my grip.

"I want to treat you well," he told me. "And like I said, I do have two *very* opinionated sisters."

"Would they be opinionated about me?" Not that I was going to meet his family. *Slow down, Kennedy.* What was wrong with me?

"Yes," he said. "But their opinions will be that you're too good for me. They are going to love you when they meet you."

"How do you know that? We just met."

He shrugged, his bicep flexing against my shoulder. I breathed in the faintest scent of his spicy aftershave, which made me want to push my face against his throat to smell it better.

He might smell even better than chai tea.

"I feel like I know you already," he said. "Strange as that may sound."

"Well, I'm a few beats behind you," I told him. "So tell me all about yourself."

As we walked, he told me about his life. He loved to cook,

he had two dogs at home who judged him even more than his sisters did, and since he didn't play hockey anymore, he'd taken up martials arts to stay fit.

He had stayed very fit.

"My childhood was pretty chaotic," he told me. "Hockey was my safe place when I found it. Like a found family with the team, you know? A coach who felt like a father to me. My relationship with my own father was...complicated."

"It sounds nice," I told him.

"I started karate my senior year when I needed to blow off some steam. I was starting to feel angry all the time..." He shook his head. "It really helped. But I was terrible at first, even though I was pretty good on the ice."

I had the feeling that he had been better than pretty good on the ice. It was just an impression I had based on the way he carried himself.

"Tell me a story about you being bad at something," I teased him. "Because it's hard for me to imagine."

"Oh, is it?" His grin brought out a dimple in his cheek. "Well. When I started, the other students were breaking boards and doing flying kicks. Not a lot of people start off when they're my size—I was standing in line with fifth graders."

I grinned at the mental image of him towering over his class.

"But I was determined to get better, so I started practicing in my backyard. One day, I decided to try a flying side kick on a soccer ball hanging from a tree. I took a running start, leapt into the air...and sailed right through it. Into a trash can."

I laughed.

"We didn't have a very big backyard," he said. "Not big enough for me. And we also didn't have enough privacy for me, because as I extricated myself, my neighbor called over the fence, "That's not how Bruce Lee did it!"

I giggled, and he looked down at my face, smiling with a twinkle in his eye. "I've never told anyone that story before. It's just between you, me, and Old Man Johnson."

"It's nice that you told me, then."

"Anything to see this smile," he murmured.

And it felt like he meant it.

Our date seemed like one fun thing after another. He took me to the best diner ever, where they had pancakes that melted in my mouth. I rolled my eyes heavenward and let out a moan, and he stared at me as if he might eat me up instead of his burger.

But I didn't mind. There was something about the way he looked at me that made me feel seen. Powerful.

Then he took me for ice cream.

"What should I get?" I asked as I perused the menu.

"You could let me order for you," he said mischievously.

"Okay," I said. "I don't think you can do it twice in a row."

"Try me," he said before heading to the counter. He ordered two vanilla soft serve, chocolate dipped cones with chocolate sprinkles.

"I've never even heard of that combination before," I said.

"All the chocolate, but not too much chocolate," he said in an airy way, as if he were quoting someone.

I bit through the crisp shell into the creamy, sweet ice cream. It was so delicious that I sighed. "Alright, you win. What kind of magic is this, anyway?"

"What do you mean?"

"It's like you have this supernatural sense of what I'll like."

"Like a god?" he asked innocently.

I burst out laughing. A slightly offended look crossed his handsome features, and I found myself laughing harder. "Oh my god, I swear you looked hurt when I laughed at the idea of you being a god!"

He chuckled too.

"I don't remember when I last laughed so much," I told him.

"Me too," he said. "Being with you feels like sunshine and a spring day after a long, long winter."

We went window-shopping. "Ooh, I love that," I said, peering into the window at a gorgeous dress.

"It would be beautiful on you."

"Someday when I'm a millionaire," I joked.

His eyes crinkled at the corners. "Come on. Let's pick out the jewelry you want to wear with it. Tiffany's is right next door."

The two of us ambled down the sidewalk to look at the Tiffany's window. "It's all so overpriced for what it is," I said.

"Some people want to spend money on the ones they love," he noted.

"But you could buy something cheaper *and* go on vacation," I said.

He leaned against the brick wall as he turned to face me. "Is that an invitation, Kennedy?"

"I don't think we know each other quite well enough yet."

"We could get to know each other in Paris."

"I've always wanted to go," I said, giving in to the fantasy. I looped my arm through his again and we started to walk again. "We could eat at that restaurant at the top of the Eiffel Tower."

"We should order champagne."

"Definitely. I'm only going to climb all those stairs to the Eiffel Tower once. We have to make it worth it."

"There's an elevator."

"I know, but I've always imagined myself taking the stairs. And I'm making you climb the stairs with me."

"As if you could get rid of me," he teased. "Then what? Will it be late?"

"Oh, we're going back to our hotel, of course," I said. "By the time you take me to Paris, we'll be..." I couldn't follow through with the thought, but I smiled.

"That blush is so beautiful," he murmured, stopping to face me. He touched his fingers to my cheek. It was a slow touch that I could only describe as careful. "You're so innocent."

"Not once we get to Paris," I said back.

"No," he agreed. "Not once we get to Paris."

His eyes darkened. "If you knew all the things I want to do to you, you would blush a lot more."

I felt my cheeks darken. "Maybe not," I lied. "Maybe I've done it all before."

"Have you?" He quirked an eyebrow. "Who do I have to kill?"

I laughed.

"They must not have realized you were mine," he said, his tone still light. He took my hand. "But I promise you, Kennedy. Everyone is going to know who you belong to."

"Only if you belong to me too."

"Of course I do."

"I shouldn't have you walk me all the way home."

"It would be a bad idea," he agreed. "But your crazy friend *did* memorize my face."

"For the sketch artist."

"For when I kidnap you."

I laughed. "After you kidnap me, are you going to take me to Paris?"

"Definitely."

And maybe there was a part of me that did want to be pulled out of my boring, ordinary life to be stolen away by the most interesting, confident man I'd ever met.

Because I let him walk me to my door.

As we stood in front of my crappy apartment building, I felt tongue tied. There was a part of me that wanted to invite him up, that wanted the night to never end.

But then there was still a part of me that hadn't lost my mind when I met Greyson.

"If you plan to kiss me goodnight," I said lightly, despite what talking about a kiss did to my cheeks, "I should warn you now it probably won't be very good."

"Why do you say that?"

"I haven't...kissed anyone," I said. "At least, not that I remember."

I stumbled over the words. I hadn't told him yet about my amnesia. Maybe I should before things went any further.

"I bet you'll be good at it," he told me confidently. "I had another girl's first kiss a long time ago, and even if she was new to it, it was still...amazing."

"Are you really talking to me about other girls?"

"No," he said, then added with a smile, "Just trying to get you into the competitive spirit before you kiss me."

"A little healthy competition?"

"Exactly."

I held out my arms for a hug. "I think you've scared me out of it."

"There will be plenty of other dates," he said so confidently that it made me smile.

"Will there?"

When he hugged me, he felt so warm and solid. It was the most comforting thing I'd ever felt, and I melted into his hug.

I had friends who cared about me. But we didn't really touch. I hadn't realized until this moment how starved for affection I felt. Greyson had touched me all night, in small, non-threatening ways, and I had loved the tingle it sent through my body, the swoop of joy.

But this hug felt incredible. It felt like coming home, with his strong arms wrapped around me and the cool sleek fabric of his jacket pressed against my cheek. If I lingered a little longer, I might be able to hear his heart.

I might be able to tell if it was beating faster too.

* * *

The next day at work, my new friend Amanda smiled at me while we were refilling ketchup bottles. "Going to skate today?"

"If I have the energy," I said. "I was up way too late last night."

"Hot date?"

"Amazingly, yes." I looked up to find Carter.

My gaze met his in surprise.

He was staring at me.

"Can I help you with something?" I asked.

"No," he said. "I came to get a bottle of water."

"Oh," I said, surprised.

Amanda had already gotten his bottle of water. He took it from her, finally pulling his gaze away from me to tell her, "Thank you."

"No problem," she said. "I'll ring you up."

He headed to the register with her. It was amazing to me that such a big, broad shouldered guy moved with so much grace off the ice. It seemed like he was built for hockey.

"So was this with your mystery man?" she asked me, then turned to him with a smile. "Two dollars."

That was with the discount we got for the countless hours we spent here at the arena. A bottle of water was seven dollars for the people who bought tickets.

He handed her his credit card.

"Yes, with my mystery man," I said, feeling the way he was suddenly very intent on absolutely nothing, not looking at me.

"Who would've known meeting someone on the street could work out so well?"

His jaw went tight. "Seems like a bad idea."

"It worked out," I disagreed.

I thought he didn't want to talk to me. But he suddenly seemed very interested in critiquing my life choices.

Once he had gone, Amanda and I went back to doing the little tasks that had to be done before setup, wrapping utensils and refilling the ketchup bottles. I didn't mind it. The mindless work was a chance to chat, and I enjoyed the people I worked with so far.

"So tell me all about it," she said.

I filled her in on all the details.

Later that day, I walked out of the arena at the end of my shift to find Jack lingering in the lobby. At this time of day, it was almost empty.

My gaze was drawn to the tall, broad-shouldered man who was leaning against the wall, like he was waiting for someone. Maybe it was Carter or Sebastian and not yet another puck bunny.

I was tempted to say something to him, but given how friendly Carter had been when I approached him, I wasn't going to bother. That rejection had stung a little, but I could understand it. They were rushed by fans and puck bunnies all the time. It must get old, no matter how much Jack smiled that gorgeous smile for everyone he met.

He glanced up at me, and I could feel his attention radiating from him, but I didn't look toward him. I was too aware of him in my peripheral vision though as I headed across the lobby. I wasn't going to throw myself at these men.

Instead, I walked outside to find Greyson waiting.

"It's probably too soon for normal people to have a second date," I teased him as I walked down the steps.

He pulled flowers out from behind his back. Tiger lilies. The name came to me even though I didn't remember seeing them before.

"We're not normal people," he told me with a smile, handing the lilies over to me.

I held them to my face and breathed in. "I think these just might be my favorite."

"Imagine that," he said quietly, giving me a smile. "And I might just be your favorite, too."

7

Greyson

O ne minute, the most beautiful girl in the world was standing on the step above me, looking down at the tiger lillies as if no one had ever brought her flowers before. Pride surged in my chest: I could be the one to give her all these things she had lost, like the memory of a man who loved her, giving her flowers.

The breeze caught her long brown hair and teased it around her face, and all I wanted to do was lean forward and kiss her smiling mouth.

In high school, I hadn't been the one who had thought to bring her flowers first. That had been Jack. But I was older and wiser, and I was going to be so fucking good to her that I would never, ever lose her again.

The next minute, as if I had summoned a certain blond-haired, sheep-dog-looking oversized hockey player, Jack shouldered out the doors then and barreled down toward us.

"Let's go," I told Kennedy, offering her my hand. "The area around the rink gets so trashy at night. Let me take you somewhere nice."

She grinned and reached out for my hand.

"Kennedy! Get away from him!" Jack's voice split the quiet night air.

She twisted, her lips parting in surprise.

This fucking asshole.

Now that she was happy, now that she had someone who cared about her, now that I would take care of her...he couldn't stay away. But he had ignored her for five fucking years.

"Is that the first thing he's ever said to you?" My voice came out harsh.

She twisted back to face me. "Well—practically. But..."

Her brows dimpled in a way that was adorable when that frown wasn't directed toward me. I never should have said that.

"Because he fucks all the puck bunnies," I went on. "He wants you now because he sees you with me."

"He wants me?" Her brows arched. "What is happening?"

Carter slammed the doors open and headed down the stairs too.

"Fantastic," I muttered. "I planned a nice night with you, but I guess a douchebag convention could be fun too."

"Kennedy." Jack reached her first, with Carter at his elbow; typical of the two of them even though Carter was supposed to be captain. "Where are you going with this guy?"

Kennedy's lips parted as if she were going to answer him, and then her face changed as if she'd just edited everything she was going to say. "What business is it of yours?"

Jack looked as if she had just slapped him. *Keep up, golden boy. You lost privileges of keeping tabs and protecting her about five years ago, when you abandoned her in the hospital.*

When you stole her from me.

He should be thankful I was just taking her and not ending his miserable life.

"I told you," I said smoothly. "They're just a couple of jealous bastards. They've always wanted what I have—"

"I don't want to be anything like you," Jack snarled back. He turned his attention back to Kennedy. "Please, listen to me. Come with me."

He held out his hand.

"You have got to be kidding me," she said.

As if I wasn't already so fucking in love with her.

But while Jack tried to win her over, Carter stepped between her and me.

It was a bad fucking idea to get between Kennedy and me again.

"Leave her alone," he said, his face dark with anger. "You're just going to get her hurt."

His voice dropped so that Kennedy wouldn't overhear. "Again."

"Don't whisper sweet fucking nothings to me, Carter, I don't want to hear them any more than she does." I pushed him out of my way.

Or tried to.

Carter was still built like a truck.

"Get out of here," Carter warned me, grabbing my arm to hold me back. "Stay away from her. Or I'm going to—"

I was so curious what the hell kind of threat he was going to make.

But apparently not curious enough, because instinct took over, and I decked Carter across the jaw.

He should've seen it coming. His winning personality meant he'd taken plenty of hits off the ice and on, even though he was supposed to be safe as goalie. But apparently he'd gotten soft since he ran away from my world, because he rocked back.

Then he threw himself at me.

I hadn't spent the last few years training for nothing. I

swiveled out of his way and then, because I kept close tabs on my old friends, I aimed a quick, snappy kick at his fucked-up right knee.

Carter was already pivoting to lock up on me, but the kick took his leg out from underneath him. His face was shocked as his knee gave way and he stumbled down one of the steps, before losing his balance completely. His big body slammed down the last few steps.

"What the fuck!" Jack yelled, shoving away from Kennedy. He threw one horrified look at Carter, then threw himself into me.

But these days, Jack was used to his fights being on the ice, not off. He wasn't the young mafia enforcer he'd once been. He grabbed my jacket like he would've grabbed another player's jersey, and I let him rip it off me as I buried my fist in his gut.

"Stop!" Kennedy cried out.

Jack and I closed up, throwing punches, jockeying to take each other down. The world went into a red blur of violence as my training took over.

The only thing that grounded me in this world and kept me from beating Carter to death was the way that Kennedy screamed.

Kennedy

I stood uncertainly on the steps for a few seconds that seemed to last a lifetime, trying to figure out what to do.

I didn't even understand what had just happened. I certainly couldn't figure out what to do next. Carter and Jack ignored me like I was dressed in wallpaper and drywall. Why the hell had they come flying out here like Greyson was some kind of threat?

But then...

Carter was at the bottom of the steps, rolling up to one knee and forcing himself up, with pain etched across his features. He was obviously struggling to put any weight on his wounded leg.

Meanwhile, Jack and Greyson were trading punches. Jack was strong and dangerous on the ice, but here Greyson seemed to have the advantage as Greyson launched a brutal, punishing volley of punches. Jack blocked most of them and got in a punch across Greyson's jaw that sent him flying back a step, but Greyson was unphased, shaking it off and dancing forward again.

"I'm going to kill you!" Jack told Greyson. "Stay away from her!"

Greyson didn't respond, but the next second the two of them had locked up. Jack threw two punches into Greyson's side that should've made a normal man stagger with some serious internal bleeding, but Greyson seemed immune.

Then suddenly, Greyson did some quick martial arts move that sent Jack off balance before tossing him over his shoulder. Jack landed on his back on the steps, with a crack that seemed like it must've broken his spine.

"I'd be more frightened that was a real threat if you weren't falling on your ass like Carter," Greyson told him, right before Carter barreled into him.

Greyson grinned at him, a quick flash of his teeth. "Finally. I've wanted to kick your ass for so long."

"Stop it!" I cried, throwing myself between them.

The two of them closed around me for a second, a

wall of muscle and fury. I threw up my hands to stop them, my eyes blurring with tears and panic. I couldn't stand this.

Greyson came to a halt. His hands fell on my waist, steadying me, as he looked over my head to Carter.

"It's alright, Kennedy," Greyson said quietly. "I've got you now."

"Stop fighting, please." I looked around, suddenly cognizant of the fact that a brawl on the arena steps was a bad look. "What the hell is going on?"

"It's alright." Greyson stroked his hands up my waist in a way that would've normally been soothing, that would have made me melt back into him. Part of me still wanted to, even as I stayed planted.

Carter stared down at the way Greyson was touching me, his eyes lit with fury, and I had the feeling he was about to attack Greyson again.

"If any of you hit each other again," I said, "I'll never talk to you again. I'm not going to listen to anything you have to say. Do you understand me?"

Carter's jaw worked once. Jack got to his feet and limped toward us, one hand at the small of his back as if he had strained something.

But Jack still gave me a nod. "Yes, ma'am. That's enough violence."

I didn't have to look back at Greyson to feel his scorn. Greyson was not the type to say yes, ma'am.

Jack raised his hands as if he were the one innocent one in this whole mess. "Just hear us out, okay?"

"What do you want to tell me?" I demanded.

In the distance, sirens split the air.

"Sounds like that's your cue to leave," Carter told Greyson. "Aren't you already a wanted man?"

"No." Greyson shook his head. "Found innocent, if you recall."

"Because you paid off the jury."

"Stop!" I interrupted the men before they could snarl at each other anymore. "Talk to me, not each other. I don't understand what the hell is going on."

Carter held his hand up like he was fending Greyson off, like Chris Pratt facing down velociraptors.

Greyson touched two long fingers to his newly split lip, and a look of annoyance crossed his face as if he realized just how busted-up he looked. I had the feeling not many people managed to land a punch on him. But his nose and cheekbone were swollen already, and his cheek was cut open.

"Let's go inside," I said again, keenly aware that people were gathering on the sidewalk across the street from the arena--very much keeping a safe distance–and taking photos. This was not a good look for the Devils.

"Greyson's got to run though, don't you?" Carter didn't even look at Greyson. "I'm sure you've got something illegal on you. Guns, drugs...you always have before."

"I'm not a wayward sixteen-year-old anymore, selling pot to make sure my sisters are fed," Greyson sounded amused.

"Right, Saint Greyson. That's the only reason you ever got on the wrong side of the law. It was always because you were rescuing puppies, wrong place, wrong time."

"Something like that," Greyson agreed.

My stomach dropped.

"He's mafia." Jack's eyes were serious as they met mine, and I didn't have any doubt he was telling me the truth. What he believed the truth was, anyway.

But Greyson had been so sweet and kind...

"A little respect," Greyson chided. "I'm more than some mafia goon at this point."

"You're so arrogant, you can't resist bragging to her that you're a mafia kingpin," Carter shot back. "Like you can't see she's too good for you."

I took a step back down the steps.

"Kennedy," Jack said.

"I've heard enough," I said. "I don't want to talk to any of you."

I turned and stumbled off down the steps.

Carter started to follow me.

"Leave her alone," Greyson growled at him. "Unless you want to lose the other knee. Give her space."

"Come on," Jack told Carter, clapping his shoulder. "We need to get back inside. Away from this...PR mess."

When I turned back, Jack and Carter were limping up the steps. They didn't turn back to look at me. Of course. They never cared about me. Greyson was probably right: they had some old vendetta, and they just cared about making sure he didn't have me.

Greyson, though, was watching me. His sharp jaw worked back and forth once, and he looked as if he had forgotten to staunch the wound across his cheek, he was so focused on me. Then a police car turned the corner, lights and sirens blazing, and with one last look after me, he cut into an alley and disappeared.

I couldn't help feeling as if I'd never see him again. After all, I had disappeared once, only to have no one ever come looking to find me.

I was halfway down the block when I realized I was still carrying Greyson's bouquet of flowers, and I had no idea what to do with it. The strangest frantic sensation came over me, like someone would realize I was connected to him because of the flowers. Like an FBI raid would descend on my apartment.

I turned back to make sure none of the guys were following

me. Part of me still didn't want to hurt Greyson's feelings. He had been so kind to me. But panic made my hands shake as I pushed open a trash can and deposited the bouquet inside. Tiger lilies joined old Burger King trash. I stared down at the beautiful petals for a second, feeling as if I'd just made the wrong choice.

But I couldn't make sense of anything that had just happened. Even as I wanted to run back to the arena, to get Greyson's side of the story, I made myself turn my back on the flowers.

Tears blurred my vision as I walked the dark city streets.

Alone.

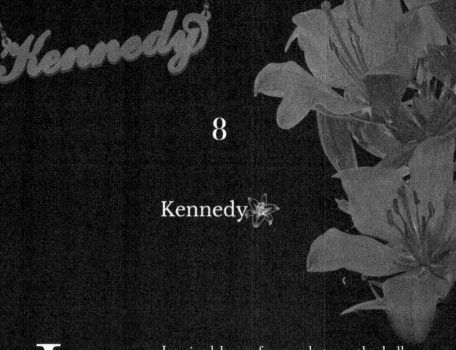

8

Kennedy

I was a mess as I arrived home from—whatever the hell that was. Confusion and loneliness were sparring in my chest. I'd thought waking up in the hospital five years ago with no idea who I was was the worst thing that could happen to me.

And the last five years of trying to figure things out had certainly not been a picnic...

But this? These men seeming to know me, or at least the whiplash they were giving me by being interested one second and then not the next...it was going to drive me insane.

Why were Jack and Carter so worried about me hanging out with Greyson? What did they know about me that they weren't saying? And what was the truth about Greyson?

Questions swirled in my mind like a never-ending storm, tearing at the never healing wound inside of me that had formed in the hospital on the day I woke up. It was as though I was trapped in a web of secrets, and every attempt to unravel them only seemed to entangle me further.

I'd discovered one thing about myself though...the little bit of kindness and affection Greyson had shown me...it had done something to me. Or at the very least showed me how desperately pathetic I was.

Because I realized I was willing to overlook a lot if it meant getting more of that.

The fact that I'd lost my memory, that there were pieces of my past that had been stolen from me—that was one thing. But since I'd stumbled into that hockey arena, it was the fragments of the present that haunted me the most. The feeling of being watched, the cryptic warnings, the feeling of deja vu...combine that with the inexplicable connection I felt with Jack, Carter, Sebastian, and Greyson...and I was feeling like a pawn in a game I couldn't understand.

With each step I took, the loneliness of the night seemed to close in around me, and everything felt...hopeless. Like I'd never find the answers I so desperately sought. The darkness of the night matched the darkness in my heart.

I fucking hated it.

I needed an escape.

A way to forget...

My phone buzzed, and I saw Carrie's name flashing on the screen. I hesitated for a moment, contemplating whether to answer or not. But maybe she could distract me from the shit show my life had suddenly turned into—if losing your memory to begin with wasn't considered a shit show already.

I swiped to accept the call.

"Hey," I greeted her, my voice laced with weariness.

"Kennedy, girl, what's going on?" Carrie's voice was immediately concerned, because after five years she could read my tone like a book..."Who do I need to kill?"

I snickered, because her attempting homicide would actually be hilarious rather than scary...but then I remembered why I was upset.

I sighed, running a hand through my hair. "It's been a day," I muttered as I stomped up the steps to my apartment, the steps groaning under my feet like they were seconds away from collapse.

"Complicated how—fuck! Don't eat that!" she snapped, and I found another grin on my face. Her kids were so freaking cute...but also handfuls.

"Just a second." She swore. "We don't eat poop!"

I waited as I unlocked my door and walked into my apartment, a big smile on my face as I imagined what was going on, and then she was back.

"Okay, crisis averted. You were saying?" she huffed.

I hesitated, not sure how much to reveal. "Let's just say I found out some things. And hockey players are assholes, and I'm feeling...weird."

There was a pause on the other end of the line before Carrie responded, her tone softening. "I mean that was definitely more vague than I was going for. But if you don't want to talk about it, that's fine too. But you know what always helps in these situations?"

I raised an eyebrow, even though she couldn't see it. "What?"

"Alcohol," Carrie declared. "Let's go out, get drunk, and forget about whatever is going on."

"Sure you're not running from the poop?" I teased.

She giggled. "Of course I'm running from the poop. Going out will be killing two birds with one stone...and you know I love multitasking."

"Okay, alcohol it is..."

Carrie sounded triumphant. "That's the spirit! Meet me at The Tipsy Unicorn in an hour. We'll drink until we can't remember what's bothering us."

I hung up the phone, anticipation and...relief washing over

me. Sometimes, all you needed was a bestie and a drink to put things in perspective, or at the very least, temporarily make you forget.

Not that I needed anymore forgetting...

* * *

The Tipsy Unicorn lived up to its name, with its dimly lit interior and the sound of laughter and clinking glasses filling the air. Carrie and I had already downed a few shots, and the world was starting to take on a hazy, carefree quality. It was exactly what I needed, a temporary escape from the confusing mess that had become my life.

It helped that Carrie always had a good story for me.

"So we hear banging against our door, and the knob jiggles...like someone was trying to get in."

She and her husband had just gotten back from a visit to Vegas, and evidently it had gotten a little crazy.

"What did you do?" I asked, a slight slur to my words as the shots kicked in.

"Well, as soon as we heard moans, we headed towards the peephole!"

"Moans?"

"Yeah, we thought someone had picked our door to have sex against."

"Were you close to the elevators?"

"No," she snorted, shaking her head as she threw back another shot of tequila.

"Okay...so were there people having sex?"

She shook her head, starting to laugh so hard that tears were gathering in her eyes. "There was a girl—" more hysterical laughter "—that was half naked...pleasuring herself against our door. Like you looked out and whoops, there was her vagina. All she had on was a sweater and some socks."

I stared at her incredulously...but evidently, Carrie wasn't done.

"So then she gets up, gets on all fours in the middle of the hallway, and starts rutting back like someone's fucking her, moaning to some invisible guy named Jeffrey about how good it feels."

"There's no way that happened."

"I swear on my dog's life," she said, with wide eyes.

"You'd swear on Pudding's life?" Carrie's dog was a million years old and senile. But we loved the old guy.

Carrie continued to regale me with details from the rest of the night, both of us taking a shot in between stories, getting drunker and drunker as the night wore on.

Eventually, groups of guys started to approach. They were a mix of confidence and swagger, clearly emboldened by alcohol. One of them, with a cocky grin, leaned in a little too close to me.

"Hey there, beautiful," he slurred, his breath heavy with the scent of alcohol. "You look like you want me."

Not the best pickup line...

I rolled my eyes, a burst of liquid courage fueling my response. "Sorry, this vagina is a man-free zone tonight. I'm just here to drink."

Carrie burst into laughter beside me, clinking her glass against mine. "She's not kidding, boys. Her vagina's got a strict no-man policy for the evening."

The guys backed off, a mix of disappointment and amusement on their faces, and we continued to enjoy our drinks in peace.

Carrie's gaze suddenly went wide-eyed as she stared at something behind me. "Wow," she mouthed.

I frowned and turned around, my own jaw dropping when I saw Jack standing there, looking like a figment of my hottest imagination. I blinked at him in disbelief, convinced I must be seeing things.

"Carrie," I slurred, nudging her with my elbow, "I think I've had too much to drink. Jack is standing there. I must be hallucinating."

Carrie was still wide-eyed, like a demented owl. "You're not hallucinating," she whisper yelled. "He's standing right there."

Jack's lips were amused as he stared at the two of us. "Hey there, ladies. Mind if I join you?"

"Don't look into his eyes," I muttered to Carrie. "He has superpowers. Makes you go all stupid."

"Oh, do I?" Jack purred, his hands settling on my shoulders.

I couldn't help but feel my cheeks flush. I was mad at him. I needed to remember that. "I'm mad at you," I said, but for some reason my words were tinged with a flirtatious tone.

Carrie shot me a knowing look, her eyebrow raised, "Blink once if you want me to hit him in the balls."

"Hey," Jack murmured, his fingers massaging expertly into my shoulders.

My brain was still trying to catch up to the fact that a little while ago he'd been fighting over me, and before that, he'd been ignoring me.

And now he was here...touching me.

"Okay?" he asked, his gold eyes beaming down at me like they did indeed hold magical powers.

I nodded, telling myself I was touch-starved, and that was why his touch felt so good. It could be anyone...it wasn't him.

Jack leaned in. "Good girl," he whispered, and I turned into a puddle, the words reverberating through me.

I wondered if the old me had liked the sound of those two little words as much as I was liking them now.

His grin grew wider, like he could see my thoughts, and then he ordered more drinks for Carrie and me.

"So Jack," Carrie said with a curl to her lip. "Why are you here?" She winked at me afterwards like she knew she was doing me a favor.

Jack had an arm slung around the back of my chair, and the warmth of his skin against my bare skin was a bit addicting.

Okay...it was *a lot* addicting.

I really was drunk.

"Couldn't stay away," he said. I glanced at him, because even in my lemon shot fueled stupor, I could hear the distress in his tone.

"Why is that a bad thing?" I asked, and he just shook his head, his finger reaching up and tracing my lips...effectively distracting me.

The hours clicked by, with Jack continuing to supply us with drinks, nursing a beer in his hand that I didn't really see him drinking. My head was currently thrown back as I laughed hard about a story he was telling us about his rookie year.

"You didn't do it. Tell me you didn't," Carrie cackled as she slapped her hand down. The alcohol flowed freely, and our laughter became increasingly raucous. The bar seemed to spin and sway with the rhythm of our merriment, and it was as if the complications of life had temporarily vanished into the haze of intoxication.

Jack winked and lifted up his shirt, showcasing the hottest set of abs I'd ever seen...and a large bass fish with *Sebastian* etched into the scales.

Carrie fell off her chair laughing so hard.

I of course had to be an idiot, and I reached out to touch the tattooed fish.

Jack flinched at my touch, but when I tried to rear back, he grabbed my wrist and kept my hand on his skin. I was trembling as I glanced up at his face, wondering if I'd just over-stepped. But it wasn't annoyance I saw...it was hunger. His golden gaze had darkened into simmering embers, and there was a faint flush to his cheeks.

"Love your touch, princess. But I only have so much control," he said roughly.

Wow. I swooned in my chair, heat spreading through me. I was feeling...lusty all of a sudden.

"Shoooots!" Carrie yelled, having picked herself up off the floor and settled back in her chair. By now there was a crowd around us, all of them eager to get some facetime with the star NHL player in their midst. Jack had bought several rounds for the bar already, and by their cheer, they were ready for more.

"What brought you to the arena in the first place?" he asked later, when Carrie decided to have a deep conversation about *dogs* with the person sitting next to her.

I bit down on my lip, his mention of the arena reminding me there was something fishy...and confusing about Jack.

"I woke up with no memories years ago, and afterwards...I started wandering the streets, thinking maybe something would jog my memory. The hockey arena was the first place that did."

"That's how you found it?" he murmured, almost to himself.

"You seem familiar too," I slurred, the alcohol making me bold. "Like we've met before?"

"Mmmh," he said in response, handing me another shot.

And this one made me forget that he hadn't actually answered my question.

The night continued, and it was hard to keep my eyes off of Jack. Did he know how hot he was?

"Yes," he said, amusement glimmering in his gaze.

Hmmm. Didn't think I'd said that out loud.

He was total book boyfriend material.

"You should fuck him," said Carrie in a sing-song voice, looking like a hot mess with her hair everywhere and her eyes unfocused.

"Shhhhh. He'll hear you!" I said, my eyes locked on Jack who was shaking his head as he stared at the two of us.

Carrie giggled. "I think he already did."

"Dance with me," Jack suddenly murmured, standing much closer than he had been just moments before. The air had taken on a sparkly effect, whirling around me like I'd found myself in some sort of fantastical wonderland...but dancing sounded like so much fun.

"Go!" Carrie said, lifting her drink. "I'll keep talking about dogs."

Jack snorted as he pulled me towards where people had been dry humping each other for the last few hours.

As we stepped out onto the dimly lit dance floor, the throbbing beat of the music enveloped us. The atmosphere was electric, the bass pulsating through my body as I swayed to the rhythm. In my inebriated state, everything felt heightened, and the dreamlike quality of the world around me continued.

I glanced up at Jack, my words slurring slightly as I spoke, "I think...I think this is my favorite song."

Jack chuckled, his eyes sparkling with amusement as he responded, "Is it now? Well, we're in luck then."

He didn't seem like he believed me, but I also didn't know if it was my favorite song or not...I just knew I really liked it at that moment.

The song that played had a sultry, sensual melody that seemed to resonate with the energy between us. As we moved together on the dance floor, there was a palpable tension in the air, a magnetic pull that drew us closer. It was as if the music had become a conduit for the unspoken emotions that simmered just beneath the surface.

Our bodies swayed in perfect sync, each movement deliberate and sensuous. I could feel Jack's strong arms around me, his hands guiding me with a gentle confidence that sent shivers down my spine. There was an undeniable chemistry between us, an unspoken understanding that transcended words.

As the song continued, the world around us faded away, and it was just Jack and me, lost in the rhythm and the allure of the moment. Our gazes locked, and for a heartbeat, time seemed to stand still.

"Why does it feel like we've done this before?" I whispered.

His fingers tightened against my skin, and there was a tic in his cheek as he stared beyond me.

"No questions tonight, okay?" he asked, his voice husky and filled with pent-up emotion.

If I was sober, I would have pushed back, demanded answers. But right then in his arms, I couldn't find it in me to ask anything else. It just felt too good to be held like this. Like he'd been made just for me.

I'd had Carrie these last five years...but for the most part, I'd been alone.

I didn't feel so alone right then.

I didn't feel alone when I was with Greyson either...

I finally nodded, my throat tight with unspoken desire as I laid my head against his chest. I'd seen it though...a hunger in his eyes that mirrored my own, a longing just the same as me.

Our bodies pressed closer together. Suddenly, close wasn't close enough. A wave of lust crashed over me. It was everything, the heat of his breath against my skin, the feel of his arms around me, his hard length pressing against my stomach.

I whimpered and his hand came up to cradle my head against his chest.

My drunk brain couldn't figure out why I wanted to climb him like a tree.

Wanted wasn't the right word. *Desperate* was actually how I was feeling.

I lifted my head up, burning for the touch of his lips. His head bent, lips getting closer and closer...

"Fuck!" he swore, snapping his head up abruptly and shaking his head.

Shame and embarrassment coursed through me.

They were playing with me. Even my alcohol clogged brain could understand that.

I tried to push away and his arms tightened around me.

"Let me go," I snarled. "I don't know if this is something you and your friends do as fucked up fun—but stop doing it with me." My words were slurred and embarrassing, and hot tears were gathering in my eyes.

"It's not like that. I promise," he said desperately.

"I don't understand," I cried out, still trying to push away from him.

Jack swore again...

And then his lips crashed against mine, a searing kiss that scorched my insides, spreading warmth through my veins where there had only been cold. Our tongues danced together, and the world seemed to disappear as we lost ourselves in each other.

His kiss felt like coming home.

I'd thought about having some sloppy kisses since waking up in that hospital, times when I'd let Carrie set me up on a date—where I'd think about letting some guy stick his tongue down my throat to see if I could feel anything.

This was the opposite of sloppy. It was like we'd done this dance a million times before, like his lips were meant to be mine. A tear slid down my cheek at the pure emotion I felt passing between us.

He licked and sucked at my mouth, like I was the oxygen

he needed to breathe. The music played around us, a room full of people but we might as well have been alone. His hard cock pressed into me and I moaned, wanting more. He had one hand on my ass and the other one tangled in my hair, sliding my head exactly where he wanted me.

I needed more. I'd never craved anything since I'd woken up.

But I was definitely craving him.

His hand tightened on my ass and then...

Someone nearby whooped loudly, bringing reality crashing over us.

"Fuck, Fuck, Fuck," Jack hissed as we pulled apart abruptly. He glanced around us with a glare, like he was trying to find who had dared to break up our kiss. He was still holding me against him, and when he glanced down at me again, he pressed one last kiss on my mouth, like he couldn't help himself. Our breaths were ragged and a rosy warmth was spread all over my chest and I'm sure my cheeks.

His thumb caressed my skin, desire simmering in the golden hue of his gaze.

"A drink. I need another drink," I blurted out, suddenly extremely uncomfortable with all the emotions slashing between us.

He smiled, amused. Like he once again knew something I didn't.

"Okay, pretty girl. We'll get you a drink."

We headed back to the bar where Carrie was still holding court, a crowd of people hanging on whatever story she was telling.

At least it sounded like she'd moved on from dogs.

As soon as she saw me, she started waving her hands in her face like she was trying to cool off.

"Fuck, Kennedy. Are you pregnant yet?"

I choked out a surprised...and embarrassed cough, Jack's chest shaking in laughter against my back.

Carrie grabbed her phone and blearily tapped at the screen, aiming it at Jack. She leaned in close to me, her voice a drunken whisper-yell. "This one's for your 'spank bank,' Kennedy."

I snorted, my cheeks flushing with embarrassment. But it actually sounded like a genius idea.

Carrie's attempts at taking a picture were abandoned when the door of the bar opened, and a tall, handsome man walked in. Because I was so drunk, it took me a moment to realize it was Carrie's husband. Keith.

She let out an excited squeal and launched herself forward, throwing her arms around him. "Baby! You're here!"

Her husband caught her in his arms, his face breaking into a fond smile. "You look like you're having a good time," he murmured, his hands caressing her face.

Sharp longing shot through me as I watched them. They were so in love. I wanted something like that.

Carrie began to whisper loudly to him, her words punctuated with playful giggles. "Oh, you have no idea what I'm going to do to you when we get home. It involves whipped cream and your dick...and you're definitely fucking me in the ass."

Keith coughed out a laugh, shaking his head, completely unfazed by her enthusiastic declarations since a drunk Carrie was always a horny Carrie. He shook his head at Jack. "She always says things like this. But the follow through is shit. She'll be passed out and snoring as soon as I get her in the front seat."

I giggled, and Jack's laughter floated over me. I glanced up, a little dazed at how gorgeous he looked with that wide grin.

A smile like that should be illegal. Or come with a warning. Because it was hazardous to your ovaries for sure.

"A warning label, huh?" he smirked, wrapping his arms around me. Shoot, I'd said that out loud.

"You're still saying it out loud," Keith said as Carrie tried to grab his dick.

"Whoa girl," he said, holding her hands above her head.

"Just like that, daddy," she purred, and Keith's cheeks went scarlet.

"Okay, it's time to get you home," he murmured, leaning down to whisper something against her ear that had Carrie melting against him.

Keith's gaze suddenly went wide. "Holy fuck. You're Jack Cameron! From the Devils! I'm a huge fucking fan, man."

Oh yeah, I'd forgotten he was famous for a minute.

For a minute...he'd just felt like mine.

Jack's hand squeezed my hip, like he'd just read my mind.

"Nice to meet you, man," Jack said, making no move to release me.

Keith glanced at me...and then at Jack's hand on my hip. "Ummm, Kennedy...you need a ride?"

"She's fine. I'll make sure she gets home safely," Jack murmured before I could say anything.

I stared up at him in shock, but he had the audacity to just wink at me.

"Kennedy?" Keith asked, even as Carrie started to do a weird dry humping thing against his leg.

"I'm—I'm good to go with him," I answered as his fingers started to trail across the skin peeking out between my shirt and my jeans.

I shivered as Carrie lifted a fist and yelled, "That's my girl! Get some hot hockey dick!"

Keith's eyes widened. "I'm so sorry," he mouthed to Jack as he led Carrie towards the door. A couple of stumbling steps in, and he swept her up in his arms.

"They're perfect together," I murmured, right before I was suddenly lifted up into a pair of strong arms.

"What are you doing?" I asked...as I nuzzled into Jack's hard chest.

"Didn't want to be shown up," he said, with another one of those dangerous winks that had my traitorous pussy flooding.

Somehow holding me with one arm, Jack dug in his pocket and pulled out a few hundred dollar bills. He tossed them on the counter and gave a head nod to the staring bartender before starting for the door.

I should definitely make him put me down.

Definitely. Definitely.

But when the door opened and the cool night air hit my skin, I decided I could stay in his arms...just for a little while longer.

Just for warmth, of course.

Jack strode us towards a giant truck, opening the door and setting me in the passenger seat...gently...like I was some kind of precious cargo. He grabbed the seatbelt and buckled it around me, and—

"Hey pretty girl," he murmured, tucking his letterman jacket around me as I groggily opened my eyes.

"Oh, did I fall asleep?" My hand went to my mouth quickly, desperately hoping I didn't have drool on my face.

I glanced around, realizing we'd pulled into his driveway.

Fuck. This was where I had to say goodbye for the night...go back to the hellish trailer park across the road. I was never going to understand how the neighborhood of mansions had ended up so close to the trailer park. It had to drive these rich people crazy that they had trash like me so close by.

"Kennedy—" he started, his hand caressing my cheek. Butterflies went wild in my insides, dancing frantically around because the way he was looking at me...

Time froze as our gazes locked, each passing moment imbued with a sense of anticipation, an electric charge. Was I imagining this? Was he—he leaned in, his lips tantalizingly close to mine.

And then his lips brushed against me, like a whispered secret that did nothing but make me want him more.

"Kennedy, I—"

"Everything okay?" Jack asked, and I crashed back into the cab of his truck, struggling to hold onto the pieces of what felt like a memory skittering through my head.

A strange sense of deja vu crept up my spine, and I shook my head, trying to get ahold of myself.

Jack was staring at me, his eyebrows arched in concern.

"Yeah, I'm fine. Just...just a little drunk," I murmured unsteadily, wanting to cry because whatever memories I'd just had...they were gone.

Stupid. Stupid. Brain.

He stared at me for a second more, before starting the truck, his arm going across the headrest behind me in that universal hot guy move as he glanced behind us and pulled out into the street.

"I'm on Wakefield Street," I murmured groggily, leaning my head against the cool window.

His hand that wasn't on the steering wheel was still stretched behind me, playing with strands of my hair.

The touch of his hand, the gentle purr of his truck, the soft music playing on the radio...

Within just a few minutes...I was asleep.

"All mine," he growled against my skin, grabbing me from behind as he pulled me tight against his chest.

"Mine," he murmured against my lips as his tongue licked against my skin. His hand covered my breast, kneading it as his other hand dragged down my stomach and in between my legs.

I whimpered as his fingers slid against my slit as he bit and sucked at my skin.

He bent his knees, lining our bodies up...his hard dick rubbed against the crease of my ass as he pressed against my clit, rubbing it expertly through my jeans.

"My pussy," he whispered as his other hand began to tug and pinch against my nipple.

I was writhing against him, crying out as pleasure streaked through me.

He bit down hard at my pulse point, immediately licking and sucking at the spot when I gasped in pain.

Suddenly, I was spun around and lifted up. My legs immediately wrapped around him, nestling his dick against my core. He strode towards his bedroom, every step pressing his cock against the seam of my jeans and somehow hitting my clit just right.

"Fuck, you're perfect. My perfect, good girl," he soothed as I buried my face against his neck.

"Give me your mouth," he ordered suddenly, stopping and pressing my back against the wall just outside his bedroom. His mouth claimed mine in a hungry, desperate kiss, his tongue tangling with me as he licked in and out.

"Please," I murmured, and his answering smile lit up my insides.

"I'll take such good care of you," he promised as his lips met mine. He grinned as his hips pressed against me, so I could feel every inch of his hard cock. He thrust against my core, pushing me closer to the edge as he hit that perfect spot between my legs. I buried my face in his neck, not wanting the others to hear.

"Let them hear you," he said in that way he always did, like he had a direct line to the thoughts in my head. "I want them to hear how good I take care of you."

He thrust against me again, and just like that, I was coming, my soft whimpers floating through the air.

"That's one. But we can do much better than that." He strode

over to his bed and threw me on the soft sheets. And then he stood at the edge, staring down at me, almost reverently, like he couldn't believe I was there. I didn't know why they looked at me like that. When they were Gods among men...And I was no one.

He slowly lowered himself to the floor and gripped my thighs, pulling me forward until my legs were hanging off the bed.

"These need to come off," he murmured as he tugged on my jeans, every whispered word out his mouth seducing me. In just a moment, my sandals were off, then my jeans, his fingers stroking along my skin as he pulled them down my legs. Soon I was lying there in nothing but my T-shirt and panties.

He stared at my thong, a tic in his cheek as he softly touched the wet spot on the fabric, evidence of the orgasm he'd just given me. His eyes closed, and there was a pained expression on his face.

With a growl, he abruptly ripped my underwear off so I was bare to the cool air. He grabbed my legs, throwing them over his shoulders while he buried his face in my core.

I whined desperately as his tongue licked through my folds, a finger working its way inside me.

"Fuck," I cried out as he hit that perfect spot. He chuckled against my core, licking and sucking at my skin, circling around my clit but never hitting where I wanted him to.

Where I needed him to.

"Please," I begged. "Please let me come."

"Are you my good girl?" he said lazily as his tongue licked through my slit, his finger still inside me.

"Yes. I promise. Please," I whimpered desperately.

"Fuck. You're sweet," he growled.

My heart was a staccato drum beat in my chest. He was usually the sweet one, the perfect boyfriend of your dreams...but he happened to have the dirtiest mouth.

And I loved it.

"Please fuck me," I panted.

"Please fuck me what?" he taunted, slowly sliding his finger out of me all the way.

I was close to tears with how empty I felt.

"Please, sir," I pleaded.

"That's it, baby."

He growled as he shifted forward, shoving my shirt over my head and flicking off my bra so I was completely bare. I never liked to think about why they were all so smooth at that.

There must have been a frown on my face because he gently gripped my chin, yanking my attention back to him. "Stop thinking," he snapped. "Unless you're thinking about my fingers, my cock, or my tongue—and what they're doing to you—you're only feeling. Understand."

I nodded in his grip and he rewarded me with his mouth on my chest, his teeth biting down gently and suckling on my nipples as he thrust two fingers inside me, the heel of his hand pressing against my clit with each thrust of his hand.

"Yes, yes, yes," I cried out as I thrashed on the bed. His arms tightened over my legs, pinning me down as his fingers fucked in and out of me. His tongue on my nipples was rough, sliding on the edge of pain as much as pleasure.

And I loved it.

Whimpers streamed from my mouth as his tongue joined his fingers, licking and sucking and finally focusing on my clit.

With just one more slide of his tongue, I was coming, my core squeezing his fingers. He continued to thrust them in and out of me until I was writhing from how sensitive I was.

When it was almost too much, he finally lifted his head, his lips shiny from my cum. He slid his fingers out of my pussy and brought them to his mouth, making a big deal about licking me off him.

He surged forward, his lips capturing mine so that I could taste myself on his tongue.

"Your pussy tastes so good," he murmured against my lips. "I could stay down there all day. But my cock is desperate for you."

"Just your cock?" I whispered.

"All of me is desperate for you." There was an ache in his voice and a burning vulnerability in his gaze. And I understood what he was feeling, because sometimes this all just felt like too much.

Like we were living in a dream world, the five of us, and if we blinked, it would all go away.

He lifted off me, and slid up his shirt—I'd never get used to his perfection. That eight pack, the sexy v that dipped to his hips. Self-consciousness slithered through me.

My body was all soft curves, none of the hard perfection of his body present anywhere on me.

"You're perfect," he promised as he pushed down his pants, revealing the swollen, glistening head of his huge cock.

He rubbed it through my dripping wet folds, once...twice, his gaze searching mine.

I nodded, a smile tipping my lips as he pushed in slowly, carefully, his eyes never leaving mine.

I gasped at the stretch. No matter how many times they took me, it always felt like this, the perfect stretch as they filled me completely.

His lips descended, sweetly moving against me, his tongue dancing and tangling with mine.

"I love you," he murmured as he slowly drew back.

Before I could answer him, he slammed forward, until he was sheathed completely inside me, my cry filling the room as he completely stretched me open.

"That's it, baby. You take me so good. Like you were made just for me," he groaned as he kissed me softly. "You're so *fucking beautiful." He sounded kind of dazed as his fingertips trailed along my jaw.*

My breath caught as he started moving, the tip of his cock hitting that perfect spot. His arms caged me in so I felt completely possessed by him.

Completely owned.

He thrust in and out of me as I wrapped my legs around his hips, pleasure spiraling through me.

"Fuck." He flipped us over until I was on top of him, his fingers digging into my hips, his cock filling me.

I flushed as his gaze slid down my face, to my breasts, to where we were connected. He bit down sexily on his bottom lip and I almost came just from that.

"Ride me, sweetheart. Show me how much you own me," he ordered in a gruff voice.

I shifted my hips, lifting myself off him, still keeping him inside me before I thrust down.

"That's it. Choke my big dick. I love your tight cunt, princess," he growled.

Suddenly I was awake, completely on top of a hard body, my core rubbing against his leg like I was a dog in heat.

Coming.

My whole body contracting as pleasure surged through me.

It took a second for the horror to flash through me. Lifting my head, I stared up at...

Carter.

I was in bed with Carter.

I'd just fucking dry humped Carter.

And judging by the monster dick pressing against my hip... I'd been doing it for awhile.

"Oh crap. Oh crap. Oh crap. Oh crap," I screeched as I launched myself off him.

We were both still clothed...well, he was half clothed,

wearing a pair of basketball shorts, his golden skin and abs, and way too many perfect muscle visible at the moment.

"I'm so sorry," I told him as I scrambled off the bed.

I froze for a minute, trying to figure out how I'd ended up here. Was I still dreaming? My hangover hit me then, my skull feeling like a drum had taken up residence and was beating me with its sticks.

I'd gotten drunk. I remembered that. Being at the Tipsy Unicorn with Carrie. We'd been doing shots...

And Jack! He'd shown up at some point.

Flashes of images hit me. The two of us on a crowded dance floor. Had he kissed me? His hands lifting me into a truck.

And then...

"How did I get here?" I asked, cringing at how hoarse my voice sounded. "With you?"

He was propped up on one muscly arm right then, staring at me with a smirk on his lips, his dick still saying "top of the morning" to me through his basketball shorts.

Don't look at his dick, I yelled at my apparently thirsty self. I was still feeling achy inside from the orgasm, my body primed and ready for more.

The door suddenly opened next to me and Sebastian, of all people, poked his head in, not seeming surprised at all that I was plastered against the wall.

"Oh good. The Sleeping Beauties are up. Jack's making pancakes downstairs." His gaze hovered on me for a moment, sliding from my toes, up to my head, leaving a trail of heat across my skin. "Come down when you're ready."

"You all live together?" I guessed, trying to plan out how fast I could move out of the state. Or maybe even the country.

I wasn't sure that there was a place far enough to outrun the embarrassment I was feeling at the moment.

Carter slid out of bed, stretching his arms above his head. And sue me, but I couldn't look away. There was just too much hot perfection in front of me. His dark hair was tousled, somehow looking even sexier than it normally did. He caught me looking...not that it wasn't obvious since I was practically drooling over him as I stood there, and he ambled towards me.

His hand cupped my thigh and he leaned towards my ear, his dick poking into my side. "Just for the record, sweetheart, you can ride me anytime you like. I'll even call you 'good girl' while you do it." He leaned back so he could see the full weight of my mortification. "It's more Jack's thing. But I can work with it."

I literally slithered to the ground, melting into a puddle of lust and horror, and he chuckled and left the room, leaving me sitting there.

Despite the fact that I was currently dying of embarrassment, I couldn't help but notice the room.

How nice it was.

The walls were a ritzy combination of dark wood paneling and light, neutral tones, the centerpiece of the room the large, king-sized bed that I'd woken up in. The headboard and gray silk sheets looked expensive, a world above the thrift store furniture that made up my tiny apartment. Soft, ambient lighting radiated from strategically placed wall sconces, casting a warm and inviting glow.

A floor-to-ceiling window stretched along one wall, offering a breathtaking view of the city skyline. Heavy, velvet curtains in a rich shade of midnight blue framed the view, and I realized as I dragged myself off the floor and looked out...we were really high up.

As I glanced around the room, my gaze caught on a framed photograph of four kids. I was pretty sure that three of the kids were Carter, Jack, and Sebastian, cheeky smiles and mud spread over their cheeks. I leaned forward, wondering who the fourth person in the photograph was. He was staring at the other boys though, so his face was partially obscured by the angle of the shot. His smile was more somber, a haunted look in his eyes that was different from the others.

A door slammed somewhere down the hall and I jumped, feeling like I was doing something I wasn't supposed to.

Not that I was supposed to be here at all.

I followed the tempting scent of sizzling bacon and the faint clatter of dishes down a set of stairs, my heart sinking with every step. There was no doubt in my mind that Carter had shared the details of me...coming on his leg with the others, and the thought of facing all three of them after that little rendezvous meant that my embarrassment was now going to be multiplied by three.

If I couldn't move, I was going to have to find another job. I mean, how did one come back from dry humping a stranger's leg?

The better question was...how had I ended up in his bed to begin with? I had faint memories of Jack offering to take me home.

So how had I gotten back to his place?

As I descended the staircase, the sound of their voices grew louder, mingling with laughter and snippets of inside jokes I didn't understand. Another wave of...familiarity passed over me.

My insides clenched. You'd think after five years I'd get used to not remembering things. But these last couple of weeks had been excruciating, feeling like I was on the edge of something, but not able to understand what the "something" was.

The aroma of breakfast grew stronger as I reached the bottom of the stairs, and my stomach churned with a mix of hunger and apprehension, wishing there was a way to sneak out unnoticed. But it looked like the front door of the place was on the other side of the kitchen.

There was no way but *through*, evidently.

Taking a deep breath, I stepped into the kitchen, my eyes widening at how...fancy it was. I guess I should have expected that though, with how nice Carter's bedroom had been. The kitchen had sleek gray marble countertops, stainless steel appliances, and a large island in the center surrounded by leather barstools.

It was the nicest kitchen I'd ever seen...but it couldn't hold my attention compared to the three guys in it—Carter, Jack, and Sebastian.

Who were all shirtless.

Carter, with his chiseled jawline and a scattering of dark tattoos across his broad chest, was leaning against the island, sipping a cup of coffee. His dark hair was still tousled in a way that screamed "just out of bed," and his warm emerald eyes were full of mischief as he stared at me.

Knowingly. Like he knew what I sounded like when I came.

Which he did.

Jack was by the stove, expertly flipping a pancake. His ash-blond hair fell in disheveled waves, his sculpted back and arms flexed with each graceful movement, and I felt a little dazzled at the sight.

Sebastian was snacking on a piece of bacon from a plate piled high in front of him on the island. His dark blond hair was slightly mussed, and I got caught staring at his tattoos. One of them said "Princess."

A flash of jealousy coursed through me thinking of another girl's nickname on his body.

That was weird.

His dark blue eyes met mine, and a smile tugged at the corners of his lips.

Is this what it felt like to be high?

My thoughts swirled in a dizzying mix of desire and admiration as I struggled to form coherent sentences. My cheeks felt like they were on fire, and my pulse was racing. I was also embarrassingly wet between my thighs. The three of them like this was too much.

Just think about what it would be like if they were all naked.

It was as if the kitchen was really a siren's den, and I'd been hopelessly ensnared.

Do not embarrass yourself anymore, I screamed internally.

"We would have let you sleep longer, but we have practice. Didn't want you waking up somewhere unfamiliar..." Jack said, sounding like he'd cut himself off.

"Umm, thanks for that," I murmured as Sebastian handed me a cup of...chai. A steaming cup of chai tea. I stared at it for a moment before taking a sip.

Yep, I still really liked it.

But how on earth would they have known that?

I glanced at Sebastian suspiciously, but he was back to chomping on a piece of bacon, definitely not on the edge of his seat about whether I was a coffee or tea drinker.

"Grab a plate, babe," Carter said, that stupid, hot grin still on his face, like he meant every word out of his mouth as a tease.

"Thanks," I murmured, rubbing at my forehead, my hangover headache still thrashing through me.

"And here's some Advil," Carter said, handing me a bottle.

"That obvious, huh?" I groaned as I grabbed the pill bottle and poured some into my hand.

"You've been playing it pretty cool, but there was no way

you weren't going to have a headache after last night," said Jack casually as he flipped another pancake expertly.

I bit down on my lip, almost jumping when I realized Sebastian was staring at my lip like it had personally offended him. I released it and he sighed, tearing into another piece of bacon while still staring way too intensely at me.

"Um...about last night. How exactly did I end up here?"

Everyone was silent for a moment, and then Jack slid some pancakes onto a plate for me. "You asked to come over. And you were pretty drunk. So it seemed like a good idea to have someone watch over you."

My cheeks flushed darker and I wanted to sink into the polished wood floor. If I'd been dry humping Carter this morning...I could only imagine what I'd been like last night.

"Right," I said, pouring some syrup over the pancakes and stuffing a bite in my mouth so I didn't have to say anything else for a minute.

All three of them were watching me, and just like the whole shirtless god thing they had going on...their attention all at once was way too much.

Why did Carter have to eat like that? I didn't even know you could make eating sexy. I certainly hadn't mastered the art since I was shoveling pancakes into my mouth like it was my job. Chocolate chip pancakes? I loved them. It was one of the few things since I'd woken up that I'd discovered pretty early on and I knew without a doubt—they were my favorite breakfast food.

"Like those pancakes, princess?" Sebastian drawled, and my fork froze halfway to my mouth at the nickname...that was tattooed on his hot as fuck body.

Maybe it was just his thing. He called girls "princess." After all, it was a nickname you saw constantly in romance books.

The thought of him using that on another person made me feel sick inside. I set my fork down.

"Yeah, they're my favorite," I answered, trying not to sound despondent.

It was official. I'd gone crazy. Or at least more crazy than I'd been before. I really needed to get out of here.

But there was just one more thing I really needed to know.

"And, uh, how exactly did I end up in Carter's bedroom, um, in his bed." The word bed came out choked sounding, and Carter's grin was so wide at that point, he almost looked like a caricature.

A very hot caricature, but a caricature nonetheless.

"Well, you started off in the guest room," Jack said...a little too innocently.

"And then around two am, you went exploring into my room," continued Sebastian.

"Eventually ending up in mine," Carter finished, giving me a casual shrug like this wasn't the most awful, embarrassing thing I'd ever done.

I was never drinking again.

And I was never telling Carrie about this.

She'd be way too excited. Didn't want to give my bestie a heart attack or anything.

I covered my face with my hands. "I'm so fucking sorry," I squeaked. Suddenly, warm hands were pulling mine away from my face.

"I'm not," Carter freaking purred as he stared down at me.

"Breathe, baby," Jack murmured with a snort. And my breath came out in a gasp since, evidently, I'd been holding it the whole time Carter had been touching me.

I stepped away from Carter and shoveled the rest of my pancakes into my mouth like it was my job.

Plus, they did taste freaking amazing.

As soon as the last bite had been swallowed–without me choking, thank fuck–I was ready to get out of there.

Or at least it felt like the socially right thing to do.

There was something comforting about being around them though. Something safe.

Just another thing to unravel when I was alone. When I wasn't humping some stranger's leg after I'd slipped into his bed like a creepy stalker in the middle of the night.

"Can I have the address so I can grab an Uber? I know you guys have to get ready for practice." I said the last word slowly. Because all three of them looked alarmed that I'd asked.

"I promise I'm not going to start stalking any of you...I just need to know where to be picked up."

"I'll drive you," said Jack, turning off the burner on the stove and wiping his hands off on a dishtowel.

It was all so...domestic. Nothing that I would expect from three superstar athletes.

"You can stay though," blurted out Sebastian, before he rubbed a tattooed hand down his face.

I stared at him curiously, comparing his—all of their behavior before the fight the other day.

What on earth was going on?

"I have laundry to do before my shift tonight," I said lamely, even though something was screaming inside me to take him up on it.

"Right," he said, looking so disappointed...I had the urge to hug him.

Okay. I had to get out of here. Now.

"Let me grab my keys," Jack said, but even his golden personality seemed muted, like all the energy had been sucked out of the room.

"See ya," Carter said gruffly, stalking past me as Jack got the keys.

Maybe I *was* going to have to talk to Carrie about this. Maybe we needed to go over every detail and analyze why it felt like all three of them were upset about me leaving after I'd prowled into their bedrooms in a drunken haze and mounted one of them.

The ride was mostly silent back to my place. It was a surprisingly quick ride. Their fancy high rise was surprisingly close to the poorer side of town where I lived.

For some reason, that thought made my head hurt, and I shifted in my seat at the weird sensation crawling over my skin.

He stopped outside my apartment, shooting it a look of distaste as he put the truck in park. I moved to open my door, but he grabbed my hand before I could.

"Let me," he murmured, before hopping out of his truck and jogging around to open my door.

Had I mentioned how hot Jack's truck was? It was red and lifted, which I wouldn't usually be a fan of. But because I'd felt first hand how big his dick was when I'd been dancing against him last night, it was firmly in the sexy category. There was no overcompensating happening there. Jack and his dick were made for this truck.

"What's in that pretty head that has you blushing so much?" Jack teased as he helped me out of the truck.

Fuck. My cheeks *were* blazing.

"Embarrassment," I quickly said. "Pure embarrassment. I'm sorry again. Thanks for taking care of me. Who knows what I would have done last night if I'd been left to my own devices. Probably streaked across the complex or something."

He chuckled, walking me towards my apartment building.

"I'm good here. Thanks so much again," I blurted out, not wanting him anywhere near my shitty apartment after I'd just seen the palace he and the others lived in.

Let's just say he wouldn't be impressed.

Not even the cockroaches that made an appearance every few weeks despite all my traps and my unhealthy obsession with bleach were impressed.

Jack bit down on his lip again, like he was trying to decide if he wanted to listen to me, but finally, he pulled me towards him.

"You should try my dick next time if you want to orgasm, sweetheart. It's much better than Carter's leg," he said offhand, his lips so close to my ear that they grazed my skin, sending starry shivers pulsing over my skin.

With that very unexpected parting thought, he walked back to his truck—whistling like a psychopath as he left me there...a mess.

It took me the rest of the day to get over my embarrassment and think about how impressive it was he'd remembered the address I'd given him last night, and taken me home without a reminder.

Almost like he already knew it to begin with...

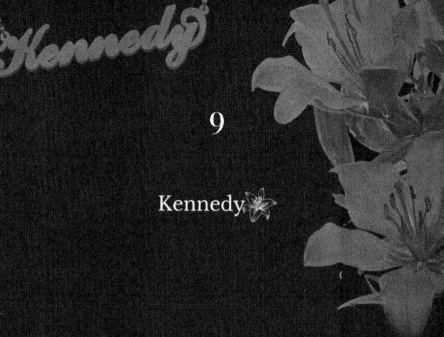

9

Kennedy

When I walked into my apartment, it seemed so small and sad compared to the penthouse. From the doorway, I could see the entirety of the galley kitchen, the small living room that felt cramped with just my couch, coffee table, and television, and the hallway to my bedroom.

Worst of all, everything I'd done to make it homey looked like a pathetic attempt, as if I were seeing it through their eyes. The Dollar Store lights I'd strung so carefully around the ceiling; the power always dimmed when I plugged them in at night. The Target dollar spot kitchen towels, hung neatly from the oven handle, that declared *It's Fall, Y'all*. The threadbare couch covered with a blanket.

Did they see me as pathetic?

After all, I'd slept in their beds, even though for weeks, they'd treated me like a pariah. For a few moments though, it had felt as if getting to know them was key to unlocking my memories.

And for a few minutes, it had felt nice...

I did my best to shake it off, focusing on dragging my laundry down to the apartment building's laundromat and getting it started. I babysat my laundry until it had made it through the dryer—there was a creepy old man on the fourth floor that I was pretty sure had stolen my underwear before—while I read my romance novel.

But as much as I loved a good book, it was hard to get lost in that fantasy when my mind kept returning to *them*.

I'd just staggered to my room with the laundry basket and dropped it on my bed when someone knocked on the door.

I wiped sweat off my forehead—the laundry room was so hot and humid—before I checked the peep hole.

Handsome face, even with a bruise marring one high cheekbone and a split across his kissable lips. Dark hair, artfully mussed. And big shoulders in a jacket, clutching a new bouquet of tiger lilies.

I should pretend I wasn't here.

His icy blue eyes seemed to stare right through the peep-hole and reach me, and I felt myself freeze, as if he could see right through and know I was there. I turned and tried to tiptoe away across the apartment.

"Kennedy." His voice was soft but stern, and it carried through the door. It felt like his voice went straight to my heart. "Please talk to me. Don't assume what I am because of what someone else said."

I hesitated for a few long seconds.

Then I pulled the door open. His face relaxed when he saw me, a smile breaking across his lips. He was so handsome it made me want to melt.

"I'm not assuming based on what someone else said," I told him, reminding myself as much as I was reminding him. "I'm assuming because of what *you* said."

"Can we go somewhere and talk?" A playful smile

crossed his lips, as if even if I'd run away from him before, he knew our future was inevitable. All his stress seemed to have melted away the second I opened the door. "Somewhere public?"

My gaze flickered down to the bouquet he held in one hand.

He raised them, holding them toward me. "I thought you might need a new bouquet."

"No one needs flowers."

"I disagree. As far as I'm concerned, Kennedy, anything you want is a need... and anything you need, I'm going to make yours."

I raised my eyebrows. "You're a little creepy and over-bearing."

He smiled back at me, without a trace of apology or regret. "Or...Possessive and protective?"

"It sounds better." I hesitated, then told him, "Wait here."

I closed the door on him, curious if some dangerous mafia guy who could obviously more than hold his own in a fight would really just wait in the hall for me. So I took my time, pulling out the big mason jar I used as a flower vase or cookie jar, depending on circumstances, trimming the stems, and arranging my flowers.

When I set them on the coffee table, I had to admit, they made the room look a whole lot nicer.

I swung the door open again, expecting he might be gone. For a second, the hallway seemed empty, and my heart dropped.

Well. I hadn't expected to feel so completely deflated.

I shouldn't trust him anyway. I should be glad he'd lost interest.

Shouldn't I?

Then I saw him, sauntering down the hall toward me. His

hands were in his pockets, highlighting his powerful shoulders, pushing up his jacket so I could see the lean taper of his waist.

"Where did you go?" I asked.

"I wanted to put together a nice date for us," he said with a smile. "I promise, we won't be alone."

"No?"

"You know what I am now," he said. "So you know I have some money."

Why did that feel like an understatement?

"I have a lot of questions."

"And I have answers." He held out his hand.

I sighed and took his hand. His palm was warm and firm, slightly calloused. I breathed in the spicy, addictive scent of his aftershave. "You'd better."

His answering smile crinkled the corner of those intense blue eyes.

"I'd better go change," I said.

"You're perfect the way you are," he promised me.

I glanced down at my joggers and *The Sound of Us* t-shirt. "Now I know you're lying to me, Greyson."

He laughed and pulled me out into the hall. "Just get your purse."

Evening was falling as we walked outside to where a nice car was waiting. I glanced inside at the driver, and my stomach dropped at the thought of how much wealth was on display. Why was this gorgeous, well-off man so interested in a girl like me, who didn't have anything special to offer? "Is this your idea of staying in public places?"

"I promised we wouldn't be alone."

I hesitated as Greyson pulled the car door open for me.

"Kennedy," he said gently, his voice low and sexy, traveling right to my spine as if his hand had caressed my lower back. "Do you know I would never hurt you?"

"I don't," I reminded him.

But I had a feeling.

"What can I do to make you feel better?" he asked me. "Do you want to carry a knife? A gun?"

"No." My eyes had gone wide, and he let out a soft chuckle, as if he appreciated my innocence. I looked up at him, reminded once again of the height difference between us—and the ninety pounds of pure muscle he had on me. "Also, I saw you fight with Carter and Jack. I don't think I'd have a chance even with a gun."

"You're always safe with me," he promised, touching my cheek tenderly before tucking a strand of hair back behind my ear. "I'd kill myself before I let someone hurt you. I'd kill myself before I'd ever hurt you."

"Why?" I whispered.

"Because it feels like I waited for you all my life," he told me. "Do you believe in soul mates?"

"No."

"That's alright." His answering smile was so confident and magnetic that it made the words convincing. "I'll believe for both of us."

I was suddenly keenly aware of the fact we were standing outside my crappy apartment building, with people doing double takes at this handsome man in the suit and the fancy car.

"We're about to get carjacked," I said with a smile. "Get in the car, Greyson."

"You need a nicer place," he told me, as I slid into the car seat. He glanced around at the dingy surroundings before he swung into the seat beside me.

The car had that nice new leather scent, but when I inhaled, I caught another scent of his aftershave. It made me want to lean over and press my nose into the smooth shaven

117

skin above his collar. A faint hint of a tattoo peeked over the collar, just a line, and it made me curious. There were no tattoos visible the way he normally dressed.

He turned and met my gaze, and it felt as if the two of us were intimately close. There was an amused sparkle in his eyes, like he noticed me noticing. "Yes, Kennedy?"

"Questions," I said, my stomach flip-flopping. My gaze flickered toward the driver.

Greyson handed me a remote, and as he held it out, he pressed his thumb to one of the buttons. A soundproofing screen slid up between us and the driver.

When I gripped the remote, our hands lingered together for a second. Then I dropped it between us. I didn't feel like I really needed to stick to public places with Greyson.

Somehow, Greyson felt like he was dangerous to everyone else...but safe for me.

"The mafia?" I asked. "Really?"

He nodded. "Did Carter, Jack, and Sebastian mention we were all mixed up with the mafia for a while? We all had our reasons. I can show you mine."

He pulled out his cell phone, and I leaned in to him as he pulled up a series of photos.

In them, he was much younger—but still handsome: a tall, muscular teenager with a hint of baby fat still in his cheeks and a wide, open smile. He had his arms around two younger girls, who had deep olive skin and curly dark hair. They grinned out from the photos.

"Alli and Alexa," he told me. "My half sisters. This was when I was sixteen...maybe the happiest I've ever been, despite everything. They were eleven and nine."

"What was despite everything?"

"Our mom is an alcoholic," he said matter-of-factly. "She was sober when she had Alli and Alexa, thank fuck. But then she fell off the wagon again. Their dad split—can't blame him—and I went looking for mine as a way to keep the lights on. He was this mafia thug. Not much of a paternal type. But I proved I could be useful, and he did let me come work for his organization."

"Where are they now?" I tried to do the math, then asked, "How old are you, anyway?"

"I'm twenty-three," he told me. "The same as you, probably."

"I wish I knew when my birthday was," I told him.

He hesitated for a second. "We'll find a day to celebrate. We'll make it good."

My lips parted, not sure how to answer. I wasn't sure I wanted a birthday if it wasn't the real day. But he was already answering my earlier question. "They're eighteen and sixteen. Alexa is going to my old high school and doing a lot better than I ever could. Alli graduated and she is rocking her freshman year at Yale." He grinned, pride evident across his face. "They are about a hundred times smarter than me."

"I'm pretty sure you're quite smart, Greyson," I told him, laying my hand over his on the cell phone. His eyes met mine, and I was keenly reminded all over again of how close together we were. A charged moment seemed to pass between us.

"After all," I added, determined to lighten the mood, "You're obsessed with me."

He let out a laugh. "True."

I wasn't sure what to make of the fact he didn't deny an obsession. "Show me more photos. I like baby-faced Greyson."

His brow dimpled. "Baby faced?"

He showed me a few more photos. In one of them, Alli was sitting on top of a wooden sign that said, Blue Creek Estates. In the background, the edge of a trailer was visible, along with a bike on its side.

A strange feeling jolted me.

Something like... longing? Nostalgia? I wasn't sure exactly what that felt like. I'd never had a past that I could be nostalgic about.

I raised my gaze to find him watching me closely.

"Where were these taken?" I asked. "Is that where you grew up?"

"Yeah," he said. "Only the finest trailer park with the finest people."

I had the strange feeling I should go find it. "Is it still there?"

"I'm pretty sure. Trailer parks never die."

"What happened to your mom?"

"She went through rehab, and she's sober and a decent mom to Alexa now." There was a faint spark of something in his gaze. "Whether she likes it or not."

My knee bounced up and down nervously until I noticed what I was doing and forced myself to be still.

There was something Greyson wasn't telling me. No one just saw a woman on the street and became so obsessed, so... thoughtful and caring. There had to be a reason.

What if I had seen some kind of crime? What if he was trying to find out something I knew?

What if he already knew I had amnesia, and he was trying to unlock my memories?

The thought struck me powerfully, especially when I had that weird, creepy sense of nostalgia looking at the photo.

"Do you know I have amnesia?" I asked bluntly.

His brows arched. "Amnesia?"

I nodded.

"That really happens to people?" he asked. "You're living a normal life, but you don't remember anything about your past?"

"I don't know how normal my life has been since you walked into it," I teased him.

The car came to a stop.

"Where are we?" I asked.

He pulled a face. "Proving your point about your life not being normal since I walked into it. But I hope you'll see that normal is overrated."

He got out and opened the door for me, I blinked at the bright lights outside flickering against the dying sunlight.

I'd been so focused on my conversation with Greyson, and my sudden suspicions, I hadn't noticed us driving into the airport...or onto the tarmac.

We were surrounded by massive planes.

"Isn't this illegal?" I asked, looking around. "We shouldn't be here without going through security–"

"Not when you're taking a private jet," he assured me. "Come on."

"Where are we going?'"

He was already walking toward a smaller, sleek silver plane. Over his shoulder, he told me, "Paris."

I just stared after him, trying to catch up.

"Greyson! You can't take me to Paris!"

"I can."

"It's too extravagant!"

"Now that you know...nothing is too extravagant. Don't make me kidnap you." He was smiling. Obviously not serious.

I didn't know what to do with this man who wanted to give me everything...or said he did. What was really going on? What did he want from me?

And if what he wanted from me was tied to my past...

How could I say no?

"This flight had better be going to Paris and you're not like, kidnapping me to your private island."

"I don't have a private island." Another playful, panty-melting smile. "Yet."

I didn't have any doubt Greyson was a man who would get whatever he wanted.

I followed him, drawn to the promise of more answers...and to the magnetic man he was. Despite whatever dangers sounded, this man had gone beyond red flags to alarm klaxons.

"I see you make no promises about the kidnapping," I teased as I joined him at the base of the steps leading up the private jet.

"I see you're getting on the plane."

He followed me up the stairs, resting one hand on the small of my back to guide me through when we reached the top. We stepped into the sumptuous interior, all white leather with cozy seats facing each other across a real mahogany table. A flight steward greeted us with two glasses of champagne.

Once we were seated, I faced him across the table. "I'm surprised you have a male flight attendant."

"I don't like having random women hit on me," he explained.

I wasn't sure what to make of that, but I couldn't help thinking of how my heart had lurched when Jack and Sebastian left with those other women.

"Have you been to Paris before?" I asked. Then I buried my head in my hands. "What am I doing? I have to work the day after tomorrow!"

"We'll sleep on the plane, spend one perfect day in Paris, fly home, and you'll make it to work," he told me. "If you insist on keeping that terrible job."

"I do." I needed to figure out how it seemed like Carter, Jack, and Sebastian knew me.

"And yes, I've been to Paris before. For Alli's eighteenth birthday. Which is why I know how to be your tour guide."

That smile was playing around his lips again. The magnetic, charming one that I couldn't quite resist, even when I knew I should.

"It seems like you are the dream big brother."

"I try."

"Even though you do...what, exactly?"

"Illegal arms shipments." His gaze met mine evenly. "I stay away from the skin trade, and I don't deal with drugs anymore. If people want guns to kill each other with, well... I'm not sure that the criminal elements of this city are any loss."

I shivered. "Thanks for just telling me."

"I'm not going to lie to you."

I stared at him, wondering if I should just ask him if he knew me already.

But I didn't want for him to just deny it. I wanted to have evidence first. To know what answer I expected before I asked the question.

"Have you ever killed anyone?"

"Yes. But no one who didn't deserve it. I've done some bad things, Kennedy. But I'm not a bad man."

"I still want to know how you went from the poor kid in those photos to here." I swept my arm around to encompass the beautiful setting.

The plane was starting to accelerate. My stomach lifted with the sense of velocity, the way the plane was beginning to leave the ground.

I'd been crazy to get on the plane with this man.

But it would have been crazier not to go to Paris with him on his private jet, wouldn't it?

"My father staged a coup and took over his boss's business. A criminal group called The Jackals. Then I did the same to him." Greyson's icy blue eyes could be cold and terrifying when they weren't lit with the warmth he usually had when he looked at me. "The strongest rule...as long as they can."

"I see." My voice came out soft.

"I know what I do is a lot for you to take in, but you're safe with me," he reminded me, touching my hand gently as if he realized how cold and frightening he came across when he talked about work.

He seemed like a psychopath.

But he also seemed so sweet with me...

"Even if I never wanted to see you again?"

"Even then." His lips parted in a smile. "But I think we both know that's not going to happen."

"If people see me with you...will I be in danger?"

"I have enemies, I admit. But I also have powerful friends." His fingers tangled with mine, and he stroked his thumb over the back of my hand in a way that was both sensual and comforting. "And I'll keep you safe. The thought of you out there in the world alone, with no one to look after you...I don't like it."

He said those last four words as if they were an understatement.

"Why? When you barely know me?"

"You seem so innocent."

"It's the head injury." I said dryly

"Well. It might be the head injury, but it's also a rarity in my world."

"I thought you were going to take me to Paris, and then I was going to come home less innocent," I teased him, my eyebrows arching.

"I'm not going to rush you," he told me. "But I do have plans to take you to bed."

Heat touched my cheeks, but he was already standing up. "Come on. Let me show you to the bedroom. They're making dinner now, but then you can get some rest before we land. Tomorrow is a big day."

"I don't have a passport," I said suddenly, stricken with horror. "I mean, I came here with just my purse—"

"You don't need a passport," he told me. "You have me. It's all set."

He showed me the bedroom tucked behind the cabin, which was sleek and beautiful, and then we had dinner. My head was spinning. There was so much to absorb.

But for now, I focused on the delicious, tender filet mignon and the lobster macaroni and cheese on my plate and the handsome, charming man sitting across from me, and I let myself worry later.

I might not feel in control of the wheel when I was with Greyson, but I was sure I was driving closer to answers about my past.

10

Kennedy

I didn't expect to sleep on a private jet to Paris with a highly questionable man in the next room, but I slept like a baby. It was surreal to wake up once at night and realize I was flying over the Atlantic ocean, snuggled under blankets and in crisp, clean scented sheets.

The next morning, I woke up with a bump and a jerk. I sat up with the feeling of movement shifting my stomach, and I knew we were taxiing across the tarmac in Paris.

I opened the door and found Greyson looking immaculate as always. Somehow. I had some wicked bedhead and a crease across one cheek from sleeping like the dead all night.

"Good morning, sleeping beauty." He laid his tablet down and indicated the table, where there were two mugs–black coffee for him and chai for me.

"You definitely should've let me change," I said, plucking at the t-shirt I was still wearing.

He shook his head. "No, that was perfect. You were wearing pajamas."

"Do you even own pajamas?" I asked. "You always look perfect."

He chuckled. "No, I don't wear pajamas, Kennedy."

God. Now I had a mental image of Greyson dressed for bed in nothing but whatever tattoos were hiding under his clothes...

It was hard for me to bring my attention back to the present. Probably because I needed coffee. "But now I have nothing to wear. In Paris."

I was going to be extra schlubby, even more than the stereo-typical American in Europe.

"Is that so?" He took a sip of his coffee. "Did you look for something to wear in the bedroom?"

I raised my eyebrows. "You are..."

I didn't even know how to finish that sentence.

I was so overwhelmed by Greyson.

But it felt nice, too.

Back in the bedroom, I found clothes hanging in the closet. There was a beautiful flowing DVF dress I'd pointed out when we were window shopping and a cute pair of black Tieks to match. Practical but chic. I took a shower and then got dressed.

"You are ridiculous," I told him when I opened the doors.

His eyes lit up when he saw me in a way that no one could fake. "And you are beautiful."

I pushed my wet hair back behind my ears, suddenly feeling shy. Which was a little late, since I'd already let him take me to a whole new continent.

"What are we going to see in Paris in one day?" I asked.

"Did I steer you wrong on our last date? Trust me."

"You keep saying *trust me,* as if we both know it's a bad idea."

He just chuckled. Before I could say anything else, the flight attendant opened the door for a French customs offi-cial. He checked the passports the attendant handed him—

once again, I had so many questions—and then disappeared again.

"Your car is waiting," our attendant told us.

"Thank you," Greyson said.

The door was open to the pilots' cabin, and I caught a glimpse of a few men in dark suits. They had serious faces, and I would bet money they were carrying. A sudden weight descended on me.

Greyson could make the world feel like a fantasy for me, for a while. But his world definitely wasn't a fantasy.

Still, when we headed out to the car, excitement made my heart race. Paris, really?

We drove into the city and stopped at a little café, where we had croissants and the world's best hot chocolate. We took a boat tour down the Seine, visited the Louvre and the Mona Lisa, then walked across the gardens at Jardin de Tuileries to the Musée de l'Orangerie.

"Another art museum?" I teased Greyson.

"I think you'll like this one better than the Mona Lisa," Greyson said.

"She's iconic."

"She's also surprisingly small, and I almost had to throat-punch someone to get you in front of it," he said dryly, since there had been quite the crowd gathered at the ropes in front of the Mona Lisa.

In the Musée de l'Orangerie, there was an enormous Monet exhibit. I wandered in front of the water lily paintings, feeling as if I'd been transported into his gardens.

"It's so beautiful," I murmured.

"I knew you would like it."

"How?"

He held my gaze. "What do you mean, how?"

"How do you always seem to know exactly what I'd like?"

"Kennedy." He stepped close to me, but it didn't feel over-whelming when he looked down at me, even though he was so much bigger. It felt comforting. "When I came here with my little sisters, I thought, someday, I'll find someone I want to bring here. And now here you are. That's all this is." His smile widened. "It's not some kind of magic or witchcraft."

"I didn't think it was magic," I said lightly. I turned back to the water lilies. Why did I feel the same lurch of familiarity when I looked at them, the same sense of longing?

I wondered if I could get my hands on Greyson's phone. If it was unlocked. I'd never even seen him use it when we were together, as if all his focus were on me.

But if I were going to do that, I'd better wait until we made it back to the states first.

I didn't need to end up stranded in France without a passport.

"Let's go have dinner," he told me. "We have a reservation."

"Where?"

"At the top of the Eiffel Tower."

* * *

It was the most magical day of my life.

Of course, I didn't remember most of my life, so perhaps that was no surprise.

Still, I had to admit...I didn't think anyone could have resisted being charmed by such a day and such a man.

As we boarded Greyson's private jet, I couldn't help but shake the feeling that something was off. I didn't quite trust him, and yet, I found myself falling for him despite my doubts. His obsession with me seemed too good to be true. Was I too eager because I'd been alone so long?

Carrie had introduced me to the world of dating and given

me ridiculously low expectations, and Greyson made me feel like the world was a magical place.

"Champagne?" Greyson asked, offering me a glass as we settled into our plush leather seats for the flight home.

"I'm too tired," I said with a yawn. The view of Paris from the Eiffel Tower had been amazing as lights came on all over the city. But I was exhausted.

Greyson's cell phone went off, and after he checked the number, he said, "Sorry. I need to take this."

"That's fine."

It was the first call I'd ever seen him take. He gave me an apologetic look, then disappeared into the bedroom for some privacy. I chewed my lower lip, feeling as if Greyson was keeping scary secrets...and feeling as if it might be dangerous to pry into those secrets.

But I had told myself I could indulge in Greyson's overwhelming affection because it was leading me down the road to the truth.

I was afraid it was really leading me down the road to being...in love with him.

Carter and Jack had been so eager to let me know the truth about him, sure it would scare me off, but it had done the opposite.

"I'm sorry about that," Greyson told me when he emerged. "I just need a moment to speak with the pilot."

Totally normal. Sure. Not sketchy at all. I smiled at him, no matter how anxious I felt.

He headed into the cockpit, leaving me alone in the lavishly decorated cabin.

I decided to head into the bedroom and get myself ready for bed.

As I entered the bedroom, I noticed Greyson's cell phone lying on the bed. To my surprise, it was unlocked. My heart raced as I picked it up and began scrolling through his text messages, hoping to find some clue about his intentions.

"Kennedy," Greyson's voice startled me as he entered the bedroom. "What are you doing?"

"Oh, I was just so tired. I thought I'd get ready to turn in." I stuttered, hiding the phone behind my back as I turned to face him.

"Really?" He gave me a long look, his gaze lingering on me just a moment too long. The phone felt like a lead weight in my hand. How the hell was I going to get rid of it without him knowing I'd been snooping?

"You wore me out with the most perfect day in Paris I could imagine," I said softly, stepping closer to him. "Thank you."

Heat sparked in his gaze.

My heart raced as I leaned in, pressing my lips against his in what I hoped would be a convincing distraction.

Greyson hesitated, and my heart stuttered in desperate panic.

I knew what he was. I knew I should wait. Why had I been so stupid as to go through his phone now?

But then, his hands gripped my hips. He returned the kiss, slowly deepening it.

As his tongue teased the seam of my mouth, I let my lips part. I felt the familiar pull of desire take over. Greyson's strong arms encircled my waist, drawing me even closer. In that brief moment of closeness, I slipped the cell phone from behind my back and dropped it soundlessly onto the bed.

"Kennedy," Greyson murmured. "My good girl. Look at you, taking charge and kissing me first."

"I've wanted to kiss you since I met you," I admitted, trying to keep my voice steady despite the turmoil of emotions inside me.

"I'm glad you gave in to the impulse."

My mind screamed at me to stop, to not let myself get carried away by Greyson's touch, but my body betrayed me. The heat of his hands on my skin was intoxicating, and I couldn't help but respond. His fingers slowly worked the zipper on the back of my dress, and I didn't try to stop him.

Greyson's lips trailed down my neck, leaving a trail of goosebumps in their wake. My breath hitched as he nipped gently at my collarbone. I was losing control. I tangled my fingers in his hair, pulling him back up to meet my lips once more.

"Greyson," I whispered, my voice wavering. "This...we shouldn't be doing this."

"Why?" he asked simply.

"I don't know who you really are," I whispered back, the words too painfully true. "And I don't know who I really am."

"I do," he promised me. His hand cupped my cheek. "I know you."

"Greyson," I whispered, but I didn't know what I was even asking for.

"Tell me to stop, and I will," he replied, his eyes searching mine for an answer.

I should say it. I should put an end to whatever dangerous game we were playing. But when I opened my mouth to speak, the words failed me. Instead, I wrapped my arms around his neck and pulled him into another searing kiss.

As Greyson's lips moved hungrily against mine, I couldn't shake the feeling that there was still so much more to discover about the man who had whisked me away on this whirlwind trip, and about the secrets hidden within my own forgotten past.

* * *

Greyson

Kennedy had tried to sneak into my phone. It bothered me that she didn't trust me.

Of course, I was breaking into her apartment while she slept, so perhaps she had some decent gut instincts.

I had driven her to work at the rink this morning once our flight landed. She had kissed me goodbye, which had made me smile.

And then my smile faded as she ran up the steps where I'd fought Carter and Jack. It took everything I had to let her go.

She belonged with me. Once they saw her, they would try to fill her head with lies again.

And with the truth too, of course, which was probably worse.

We hadn't talked since I dropped her off. Not hearing her voice or seeing her smile for the past twenty-four hours, especially when those assholes were getting to see her—though they were probably wasting the opportunity—was driving me a little mad.

It was a pity I couldn't kill them. But if she ever recovered her memories, she wouldn't forgive those particular murders. I wasn't petty enough to risk losing Kennedy to the ghosts of Carter, Jack, and Sebastian.

Besides, the stupid bastards would lose her on their own. They were more of a risk to me dead than they were living, breathing, and acting like assholes.

I eased her front door open slowly. This place was such a

shithole. I could break into almost any door, but this one was too easy. I hated that she was staying somewhere she was so vulnerable. Sooner or later, the people who had run her down in the street would realize she was alive, and they would come for her.

I intended to be standing in their way.

Unfortunately, she was probably going to be stubborn about her relocation. I'd have to figure out something to make this shithole untenable, because no woman of mine was going to stay someplace with such flimsy security.

I closed the door softly behind me, taking in the apartment from this angle, this time of night. I already knew she was asleep, so I could take my time.

She had strung little lights along the ceiling, and they cast soft, twinkling light over the small living room and kitchen. She had made the living room cozy with a blanket and a few throw pillows, and framed posters hung on the walls. She'd apparently rediscovered her love for Audrey Hepburn, and I found myself smiling.

Such a drab little place, but she'd made it into a home. I knew she'd do the same for my mansion. It wouldn't feel like home until it was hers.

I moved quietly through the apartment. The only clutter was her stack of library books, piled up beside the couch. I crouched to look at the titles, which I hadn't been able to see from the camera, then pulled my phone out to take a photo of the spines. I wanted to remember what she was reading.

I glanced up at the vent, knowing I was making eye contact with one of my cameras. Then I moved on to the narrow hallway. Her bedroom door was shut—a habit from her teenage years, when she'd pushed a laundry basket in front of the doorway every night so she would know if her stepfather tried to open the door.

135

I touched the door lightly, wishing that I could rewind all the way back to before we first met.

Wishing I could always have protected her.

Wishing we could've killed her stepfather sooner.

I went into her bathroom, closed the door, tucked her bathmat along the doorway so there would be no crack of light escaping into the hallway. Then I flicked the lights on. My own reflection flickered to life in the mirror before I opened the medicine cabinet doors.

In between the Tylenol and face wash, her little pink birth control pills sat in their round silver foil. I pulled them out, taking note of how many pills were gone, and slid them into my pocket. Then I pulled out my version, which was all sugar pills, and carefully poked my thumbnail into the first six pill pockets and popped out the pills.

She didn't need these anymore. She had always talked about having kids someday when we were young. She was going to be a great mother. Fucking her was going to be even more magical knowing she might end up carrying my baby. The thought made a smile break across my face as I imagined how she would look pregnant, how she would smile when she was cradling our baby.

I set them back in the medicine cabinet and closed the doors, tidying up after myself before I went back out into the hall.

I hesitated, then pulled out my cell phone and brought up the video footage. I toggled with my thumb to her bedroom. In the best black-and-white footage money could buy, I could see her sleeping deeply, one arm tucked beneath her head.

I shouldn't.

But I was already opening the door and letting myself in.

Seeing her through the cameras wasn't good enough. She was so beautiful, asleep and innocent. Her dark hair fell across the pillow. She was wearing a thin camisole, one strap slipping off her shoulder; her breasts were covered by the blanket, and I almost reached out to tease the blanket down so I could get a better look at my perfect girl.

But if she woke, seeing me looming over her in bed would be hard to explain. I took a step back again, committing her to memory.

Her pouty lips moved, talking in her sleep. "Greyson..." she murmured, and I stiffened, but she was still asleep.

Pride surged through my chest.

"You're in my dreams too, angel," I whispered.

Her lips parted slightly, a faint sigh escaping her, as if she were working toward an orgasm in her dream. I'd heard that wistful hint of a sigh before when she was close to coming on my hand or my tongue.

My cock was so hard, I felt like I'd explode.

When her lips were parted like that, all I wanted to do was rub the tip of my dick against that sweet, rounded lower lip. Would she take my dick into her mouth in her dreams? She used to love to give us blowjobs, her eyes sparkling with mischief when she knelt, knowing she had all the power over us.

Might as well join her in her dreams.

I unzipped my jeans and pulled out my cock, which was already beaded with precum on the tip from just watching her. God, I was so close, just having her here. I needed her.

I glanced around the room and found her laundry basket in one corner. I picked up her panties and lifted them up to my face, inhaling the faint honey-and-roses scent of her that clung to the lace-trimmed cotton.

I wrapped the panties around my cock and began to stroke myself, watching her face shift in her dreams. She smiled slightly, her lips still parted. Was she taking my cock in her dreams, smiling up at me as she gripped my balls? Her fingers used to dig into my thighs, urging me forward, letting me fuck her mouth harder and harder.

She was such a dream.

I'd always loved doing the same for her. Spreading her legs wide to run my tongue through her folds, working my thumb against her clit while I ate her out like my life depended on it, feeling her thighs shake around me. She was the only dessert I wanted.

I threw my head back and wrenched down on my lower lip, trying to make myself come silently, even though just being near her made for the best orgasm I'd had in five years.

I couldn't fucking wait until I was coming where I belonged, buried deep inside her, watching her come along with me. I loved the way she blushed when she orgasmed, her eyes wide and sparkling, her fingers tangling in that gorgeous, thick dark hair.

I put myself away, then dropped the cum-soaked panties back into her laundry basket. I'd love to keep a pair of her panties...but soon she was going to be mine.

All of the time.

11

Kennedy

I went into work two hours early so I could skate before my shift. There was a huge fundraiser coming up, and as I walked through the lobby, I could see they were already setting up the lobby for the event. The black tie affair was a little less exciting for me when I'd be wearing my usual black Devils polo and passing out little crostini appetizers, but I was excited for it. The Devils had partnered with a really wonderful sounding charity.

And I didn't mind the idea of seeing Carter, Jack, and Sebastian in their tuxes, either.

Greyson probably wouldn't have appreciated that sentiment, but I couldn't imagine my life without any of them now that I'd met the four of them. Even though it was hard to imagine a life where the four of them ever came into contact with each other without throwing angry words...and fists.

They had history.

I got my cheap rental skates and carried them down to the ice for open skate.

Apparently something had changed about open skate

because it was packed today. And not with the usual weekday collection of elderly couples who chatted as they skated at a leisurely pace and stay-at-home-moms with wobbly toddlers on skates. There were a ton of young women and middle-aged men tugging at skate laces. I stared around me, curious what had changed. But skating was fun for everyone.

As I sat there lacing up my skates, it occurred to me that something about the history between my guys might be out there on the internet. Jack had accused Greyson of being wanted by the law at some point.

I pulled out my cell phone and began to search the guys' history. Soon, I was pulling up stats from their high school hockey days. I stared at a grainy photo of them from the archive of The Green Ridge Courier, the newspaper from one of the suburbs of our city. In it, younger versions of Greyson, Jack, Carter, and Sebastian posed together with their hockey sticks.

I saved the photo, feeling the familiar tug of my past.

Of memories bubbling in my subconscious, that fell apart the second I tried to pull them out.

Of course, when I looked up, Jack, Carter, and Sebastian were literally hanging on the flags above the rink. So perhaps it wasn't surprising they felt familiar whenever I saw their photos. Carter glared out of his photo—that seemed fitting—and Jack had that gorgeous, boyish grin. Sebastian, though, looked serious, except for one corner of his mouth tilting up just slightly. It was a look that made me wish I could do something to make him smile. I wanted to see his full-hearted grin.

If Greyson had played with them...I needed to figure out why he had stopped. They were never going to tell me that answer. I'd have to find out on my own.

I threw my cell phone back into my bag, decision made. I was going to the suburb on the edge of the city where the guys had grown up, I was going to find the trailer park where

Greyson had lived, and I was going to start to unravel whatever had happened in the past.

I just needed a day off work.

I'd let the arena take over my life. My manager was always happy to give me more hours, and I loved being here.

Now I finished tying my laces and did the clumsy toddler-walk everyone did in skates across the black mats until I could step onto the ice. The ice was already marked with more curling divots from skates than it usually would've been at this hour, so my gliding didn't feel as smooth.

The girl who sold wristbands for the open skate, Katie, also put on the music. It turned out she was a total Swiftie too, so I'd convinced her to play Taylor's latest. The music, the plan percolating under my skin, and the freedom of flying across the ice all put me into the best mood.

"Isn't that the girl who was there when Carter and Jack got into that fight?" I heard a girl murmur to my side.

I didn't look at them, but from the corner of my vision, I could see the two girls who were skating together. It made me wish Carrie was here to skate with. They looked like they were around my age. One of them gripped the wall, floundering along on her skates awkwardly. Her friend was skating smoothly, but she had to be cold, given how much of her cleavage her sweater exposed.

So, they probably weren't here for the pure love of skating. They were probably here because they were wanna-be puck bunnies. Well, based on what I had seen of the guys' behavior, they were probably in luck. It seemed like Jack, Carter, and Sebastian were always leaving with one puck bunny or another.

"No, I don't think so," the floundering girl said with a lot more confidence in her words than she had in her skates. "She doesn't look like the kind of girl they would fight over."

"True," the other girl said. "They could have anyone. It's

hard to imagine why they would even fight over a girl. Maybe if she was—"

"Right here?" I asked, swiveling on my blades and sending up a little spray of ice fragments. I skated backwards. OK, I was showing off. "You know that I can hear you, right? You could at least wait for me to skate off before you have this conversation about how I'm not good enough for them."

"At least you know it," the girl who was clinging to the wall said.

The two of them giggled as if that had actually been funny.

"Do you know her?" the girl with the sweater cleavage asked. "The girl they were fighting over? We saw a photo of the fight but she was like, so grainy."

"Who could even really see her with the guys in the frame anyway?" The girl suddenly hit a pit in the ice and came to a stop, turning to grip the wall with both hands as an oh-shit look came over her face.

I gave them a look and turned to skate away.

"Oookay," Cleavage said, since her friend was still focused on clinging to the wall for life. "Someone is jealous."

I started to skate off, wondering why that had bothered me so much. It was another moment that felt like an echo, like something from my past that I couldn't even remember.

It had stung. Like maybe I'd heard that accusation of jealousy, of being unworthy, before.

Suddenly, I collided with a rock hard chest. Strong hands wrapped my arms, holding me upright. A crisp and clean scent wrapped around me.

Behind me, the girls let out a little squeal, and I knew even before I looked up into a big, hard jaw and tousled dark blond hair that I'd just run into Sebastian.

"Hey," he said, frowning down at me as if he'd come to find me. "What are you doing here?"

"What am I doing here?" I asked.

"You're supposed to skate on the team side," he said, jerking his head at the other rink on the other side of the arena. The professional rink was on the opposite side. "Not here with all the trash that wandered in trying to get a glimpse of the team."

His lips curled up at the corners, just faintly. The way that filled me with longing.

"I see too much of the team," I told him dryly, skating back out of his reach. He let his hands fall to his sides.

"Is that so?" He patted my purse, which was slung over his shoulder. I hadn't noticed until now. "Well, you're going to get robbed leaving your stuff around. I'll keep it safe for you."

He turned around and skated off, a thing of beauty as always. I stared after him in shock for a second. The girls were whispering together, but they barely registered for me now.

"What are you doing?" I hissed as I skated after him.

He pulled my purse off his shoulder as he skated up to the gate and stepped with perfect ease onto the black mats, transitioning to a walk. "Saving you from being robbed. How naïve are you?"

"Pretty naïve," I shot back, "but not naïve enough to trust you."

All the hurt and frustration I'd felt watching them watch me spilled out now.

"Ouch," he said. "Luckily for you, I don't need the two hundred dollars you can probably access with your ATM card, your Costco card, or an unreasonable amount of lipgloss."

"Did you look through my purse?"

"No, of course not."

He was still holding my purse and walking far too quickly ahead of me. I strode along as quickly as I could. It was hard to feel remotely graceful and non-ridiculous when walking on skates, although Sebastian made it look good, the asshole.

143

"Someone did start going through your purse," he told me without looking back. "That was what brought me onto the ice. I had them removed—"

Why did that feel like an understatement?

"And then I grabbed my skates so I could bring your purse to you and tell you not to be an idiot. But then I overheard those girls."

I chased him through the doors to the team side of the rink. He finally stopped and faced me. He towered over me, a warm and solid presence. The rink was cold and deeply quiet, this early before their practice. It felt so different from the other side. It was huge, and standing down here in front of the plexiglass, the tiers of seats seemed to rise up a mile above us. They played for so many people.

"Here's your purse," he said blandly, handing it over.

"Why?" I asked, finally taking it from him. "Why help me?"

"Like I said before. You're part of the team now."

I shook my head. That wasn't true, or at least, it wasn't that simple. I believed Sebastian would've intervened for anyone who was being stolen from. I could even believe he might come to the rescue of anyone who was being baited or bullied.

But this was more complicated than that.

"Skate with me," I said.

He shook his head.

"Come on, if anyone else comes in here and sees me skating, they'll kick me out. You're going to get me fired." Suddenly, it occurred to me that maybe that was what he wanted.

"No one's going to kick you out," he scoffed. "Don't worry. I'll take care of it."

Doubt still lingered for me...along with a desire to keep talking to him.

"You don't have anything else to do before practice," I told him. "Or are you worried I'll outskate you?"

It was such a totally outlandish claim. It still made his lips twitch a little more.

"Fine," he said. "But you have to come here to skate from now on. I don't want anyone hassling you like on the other side."

"We'll see." I wasn't going to make any promises.

He stepped out onto the ice. Then he turned, skating backward without any apparent effort. He was wearing a sweatshirt that hugged his shoulders and a pair of gray sweatpants, his dark blond hair wild around the hard angles of his face. His jaw and cheekbones were so sharp, he didn't look like he was quite the same species as the rest of us.

"You need better skates," he told me, skating backward.

I glanced down at the frayed black hockey skates that the rink rented out. "Ah yes. The old skates...that's the only reason I can't outskate you."

He chuckled, and my gaze flew to his face. Warmth blossomed in my chest. I'd made him laugh.

"You have a competitive streak, hm?" he teased me.

I skated after him. "It's nothing compared to yours."

"I don't know about that."

"How's Carter doing?"

His lips tightened. "He'll be fine."

I hated that he had stopped smiling, and I hated that I was so far from their tight little circle of friendship. He wasn't going to tell me how Carter was really doing.

"Are you looking forward to the charity auction?" I asked him.

"Not at all."

"Do you ever answer a question with more than six words?" I asked in exasperation.

145

He held up six fingers, put one down with each word. "Not. If. I. Can. Help. It."

I burst out laughing. "You're impossible."

The two of us skated around the rink as I tried to get my wild heartbeat under control.

Skating always felt right to me, like freedom. But skating with him at my side felt even better. Even though Sebastian wasn't very talkative, there was companionable silence in the swish-swish of our blades moving across the ice. He pushed me to skate faster to keep up with him, but it felt good; it felt more like flying than ever. His towering presence beside me felt warm and solid as we raced across the ice.

I didn't ever want it to end.

But that was exactly why I needed to know what was going on. Why these men kept watching me.

Why I felt a pull toward them.

I skated ahead, then turned to face him.

He stopped, a plume of ice flying up from his blades as he turned his body. Our bodies were just inches apart.

My heart raced faster than ever. Maybe I shouldn't. Maybe I should just enjoy these moments of skating together, the burst of reckless joy.

But would he go back to ignoring me tomorrow?

"What is it?" he murmured, looking down into my face.

I couldn't get my voice to come out as more than a whisper. "Do you know me?"

He jolted back as if I'd just slapped him. "What are you talking about?"

"I have amnesia," I explained, trying to smooth things over. "I don't remember anything about who I was."

"Then...how do you know your name?" he asked me, frowning. "You don't remember anything else?"

I touched the repaired necklace, which I wore under my

sweatshirt. I wore it almost all the time. "I had a name necklace on."

His face clouded. It had to be because he was shocked I had amnesia...didn't it? "That was convenient."

"Yep," I said, feeling suddenly exasperated. "That's been the whole story of my amnesia. Super convenient."

He crossed his arms over his chest.

"And no, I don't remember anything else," I said. "But I know that when I come into this rink, it feels like...home."

The closest I'd come to home so far, at least.

"Maybe you used to skate," he said.

"I'm sure I used to skate. But...do you remember me? Maybe we saw each other at a rink sometime, or..." I couldn't go any further with ways we might have known each other, in another world. "You just look at me sometimes like you recognize me."

He shook his head. "Nope."

His face was closed off. It was the same stoic, serious expression he wore on the flags, as if he were facing an opponent.

"I'm sorry," he said, a beat too late, as if he were remembering the lines a normal person would say talking to someone who had lost their memories. "I wish I could tell you something."

"I wish you would too." It felt like he was lying to me, and fury pulsed through my gut. Why would he be lying to me? Why would anyone keep the truth about my background away from me?

I started to skate away. I was almost to the open gate to the penalty box where Jack seemed to spend too much time. Then I turned back.

"Was I Greyson's girlfriend?" I demanded. "Did you know me back then? Before you guys started to hate each other?"

Expressions flickered across his face, too fast for me to read. Anger? Jealousy? Worry? By the time he skated toward me, his face was unreadable.

"Greyson's girlfriend?" he scoffed, as if that were a ridiculous idea. "You're too good for him, obviously."

"I don't think I am," I said, prodding him deliberately, because he obviously couldn't stand Greyson. "Greyson's been good to me."

"Is that so?"

"He took me to Paris." I tilted my head, studying him, looking for another flash of reaction before he could school his face. "I bet he wouldn't lie to me."

He let out a disbelieving scoff. "You should definitely test that theory, then. Greyson is always lying."

"What happened between you guys?"

He raked his fingers through his hair. "It's in the past. I don't like to think about it." He glanced away. "I didn't like losing a friend. Especially one like Greyson."

Ruddy color had bloomed across his chiseled cheekbones. From anger and emotion more than the exertion of being on the ice, I was sure.

But I believed he meant that one thing. He hadn't liked losing his friendship with Greyson.

"I think you know more than you'll tell me about my past," I whispered, afraid my voice would shake if I said the words louder. "And I'm going to figure it out, Sebastian. You're always watching me. Protecting me. Like you knew me before—"

"I didn't have to know you before to want to protect you now," he interrupted me hotly. "I want you, Kennedy. From the first time I saw you. It's as simple as that."

"No," I started to say, but then suddenly, his big body was against mine.

His hands wrapped my waist, steadying me.

I looked up at him, my lips parting in surprise, right before he bent his head and kissed me.

His lips brushed against mine, soft and cool to the touch. He tasted like cinnamon gum, and the taste and scent was another tease at the back of my memory. My lips parted against his, welcoming him in, despite myself. An ache opened between my thighs.

One of his big hands cupped my cheek. His palm felt rough, calloused against my skin, but in a good way. "Is this alright?" he asked me.

I wanted to kiss him again so badly.

"Kissing me to shut me up?" I asked back archly. "It's fine, as long as you realize I'm not going to stay shut up."

He was already leaning forward to kiss me again. His lips tilted against mine in a smile, and it made me smile too. I loved when Sebastian softened into a smile. It made me feel like I'd won some kind of victory.

He lifted me off the ice easily, and I let out a little cry of shock as my blades left the ice. But he was holding me firmly as he set me on top of the low wall of the penalty box. "You're just so short," he chided me, as if I'd done it to him on purpose. "I'm going to sprain something trying to bend down to kiss you."

"Are you really going to insult me in the middle of kissing me?" I demanded, wrapping my thighs around his lean waist to steady myself.

"It's not an insult. I've always liked short girls." His lips tilted a little more, on the verge of a full smile.

"You're better at kissing than talking," I told him, grabbing the front of his sweatshirt and pulling him in toward me again.

His lips pressed mine in a soft, tender kiss. I felt myself sigh against his mouth at the feel of his body against mine. My hands rested on the hard planes of his chest, feeling them flex and move as he bent forward to kiss me. The scent of his aftershave seemed to engulf me, along with the deeper scent that was just him.

He deepened the kiss. One of his big hands slid into my hair, cupping the back of my head. Then he tugged my hair back, exposing my throat. It felt good to have him pull my hair, and it felt even better when his lips brushed against the curve of my throat. My whole body tightened, my core pulsing with desire, as his mouth teased along my throat and into the intimate spot just below my ear.

In the distance, a door banged open. He suddenly pulled away, his arms still wrapped around my waist. His concerned dark blue eyes met mine.

"Penalty box," I whispered, already easing one leg over. We could hide in there and no one would see us.

He nodded, and in a second, he had jumped over the wall of the penalty box. His arm wrapped my waist and he helped me over, the two of us sinking to the ground with our backs against the wall.

His big shoulder pressed mine. For a few long heartbeats, the two of us were silent, listening to the voices coming down the stairs toward the rink.

I didn't recognize the first voice.

"Coach Reed," he told me quietly. "Goalie coach."

He pinched the bridge of his nose, a look of bemusement coming over his face before he whispered, "This was so stupid. We weren't doing anything wrong. We didn't need to hide."

"Then do you want to go back to skating?" I whispered back.

"Not now. It'll look sketchy as hell, the two of us popping out of the penalty box."

"You are sketchy as hell," I whispered back. "You know something you aren't telling me. Or you're a creepy serial killer who watches me all the time because you're planning to make a shrine out of my clavicles—"

His brows arched. I expected a denial, but he ran his fingertip over one of my clavicles, the movement sensual even through my hoodie. "One of these tiny things? I could find better clavicles for a shrine."

My lips parted in mock offense. Then I remembered not to let the cute hockey boy distract me. "Just talk to me. Please."

"You already said I'm better at kissing than talking," he reminded me, then suddenly shifted onto his back, lying on the cold, hard floor. He grabbed my hips and swung me over so I straddled him.

"You're insane," I whispered. "And extremely transparent."

"When it comes to you," he admitted. Then his big hand wound through my hair before he used my hair to pull me down to him, until we were nose to nose. "I just can't resist you, Kennedy. I'm sorry. I can't stay away."

His tone, and his words, seemed teasing.

But there was an edge that looked like genuine anguish in his gaze.

He tugged my face down to his for a long, slow kiss. I felt myself rock forward against him greedily, wanting more of him. A faint sigh escaped my lips, and I pressed them together tightly, afraid to make any sound. From the faint sounds, it seemed as if the coach and player were so close to us now.

Then mercifully, they stopped.

"You get me into so much trouble," Sebastian mouthed, looking amused as he gazed up at me. His fingers gently stroked my hair, pushing it back behind my ear. His deep blue eyes danced as he surveyed my face, as if he liked to look at me. Needed to look at me.

"You're telling me the trainer is wrong?" Reed sounded

disbelieving. "You're sure you'll be fine on the ice for the rest of the season?"

"I'm saying I'm fine for this week's game. She's too careful, you know she is." It was Carter's rough voice.

Sebastian froze, and a look of worry crossed his face. God, the way these guys looked out for each other was too cute.

"You don't think he's ready," I whispered back to him.

He shook his head. Then he pulled me close, so my head was pillowed on his chest, and pressed a kiss to my forehead. It felt sweet and cozy, being here like this with him, even when we were hiding.

I turned my face to kiss his throat, his smooth-shaven cheek. He let out a faint groan of longing, then captured my lips with his. The two of us traded more wild kisses, and I shifted onto my knees on top of him so I could kiss him more deeply.

He tugged my hoodie up, bringing my shirt along with it. The cold air of the stadium nipped at my exposed skin, and when he pushed my bra cup down, my nipple beaded against the frosty air—before he captured it in his warm mouth.

"Did you think about what I said?" the coach's deep voice echoed through the empty space around us.

"I promise, I've got it," Carter said.

Their footsteps faded away as they exited the rink.

I didn't want to stop, and I was afraid that Sebastian would pull away now that we didn't have to hide any longer.

Instead, his fingertips played across my skin like a seasoned pianist playing a familiar tune. His hand cupped my breast, tweaking my nipple in a way that sent a surge of longing through my aching core, as his lips teased against my throat again. I rocked against him hungrily, and I couldn't help but reach out to him, gripping him through his pants.

"Damn, you're good at this," Sebastian murmured, his

breath hot against my neck. I could feel his excitement growing beneath my touch, mirroring my own.

"Have to keep up with you somehow," I teased, brushing my fingers against his growing erection. He bit back a groan, the sound sending thrills down my spine.

"Keep going and you might just find yourself in more trouble than you bargained for," he warned playfully before capturing my lips in a fiery kiss.

Funny that getting fired felt like the least of my fears when it came to these men. Somehow, I felt sure that they were the doorway to my past...or the doorway to my destruction.

But for now, it didn't matter. All that mattered was the warmth of our bodies pressed together.

Sebastian's breath was warm on my skin as he shifted me up, my breasts swaying above his face, so his mouth could reach my nipples. I let out a moan as he continued to suckle and caress me.

The taste of his kisses lingered on my tongue, spurring me on as I finally pulled away. My nipples were damp from his mouth as I rocked back and began to unzip his pants, my fingers trembling with anticipation.

"Are you sure about this?" His voice was a husky whisper.

"More than anything," I whispered back.

Hunger flared in his eyes, mirroring my own need.

He let out a groan and let his head fall back against the cold floor, as if he were surrendering to my touch, to the need we had for each other.

I finally drew him out. My grip tightened around him, eliciting a groan of approval. I stroked him gently at first, then more firmly, finding a rhythm that matched the beating of our hearts. His thighs tensed, his hard abs rippling against my body.

"God, you're incredible," he breathed between fervent kisses.

He trailed his lips along my stomach, before lavishing my breasts with attention. When his teeth grazed my sensitive skin, my hips bucked against him. I wanted more of him, but even more than that, I wanted the power I had over him to please him. I wanted to see him come. To lose control.

In response to my touch, Sebastian moaned softly between my breasts. Then he captured one of my nipples in his mouth again, and I felt the pooling of lust between my thighs, so intense that I might come from just his lips on my breasts. I couldn't help but imagine what it would be like to fully surrender to him, to give myself over completely.

"Almost there," he gasped, his face flushed with pleasure. "Don't stop."

I quickened my pace, tightening my hold. When he finally came, his hot release sprayed against my stomach.

Panting, he gazed into my eyes. A soft smile came over his lips, awe and gratitude mixed in his gaze.

"Thank you," he whispered, pressing a tender kiss to my forehead. "My beautiful girl, my good girl."

"I don't know that a good girl would've done any of that," I said, feeling his cum soaking against the inside of my hoodie. I was sticky with him. "I'm going to be wearing your cum all day."

"Good," he said, pressing another kiss to my head. "You're not just some good girl. You're *mine.*"

I laid there, feeling more comfortable than I probably should. No matter how cold it was, my body felt warm from arousal and from Sebastian.

"I wish we could stay," I whispered. "But I've got to get to work."

"Me too," he admitted reluctantly. "Practice will start soon."

"Maybe I can get a shower first."

He sat up on his elbows, looked at me with smoldering eyes.

"Don't shower," he said. "I want you wearing my cum all day. I want to smell myself on you. Most important...I want to make sure other men know you're mine."

"You're a pervert," I told him, but I couldn't help smiling.

"Only for you," he told me with a wink.

It was one of the many, many things Sebastian said to me that I wished I could believe.

12

Kennedy

The next day, I called out sick to work. Somehow, I felt like if I saw the guys, it would just make me more confused about what I was doing and what I wanted.

I sat on my couch and stared at the two missed calls and missed texts from Greyson. I started to tap out a response, then deleted it. I was glad he couldn't see me deliberate over such a simple message.

Finally, I called out sick on Greyson too.

Down with a cold. Super gross. You don't want any of this.

It was exactly what I had texted to Carrie two months before, so I knew it sounded authentic. Of course, she'd texted me back that I didn't have to worry, because her children had brought home every germ within a 500 mile radius. She claimed I'd probably gotten sick from her gremlins, and it was probably true.

Greyson, on the other hand, texted me back offering to bring me soup and take care of me once he got away from work. I didn't want to think about what urgent things Greyson had to

I just needed a break from all of them, and from the way it felt like they were sweeping me away into a new future, but away from my real past.

I got into the Civic and drove to the outskirts of the city.

Greyson, Carter, Jack, and Sebastian had gone to high school on the outskirts of the city. I drove past the hospital that had once been my home, then found myself stuck in rush hour traffic until I reached the outskirts of the city and the traffic eased. Everyone was trying to get into the city, not out of it, this early.

A restless, anxious feeling swept over me. My knee jiggled anxiously, and I tapped to the steering wheel, not quite in tune with the music I was listening to. I couldn't shake the feeling that I was making a terrible mistake. But I had to know.

And what did it say about the secrets in my past that it seemed as if my brain went into full nervous alert about the thought of untangling them? What had happened in my past?

I drove to the high school first. If the guys had gone to school together, maybe I had gone to school with them. Maybe they knew me from when we were teenagers.

I pulled into the parking lot of the school, a squat gray brick building. It definitely didn't look like one of the high schools from one of my favorite teen movies, like *Clueless* or *Ten Things I Hate About You.*

I went up to the door and tried it before realizing there was a sign telling me to buzz in. I pressed the doorbell, and a voice came over the intercom. "What can I help you with?"

I'd thought that I would be face to face with a person when I asked these vulnerable questions. I stared at the intercom, trying to figure out a way to ask for what I wanted that didn't sound insane.

Nothing came to me.

"I wanted to find out if a student ever attended here."

"Why?"

"Well, I have amnesia, and I think I might have been a student here at one point..."

"Is this for real, or is this a plot point from a soap opera?" a young voice asked behind me.

"This definitely seems like one of those fake TikTok stories," another kid said.

I turned to face two teenage girls, who smiled at me, then waved to the admin through the window, and I realized for the first time that there was a magenta-haired older lady watching us. She visibly sighed and pressed the buzzer. A little alarm sounded, and one of the kids reached out and grabbed the door.

"Come on in," she said in a friendly voice. "I am dying to know how your story ends."

"Me too," I said.

The three of us went together through the little lobby and into the door of the office.

"So you two are late again, absolutely shocking," the elderly lady said to the two of them. To me, she said, "Just give me a second to get them into class. Hopefully in time to learn something today."

"I am so ready to be educated," one of the girls said, wide eyed.

The woman scoffed and gave them each a little paper slip.

Then she turned to me. "How can I help you, again?"

The two girls lingered in the doorway. She didn't even look at them as she raised a finger to point. "Out. Stop trying to miss math class on purpose."

"I don't think we should be blamed for trying to escape algebra," one girl murmured to the other one as they headed down the hall.

The lady's look on her face said, *I don't get paid enough.*

I agreed with her. On general principle.

"My name is Kennedy," I explained. "And five years ago, I was in an accident. I've had amnesia ever since. And I think I might have gone to this high school."

"What's your last name?" she asked, giving me a suspicious look as if she weren't sure yet if she should be sympathetic or expect to see a video of herself floating around the Internet.

"I–don't know," I stammered.

"When would you have been a student here?" she asked.

"About six years ago?"

"So you want me to tell you if there was a Kennedy at the school six years ago?"

"Yes," I said in relief.

"I can tell you that there was a Kennedy at the school six years ago," she said. "There are also four Kennedys at the school this year."

"Oh," I said. "Can you tell me the last names of the old Kennedys?"

"I can't," she said. "Students have our right to privacy regarding their data. If you gave me a first and last name, I could tell you if they graduated from the school." She gave me a sympathetic smile. "I'm sorry. That's all I can do."

"It's alright," I said, a slight hitch in my voice. "Thank you for trying."

"For what it's worth," she said as I headed for the door, "I hope you find out who you were. What your past was. And I hope it was something nice."

"Thank you," I said with an automatic smile, even though something about the word she just said felt like a premonition.

Like a curse.

As if I might find out who I really was and regret not leaving my past buried deep in my subconscious.

Feeling as if I was on a fool's errand, I drove to my next stop. Greyson had shown me that photo of his sister in front of the sign for the trailer park. Would he have done that if he'd known me in the past, if he was trying to hide something from me?

All the tangled pieces of my puzzle felt as if they were slipping through my hands as I drove to the trailer park. On my way, I drove past a gorgeous series of mansions. I wondered about the people who lived there, on these huge rolling plots of lush green grass and these enormous houses.

I felt an ache of longing looking at a beautiful white stone and gray paneled house. I'd never been very materialistic–at least not that I remembered–but the house was so beautiful, and it felt like the brightly lit windows were calling to me like home.

But I drove past it and almost missed the left turn onto the sandy driveway of the trailer park. I passed the same sign where Greyson's sister had posed, but it looked like the sign had deteriorated since then. It barely seemed to be hanging on to its posts, and someone had used it for target practice, leaving it dented with a few stray bullet holes.

Very inviting. Goosebumps prickled on my arms, but I parked anyway and got out.

As I walked through the trailer park, I kept expecting to be hit with some kind of jolt of memory. But I didn't feel anything. Instead, I walked down the little roads, past children's bikes laying on their sides in the yards and broken down cars and the little gardens people had started in pots. None of it felt familiar.

I turned a corner to walk back, and saw an older woman, sitting in a camping chair in front of her trailer. She waved at me, her face lighting up as if she knew me.

I knew that couldn't be the case, but I still felt drawn to her.

I went over hesitantly, worried that I would come across as odd. "Hi."

"Hey there! I haven't seen you in a long time. How have you been doing?"

My heart leapt into my throat. For a few long seconds, I couldn't even speak. I couldn't even think of what to say.

I took a few more steps toward her. She took another sip from her mug of tea, blinking at me with watery eyes. I realized that she might not be able to see very well.

I took another step, so she would be able to see my face. "Do you remember me?"

"Of course I do," she said. She tapped two fingers against her temple. "I am terrible with names, but I never forget a face. I'm so glad you got better!"

"Better?" I echoed.

"Oh, the rumors about where you went were crazy. I heard that you died, but obviously, you got better." She let out a cackle of a laugh. "And some people said that you went to live with your stepfather, but I knew that was never something you would do on purpose."

"My stepfather?"

"Well, no loss if you don't remember him. You were the sweetest girl, and everyone just felt so sorry for how they treated you once we heard about...well. Everyone just turned a blind eye, but we all knew your stepfather was not a very nice man."

"What was his name?" I asked.

She chewed her narrow lower lip. "Like I said, I've never been good with names. I'd hear him yelling at you and your mom, but I didn't exactly spend a lot of time chit chatting with him. He was not my kind of people."

"It sounds like he wasn't my kind of people either," I said, trying frantically to gather all the facts I could and remember everything I could to process later. "You could hear him? So I must have lived close by? Can you point out where I lived?"

"Don't you remember?" she asked.

"It's a long story," I said.

"Well, I'm not going anywhere. I've got time," she said with a cackle. "Anyway, you lived in that next place over."

She pointed to a boarded up trailer.

When I looked at it, nothing seemed familiar.

"No one's living there now," I said. "Do you know where my mom went?"

"I guess she went with your stepdad."

"Do you remember her name?"

"Now, she wasn't real friendly either. Not like you. We always wondered where you got your sweetness from."

"Thank you," I said.

Before I could ask anything else, the door to the house behind her opened. " Louisa, are you talking this young lady's ear off?"

An older lady, but still young compared to my new friend, stepped out of the house. She came down the stairs, giving me a slightly confused but friendly look, as if she didn't know why I was standing in her front yard.

"She had a lot of questions and I was trying to answer them for her," Louisa explained.

"You're answering questions for her," the new lady said in a bemused voice.

"I'm trying to find someone who used to live around here," I explained, figuring it was easier than explaining my amnesia to everyone I ran across.

"Well, Louisa is probably not your best source," the lady said with a smile, putting her arm around the elderly lady's shoulders affectionately. "My mother has Alzheimer's. Sometimes she thinks she recognizes someone..."

My heart plummeted.

"No," Louisa protested. "I know my memory isn't great, but I remember her! That's that sweet Shannon girl!"

The lady looked back up at me. "All right, Shannon. It was nice meeting you." Her tone said that I should just play along.

"Did you live here six years ago?" I asked the lady, trying again.

She shook her head. "I just moved in when Mom got real sick last year. I'm sorry, honey. I hope you find whoever you're looking for."

Me too.

* * *

Sebastian

It was a text from a number I didn't know.

What the hell did you do to Kennedy?

I paused, in the midst of drinking my morning smoothie, and then put the cell phone down on the kitchen table and pushed it across to Carter. "Does that seem like the voice of our least favorite former wing?"

"Jealousy and angry accusations? Yep," Carter answered.

Jack leaned over Carter's shoulder to read the text. "At least we have his number again for when he inevitably tries to get Kennedy away from us, like the possessive psychopath he is."

"He thinks you're the psychopath," I reminded him. "You're the one who killed for her first."

"As if you all weren't jealous that it wasn't you," Jack said. "We'd all kill for her in a heartbeat."

"She can't exactly know about that, can she?" I demanded. "As far as she knows, we're just the assholes who won't answer any questions."

I reached for my phone again.

But Jack had already grabbed it. He was typing.

Give her an orgasm?

No response.

"What's wrong with Kennedy?" I demanded as I got my phone back from Jack. "God damn it, why antagonize him? He's already both petty and murderous. You could just leave him alone."

Jack didn't look apologetic. He just shrugged. I'd have accused him that this was all just a game for him, but I'd seen what he'd been willing to do for Kennedy.

"I'll find out where she is," Carter said.

"If she ever finds out you've got a tracker on her car," I reminded him.

"She's not going to find out." Carter was already pulling out his cell phone and clicking away to dial in her location. "But you know Greyson will take her from us if he gets the chance. I'm not running the risk that she just disappears one day and we never see her again."

"Because he's going to take her in the Civic," Jack said in disbelief. He pointed out the window. "He's going to take her in his private jet, take her to his mansion, he's going to give her all the shit we should be giving her, but with us, she'd be with men who are actually sane and law-abiding citizens—"

"Mostly," Carter interrupted.

"Whatever," Jack said, throwing up his hands. "I can't do

this, that's all I'm saying. You've been keeping your distance, but I can't fucking do it—"

Carter was on his feet so fast the table legs scraped across the floor with an unholy squeal. "I never wanted to do this! I was never on board with making her disappear!"

"You agreed to it! To keep her safe!"

"I'd do anything to keep her safe!" He raked his hand through his hair. "Then the second she comes in the door, you two are ready to abandon the plan—"

"It doesn't work anymore. Not now that Greyson's found her."

"God, you know Greyson. He was never going to stop searching for her. And if he's found her, then what if whoever tried to kill her before finds her now too?" Carter demanded.

We'd hidden her from Greyson, but more importantly... we'd hidden her from the people who tried to kill her.

We'd started half a dozen rumors back home about what happened to her. The fact her stepfather and mom had disappeared had made it easy to pretend they'd all skipped town. But just in case someone ever found a body—or pieces thereof— we'd scattered other stories around, too.

"Guys," Jack said urgently, his face worried as he gazed over Carter's shoulder. "Kennedy's searching too."

My heart dropped. "Where is she?"

"She's gone back home. She's at the trailer park."

Ten minutes later, we were all in the car.

I drove like a bat out of hell.

"Easy, Jesus," Jack said, putting his hand up on the dash as I took a corner. "She's not in imminent risk of death. We've got to tell her."

"That's what you want to do now?" Carter demanded. "Five years of staying away from her, and everything that cost us, and now that she's hanging around the arena giving you

166

guys those innocent, wide eyes... you want to just dump the truth on her?"

Jack and I had struggled to convince Carter to hide her in the first place. Now we couldn't talk him into giving up.

We all wanted to protect her so badly.

"How are we going to protect her if she's not with us?" I asked, sounded totally reasonable...as if I'd ever been reasonable when it came to Kennedy.

"Why do we have to tell her to have her with us?" Carter demanded. "We could just...win her over. Stop acting like assholes, but that doesn't have to mean telling her the truth."

"Maybe not the whole truth," Jack admitted, "but we do need to tell her something."

"She's better off not remembering," I said, feeling haunted by the memories of what Kennedy had experienced.

She'd been helping me wash the dishes after Jack's mom had cooked for us. Jack had disappeared, as he did. She'd barely pushed her sweatshirt sleeves up, even though they'd gotten soaked with water.

"What's going on?" I'd asked her.

"Mm?"

I'd pulled her sleeve up. She'd tried to pull away, but I'd caught her hand in mine and held her still.

"Kennedy," I'd whispered. "Trust me."

We'd stood there under the bright lights in Jack's huge kitchen. The window had reflected back our faces. She'd looked so innocent that day, her hair pulled back in a ponytail, her lips shiny with pink gloss. Our girl.

"I do," she'd whispered back. "I don't want you to get hurt."

"The only one who can hurt me, baby girl, is you," I'd promised her, right before I reached for her sleeve again, and this time she'd let me.

There had been bands of bruises around her wrists.

167

"We'll be out of here soon," she'd said with a smile, even though her eyes had suddenly been shiny with tears.

It hadn't been the worst thing her stepfather did to her. But the thought that she would try to get those memories back bothered me.

She was better off without them. Better off laughing the way I heard her laugh now, as if she'd been born five years ago, new and bright and unbruised.

"Maybe we don't get to decide that for her," Jack said.

I turned to give him a disbelieving look, and Carter said urgently, "The road does *turn*, Sebastian."

I looked back at the road in time to make the turn, but told them, "We made that decision for her five years ago. We could have been there for her. It must've been hell for her, having no memories, no family—"

"She made a nice life for herself," Jack interrupted. "Kennedy always finds a way."

Jack had that rich boy optimism.

We drove past Jack's old house.

"What are we doing when we get there?" Jack demanded. "We didn't think this through."

"You grew up across the street, you can go talk to her," I said, even though I wanted so badly to be the one who wrapped her up in my arms.

What the hell had she learned out there?

My phone chimed again as I was pulling into the trailer park.

Greyson.

In the photo, Kennedy was sitting on the hood of the Civic, licking an ice cream cone. This was our *now* Kennedy, with her hair loose around her shoulders and a smile that crinkled little laugh lines at the corners of her eyes.

I swore and hit the brakes.

"There's no fucking reason for us to be here, anyway," I said. "Greyson already got to her. Picked up all the pieces, bought her ice cream, and probably told her some bullshit story."

"So we tell her," Jack said. "We've got to tell her."

"Tell her what exactly? Your stepfather was an abusive creep who worked for some real bad dudes, and after we disappeared him, those dudes came after you? Maybe? Or maybe it was some of Greyson's pals, since he was busy crawling his way up the ladder at the time?" Carter asked.

That wasn't the stuff I was afraid to tell her.

It was what came later.

I'd seen the car fly around the corner. As she tried to escape, she leapt toward me, her arms outstretched. Thinking we were her safety when for whatever reason they'd come after her, it had to be us.

I'd raced toward her, but it had all happened in a second.

No one would ever want to hurt Kennedy.

They would hurt her to punish us.

Because anyone could tell how much she meant to us...

We'd ruined her life by loving her.

The car had slammed into her, sending her flying into the brick wall. I'd run as fast as I could, but I couldn't get a glimpse of the driver or the license plate.

Then all I'd been able to see was Kennedy's still, bloodied form.

But when I'd pressed my fingers to her throat, she'd still been alive. Her eyes were open, unfocused, her pupils uneven.

"Fuck, Kennedy," I'd said, hearing my voice closer to tears than it had been since I was a kid. "Just hold on, sweetheart. You're going to be okay. We're going to take care of you."

But of course, we fucking hadn't. I'd been right there and I hadn't been able to protect her, so as much as I'd hated keeping my distance from Kennedy, I'd hoped it would be the way to keep her safe.

Jack added, "Carter's right. We've lied to her this long. We've got to tell her something, got to get her to trust us, got to make sure we can keep her close enough to protect, but..."

Jack shook his head. "Maybe she's better off not knowing."

"I can't lie to her," I said.

A week ago, I would've told him that meant he had better stay away from her.

They hadn't let us ride in the ambulance with her. We'd followed in a car.

"We've got a chance here," Jack had said slowly when we found out she had brain damage. That she was in a coma. That she was going to have amnesia.

That we could erase her from our lives so no one would ever come after her again.

I'd searched her bleeding body for the name necklace. It wasn't around her neck. It must have broken off in the accident.

I'd choked up at the thought of taking her name away, increasingly frantic as I searched for it.

Jack and Carter had dragged me away.

And before that...

"I have a gift for you," I'd told her, leaning over her as she stood at her locker. I'd been too excited to wait.

I'd dangled the necklace in front of her, and she had turned, flashing me the most perfect smile in the world.

"What's this?"

"I want you wearing my jersey tonight," I told her. "And I want you wearing this."

"You have an awful lot of demands," she teased me, taking the delicate gold necklace from me. Her eyes lit up when she saw it, then she grabbed me and bobbed up onto her toes. She still

wasn't quite tall enough, so I lifted her off the ground with one arm around her waist. She pressed a kiss to my cheek.

I'd always lived to give Kennedy presents.

"Fine. We'll win her over," I said. "It's the best plan."

Jack raised his eyebrows, as if he didn't have a lot of faith.

Could we make Kennedy happy while leaving the truth in the shadows of the past?

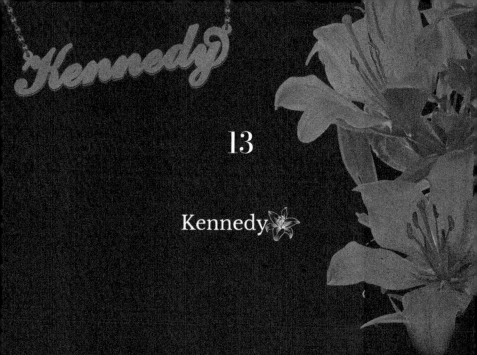

13

Kennedy

I was in the midst of my shift at the charity auction, navigating through the elegant crowd of donors and guests in my work uniform, a tray laden with stuffed mushrooms in my hand. Working events at the arena had been exciting so far, but tonight's event took things to a whole new level. The events room was transformed into a sparkling wonderland, adorned with twinkling lights and elegant decorations. Guests in their finest attire mingled, laughter and animated conversations filling the air.

Dressed in my simple work uniform of a fitted white button up and black dress pants, I felt distinctly out of place amidst the sea of glamorous gowns and fitted expensive suits. My hair was pulled back into a no-nonsense ponytail, and my makeup was minimal, just enough to look presentable, but definitely nothing that would stand out in the perfection and glamour that surrounded me.

Jack, Sebastian, and Carter were on the other side of the room, surrounded by donors desperate for some of their star power. I'd never felt weird about the inequality between us, that they were everything...and I was...nothing.

But tonight it stood out in stark relief.

Even amidst the glitz and glamour of the event, they stood out. Every eye on them. The trio had a magnetic presence that drew everyone's attention. As our eyes met, a shiver of recognition and connection passed between us, a silent acknowledgment of the history we shared.

I kept calling them gods in my head, but tonight they looked the part more than ever. The sight of them in fitted tuxes was going to be starring in my daydreams for quite some time.

And my dreams at night.

Vibrator material for sure.

As I worked, I couldn't help but steal glances in their direction. They were watching me too. One of them had eyes on me every time I looked over.

Sebastian shot me a grin, his gaze trailing down my body exaggeratedly. I flushed and rolled my eyes, my smile falling as I saw the pack of women hovering behind him, ready to try and stake their claim.

I didn't want to be that girl. And I'd jacked Sebastian off knowing it probably meant nothing to him.

I just wish it had meant nothing to me.

An announcement came on that the date auction was about to begin, and the room crackled with electric excitement. Guests headed towards their seats and I went to exchange my tray of mushrooms—which almost no one had touched—with a tray full of flutes of champagne. Dinner would be starting but they could get some champagne down their throats while they watched the auction. The stage across the room was a spectacle of its own, adorned with luxurious drapes and bathed in soft, dimmed lighting that set a romantic tone.

I winced when some asshole pinched my asscheek. Hopefully that wouldn't be the trend for the rest of the night. There was a plethora of gorgeous women to choose from.

They didn't need to harass the sweaty server.

The auction began. One by one, the participants made their entrances, each arrival a dazzling spectacle that left the crowd in awe. The women who graced the stage were all stunning, exuding confidence and grace, their beauty accentuated by expertly styled hair and professionally done makeup. Their gowns shimmered and sparkled under the spotlight, each outfit a work of art, donated by designers for the night.

From flowing, floor-length dresses that cascaded like waterfalls to sleek, figure-hugging ensembles that accentuated every curve, each of them looked like a model. As they strutted and posed with sassy confidence, the room erupted in applause and wolf whistles.

"Five thousand dollars," a guy yelled as a gorgeous brunette sashayed down the stage. She winked at him and he called out a bid for seven thousand dollars—even though no one had beat his bet.

The rest of the bidders in the audience were far from reserved. They yelled out their bids, their paddles held high as they desperately competed for a date. Besides the athletes in the room, a lot of these men were never going to have a chance with women that looked like this in real life.

This might be their only chance.

And apparently they understood that fact since that guy over there with no neck and three strands of hair on his head had just bid ten thousand dollars for a date with a beautiful redhead.

I drifted around, handing out champagne as the auctioneer's voice, commanding and charismatic, boomed through the room, driving the bidding wars to greater heights.

I tried not to look where the guys were sitting, not wanting to know if they were bidding on any of the girls, but my gaze kept darting over anyway.

They seemed...bored almost, picking at their salad and talking amongst themselves, seeming to pay no attention to the girls on the stage.

That doesn't mean anything, Kennedy. You saw them leave with girls just the other night, I tried to remind myself.

Didn't stop the thrill of satisfaction every time I saw them so uninterested though.

I'd just gone to grab a tray of bread baskets when I saw my boss, Todd, searching the crowd of people, his cheeks flushed and a pinched, panicked look in his eyes. When his gaze fell upon me, his eyes lit up with a mixture of relief and desperation.

"Kennedy," he said, his voice filled with urgency, "I need a favor."

I nodded, eager to help out in any way I could. "Of course, what's up?"

He took a deep breath, clearly hesitant about what he was about to ask. "We're short on volunteers for the auction," he explained, "and it's for such a good cause—helping abused kids. We need as many participants as we can get to raise money for them."

I tensed, hoping the conversation wasn't heading where I thought it was. I'd gladly start soliciting women on the streets to be in the auction as long as I—

"I need you to be in the auction, Kennedy," he implored. "*Please*, the goal is to get *all* the kids at that shelter's lunches paid at school, and get them clothes, toys, and bikes."

I glanced over right as a blonde stepped out in a long emerald gown, her golden hair done in soft waves down her back. I compared that to the uniform I was wearing.

176

I smelled like stuffed mushrooms.

I was sure of it.

My cheeks flushed with embarrassment just thinking of being auctioned off in my current state. I would be a laughingstock.

Even more than I had been after coming on a stranger's leg because of a dirty dream.

"Look at this picture," Todd pleaded when I continued to hesitate, tugging a photograph out of his pocket. The cutest little boy with soulful blue eyes, and tousled black hair stared back at me from the picture.

"This isn't fair," I growled, feeling like he'd just declared war on my emotions. I was a sucker for helping little kids. I'd basically do *anything* if it helped them.

I threw back my head and sighed. Todd was already smiling in victory when I finally glanced at him.

"I'll do it."

"You're a goddess, Kennedy,"

"Right," I said, giving him a weak smile, dread already pulsing through me.

He started to push me to the side of the room, towards the hallway that led to the rooms where the other participants had gotten ready.

"Is there a dress I can borrow?" I hissed. I glanced over at the guys. Because I had a problem, obviously. They were staring at me, confused, and I shrugged my shoulders before turning back to Todd.

"Ummm, I have no idea," he said sheepishly.

"Todd!" I said, my voice coming out in a squeak. "I'm not going on that stage in my uniform."

"You look great," he cajoled, a big fat liar face if there ever was one. "I promise!" he said as he pushed me towards a haughty looking woman with an earpiece who eyed me like I was a bug she wanted to be as far away from as possible.

"I hate you," I spit at Todd as my full freak out commenced. He blew me a kiss and hustled away.

"You're the volunteer?" she asked disdainfully, her nose actually wrinkling up as she stared at my uniform.

A charmer if I'd ever met one.

"Yep," I said through gritted teeth.

I'm doing this for the kids. I'm doing this for the kids, I chanted over and over so I didn't punch her in the face or run screaming out of the room.

"This way, please," she sighed, leading me down a hallway and into rooms filled with makeshift mirrored stations. There weren't many girls in the room; the auction was going to be over pretty soon.

Maybe they wouldn't need me after all?

"We have one dress left," she said, gesturing to a garment back hanging at one of the stations. A pretty blonde with her hair in a neat chignon, clad in a sparkling gold dress, eyed me in the mirror. At least she wasn't wrinkling her nose at me.

Progress.

"Put on the dress...try and...fix your face. And you're up at the end," the woman said before turning to leave.

I reached out, practically clawing at her arm. "Sorry—did you say I was up at the end?" I asked, panic dripping from my words.

She smiled—well, it was definitely more of a "it's going to be hilarious to watch you up on stage" kind of smirk. "You're at the end. Don't mess up my schedule."

She shrugged off my hand that I belatedly realized had still been holding on to her and stalked away.

"Isn't this so fun?" the blonde gushed, powdering her nose.

"So fun," I repeated numbly, turning my attention back to the garment bag.

At least I didn't have to wear my uniform up there.

I pulled the zipper down, revealing a gorgeous, sparkly black cocktail dress, the fabric a rich, lustrous black that seemed to absorb the ambient light, making it even more alluring. It was...stunning, the kind of dress that I had never dreamed of wearing.

Except there was one small problem.

It was at least a size too small.

"Do you know if there are any dresses available?" I asked the blonde.

"That's the last one. I think it was too big for most of the girls," she said innocently.

Of course it was too big for them.

Of courseeeee.

I moved behind a privacy partition and stripped off my work clothes. Taking a deep inhale, I stepped into the dress, inching it up as far as it could go.

Fuck.

I stared at myself in the mirror, wondering if my work uniform would be a better bet.

The dress clung to me like a second skin, every seam and stitch straining to contain the curves of my body. With each delicate tug and careful adjustment, I fought to stuff myself into the dress, the fabric protesting with a faint but persistent groan.

Hey, at least it zipped.

I stared at myself in the mirror, shaking my head at the sight. I was fine with it accentuating my curves.

But my boobs...they were now defying gravity, spilling out *everywhere.*

My nipples were basically an inch from popping out.

Good thing the dress was so tight, I guess.

"You're up," a voice hissed, and the woman who'd shown me in popped her head behind the privacy screen, her scowl widening as she stared at me. "We have a schedule!"

"Sorry," I muttered, my hands fluttering around my chest, trying to lessen the impact of so much boob. I walked around the partition, my eyes widening when I saw the room was completely empty. Evidently, I'd taken longer than I thought to squeeze into that dress.

"Just walk out on the stage, wave at the crowd, and walk to the side," Ms. Golden-Ray-of-Sunshine explained in a bored tone as she all but pushed me towards the hallway that led out to the stage.

"Right," I muttered, feeling like a swarm of bats had taken up residence in my insides.

I was going to throw up. Yep. It was going to happen.

"Do not throw up," she snarked at me like she could read my mind. Or maybe it didn't take a mind reader—I was sure my face was a lovely shade of putrid green at the moment.

Terror. That was what I was feeling. The dress, beautiful yet so unforgivingly tight, clung to me like a second skin. How had I ended up here? Was this real life?

As I walked onto the stage, the blistering spotlight focused its intense heat on me, making my skin tingle and prickle with discomfort. The brightness was overwhelming at first, causing me to squint and blink as the relentless glare threatened to blind me. The world beyond the spotlight's boundary became a hazy blur, and the faces in the audience seemed distant and indistinct.

The heat seemed to intensify, and I suddenly had a vision of myself looking like a stuffed pig on the stage, sweat trickling down my skin.

As the initial shock wore off, my eyes slowly adjusted to the brilliance of the spotlight. The world beyond it came into focus, revealing the eager faces of the audience, the glittering decorations, and the grandeur of the room. Though I still felt the intensity of the spotlight's heat, I was no longer blinded by it.

The MC, one of the team's game announcers, stepped forward, his voice carrying through the room.

"Ladies and gentlemen," he began, his voice dripping with charisma, "may I have your attention, please? We have our last participant for the night, and might I say, gentlemen, that dress and the woman who's in it is leaving us breathless, am I right?"

Pig.

Now I wasn't thinking of myself looking like a stuffed pig, because there was one right by the stage.

My hands itched to cover my chest, as my cheeks blazed with embarrassment. But I kept them at my sides, trying to plaster a hopefully pleasant looking smile on my face as he continued his idiotic diatribe. Had he been this annoying with the other women and I just hadn't noticed?

I focused my gaze on the wall behind the crowd, unable to look at anyone too closely. Especially the three of them. I couldn't take it if they were laughing at me. Or disgusted. That would suck too.

What was the advice people gave when in front of a crowd? Imagine that they were all naked? That didn't seem very fitting. My gaze accidentally fell on the owner of the team, who while seemingly nice...was sporting a blond bowl cut. Definitely didn't want to imagine him naked.

I realized the announcer had stopped speaking and there was silence in the room. An excruciating, uncomfortable silence.

Fuck, this was it. Here I was up here. And no one was going to bid on me. Insecurity lashed at my chest and I was seconds away from running off the stage whereafter I'd become a nun in a far-away country where no one would hear from me again.

Just as I was almost to the point of no return with my delusion...as if a dam had burst, the room erupted in a roar of voices. Bids were called out from every direction, the numbers rising faster than I could comprehend. My eyes widened in shock, my heart racing even faster as I struggled to process what was happening.

Amidst the chaos of competing bids, one voice cut through the crowd like a beacon of clarity. It was Carter's voice, strong and unwavering.

"Ten thousand dollars," he yelled, his bid resounding through the room with undeniable determination. Carter was wearing a midnight blue colored velvet suit. On anyone else, it would have probably looked ridiculous. But he looked straight off the runway, his deep green eyes gleaming as he stared at me. For a second, I remembered how his hard body had felt underneath me, the way his...

"Eleven thousand," Sebastian threw out, standing up from his seat. My mouth dropped. What were they doing?

Carter shot him a glare. "What the fuck are you doing?" I saw him mouth. Sebastian just winked at him.

"Twelve thousand," Sebastian said, even though no one else had said anything yet.

My insides heated as Sebastian turned his attention to me, his tongue trailing along his bottom lip, reminding me of just how that tongue had felt on my skin. And the sounds he'd made when he'd come.

"Fifteen thousand!" Jack snapped, also leaping out from his seat. Sebastian's smirk fell as he stared at him incredulously. Jack flipped him off.

If I'd thought that the opening bids were outrageous, the ones that followed were even crazier. It was like the fact that the three stars of the team had decided I was worth their effort spurred everyone in the room to try and win me.

"Twenty thousand!" a man in front of the stage bellowed, holding up his glass tumbler instead of his bidding sign.

"Twenty-five!" Carter called out.

"Twenty-seven!"

"Thirty!"

"Thirty-five!"

The bids continued to go up. I glanced at the announcer, and he was staring at the room, bemused, like he couldn't believe it either.

"Fifty thousand!" Sebastian had just yelled.

Carter's hands were fisted at his sides, and he looked seconds away from decking his best friend.

"Fifty-five!" Jack shouted.

This was insanity. Lunacy in its finest form.

"Sixty-five," the guy in front suddenly said, his beady eyes glinting with determination.

Oh fuck. Please don't let him be the winner.

"One hundred thousand!" Carter bellowed.

There was a wave of shock that shot across the crowd at that bid. I gaped at him, probably looking like a deranged farm animal, but honestly...

The guy in front sat down, his lips moving silently as he muttered obscenities to himself.

Thank fuck.

"Two hundred thousand," Sebastian said, wacking his sign on the table for emphasis.

"Three hundred!" Jack answered. I mean, I knew hockey players made a lot of money...but this was a lot, even for them...right?

"Five hundred thousand dollars," Carter snarled. He leaned over and said something to Jack and Sebastian that I couldn't hear. They both had twin looks of amusement on their faces though, and Jack was rolling his eyes at whatever Carter was saying.

They both sat down though.

"Five hundred going once. Five hundred going twice!" The auctioneer banged his gavel on the podium in front of him. "Sold to team captain Carter Hayes for five hundred thousand dollars!"

The crowd erupted in thunderous applause, their whispers almost as loud as their cheering. People's gazes were darting from me to Carter, speculation in their eyes.

For once, I didn't care.

Carter and I were just staring at each other. He looked extremely proud of himself...and me...well, if you'd told me that after an archaic, sexist event like this I would actually feel confident about myself...

I wouldn't have believed you.

The high school hallway was a bustling, frenetic space filled with gossiping teenagers. Rows of dull gray lockers lined both sides of the corridor, their metal surfaces marred by years of scuffs and stickers, bearing the memories of countless students who had passed through these halls. The scent of teenage angst and anticipation hung in the air, a heady mix of body sprays, cafeteria food, and the faintest trace of pencil shavings.

As I walked down the hall, I pretended to be unaware of all the eyes on me. Packs of friends chatted animatedly, their laughter and gossip mingling in the air. Some leaned against the lockers, engrossed in conversations that seemed of utmost impor-tance, while others hurried along, lost in the whirlwind of their own thoughts and concerns.

"Oh, Kennedy..." I froze, immediately recognizing the cloying voice.

Sasha. I was tempted to keep walking, but it would probably make it worse. Predators always loved the chase.

I turned around to face her, and she grinned cruelly as she flicked her long, chestnut hair over her shoulder. She made a big show of staring at what I was wearing.

"Shopping at Goodwill again, Kenny?" I bit down on my lip. She was just being an asshole. This shirt was actually from Target, thank you very much. I'd done my best to work as many extra hours as I could in my after school jobs so I didn't have to shop at Goodwill this year—not that there was anything wrong with that.

"Do you need something?" I drawled, pretending to be bored even though all my senses were on high alert.

The four of them circled me like vultures, their laughter mocking.

"We're just wondering when your self respect is going to kick in," Ashley said snidely. Her blonde curls were especially volumetric today.

I sighed, shaking my head. They were never going to move on, not while Sebastian, Carter, Jack, and Greyson were paying me attention.

"We all laugh about it, ya know. How you pant after them. I really wish you would get some self respect." Sasha twirled some of her hair around her finger.

"I'll work on that," I muttered, rolling my eyes and turning to leave.

"They just feel sorry for you, you know that, right?" Tiffany said, hitting me right in my sore spot.

I'd been wondering since that first day why the guys seemed to want to be around me. It didn't make sense. I was no one, and they....they were everything.

"Ahh, but you know that already, don't you? That you're their charity project?"

185

My hands were trembling at my sides, and I was trying to hold in my tears as I slowly turned back towards them.

"Anything else?" I said, hoping my voice sounded more indifferent to them than it did to my ears.

"What's going on, baby?" Carter's voice said from behind me, a pair of strong arms wrapping around my waist.

The girls' eyes widened as they stared at him. Carter leaned over and nestled his chin on top of my head.

And I immediately felt safe.

Sheltered...

Wanted.

"The four of you wouldn't be giving my girl a hard time, would you?" Carter asked cooly. I could feel the rigidness in his body though—he wasn't happy.

Sasha's face had twisted from cruel to innocent and wide-eyed. "We're just saying hi, Carter." Her voice was breathy...and high pitched, nothing like it had been a few seconds ago. "Isn't that right, Kennedy?" Sasha pressed, a warning in her gaze to back her up or she would ruin me.

"Sasha, if you think that any of us doesn't think you're the slutty witch of the west...you've got another thing coming."

Her mouth dropped. "Carter—"

"You and your friends are trash, Sasha. Absolute trash."

"That's not what Jack thought this past summer!" she spat.

Carter laughed cruelly. "You mean when he was black out drunk and a donut hole would have done it for him."

Tears were gathering in her eyes, but I didn't feel an inch of sympathy for her. She and her friends spent their days torturing anyone they thought was below them.

"Carter, come on," Ashley said sweetly.

I couldn't see Carter's face, but I could imagine the look he'd just shot her, because she literally flinched.

"The four of you are done. Don't talk to any of us, don't look

at any of us...don't show up anywhere you think we can be. I'll ruin you. All of you," he said coldly. "And just in case I wasn't clear...'us' includes Kennedy."

Carter's protective embrace tightened for a second, and then, he released me briefly, his hands sliding down to my waist.

With a quick and fluid motion, Carter dipped me backward, his strong arms supporting my lower back, his lips crashing against mine in a searing kiss that short-circuited my brain.

Our mouths melded together, and my senses were overwhelmed by the taste of his lips, the warmth of his body pressed against mine...of him.

When he released me...the girls were gone.

"Come claim your date!" the announcer blared...and I came back to the room, blinking at the crowd as the memory slipped away. But Carter had been in it...hadn't he?

I pulled at the memory, straining to hold on...but it was no use.

Just like every other time, whatever I'd remembered had slipped away, leaving me a blank slate with only a feeling of familiarity and a blaring emptiness that reminded me there was something wrong with my brain.

Carter was coming up the stairs, nothing on his face to suggest he'd noticed I'd slipped off into lala land.

Apparently, when you cost half a million, they got to collect you on stage instead of shuttling you off to the side like the other girls had been.

"You look stunning, sweetheart," he murmured as he walked in front of me.

I blinked up at him, still in disbelief at what he'd just done.

"I can't believe you did that. Half a million dollars! Are you insane!" I whisper-yelled, my arms flailing in front of me. His gaze flicked to my breasts popping out of my dress and a sexy smirk spread across his lips.

"Worth every penny," he mused, his tongue sliding along his lip and melting me into a puddle of lust.

There was a loud cough nearby, and my gaze shot over his shoulder where I realized most of the room was staring at us interestedly.

"Can we get off the stage now?" I hissed, sure at this point the blush in my cheeks was going to become permanent.

"Of course," he grinned, interlocking our fingers in a way that felt all too right, and leading me off the stage.

We descended the stairs into the side area where other contestants had gone. It was empty, and I looked around, wondering what I was supposed to do now. I was pretty sure the auction dates didn't start tonight, so I pulled on his grip. "I think I have to go back to work..." I said.

"Not happening, sweetheart. They didn't put a time limit on the date...so I'm thinking it starts now and ends...not sure when it ends, actually."

Never. I never want the date to end.

Ignoring the ridiculousness in my head, I allowed him to lead me out into the main room, to the table where the other two were sitting with twin looks of annoyance.

Their faces immediately brightened when they saw me though.

"Hi, Princess," purred Sebastian, and I shyly said hello back, my gaze getting caught on his lips again.

"Down boy," Carter warned as he pulled out the chair between him and Jack and helped me into it. His fingers trailed along the bare skin on my back and I shivered. It was a lot. Jack and Sebastian were staring at me while Carter touched me.

A girl could only handle so much.

I leaned against Carter on the bed, his hands kneading and massaging my breasts as Jack licked and sucked at my clit.

Sebastian lounged next to us, casually jacking himself off as he watched me cum on his best friend's tongue...

Whoa there.

"Whatcha thinking about, baby?" Jack murmured in my ear, his breath dancing against my skin.

"That I'm going to embarrass myself in a minute if the three of you keep it up!" I exclaimed, leaning forward so Carter wasn't touching me anymore.

"Mmmh, this looks good," I said exaggeratedly, stabbing at the salad in front of me.

Oh. It was actually good. Apparently they got the good food for these fancy functions.

"So what are you going to do for your date?" Jack asked, crossing his arms in front of him and making his arms bulge distractingly, even through his fitted tux.

"It's a secret. But it's better than anything you assholes could plan," drawled Carter.

"I don't know. I think the best dates are pretty simple, don't you think, Kennedy?" said Sebastian.

"Lots of things could be fun," I gulped, weirdly not wanting to play favorites and make Carter worried about the date. I was the one who should be worried. He'd already paid half a million.

"It was worth every penny," Carter said all of a sudden, and I glanced over at him.

"What?" I asked distractedly, because Jack had decided to play with my hair.

"The date. I can tell you're thinking stuff you shouldn't. I would have paid double that."

My gaze widened. "Why?" I whispered.

"Because there's nothing worth more than you," he said softly, his fingers lightly caressing my cheek.

The weird thing was...staring into his eyes...I could tell he meant it.

Which begged the question. Why?

* * *

Carter

I splashed some water on my face, trying to get a fucking hold on myself. I looked wired. My constant state since Kennedy had wandered into the arena after five fucking years.

It felt like *I* was the one who'd woken up from a deep sleep. I hadn't realized how much I'd been going through the motions of life, pretending to be a man who hadn't lost everything.

I watched her nervously step onto the ice, amused and somehow turned on at the same time. She was a beautiful mess out here, wobbling like a newborn deer. Her face was determined as she tried not to faceplant.

I took her hand, my grip firm, and gave her a reassuring smile. "All right, baby, it's not rocket science. First things first, find your balance. Bend your damn knees a bit and don't be scared to lean forward. You want your center of gravity over your skates."

She nodded, her eyes wide with uncertainty, but she did as I said. Her first few steps were shaky as hell, and I could practically see the panic in her eyes. But I wasn't about to let her fall flat on her ass.

"Keep your weight on the balls of your feet," I told her patiently. "And don't overthink it."

As she continued to stumble and regain her balance, I stayed close, ready to catch her if needed. "Okay, now let's try some gliding," I said, releasing her hand but hovering nearby, just in case.

She pushed off tentatively with one foot, then the other, her movements jerky and awkward. It was like watching a damn baby giraffe trying to take its first steps. I had to bite back a chuckle.

"Relax, Kennedy," I called out, unable to hide the amusement in my voice. "You're not auditioning for the Olympics."

She gained confidence on the ice pretty quick, and I was impressed. She was no longer stumbling like a novice, and her movements were becoming smoother with each passing moment.

I clapped my hands and she glanced at me questioningly. With a grin I never seemed to get rid of around her, I bent down slightly, preparing to lift her onto my shoulders.

"Hold on tight," I warned her, my voice playful.

"What?" she'd asked, before letting out a surprised laugh as I placed my hands under her arms, lifting her off the ice with ease. Kennedy clung to my shoulders as I stood up straight.

"Ready baby?" I asked, slowly starting to skate around the rink with her on my shoulders. Her laughter filled the air, and it was like music to my ears.

As we glided across the ice together, her tension melted away. Her grip on my shoulders relaxed, and she began to enjoy the ride. I glanced up at her, feeling weirdly giddy at how wide her smile was.

It had been like that since we'd met, like my happiness was dependent on...her happiness.

After a few laps, I decided to take it up a notch. I lifted her off my shoulders and slid her down my body. "Wrap your legs around me, baby," I murmured, watching her face, mesmerized as she bit down on her lip and did as I asked.

Fuck. I hadn't thought this through. My dick was way too

close to what I knew was going to be the sweetest pussy I'd ever experience.

Her eyes met mine and I got a little dizzy staring at her.

We were so young. It wasn't supposed to feel like this. Like my soul had found its counterpart.

I wanted to kick my own ass when I said things like that, but I couldn't help it.

Something in me knew she was it for me. She was it for them.

I was still trying to wrap my head around that fact.

I started to skate. I'd been on this ice so many times, I didn't have to even think about it anymore. So I could stare at her instead of where I was going. The world around us faded away, and it was just Kennedy and me, lost in the moment.

I pulled her even closer, our bodies pressed together as closely as they could get. Our breaths mingled in the frosty air, and I could feel the heat of her body through our layers of clothing.

And then I couldn't help it. I had to kiss her. I leaned in slowly, giving her a chance to move away if she wanted. I grazed her lips, once, twice...shivers sliding down my back, my dick hardening because apparently just kissing her got me hard. She gasped and my mouth closed over hers in a supple kiss. I gently slid my tongue into her mouth, groaning at how good she tasted. I don't know how long we kissed.

I just knew it was the best fucking kiss of my life.

Finally, I forced myself to break away. I could have done that forever, but we couldn't exactly stand in the middle of the rink for the whole day.

She was smiling shyly as I set her down.

"Wow," she whispered.

I kissed the tip of her nose, noting how cold it was.

"*Wow is right,*" I commented. "*Now let's get you warm, baby.*"

I grabbed her hand and pulled her towards the exit.

"*You're getting the hang of it, by the way,*" I told her.

"*I really am,*" she said excitedly. And I had to stop and kiss her again, because now that I'd broken the seal so to speak, it was going to be really hard to stop.

I dragged myself out of memory lane, continuing to stare at myself in the mirror. They were doing a tour of the facilities for the donors and the women who had participated in the auction. I needed to get back out there—get back to Kennedy. I'd just needed a moment to get ahold of myself. Spending half a million for one date was the least that I would do to spend time with her. I felt feral, like all that time without her had done something to me, made me more animal than man when it came to her. I was trying to play it cool, but fuck, it was hard.

That fucking dress. That fucking body.

She was perfect.

The group was heading into the locker room when I rejoined them, Jack and Sebastian taking turns flirting with her as one of the employees from the team's media department droned on about our "state of the art" facilities.

I wrapped an arm around her waist and pulled her away from my two best friends.

"Mine," I teased.

"You suck," said Sebastian. I lifted an eyebrow, and he huffed. I knew for a fact he'd come to practice smelling like Kennedy the other day. Because he'd proceeded to torture us with how good her hand had felt wrapped around his dick.

I may or may not have punched him afterwards.

And Jack, Mr. Sunshine himself, had been in a mood ever since then. He was glaring at me like he was imagining my murder.

So I winked at him. To cheer him up, of course.

Sebastian and Jack stalked off to schmooze the donors, leaving me with Kennedy as we trailed behind the crowd.

"Carter," she said suddenly, anxiety threaded through her voice. "You really should get some of your money back. I know it's for charity. But I can't—"

I pressed her against the lockers, faintly aware of the far door slamming shut as the last of the group exited the room.

Kennedy went silent, her eyes wide and confused.

"I think I told you, baby...Worth. Every. Penny." She gulped and I pressed against her, letting her feel the raging hard on that I'd had since I'd seen her in that dress. She was still in it, and I wanted to rip it off her, unveil those gorgeous tits.

Fuck.

"Carter," she whispered.

I slammed my mouth against hers, finally giving in to the urge that had been clawing at my insides since I'd first seen her in the arena.

I fucked her mouth with my tongue, deep, long licks that had her writhing against me.

"Fuck, baby, you still taste so good," I murmured, freezing when I realized what I'd just said. All I could hope was that she hadn't heard me. "In my bedroom...I've been wanting to redo that since it happened. But I want to be the reason you're coming this time."

Her gaze was lust drunk and she was panting. "Yes. I want that," she whimpered.

I laughed darkly and thrust my thigh between hers.

"I want that sweet pussy to soak me," I growled. "Ruin this tux, baby. I'll never wash it again."

"Carter," she whispered, a gorgeous flush spreading across her chest.

I kissed her again, my tongue pushing aggressively into her mouth. I couldn't get enough. I couldn't get close enough to her. My hands tangled in her hair, angling her head exactly where I wanted it.

Her hands were pulling at the back of my tux. "Touch me, baby. I'm desperate for it," I said.

Her hips shifted against my leg and I groaned in delight. "That's it, Kennedy. Rub that sweet pussy. Make yourself come." I barely recognized my voice. When I'd thought earlier how she made me more animal than man...I hadn't been kidding.

I pulled at her hair, trying to rein myself in, but sucking at it as I ate at her mouth. She tasted. So. Fucking. Good.

But those tits were also calling my name. I let go of her hair, my hands sliding down her body until they were on her breasts, kneading and squeezing. Fuck. They were perfect. Just like the rest of her. More than a handful. And real.

Fuck. Fuck. Fuck. I was so hard, my dick was in danger of ripping through my pants. Or at least it felt that way.

She was full on riding my thigh now, and I grinned as I yanked at the top of her dress. Fuck, this thing was tight.

"You're going to have to wear my jersey out of here," I whispered.

"What—"

I ripped at the top of her dress, revealing the hottest set of boobs that I'd ever seen. I'd thought she was the most gorgeous girl in the world in high school, but this new, older version of her...I had to keep pinching myself to make sure she was real.

She was whimpering as her body tightened. "That's it, baby. You're almost there."

I licked at one of her pink nipples, rolling the tip of it with my tongue. She grabbed my cheeks and pushed me against her. I laughed against her skin and sucked hard on her nipple.

She came instantly.

Interesting. Apparently Kennedy had developed a little taste for pain.

Her cries as she came needed to be recorded. I just wanted to play it constantly...on repeat. Every fucking day of my life.

It could be my new warmup mix.

Her eyes were dazed, pupils blown out as her body finally started shuddering. I was still busy, playing with her breasts.

"Fucking perfect, baby," I murmured. "Now come again." I thrust my thigh up and rubbed against her pussy. Her head fell back, her chest heaving.

"Carter." Her voice sounded pained.

"I know, baby," I soothed her. "I know." This thing between us was painful. It was intense, with the power to destroy us all, and...

I'd let her go once to protect her.

I didn't think I had it in me to do it again.

My lips trailed along her neck and she pulled at my dress shirt so hard I felt a button pop.

"Are you going to do it, Kennedy? Are you going to be my good girl and come again?" I said roughly as I bit down gently on her earlobe.

I pushed her dress up more, hissing when I realized she didn't have anything on underneath.

"It was so tight. I didn't want lines," she gasped as I squeezed her ass with a groan. I ran my fingers through her slit, dying a little with how wet she was.

I had to get a taste.

I dropped to my knees, throwing one of her legs over my shoulder as I practically dove into her gorgeous cunt.

"Fuuuuck," I growled as I caught that first taste. "You taste so fucking good." I licked along her slit, gathering up every drop of her that I could get. "Ride my face, sweetheart. Give me what I want."

She froze for a moment, but then I bit down on her clit and her cries were ricocheting around the room.

I thrust two fingers into her core as I sucked hard on her clit. Kennedy finally let herself go, writhing against my face as I took what I wanted.

I squeezed her ass before brushing my fingers across her asshole. She froze, a startled yelp coming out.

I laughed as I continued to suck on her clit. Kennedy was going to love ass play soon enough. It's not somewhere we'd gone in high school, but just the thought of a toy jammed in her ass while I fucked her senseless...or better yet, two of us taking her at the same time.

Fuck. I was about to come in my pants.

"Please, please," she begged. I glanced up at her, taking in how her head was thrown back, those gorgeous breasts pushed forward as she panted. Her hands were in my hair, pulling and twisting at my locks.

So what if I was bald after this experience.

#worthit.

I pushed my finger into her ass while I massaged the bundle of nerves in her cunt.

And that was it.

She was coming, her pussy gripping at my fingers.

"That's it, baby. Just like that," I groaned as I lapped up every drop of her cum.

Those tits were distracting me though. I took a break from her sweet pussy to suck her red nipples, scraping my teeth against them so she was shaking against my mouth. I continued to fuck in and out of her cunt, needing one more orgasm before I could stop.

"You're stunning. So fucking hot. You're perfect, baby," I

growled as I shifted my attention back to her pussy. My favorite place in the world to be, I'd decided.

"One more, sweetheart," I begged as I slid another finger in. She moaned, and a second later she was orgasming again, her cries the hottest thing I'd ever heard.

I couldn't help it. I came. In my tux pants. Like a freaking teenage boy.

It was glorious.

One of the best orgasms I'd ever had. Even if my briefs were filled with cum now.

I reluctantly pulled my head from her pussy, my tongue sliding against my lips, making sure I didn't waste a drop of her.

She was staring at me, her gaze shell-shocked, like she couldn't believe what had just happened.

I kind of couldn't believe it either.

But it was the best thing ever.

It was also going to happen again and again. If I went a day without her cunt, I would probably die now.

That was just a fact.

"You probably deserve a thank you after that," she gasped, a giggle slipping out of her.

I huffed out a laugh, staggering to my feet like I was drunk.

I guess I was drunk.

On her.

"Crap," she muttered, realizing she was basically naked at the moment, her dress bunched around her waist. She struggled to pull it down, her breasts jiggling and giving me all sorts of naughty thoughts.

I was definitely going to fuck them one of these days.

"Carter, you said you had a shirt," she said, her cheeks flushed with embarrassment and desperation in her voice.

"Oh, right," I muttered, walking over to my locker and digging through it. I somehow didn't have a jersey in it, which was probably a good thing. Because her in my jersey might lead to me actually fucking her.

And I didn't think she was there yet.

I found a shirt I was 75% positive was clean, and helped her put it on. It drowned her, going down to her knees.

"Shortie," I teased, that feral feeling coming back at the sight of her in my clothes.

She stuck her tongue out at me and I shifted uncomfortably, reminded of the sticky soaked mess inside my pants.

"Do you—" she stammered, gesturing to my crotch.

"Do I what?" I asked innocently, wanting to hear her say the words.

"Do you need me to...take care of you?"

I grinned. What a fucking sweetheart. I could clearly recall how good she was at blowjobs, and I would definitely take her up on that soon.

Just not while my dick was coated with drying cum.

Now fresh cum. Her licking that off would be sexy as fuck.

Drying, cold cum...not so much.

Fuck. When did I become such a gentleman?

Only for Kennedy, obviously.

"What exactly is going on with us?" she asked.

"That should be obvious, I think, baby," I said, leaning over her, one arm propped on the locker above her.

"I really like Greyson too," she whispered, a flash of defiance in her gaze.

"That's alright. I'm not afraid of some competition." I leaned forward, enjoying the way her breath turned shaky as I got closer. "Game on," I whispered.

"Dude...they just pulled out a fucking smores bar," Jack called out as the door suddenly slammed open and he and Sebastian walked in. They both came to a screeching halt when they turned the corner and saw Kennedy and me.

Jack blinked, his mouth dropping open in shock.

Sebastian recovered much quicker. "Well. It looks like we missed some fun," he coughed out.

I growled at him and he flipped me off.

"Can I get a ride home?" Kennedy said quietly, playing with her hair like she always did when she was anxious.

Fuck. They'd made her self conscious. I shot Sebastian a glare and he immediately looked chagrined.

"Yeah, of course, sweetheart," I murmured, grabbing her hand and bringing it to my lips so I could brush a kiss against her soft skin.

"Hey, come here, princess. I was only teasing," Sebastian said softly, opening up his arms with a desperate look in his eyes.

She timidly walked over, letting him envelop her in his arms. Sebastian's whole body relaxed as he held her.

Jealousy tugged at my insides, but it was muted. Almost nothing. We'd all been in pain these last five years. I'd never want to take her away from them.

"Okay, okay. My turn," Jack said exasperatedly, pulling on Sebastian's arm until he let her go and Jack could pull her into his arms.

He rocked her back and forth, nuzzling her hair until she was laughing. The sound of it made us all grin like a bunch of loons.

I held her hand the entire drive home, everything in me protesting as I walked her up to her door.

"Tomorrow." I said, making sure there was no question in my voice. Our date was happening. I wasn't going to give her much time to think about all the reasons she shouldn't go out with me.

We'd done enough thinking on that topic for her.

"Tomorrow," she repeated softly, and I pulled her towards

me, kissing her once again. I needed a fix to hold me over until I saw her again. I didn't think I'd be sleeping at all tonight. I'd just be reliving tonight over and over again.

The door closed behind her, and I wavered in front of it for a moment, trying to decide whether I wanted to break it down, grab her, and take her to our place.

I somehow managed to drag myself away, but only because I knew I'd see her soon.

My phone rang the second I'd gotten in my car.

"Some asshole completely destroyed my truck," Jack snapped.

"What?" I growled, flipping around In the middle of the road and heading back towards the arena instead of home.

"I'll be there in twenty minutes."

"See ya," Jack sighed, sounding devastated–he fucking loved that truck.

I pulled into the arena parking lot twenty minutes later, the eerie glow of the parking lot lights casting long shadows across the asphalt. I scanned the area, looking for Jack's truck. Parked not far from the entrance, I spotted a marked police cruiser, its roof lights softly flashing in the darkness.

And then I saw Jack's truck. It was a complete wreck. The front end was a mangled mess, the hood crumpled and twisted beyond recognition. The headlights were shattered, shards of glass glinting under the harsh lights. The grill had been ripped away, leaving only a jagged, gaping hole in its place.

But it was the spray-painted message that truly sent a shiver down my spine. The words, "I see her," were written in large, crude letters that marred the truck's paint job. The white spray paint stood out starkly against the vibrant red, a chilling message that left no room for ambiguity.

Anger and frustration were etched on Jack's face as he

leaned against a nearby car, his arms crossed tightly. Sebastian, too, wore a grim expression, his jaw clenched in quiet anger.

My grip on the steering wheel tightened as I parked the car and quickly got out. There were two police officers, one of them snapping pictures of the damaged vehicle, while the other questioned Jack and Sebastian.

"Do you have any idea who the 'her' is the message is referencing, or who would do this?" the officer asked, his expression stern.

Jack leaned against a nearby car, his arms crossed, his demeanor casual despite the wreckage before us. "No idea," he replied with a nonchalant shrug. "Could be anyone."

"Steal anyone's girl?" the officer joked, his grin fading when none of us laughed.

Sebastian shifted, tension in his jaw.

We were all well aware that this act was no random act of vandalism; it was a direct threat.

"What did the surveillance footage show?" I asked, since I knew there were cameras all over the parking lot.

"Somehow the camera over this area stopped working this morning. Security hadn't gotten people out yet to fix it," the officer with the camera said, not sounding nearly as suspicious as he should be.

Convenient.

Anger...and frustration were coursing through me, and I clenched my fists, wanting to scream. The last time Kennedy had been threatened...we'd had to let her go.

"We'll keep you updated on the investigation," one of the officers said as he and his buddy got back in the cruiser. The three of us watched them drive away before any of us spoke.

"I can't let her go," I blurted out, starting to feel light headed at the thought. I sank into a crouch, my hands over my face. "I can't do it."

It was selfish of me. But I wasn't sure I'd survive without her this time.

In fact, I knew I wouldn't.

"I can't let her go either," said Sebastian quietly. I glanced at him, a little surprised he was agreeing with me. His eyes were blazing, fists clenched at his sides.

"I'll kill anyone who tries to take her away this time," said Jack, determination laced through his words like I'd never heard before. We both glanced at him. His jaw was set, and there was a coldness in his eyes.

"We can't protect her while she's in that shitty apartment," mused Jack, running a hand through his hair.

"So we get her out of it," I said.

Sebastian's voice carried in the night.

"By any means necessary."

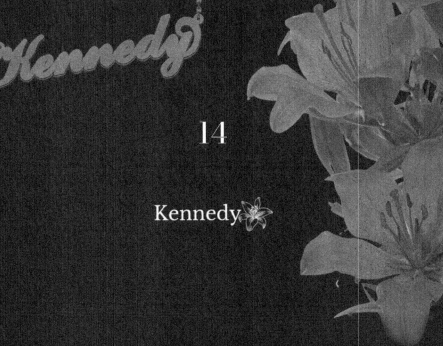

14

Kennedy

Getting ready for my date with Carter was turning out to be more nerve-wracking than I had antici-pated. He had asked me to dress up, and I'd spent hours rummaging through my closet, trying to find something that felt suitable. But everything I owned seemed either too casual or too...poor.

As I sighed in frustration, the doorbell chimed. Before I could get to it, Carrie unlocked it and walked in, holding a garment bag.

"Impatient much?" I teased.

"You know it," she said with a wink. Her eyes sparkled mischievously as she handed the bag in her hands to me. "I brought you something."

"But it's not even my birthday," I quipped, a little joke we had between us because Carrie's love language was gifts. She *loved* giving and getting gifts.

Even when it wasn't a birthday.

I unzipped the bag to reveal a stunning fiery red dress. It was sexy. The kind of dress I'd always admired on others but never dared to wear myself. The fabric was silky and draped elegantly, with a plunging neckline and a daring thigh-high slit.

"I can't wear this," I protested, my fingers running over the smooth fabric. "It's too...too sexy for me. I'm going to look ridiculous."

Carrie raised an eyebrow and crossed her arms. "Kennedy, when are you going to realize how fucking *gorgeous* you are?" she asked, her voice filled with genuine concern. "We can't walk five steps without some guy trying to dry hump you. This dress was *made* for you."

I bit my lip, feeling a mix of insecurity and gratitude. Carrie was the kind of friend that everyone searched for. And I wasn't sure how I'd gotten so lucky to wake up, in the darkest moment of my life, and find her there. She'd always been my rock, and I'd do anything for her.

She stepped closer and gently placed her hands on my shoulders. "Kennedy, I just want you to be happy," she said, her voice softening. "Carter obviously sees what everyone who meets you sees. You're something special."

Tears welled up in my eyes as I looked at my best friend, my heart overflowing with love and appreciation. I sobbed and threw my arms around her.

"Yes, yes. I know I'm the best," she murmured, but her voice sounded a little choked too.

I let her go and took a deep breath. "I'll wear the damn dress," I said, my voice steadier now.

She gave a fist pump. "That's the spirit. My girl's gonna get laid!"

"Um—"

"Did you or did you not get tongue fucked in a locker room last night?" she crowed.

"Well—"

"And did you, or did you not, jack off another hot hockey player the other day."

I nodded. "Both of those things "did" happen."

"Then tonight is the next step. Where you get well fucked."

"Well fucked?"

"I'm just assuming since you said he was amazing last night with his tongue and fingers...that his dick is going to know what it's doing," she explained.

"That—You're probably right."

"Of course I'm right," she scoffed. "And then ya gotta tell me all about it."

"Don't you have enough dick from Keith?"

Her eyes went a little dreamy, and I was sure whatever sex romp she was thinking about, I probably didn't want to hear it.

I had to see Keith all the time. And I'd rather not picture him naked.

"I have *such* good dick," she finally said, before pulling a curling iron out of another bag I hadn't seen her carrying. "Now, let's get you ready for your date."

As I stood before the mirror an hour later, wearing the red dress, I couldn't help but feel like I was gazing at a stranger. The transformation was astounding, and I barely recognized the woman staring back at me.

The dress clung to my curves in all the right places, emphasizing my figure in a much sexier way than the skin tight dress had last night. The plunging neckline showcased just the right amount of cleavage, while the daring thigh-high slit hit just low enough not to show off my goods, but to definitely catch the eye. The silky fabric felt luxurious against my skin, and the fiery red hue seemed perfect with my coloring.

Carrie had styled my hair in loose, cascading waves that framed my face, and a subtle smoky eye and a touch of red lipstick added a sultry allure to my look.

207

I had never seen myself like this.

For once I stared at myself and actually felt...gorgeous.

A knock on the door a second later sent a jolt of anticipation through me, and I couldn't help but feel a flutter of nervousness in my stomach. Carrie squealed, doing a weird little dance. "And that's my cue to leave."

I took a breath, nervous energy flickering through my veins.

"You've got this. You look perfect!" Carrie whispered.

I squeezed her hand and made my way to the door, my heart pounding in my chest as I turned the handle. And there he stood.

Carter.

Looking good enough to eat in an all-black suit with no tie. I'd never been attracted to collar bones before...but the bare tan skin peeking out from the top of his dress shirt was doing it for me.

His presence filled the room, and my breath caught in my throat as I took in the sight of him.

I'd always thought Carter was one of the most gorgeous humans I'd ever seen, but tonight, he was on a whole new level of hotness. The suit hugged his broad shoulders and lean frame perfectly, accentuating every sinew of his powerful physique. His dark hair was styled with casual elegance, and the scruff on his jawline only added to his rugged charm.

In his hand, he held a bouquet of tiger lilies, their vibrant orange petals a striking contrast against his dark attire.

My eyes locked onto the flowers, and I froze for a moment.

Tiger lilies weren't some random flower. It's not like every guy walked into a flower shop, pointed to them, and said, "I'll take those."

Roses, yes.

Tiger lillies, no.

There was no way that was a coincidence that both

Greyson and Carter had decided to get them for me. If it really was random, I needed to examine what about me made me seem like a tiger lily girl.

Although I *was* one.

Carter's gaze shifted from the bouquet to me, and he didn't seem to notice my unease, because there was an awe struck look in his gaze and he was taking his time staring at me, his mouth opening and closing several times like he couldn't figure out what to say.

"You're stunning," he said, his voice rough, like it was hard for him to form words. "Prettiest thing I've ever seen in my whole life."

Carrie pushed past me, mouthing "Told ya" over her shoulder with a smug grin as she headed towards the door. She stopped in front of Carter, pointing two fingers at her eyes and then at him. I'm sure she was trying to be all fierce and protective. But it was actually hilarious.

Carter gave her a little salute and she pretended to swoon.

"Don't do anything I wouldn't do," she yelled as she left the apartment.

"Why do I have the feeling that isn't actually a cautionary statement?" mused Carter.

Before I could say anything she popped her head back in the doorway. "Because it isn't," she sang. "Now, make sure to fuck my best friend good."

With that cheery statement, she popped out of view, leaving me an embarrassed mess and wishing there was a rock to hide under because...

COULD SHE BE ANY MORE EMBARRASSING.

Carter snorted, his face a little shell-shocked as most people were after they met my best friend.

"Well, on that note, should we go?" he asked, holding out a hand for me to take.

"You know, for five years, my life was pretty boring. And now—"

"Now what?" he asked as he pulled me towards him until I was plastered against his hard chest.

"Now it feels like I've turned into Cinderella and I'm waiting for the other shoe to drop."

"Cinderella ended up happily ever after," he murmured in what could be the sexiest voice I'd ever heard. I would have to have Jack, Sebastian—and Greyson repeat the phrase just to check.

For research purposes, of course.

Carter kissed me deep, his tongue tasting me with long, languorous sweeps. He kissed me like he never wanted to stop, like he couldn't get enough. Like he had last night when he'd blown my mind in the locker room.

I was pretty sure he'd short circuited my brain when he finally pulled away, and I took a step away, trying to clear my head.

They were all so...much. It was hard to think around them. Like they had this aura that messed with my senses every time I was around them.

It would explain why I kept letting them come around even though I just knew they were hiding things from me.

"Ready to go?" he asked.

"Yeah, let me grab my purse and put these flowers in a vase," I told him, walking the few feet to the counter to grab the black clutch Carrie had brought over for me to use.

My faded brown purse from Kohls wouldn't exactly have gone with this outfit.

I felt his questioning gaze on my back as I slipped the bouquet in with the flowers Greyson had given me the other day.

"Thank you for the flowers," I murmured as I turned around

Carter's gaze hovered on the flowers a moment, but he didn't say anything. He just grabbed my hand and led me out of the apartment. They all did that, taking my hand like it was nothing. And considering that there were four of them...

Their hands all seemed to fit in mine so perfectly considering how different they all were.

He let me go long enough to lock up the door, but when I glanced up at him, I cringed when I saw how angrily he was staring at the door.

"Everything okay?" I asked, a little shame peeking into my voice about what a shithole I lived in compared to their place.

"I could pick that lock with a toothpick, baby. We have to get you a better door." The anger dissipated when he looked down at me, his voice gentle.

"I'm not sure the landlord would be cool with a new door. We've been asking for better security for years, but he knows he has the best price in town—so it is what it is," I explained, grabbing his hand to lead him out to the street.

I thought I heard him say something like "we'll see," but I decided to let it go.

Once we got to the sidewalk, I glanced around for the silver sedan he'd driven me home in last night. Instead, Carter led me towards a black Maserati that stuck out like a sore thumb in my shitty neighborhood. The sleek, low-slung sports car gleamed under the soft glow of the streetlights, and I was relieved to see it still had all of its wheels on it.

You never knew in this neighborhood. He and Greyson were brave to bring their cars here.

The car's body was a deep, glossy black, the polished chrome accents catching the light and creating a dazzling effect.

"I love this car," I whispered, and Carter's hand squeezed mine. When I glanced at him, he looked torn.

"What is it?"

He shook his head. "Nothing," he murmured. I kept in my eye roll. Someday I would get ahold of all their secrets.

Someday.

Carter held the door open for me, and I slid into the plush leather seats, feeling a little bit like I was about to come. It was so freaking nice.

Carter got in, and the engine roared to life with a powerful growl, sending a thrill through me. An awkward giggle came out of my mouth—that was more of a moan.

I was an embarrassment, but this car was really, really hot.

"Something told me you were a Maserati kind of girl," he mused as he took my hand and set it on the gearshift, switching gears with his hand on top of mine.

Oh...I liked that.

There was a universal hot guy code of conduct, and somehow, the four men who'd swept into my life all seemed to know it.

Judging by Carrie's stories, and the few miserable dates I'd been on in the last five years, they were the lucky few who did.

Or I was the lucky one, I should say...

"Where are we going?" I asked as he sped through the streets.

"You'll see," he said with a wink that made my panties a little damp.

Honestly, sue me for being basic, but I wasn't sure what girl could resist the charm Carter was giving me tonight.

"You guys go back on the road in two weeks, right?" I asked, feeling ridiculously forlorn about it. The arena would be quiet while they were gone.

He glanced over at me, frowning. "Yeah, unfortunately we do."

"Unfortunately?"

"It's a week we'll be gone. I'm not exactly happy to be missing out on that time with you."

Seriously, was this how it was for every girl, once they met "the one." Or maybe "the four," I should say?

I was very aware there were lots of red flags flapping around these guys, but I was having trouble remembering they were red with every sweet thing that came out of their mouths.

The universal curse for all womankind, I was sure.

Carter skillfully navigated us to the heart of downtown. Towering skyscrapers reached for the night sky, their illuminated lights creating a mesmerizing contrast against the darkness.

He shot me a smile every minute, it seemed, never letting go of my hand the entire time we were driving.

Finally, we pulled up to the grand entrance of the city's most exclusive hotel, The Grand Astoria Plaza. Carrie and I had talked about trying to come here for drinks some time, when we saved up more money. A cocktail was like fifty dollars.

My eyes widened as I stared out my window at the crimson bedecked stairs that led up to the hotel. The valet attendants, dressed in sharp uniforms, rushed towards our car. Carter opened his door and handed the keys to one of them with a casual ease that showed just how used to all this luxury he was.

One of the other valet guys was reaching for my door as Carter rounded the car. I heard the muffled sound of Carter's voice and the guy backed away, leaving room for Carter to open the door instead.

"Fuck, baby. I don't know whether I want to hide you from everyone's eyes, because every asshole in this place is going to want you...or if I want to show you off," he growled, his gaze skimming over how much leg was showing through the slit in my dress.

I beamed at him and he shook his head, like he was the dazed one now.

"Show you off for sure. Because I'm the luckiest damn man in the world."

That was a stretch. A huge stretch. But I did feel pretty for once, like maybe I could go inside this fancy place and not immediately be seen as some kind of imposter.

He led me inside, and I gasped when we stepped into the hotel lobby. Crystal chandeliers hung from the ceiling, twinkling over the white and black marble floors and plush, velvet furnishings. The air was scented with the delicate fragrance of fresh flowers, a rich person scent that made me salivate. The hotel's staff greeted us with polite smiles and the soft strains of a piano playing in the background.

I'd joked about feeling like Cinderella earlier, but it really wasn't a joke. Not at all.

First Greyson whisking me away to Paris...for the day.

Now this.

And my moment with Sebastian, while not fancy, was certainly just as memorable.

Even Jack sweeping into the bar that night.

I felt like I was going to pinch myself and find out I'd been dreaming all along.

Which would majorly suck.

We headed towards the golden elevator doors across the lobby and stepped inside as they opened with a soft, elegant swoosh. Carter flashed me a charming smile that set my heart racing.

He pressed the button for the fiftieth floor, and a nervous thrill ran through me. At the top of the hotel was what was supposed to be the city's finest restaurant—except it was invite only.

Apparently, star athletes were one of the people on their list.

"Better stop smiling like that, baby," he growled suddenly in a raspy, rough voice.

"What?"

Suddenly, I was pressed against the mirrored wall, a whimper slipping from my mouth as a desperate, needy feeling washed over me. His lips caressed mine, soft and eager. I was frozen in place, not responding at first. Carter gently fisted my hair. "Kiss me," he ordered. And then his mouth descended on mine again.

Rougher.

His tongue thrust into me, fucking my mouth. Whimpers spilled from me in a constant stream as my lips closed around his tongue, sucking eagerly.

Screw the restaurant. I wanted him to do any and every thing he wanted, just as long as I got his dick inside me. Now.

I was about to suggest that we ditch the restaurant and do just that, when he abruptly yanked himself away with a "fuck", smoothing my hair into place and wiping the red lipstick off his mouth...right as the elevator doors opened.

"I hope you like French food," he said in a slightly out of breath voice. His eyes were burning with hunger, and I knew the same frantic look was echoed in mine as well.

Considering how fancy this dinner was about to be, it was going to be excruciating.

"I do," I said in a neutral voice, considering the last...and first time I'd had French food was in France...with Greyson.

It was then that I finally noticed the restaurant.

Maybe dinner wasn't going to be excruciating.

Sex could wait.

Maybe.

Because this place was gorgeous. The walls were a gleaming ivory color, paintings with gold outlines of the female form every couple of feet. Crystal chandeliers hung from the ceiling, casting a soft, warm light that danced across the room. The tables were set with crisp white linens and glistening silverware, each adorned with a single red rose in a delicate vase. Soft jazz music played in the background, and...I'd never been to a place that felt so romantic.

Not even Paris.

We stepped out of the elevator and a hostess appeared, as if from thin air. As soon as she saw Carter, her cheeks flushed and she stood up straighter, thrusting her chest forward. She was completely fixated on him, but Carter paid her no mind...he was staring at me.

"Good evening, Mr. Hayes," the hostess said in a high, breathy voice. Carter squeezed my hand and glanced over at her, a polite, disinterested mask slipping into place.

She quickly got the memo he wasn't interested, and regained her composure. "Thank you for joining us this evening. Your table is this way." She guided us to a secluded corner table, where a panoramic view of the city unfolded before us. The skyline glittered with a sea of lights, and I wished my phone was better at capturing pictures.

It was breathtaking.

We settled into our seats, the hostess informing us our server would be with us in just a moment before she walked away.

"This place is amazing," I whispered, watching Carter as he lounged in his seat. He was comfortable in his own skin, so self-assured that he belonged.

What would it be like to feel that way?

Had I ever felt that way?

"Only happy thoughts, baby," he murmured, leaning forward and grabbing my hand so he was holding it across the table.

"Sir, I'm so sorry, but you have a call at the front." The hostess was back, looking far edgier and uncomfortable than she had just a few minutes before.

"What? Who is it?" asked Carter, his forehead scrunched in confusion.

"I'm not sure, sir. But they said it was important."

"Okay," he said slowly, getting up from his seat. "I'll be right back," he murmured to me.

I watched as he left, a flicker of unease in my stomach...for no apparent reason at all.

It just seemed weird.

There was a french loaf on the table, and I decided to grab a slice...because bread was life.

But then I finished it.

And he still wasn't back yet.

Another slice in....

And he still wasn't back.

And before I knew it...twenty minutes had passed...and I was beginning to have concerns.

Just as I stood up, a furious Greyson rounded the corner, his face filled with relief when he saw me.

"Kennedy!" he murmured, stalking towards me.

"What are you doing here?" I said slowly.

He closed his eyes as if my question had caused him physical pain. "I'm so sorry, baby. Carter left."

"What?" I asked incredulously, looking over his shoulder like Carter was going to appear at any minute.

"This was all a joke. They wanted to embarrass you and leave you with a huge bill. But then Carter saw the hostess...

217

and..." He sighed and glanced away as if he couldn't bear to say the words.

"He saw the hostess and what—"

"That phone call...that was him giving an excuse to leave so he could fuck the waitress in the bathroom."

What was the word for what I was feeling right then?

Devastation.

Humiliation.

White hot shame and disgust.

"But why would he do that?" I whispered, pulling on the skirt of my dress anxiously. "I don't understand."

Greyson gently grabbed me by the arm and started walking me back towards the elevators I'd arrived in. "He and his friends are assholes like that. They thought it would be a funny joke to play. They do these sorts of things all the time."

I was walking willingly with him, but there was a numbness spreading through my veins like I'd been dipped in a cold bucket of water and my body was slowly dying.

I stopped before we made it across the dining area.

"I still don't understand," I said stupidly. "He seemed so—"

"Have you ever seen that movie, *She's All That*?" Greyson asked, urging me forward once again.

"Yeah," I said slowly.

"That's what they like to do. Get girls to fall for them...and then they embarrass them. They're the worst kind of assholes, Kennedy. I'm so fucking sorry."

We'd made it to the hostess stand...but she was nowhere to be seen.

"Probably cleaning herself up," he murmured, leading me to the elevator and pressing the button, his posture tense.

"Is he still here?" I asked in a high pitched voice. "Is he still fucking her in the bathroom right now?"

My voice sounded shrill and scary in my ears. I was quite

possibly having a mental break. I just couldn't understand how someone could be so fake. How he could act the way he did. Say the things he did.

And be that awful of a person.

Greyson stared at me, an almost pitying look on his face that made me want to shrivel up and cry. "He left, sweetheart."

Right. He'd already said that.

The elevator doors opened and I walked through them, staring unseeingly at my reflection in the mirror as the doors closed behind me.

"How did you find out?" I whispered, suddenly hating the dress I was wearing. After tonight, I was going to burn it. Carrie would understand. I'd pay her back.

"I always have my ear to the ground. It's been in the gossip rags the guys were interested in someone–I obviously knew that was referencing you. It didn't take much to find out their plan."

"But how? Like, did you tap their phone? I don't understand?"

I was a simple girl. I'd woken up five years ago with no memories, and therefore no baggage. I went to work, I did my job, I tried to be nice to people, I tried to be a good friend...this kind of thing—it was beyond my comprehension. This didn't happen in my simple little world.

But I guess going to Paris and fancy restaurants, and stupidly hot hockey players bidding half a fucking million on me to go on a date—that didn't happen either.

"Do you really want to know how I found out?" he asked gently, tilting up my chin to look at him since I'd been staring daggers into the ground, apparently.

"One of the escorts they regularly use. I pay her for information since she services most of the bigwigs in the state. It's amazing what people say in front of people they don't think matter."

Escorts?

It just kept getting better.

"I'm so stupid," I whispered. I wasn't prone to bouts of depression, but this was agony. Pure, unadulterated agony.

"I'm so sorry, baby," he said, an ache in his voice. "I'm so fucking sorry."

I took a deep breath, not wanting to be that girl that gave a fuck about an asshole guy.

But it sure was difficult.

"Can you give me a ride home?" I asked, wanting to curl up in a ball on my couch in sweats with a bucket of ice cream.

And then I needed to find another job.

That was going to be fun.

But if they were jerks enough to pull something like this, it would be in the rumor mill soon enough, and I had no interest in being laughed at by my coworkers—to my face or behind my back.

"I don't think you should be alone right now," Greyson said, rubbing my back soothingly.

"I think that's exactly what I need."

Greyson frowned, frustration in his gaze. "Why don't you let me take your mind off things? How about London this time? I actually like it more than Paris."

As amazing as that sounded, maybe I needed to stay away from boys who did things like fly to Paris...who seemed too good to be true.

But then he pulled me into his arms and he had me rethinking everything.

Maybe I was pathetic. But it was fucking comforting to be in his arms.

"Let me distract you. Make you understand what fucking

fools they are," he whispered, brushing my hair out of my face has he cradled my head gently.

"Okay," I said, even though I knew I shouldn't.

But Greyson wasn't exactly a rebound...I'd started falling for him first.

Hadn't I?

The elevator doors opened and he led me through the lobby and out the front entrance like a man on a mission. I was practically having to jog to keep up.

I mean, I definitely wanted to get away from here, but I also didn't want to break a heel. Carrie's shoes were really nice.

"Greyson, slow down," I called out when I almost tripped on the stairs.

He stopped and raked a hand through his hair. "Sorry, baby. Just eager to get you out of here. I'm so fucking mad right now."

I softened against him, some of my unease settling.

Greyson's driver was already waiting, and I let out a deep exhale at being so close to escaping this place. Greyson opened the door for me, and I was sliding in, when I heard my name suddenly called by a very familiar voice.

I glanced back, wide-eyed as Carter appeared in the hotel entrance, staggering as he tried to get down the stairs.

"Time to go, sweetheart," Greyson said calmly, pushing me all the way into the car and jumping in behind him. The car door slammed closed.

"Go!" he snapped at the driver. Tires screeched as he pulled away...right as Carter made it to the bottom of the stairs, his fist beating once on the window before we were out of reach.

"Greyson," I said in a panicked voice. "What was that? He looked—he looked like something was wrong with him!"

"That was called an inconvenience," Greyson answered,

saluting Carter before he typed something into his phone. "A big inconvenience."

"He didn't ditch me, did he?" I said softly.

"No, he didn't, Kennedy." I'd never seen a man look as satisfied as Greyson did at that moment.

"And where are you taking me?" I asked, bracing myself for him to tell me this was where I died or something like that.

"Home," he answered simply as the locks on the doors engaged around us.

And somehow, it was very clear to me that that the "home" Greyson was referring to, was not my home.

I was pretty sure he was kidnapping me.

15

Kennedy

After two attempts at trying the doors, I gave up. Apparently I was the easiest person to kidnap in the history of kidnapping.

Greyson sat there calmly in his seat the whole time, watching me avidly, a psychotic—yet hot—smile on his face, like he was watching a cute bunny and found the whole thing adorable.

Psychopath.

"If you're taking me somewhere to kill me, I warn you, you're not going to get much satisfaction out of it," I told him at one point when we'd turned into a neighborhood loaded with mega mansions tucked away behind large iron gates. "I literally have one friend. And she'll probably think the whole thing is very exciting and won't even cry because she's weird like that."

He snorted and rolled his eyes. "Why would I kill the person that means the most to me in the world?" Greyson asked the question as if that should be obvious.

I gaped at him.

"Why did you do all of that? You—you hurt me," I snapped,

223

determined to ignore his "means the most to me" comment. Because I didn't know what to do with that.

It was also fucked up because other than being mildly terrified about what he had waiting for me at the end of this drive—I was actually feeling a lot better.

Because Carter hadn't ditched me to go fuck someone in the bathroom during our date.

I still doubted I'd be wanting to go back to that restaurant any time soon—you know, if Greyson let me live.

"I don't like when you go on dates with other men, Kennedy," he said with a sigh, folding his arms and settling back into the seat with a frown on his face.

I was not distracted by the way his suit pulled against his muscles. Not distracted at all.

"You were jealous I was on a date...so you showed up, did something to Carter, and then lied to me so you could get me away from the date."

"Carter has a head like a rock. He'll be fine."

"Oh my gosh! You knocked him out?"

He raised an eyebrow. "Well, he wouldn't have exactly let me walk you out of there willingly, now would he?" Greyson's gaze drifted to the window and he straightened.

"Home sweet home."

I had so much more to say to him. But then I was distracted by the sprawling mansion rising up in front of us.

Maybe mansion wasn't the right word. Maybe castle was more accurate.

It was enormous.

"This is your house?" I whispered, staring at it in shock. I'd thought Carter, Jack, and Sebastian's penthouse was beyond impressive. But this was something else.

Greyson's home was a blend of modern design and rustic charm. Set against a backdrop of lush greenery, the building was a mix of stone and wood that gave it a warm and inviting appearance. Large, arched windows framed in wrought-iron grilles added character and made it more welcoming looking, while climbing vines crept up the walls, lending a touch of natural beauty. There was a meandering stone pathway that led up to the mansion's entrance, where there was a massive wooden door with intricate carvings. The entire estate was rustic elegance, as if it had grown organically from the surrounding landscape.

I actually loved it.

I glanced at Greyson, startling when I saw how intensely he was staring at me.

"What do you think?" he asked, and it kind of felt like my answer was a matter of life or death.

"I'm thinking you're a strange kidnapper," I mused. "But your home is gorgeous."

"*Our* home," he said with a wink as the car came to a stop. "Someday this is going to be your home."

Why did all the super hot ones have to be crazy? At least that's what Carrie would say if she was here.

Greyson gracefully exited the vehicle before holding out his hand to help me out. I was very aware of his gaze caressing my skin as I extended my leg out of the car. A similar reaction to my dress's slit as Carter had.

Something told me he probably wouldn't appreciate that comparison.

Greyson pulled on me a little too hard, causing me to fall forward against his chest.

I tried to push away—since he'd just kidnapped me. But his arms held me tight. "I might not like that you wore this dress for another man, sweetheart. But you're gorgeous. Absolutely stunning. You took my breath away when I saw you."

I stared into his ice blue eyes.

Complicated.

This man was extremely complicated.

"I don't know what to say when you tell me things like that, after what you've done tonight."

He smirked, a crazy gleam in his gaze. "I think I can convince you to forgive me."

"I doubt that," I murmured, ignoring how damp my underwear felt all of a sudden.

Greyson's grin only widened, but he allowed me at least a little space, choosing to grab my hand instead of my whole body and leading me towards the house.

My steps slowed as I noticed the men in suits situated along the perimeter of the house.

"My private security," he said casually when he noticed where I was staring. "They know better than to talk to you."

"Private security. Right," I murmured. I hadn't noticed any security people in our other...interactions.

So this was new.

"Come on, pretty girl."

"You're lucky I'm not screaming for help," I told him as he pulled me towards the side entrance in front of us.

He gave an exaggerated head nod towards the security goons, effectively pointing out that even if I did scream—nothing was going to come of it.

"Touché," I muttered.

But right as I was about to follow him into the house, he swept me up in his arms and walked through the door.

"What are you doing?" I hissed.

He laughed, a happy, boyish grin on his face that took my breath away for a second. "I'm carrying you over the threshold. This is going to be your home someday soon—so it seemed fitting."

"You're insane."

"Hmmm. Maybe. But that's your fault. I was perfectly sane before I met you..."

"A couple of weeks ago," I pressed, wondering if this was the moment he'd tell me some secrets.

"Something like that," he said instead, his grin widening, because he knew exactly what I'd been trying to do.

Greyson set me down inside the doorway, grabbing my hand again, of course. I stared around in awe...the inside of his mansion was even nicer than the outside.

We'd walked into an enormous room with high ceilings and marble flooring, adorned with a magnificent chandelier that hung like a work of art from above. The room seemed to serve no purpose, there wasn't anything in it except a black circle table with an enormous gold statue on it. A foyer...I think that's what the rich people called this kind of room.

Greyson pulled me beyond the foyer, where there was a living area type of room that opened up to reveal a vast and open-concept space. The room actually looked comfortable, with several plush, expensive looking sofas, an enormous TV, and walls adorned with abstract artwork that added a pop of color to the neutral palette. Large windows allowed natural light to flood the room, offering views of the lush grounds outside.

We didn't stop in the living room though. He continued to pull me through the house, past a dining area with a sleek, modern table that could fit a whole crowd, and a glass wall that provided a stunning backdrop of the garden. Through a kitchen that was a chef's dream, with state-of-the-art appliances and marble countertops that gleamed under the soft, recessed lighting.

There were so many rooms, I lost count...and they all disappeared from my mind when he led me into a room that could only be his master bedroom. I stared around the room, noticing

227

the high ceilings and how everything was done in soft, muted colors that offset the dark, hardwood floor. It was interesting though; the home was gorgeous, but everything was done so neutral, it almost seemed like the designer hadn't finished their job–like the couch had been waiting for some colorful throw pillows, the shelves were waiting for some more knickknacks, and the walls a few more pictures.

Maybe Greyson was really minimalistic.

My gaze got caught on the king-sized bed in the middle of the wall. It was the nicest bed I'd ever seen, with a tufted, upholstered headboard. It was dressed in crisp, white linens and fluffy pillows you could sink into. There were sleek, modern nightstands with minimalist lamps on either side of the bed. I dragged my gaze away from it, noting the large window across from it that offered a breathtaking view of the gardens outside and the moonlight sparkling across the surface of the pool.

Greyson was typing something in his phone when I glanced over to him warily. I was pretty sure this was his bedroom...but I guess it could have been a very nice guest room. Maybe he was going to "bid me goodnight" and that would be it.

My hopes were dashed when he slipped his phone into his pocket and prowled towards me. "Do you like our room?" he asked, something almost...hopeful in his voice.

"Your room, you mean. Do I like *your* room."

"Our room. Your room. It's all semantics. Everything I have belongs to you too."

"Greyson," I murmured, brushing some hair out of my face as I chuckled nervously. "You're being ridiculous."

"Am I though?"

"Okay...well, until it's officially *my* room...can you show me to the guest room for now?" I asked, taking a step back.

"Now why would I do that?" he asked, still stalking towards me.

I kept taking steps back until my back hit the wall.

"Greyson..." I whispered, holding up my hands. "What are you doing?"

"I think I need to remind you, sweetheart..."

"Remind me of what?"

"Who you belong to."

His lips crashed against mine, and I kissed him back...just for a second. I couldn't help it.

But as his tongue slipped into my mouth, I remembered that he'd basically just kidnapped me after beating up Carter—not to mention he'd lied.

I pushed on his chest and yanked my face to the side. "Greyson. No. You can't just—"

Greyson abruptly grabbed my hands, and forced them over my head, pushing his whole body into me so I could feel up close and in person his raging-hard on.

My eyes widened.

"Baby...I'm pretty sure I can do whatever I want to," he growled, before going back to licking and sucking at my lips.

"Greyson...arghhh!" I thrashed against him, but he was too heavy. Between his body and the way he'd pinned my arms above my head, I wasn't able to move at all.

He licked down my neck, and gently bit at my pulse point.

"Did he touch you in the car, baby?" he whispered as he sucked on my skin. "Did his lips touch this body that's only supposed to belong to me?"

"I don't belong to you. I don't belong to anyone," I said, but my words came out breathy and weak.

Greyson switched his grip on my wrists to one hand, and with the other, he started to massage my breast.

"You don't sound like you actually mean that," he laughed as he bit my earlobe, his tongue sliding along my skin.

"I do," I moaned as his hand did some kind of magic on my breast, pulling at my nipple in a way that sent a direct shock of lust to my core.

"Mmmh...let's see what your perfect pussy has to say..." he growled.

His hand trailed down my side, sliding across my thigh. I tried to snap my legs together, but he pushed his thigh between mine so I couldn't.

"I hate you!" I said, as his fingers pushed up the bottom of my dress...up...up until he was stroking across my underwear.

"I think you're lying," he laughed as his lips continued to scatter pleasure across my skin. His finger pushed past the edge of my underwear. Closer. Closer. And then he was stroking through my slit. "And now I know you're lying. You're fucking soaked," he groaned, abruptly removing his finger and bringing it up to his mouth where he made a big deal about tasting me.

Fuck...why was that so hot?

"Never tasted anything better, baby. But I think I need more." Before I could blink, he pulled me into his arms and carried me over to the bed, throwing me on top as he ripped off his jacket.

His gaze was hungry...unhinged...and I wasn't proud of the lust shooting through my body.

He kneeled on the bed, crawling up until he was hovering over me. "Unbutton my shirt," he growled as we stared at each other.

"Make me," I said, lifting my chin, even though I was having to do everything I could to stop myself from humping the man on top of me.

"Sure thing, sweetheart," he drawled as he grabbed my hands, bringing them up to his silk dress shirt.

Something came over me and I grabbed at the fabric, ripping it apart so the buttons flew all over the place.

"Fuck, that's hot," he said, the opposite of what I was going for. I guess I could have guessed he had a million more expensive shirts just like that waiting in his closet. "Now let me repay the favor."

He abruptly grabbed my dress and ripped it in half so that I was lying bare underneath him, with nothing but a pair of panties on.

"Greyson!" I yelped, but he just laughed darkly as his gaze ate up my naked skin.

"Look at how pretty you are, baby," he murmured as he leaned forward and lapped at my nipple. "I'm not sure what I want to play with first."

"Nothing. How about nothing," I said, but I'd stopped struggling. It felt too good as he continued to lap and suckle on my nipples, one finger lightly tracing the seam of my pussy through my underwear.

"You're such a pretty, perfect girl," he soothed as his tongue slid across my breasts.

"Greyson," I whimpered, all the fight out of my voice.

"Still trying to say you don't want my cock?" he drawled as I whimpered.

"Yes," I squeaked. "I don't want it."

My hands were tangled in his hair though, and I was holding him to my chest as he continued to torture my breasts.

Greyson made a hungry noise as he ripped my underwear off and shoved two fingers deep inside my aching core.

My cries echoed around the room as I thrashed underneath him.

"Ahhh," I screamed as he bit down on my nipple and I came, the orgasm almost painful in its intensity.

"That's it, baby. Look at you. Coming so good for me."

"More. I need it. Please," I begged.

He worked a third finger inside me. And then a fourth. I cried out again, tears slipping down my face.

"Feel me, sweetheart. I want you feeling me for days after this." He licked up my tears, and a desperate, needy feeling washed over me.

Greyson tried to kiss me, but I twisted my face to the side. "No."

His laugh sent shivers cascading down my skin. "No?"

"You're not allowed to kiss me. Just fuck me and get it over with."

I didn't know why I was choosing *now* to fight. This was a done deal. I was going to get fucked. And I was probably going to like it.

But I was spitting mad at the moment that he could make me feel like this. That he could make me feel like he was tearing me apart and rebuilding me with every brush of his skin against mine.

"Your lips are mine," he growled, grabbing my chin with his free hand, his mouth descending on mine. His tongue thrust in time with his fingers and I moaned into the kiss. I sucked on his tongue and laughed happily.

"Your pussy is mine." He twisted his fingers inside me, shockwaves shattering throughout my insides.

"You. Are. Mine."

Greyson moved his hand from my chin to my hair, fisting it roughly as he angled my head so that his lips could slide down my neck.

His fingers fucked in and out of my core harder. "You're going to come for me again. You're going to come so many fucking times tonight that you black out. And then I'll probably still make you come. When you wake up tomorrow, you're going to know that You. Are. Mine!"

My muscles trembled and my pussy clenched as I came again for him, like my body really was responding to his command.

"That's it. That's my good girl."

"Fuck," I gasped. Because it didn't matter who said it—him, Jack, Carter, Sebastian...it was like a magic button to turning me on.

Greyson fumbled with his pants, the first time he'd seemed less than perfectly in control of himself. I glanced down between us, my eyes widening as I saw his enormous...pierced cock.

"Wow."

"That's exactly the reaction I was looking for," he teased as he grabbed his monster cock and rubbed the glistening head through my folds.

"Greyson," I pleaded.

"I know, baby. I know," he soothed.

My brain came back for a moment and I grabbed his wrist right as he began to push in.

"Wait. Protection. Get a condom."

He laughed. "You'll never need protection from me," he said as he slammed into me hard, sinking in until he was balls deep and his piercings were rubbing against my inner walls.

I cried out, a sharp pinching sensation inside me where he was stretching me out. My breath was coming out in gasps as my brain ceased to function for a moment.

When my eyes fluttered open, who knew how much later, Greyson was staring at me, his eyes almost...glossy. Like the moment was making him emotional.

"Don't look at me like that," I whispered, something clenching inside my chest. Something way too emotional...way too intense after what he'd done.

Greyson leaned down and gave me a soft kiss that squeezed

my heart uncomfortably.

"My baby's perfect. Beautiful. A goddess." He kissed me again as he started moving, angling his hips so that he hit different places inside me. "I'll never let you go. I'll do anything .to keep you. You're mine."

Greyson hit a spot inside me that made my breath hitch, and so of course the bastard focused on that spot, hammering in again and again until I was falling over the edge and screaming hoarsely.

After that, things became somewhat of a blur. He was like the Energizer Bunny, a never-ending story. His hard cock thrust inside me again and again, my cries mingling with his groans.

At some point he flipped me over on all fours, fucking into me as he held a small vibrator that he'd pulled from who knows where to the edge of my asshole. He tortured the sensitive ring of muscle, never pushing in more than the tip. I came so many times I collapsed onto the bed, tears streaming down my face.

"We're not done yet. Not until you tell me you're mine," he snarled, as he flipped me to my side and spooned me from behind, his dick never missing a beat as he rubbed my clit with one hand and played with my nipples with his other.

I thrashed against him as another orgasm rushed through me.

"No, I'm not yours. I'm not," I cried.

"Your cunt knows who it belongs to. You're fucking choking my dick, baby," his voice was sweet and cajoling, not seeming upset at all that I wasn't saying it back.

He bit down on my neck then, like some kind of sexy fucking vampire, while his cock slammed into me relentlessly.

I convulsed around his cock, and I turned my head, my teeth sinking into his bicep as the pleasure tore through me. I guess we were both vampires at the moment.

It was too much though. The pleasure was sliding along the edge of pain and I was exhausted. I couldn't do any more.

"Please. I can't—please," I cried out. I'd come so many times I'd lost count. I was so sensitive though, everywhere, like all my nerves had been activated at once.

"Say it and I'll come, Kennedy. Say that you're mine."

A harsh sob burst out of me. "That's not happening."

He pulled out and flipped me to my back before sliding back inside me, making me groan because I was so freaking sore. "I can go all night. Now that my dick's finally inside you, I'm in no hurry to get out."

I was too tired to fight him, coming over and over again until eventually...I blacked out.

But I never said it.

* * *

I woke up with a groan, my arms stretching over my head. Every muscle in my body hurt for some reason. Had I worked out? I went to scratch an itchy spot on my stomach, freezing when I felt something dry and crusty on my skin. My eyes flew open and I glanced down, shocked to see a white film all over my chest, my stomach, and down between my legs. Was that— oh fuck.

It all came back then—Carter, the dinner, Greyson showing up...the all night fucking he'd subjected me too.

Cum. I had Greyson's dried cum all over my body.

"Good morning, sweetheart," Mr. Cum himself purred from nearby. I blearily looked over and saw him leaning against the doorway that led out to the hallway, looking fresh as a daisy in a perfectly pressed suit. "Chop, chop. You've got work in thirty minutes."

"Thirty minutes," I whispered. I hadn't been scheduled to

work until six thirty the next day...which meant...I'd slept for basically forever.

"A shower?" I asked, the room spinning as I slid off the bed, standing there like a newborn colt, unsteady on my feet.

"No time for that," he said cheerily, like I wasn't covered with his cum. He stalked towards me, and I noticed for the first time, he had a bag in his hand.

Greyson opened the door, pulling out my work uniform and what looked like a fresh pair of underwear and a new bra.

He moved me around like a doll as he got me dressed. I was so shell-shocked over everything that had transpired over the last twenty four hours, I just went along with it, letting him move me as he wanted. Greyson took care of everything, even brushing my hair and pulling it into a ponytail.

And he fucking whistled the whole time he did it.

I blinked and I was in the car, pulling out of the mansion's long driveway.

"Are you really driving me to the arena?" I finally asked, incredulously, after we'd been on the road for ten minutes.

"Well, I know you like your job. So until I convince you to do something else, it is what it is."

He was seated as close to me as was possible without being on top of me. One hand was strewn across the headrest playing with my hair, while the other fiddled with his phone, doing whatever mafia business a psycho like him does.

"I'm never seeing you again after this," I told him as we turned down the street that led to the arena, scratching at my chest because it turned out dried cum was in fact...very itchy.

He snorted. "You're hilarious," he said dryly as he stared at me like...like he was in love.

I crossed my arms in front of me with a huff, like a petulant teenager as he brushed a kiss against my forehead.

"Mmmh, you smell like sex and me," he growled, his tongue

teasing my ear.

I shivered. "I smell like butt, actually. Thanks for that."

He chuckled again as we pulled up to the arena. My eyes widened in surprise when I glanced out the window and saw three furious hockey players standing at the top of the steps that led into the arena.

"Oh good. Your fan club's here," Greyson drawled, nuzzling into my hair.

"Okay. See ya," I called, trying the door so I could get the heck away from the...gorgeous, confusing, CRAZY man beside me.

Of course, that wasn't quite the goodbye Greyson was contemplating. A second later, I was pinned to the leather seat, his hand in my pants as his fingers worked my clit and core until I was coming violently.

When he was done, he patted my ass and opened the door. "See you later, baby."

I stood there on the sidewalk as he drove away, completely dumbfounded by what had just happened...by all the things that had just happened.

"Kennedy," Carter yelled, running up to me and sweeping me into his embrace. "Baby, are you okay?"

"Um, that's a difficult question," I said dazedly. "A really difficult question."

It hit me then that he'd been injured yesterday. "Oh my gosh. Are you okay?" There was bruising around his left eye, but other than that, he looked healthy...and beautiful.

"He came up behind me as I went to grab the phone and sucker punched me. And then he stabbed me with some sedative for good measure and threw me in the bathroom," Carter hissed, his scowl promising pain. "But other than that, I'm great." He smashed a kiss on my forehead, pulling me tightly against him like he couldn't bear to let me go.

"What did he do to you?" Jack asked worriedly, his hand softly caressing my cheek.

My gaze darted over his shoulder, unable to look at him all of a sudden.

"I'd rather not talk about it," I whispered. And that was true. I didn't know what to say about last night. He'd wanted to transform me.

And he'd succeeded.

It was going to take awhile to unpack last night's events.

All of them.

"Hey, sorry, but I need to get into work," I told them lamely, even though I knew I owed them an explanation.

Carter froze and then he cleared his throat. "Okay," he said stiffly.

He reluctantly let me go, and I shot him a fake smile as I walked up the steps, my muscles screaming with every step.

"Princess, you okay?" Sebastian asked, hustling up the stairs next to me.

"I don't want to talk about that either," I said softly, and his cheek ticced, a dark look in his gaze like he was contemplating Greyson's murder.

The three of them followed me silently into the building. They spent the night nursing beers at the bar for my entire shift.

But I made them take me to my apartment at the end of the shift.

And I didn't let them come in with me.

I showered Greyson off me and climbed into bed.

It was only as I was falling into bed that I admitted to myself...I might not have said it.

But it didn't make it not true.

A part of me may have started to belong to Jack, Sebastian, and Carter—but Greyson owned a part of me now, too.

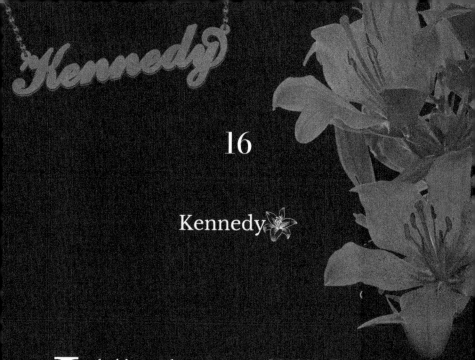

16

Kennedy

It had been a long time since I had last dreamed I was trapped in the coma again.

But even though I knew I was dreaming, I couldn't pull myself up to the surface. I was stuck, trapped in the deep black. My arms and legs felt heavy, as if they were being drawn through the mattress underneath me. There was no escape.

I tried to move, but I was entombed. I could hear sounds around me, but I couldn't open my eyes, or maybe I did but I was in the deep and couldn't see anything. But the sounds, a low crackling, a sudden rushing sound, sent a jolt of panic through me. It was so warm in my room and my breathing felt shallow and rapid, like I couldn't get enough breath. My skin felt flushed and hot, as if I were burning up.

In the distance, I heard the sound of someone slamming into a door. "Kennedy!"

I wanted to call back, "I'm here. Don't leave me alone." But I couldn't speak, when I finally managed to get my lips to part, my voice came out so rusty and weak, the same way it had when I first surfaced from the coma.

"Kennedy!" That deep, husky, desperate voice was Sebastian. The fear threading through his voice sent a rush of adrenaline through me.

I was finally able to open my eyes.

The room was almost pitch black. But there was a slice of surreal light coming through the window, bright orange. The room was filling with smoke, and the scent choked me.

My room was on fire.

And I couldn't move.

Finally, I heard the sound of the door slamming into the floor. Seconds later, Sebastian was in my room, his eyes wide. Beyond him, I could hear smoke alarms going off, and the sound of sirens.

"What are you doing?" he demanded, right before he scooped me up and cradled me against his chest.

"Is this real?" I begged to know, my fingers digging into the thick muscle of his shoulder, trying to ground myself in something real. I pushed my face against his T-shirt and the hard planes of his chest, but I couldn't smell his aftershave. All I smelled was the smoke.

Was I still trapped in my bed? In my sleep? Had I dreamt of him to comfort myself as the smoke smothered me?

"This is real, Kennedy," he told me, giving me a worried look as he carried me through the living room and over the broken down door.

Then we were out in the hallway. Everyone else seemed to be evacuating, or already outside. Firefighters were rushing in as he carried me out across the parking lot to his car.

He opened the back seat and slid me inside, then stood there with his hands braced on the door frame, studying my face. "What happened?"

"I couldn't move," I whispered. "I felt like I was back in my...And part of me still wonders if maybe this is the dream, if

I'm really still in the coma and this isn't real, but I'm about to die in a fire..."

"I am real," he said, taking my hand and pressing it to his cheek. The day's scruff was bristly against my palm. "And you're alive, Princess. You're not dying in a fire. You're with me, period. Let me show you how alive you are."

He got into the back seat with me. Then he closed the door, and through the windows, I could see the bright orange flames engulfing the building.

"Eyes on me, Princess," he said quietly.

With effort, I turned away from the devastation outside and met his deep blue eyes.

"That's better," he murmured.

He wrapped his arm around me, kissing my forehead tenderly. "I just want to take care of you," he whispered.

"Why?"

"Does there have to be a reason?" His breath was soft against my hair. "You deserve to be loved. You deserve to be cared for. And I don't think anyone has taken care of you for a long time."

The flames danced in the distance, casting Sebastian's beautiful face in harsh, flickering angles as we sat in the back-seat of his car.

"I wish I'd been there to take care of you," he whispered. "But I'm going to now."

My gaze was drawn out to the flames racing across the outside of the building. My heart raced and my breaths came in shallow gasps, panic threatening to overwhelm me as I watched my apartment burn.

"Hey," Sebastian said softly, reaching over and resting his hand on mine. His touch was warm, grounding, and my breathing began to slow. "I want to tell you about something, Kennedy. About when we–when *I* was a teenager."

"I'm listening."

"I had this odd fascination with fire." His lips parted in a playful smile. "Well, I was a bit of a pyro. I loved building campfires, watching the way the flames would lick at the logs and dance in the night."

His words painted pictures in my mind, momentarily distracting me from the chaos outside. For a second, I could imagine the flames outside were a bonfire, something fun and deliberate, not the sheer chaos unfolding outside.

"If we'd known each other back then, I would've built you the most beautiful fire, Kennedy," he continued. "We would've been wrapped up in blankets, staying warm and cozy on a winter night. And I'd have kissed you like this."

He leaned forward, and I was already smiling at the thought when his lips brushed mine. As he kissed me, slowly and tenderly, I felt the tension in my body begin to ease.

"Can I remind you how alive you are?" He whispered to me. "How much you're grounded in this body... how you're here with me."

"Yes," I whispered, surprised to hear my voice come out husky.

Sebastian's eyes met mine, filled with concern and desire. He slowly moved his hand to my sleep pants, fingertips grazing my waist before he slid inside. "Is this okay?" he asked gently, his voice laced with genuine care.

"Yeah," I replied, my heart pounding for a different reason now.

He teased his fingers across my mound as he brushed against my panties until his fingers circled my now aching clit. Something about having him touch me through my panties, which began to cling to me as I grew wet, felt irre-sistible, knowing how slow he was going to take things. My hips jerked against his hand, and he smiled. The flames danced in his eyes, reflected from outside, and I started to look again.

"Look at me," he whispered before I could turn away. His other hand caught my chin and held my face still, forcing me to make eye contact with him. Then he leaned forward and captured my lips with his in a hard, wild kiss.

His fingers slid beneath the fabric, touching me intimately. The world around us seemed to fade away as he played my clit, circling my folds, teasing inside me with two fingers.

I began to thrash against the seat, and he dragged my pants and panties down with one hand, exposing my thighs and my now wet pussy to the cool air of his car. I was too greedy now to care, my hips bucking against his hand as he worked two fingers inside me, his thumb circling my clit. Intensity sang across my skin, and I threw my head back.

"Sebastian," I moaned, and he captured my lips with his as if he wanted to swallow my moans.

Sebastian stroked me to the edge, until my thighs were shaking. When I moaned, he captured my mouth with his, his tongue sliding inside my mouth as his fingers fucked me wildly.

As our tongues tangled together, I tumbled over into a powerful orgasm. Waves of pleasure washed over me. My core squeezed around his fingers, pulsing around him hungrily. He watched me with a look of pleasure on his face, as if making me come was the most satisfying experience.

Slowly, as I came back to earth, I realized I had briefly forgotten about the burning ruins of my life outside the car.

Despite the comfort I found in Sebastian's touch, tears welled up in my eyes as reality set back in. My home was gone, swallowed by the flames.

I sobbed into Sebastian's shoulder, feeling his strong arms wrap around me. I still couldn't smell his scent over the smoke that clung to us both, and it made me feel as if I were lost in a dream again. I needed every bit of Sebastian right now—his body against mine, his deep, soothing voice, his comforting scent.

"Shh," he whispered. "Let's get you out of here. I'm going to take you home."

I nodded silently, tears still streaming down my face. "I don't have a home."

"You'll always have me, Kennedy. And that means you'll always have a home."

Sebastian started the car and began driving away from the wreckage of my life. The journey was a blur, my mind lost in memories of the home I'd lost and the fear that had gripped me when I first saw the flames. Sure, my apartment was small and grungy; I got ding-dong-ditched by an annoying group of tweens on at least a monthly basis, and one of my neighbors let her dog pee on my car. Baxter the beagle had a strong preference for the driver's side front tire.

But still. I cried, thinking that I would never go back there.

The car came to a stop, and I realized we'd pulled into the garage below their condo building. Sebastian got out and walked around to my side, opening the door and scooping me up into his arms.

I protested weakly, "I can walk."

"I know," he replied, his voice gentle but firm. "But I love taking care of you."

He carried me through the lobby, past a doorman who nodded at us, and into the elevator. The penthouse was so high up that it felt as if my ears popped. I rescued my head against his shoulder, letting myself relax into his touch. It was crazy to me how easily he carried me, as if I weighed nothing.

As we entered, I caught my breath at the sight before me. I still couldn't get over how nice their condo was. It was masculine but lavish, with dark wood furniture and rich fabrics adorning the space. Floor-to-ceiling windows offered a stunning view of the city far below. It even smelled nice in here.

Sebastian carried me into his room and set me down on my feet. His room was all dark espresso-colored wood, with a king sized bed with crisp white sheets and duvet. There were a few paintings on the wall, and a long mirror across the far wall reflected back the bed.

I immediately went to the enormous floor to ceiling windows, searching for any sign of my old apartment building or smoke still rising in the air. The guys lived so close to my old apartment—and to the hospital where I'd once been trapped in my coma—and it was strange to think that all this time, I could've stumbled into them.

"Can you see anything?" Sebastian asked softly, standing close behind me.

"Nothing," I murmured, my heart heavy with the weight of loss. He placed a comforting hand on my shoulder, and though it didn't erase the pain, it helped ground me in the present, reminding me that I wasn't alone.

I turned to face him, but of course, I was face to face with his chiseled pecs, his t-shirt clinging to his body.

"Will you help me... be grounded again?" I whispered. "Here, with you?"

His lips curled slightly at the edges. "Absolutely."

I felt the chill of the glass on my back and gasped as Sebastian pinned me against the window, his lips finding mine in a passionate kiss. His hands roamed my body, slowly teasing off my smoke-soaked shirt.

When he pulled it over my head, he groaned, his gaze reverent on my body. "God, you are so beautiful."

With trembling fingers, I reached down and gripped him, drawing a low moan from his throat.

"How did you know I needed you?" I whispered between kisses, my breath ragged with desire.

Sebastian's eyes locked onto mine with unwavering intensity. "I always know," he murmured. "I'm sorry you spent so much time alone... but you're never going to be alone again. I'm always going to be right here."

My heart swelled at his words, but as we continued to press against each other, I couldn't help but remember the acrid smell of smoke that clung to my hair and clothing. The memories of the fire threatened to overwhelm me, my breath hitching in panic. Sensing my distress, Sebastian pulled away, concern etching lines across his face.

"Kennedy? What's wrong?"

"Smoke," I choked out, tears forming at the corners of my eyes. "I can still smell it on me, and it's freaking me out."

"Hey, hey..." Sebastian's voice was soothing as balm. "Let's get you cleaned up, alright?"

Without waiting for my response, he scooped me up once more and carried me into the bathroom, where an enormous tub awaited. He set me down on the cool tile floor and began filling the tub with warm water. After adding a generous pour of bubble bath, he stripped off his own clothes and stepped into the water, beckoning me to join him.

"Come on," he urged, offering me a hand. "We'll wash away the memories of the fire together."

I hesitated, then took his hand and stepped into the tub, my body sinking into the comforting warmth of the water. As Sebastian began to wash my hair, I closed my eyes, letting the sensation of his strong fingers massaging my scalp chase away the lingering dread.

"Thank you," I whispered, leaning back against him, feeling his heartbeat against my spine.

"Always, Kennedy. Always."

Sebastian's hands moved from my hair, trailing soapy suds down my neck and across my chest. His touch was tender yet deliberate as he washed my breasts, fingers occasionally brushing over my sensitive nipples, sending sparks of pleasure coursing through me. I couldn't help but moan softly, my body responding to his intimate caress.

"Sebastian," I whispered, tilting my head back to rest on his shoulder, my eyes still closed.

"Shh, just let me take care of you, Kennedy," he murmured in reply, his breath warm against my ear.

As his hands continued their gentle exploration, they traveled downward, washing the curves of my hips and thighs. I felt myself growing more aroused by the second, my body aching for his touch. When he finally reached the apex between my legs, I gasped, an involuntary shudder rippling through me as he began to stroke me with purpose.

"Sebastian," I whimpered, gripping his forearm as waves of pleasure built within me. "I'm...I..."

"Let go, Kennedy," he urged, his voice low and commanding. "You're safe with me."

And with those words, I surrendered to the sensations. My body trembled and shook, safely cradled in his arms.

My moans echoed off the tiled walls, mingling with the sound of the cascading water.

When my breathing had steadied, Sebastian gently pulled me upright and turned off the faucet. He grabbed a plush towel, wrapping it around me before lifting me from the tub and cradling me in his arms.

"Sebastian," I murmured sleepily, clinging to him as he carried me into his bedroom and laid me down on the soft, luxurious sheets. "Promise me you'll stay with me tonight. I need to know I'm not lost in the coma again."

"Of course, Kennedy. You'll never be alone again. I promise," he reassured me, tucking the covers around my body and climbing into bed beside me.

"Your place...it feels like home," I mumbled, my eyelids heavy with the weight of exhaustion.

"It better, princess," Sebastian murmured, pressing a gentle kiss to my forehead. "This is your home. This is where you've always been meant to be."

* * *

Sebastian

There was a shadowy figure in the door of my room. I knew it wasn't a threat, but it was an asshole.

"Go away," I whispered at Carter.

Her breathing was soft and even as she lay curled against me with her head cushioned on my shoulder.

I felt more comfortable than I had in five years.

Like this place had just been a place to sleep until I carried her through the doors. But with her in my bed...we were both home.

"Not a chance," Carter said.

"You're going to wake her up, asshole."

"You don't get to go off on your own making decisions. Get your ass out here. Or I *will* wake her up."

I'd fucking die for Carter, but I also would seriously contemplate murdering him myself from time to time.

I kissed her forehead and she let out a happy little sigh that melted my heart. "Be right back, princess," I whispered, feeling my heart twist at having to get out of bed. I eased my arm out from under her head and then crept across the room.

I had been in such a good mood having her close, but my mood darkened with every step away from her. I felt pretty pissed by the time I closed the door softly behind me and met Carter and Jack in our living room.

"What the fuck couldn't wait?" I asked.

"You don't deserve to be cuddling in there with her, like you've rescued her from all her problems, when you're the one who gave her half those problems. You burned her fucking house down, you asshole."

"We all agreed that place was a shithole, and she needed to move in with us," I said.

"She brings out the absolute psycho in you." Jack sounded disbelieving.

"She does the same for you, if you recall," I answered stiffly. "Anyway, now she'll stay with us. Problem solved."

Carter swore. "We better talk through our alibi, just in case you're not as smooth anymore as you think you are, pyro. We've got a good life, a clean life, a life that she needs us to have if we're going to be good enough for her. No more fucking crimes."

"No more fucking *half cocked* crimes," Jack corrected, and we both looked at him. He shrugged. "I'm not planning anything. But I don't want to make promises I can't keep."

"I cannot handle the two of you," Carter said.

He walked away from us into the kitchen. But we followed him.

Carter turned back to face me. "Greyson is going to know it's you. When the four of us were trying to take down the Muertes gang to prove ourselves to his father, you were the one who burned down their headquarters and their entire supply. He knows your MO."

"And what's he gonna do?"

"You know he's gonna try to get Kennedy back from us."

"I hate to say it," Carter said quietly. "But maybe we need to take care of Greyson. Permanently."

I swore.

Jack shook his head.

"Come on," Carter said in exasperation. "Because you were besties in kindergarten, you've got some kind of undying loyalty to him?"

"I mean, it's a pretty low bar of loyalty. I just won't murder him," I said dryly. "And anyway, you were just talking about staying clean and not doing crimes, not being unworthy of Kennedy. No matter how we feel about the asshole at this point, Kennedy loved him. She loves him now. We can't take that away from her. Not...forever. What if she found out?"

"Well, I don't think she's gonna take it very well if she ever realizes Sebastian burnt down her apartment building either." Carter grabbed a spray bottle and began to clean the enormous granite island, even though it was already spotless. Usually, I liked it when my roommate rage cleaned.

Carter's cell phone chimed. He pulled it out of his pocket and took a look, then said, "It's for you."

He tossed it to me, and I caught it.

> Greyson: Tell Sebastian there's a lot more at stake than juvie these days.

"So, he knows," Carter said.

"I'd love to text him back a photo of Kennedy in my bed," I said. "But I need her to stay asleep."

The phone chimed again.

> You can pretend, but you three never changed your roots.

"Fair enough," I said, sliding the cell phone back across the island to Carter. "I never changed my roots. I was obsessed with Kennedy when we were kids, and I'm obsessed with her now."

"I couldn't stand her being with Greyson," Jack admitted. "This is for the best. She'll be here with us, where we can keep her safe and protected."

"He'll try to get her back," Carter reminded us.

"So it's war," I said. "That's fine. I'm ready to fight for her... the way we should have five years ago."

"Dramatic bastard," Carter muttered, as if he hadn't been ready to murder someone earlier tonight.

All of us had been losing our shit about Greyson taking Kennedy. I'd just done something about it.

And now...the spoils of war.

I slid into bed beside her, tucking the blankets carefully around her still form. She let out a happy sigh as she snuggled close to me.

I'd burn the whole world down for this girl.

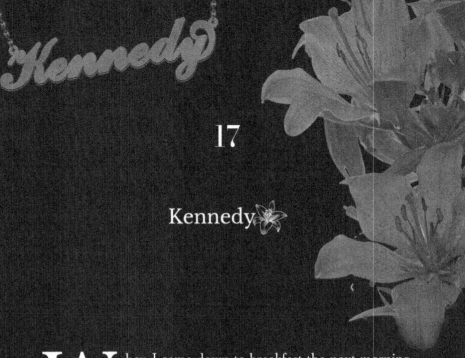

17

Kennedy

When I came down to breakfast the next morning, there was a gold wrapped box-- a big one-- sitting on the big granite island. I glanced at it curiously, sure that it was for me, knowing these men. But I didn't want to assume.

Then Sebastian caged me against the island, his big arms braced on either side of me. The hard edge of the counter brushed my belly, but his big dick pressed urgently against me through his sweatpants. It seemed even harder than the granite island.

"I got you a little something," he told me quietly, his voice low and sexy as he spoke into my ear.

"You shouldn't have," I said.

"I should do what I want," he returned. "And that includes spoiling you. Now open your present."

I couldn't help the grin that broke across my face as I tore into the wrapping paper.

Inside was a plain black box, and when I opened it up, inside were a pair of beautiful new figure skates. They were obviously custom skates, red with black and gold laces. They were so beautiful.

I knew he wasn't going to hear any of it if I protested that he shouldn't have bought me a gift, so I just turned in his arms and put my arms around his neck. "Thank you."

"You're welcome," he murmured, smiling down at me fondly as he smoothed my hair back with one hand. "That smile is my favorite smile in the world. I hope you know you're worth everything. That you deserve all the presents. Let us spoil you."

"Well..." I tapped my finger against my mouth, pretending to think about it. "I'll consider it."

"Mm, well, choose wisely, princess." his voice lowered to a husky whisper in my ear. "If I'm not allowed to spoil you, I may choose to punish you instead."

An unexpected thrill of lust ran through me at the word *punish,* but I pulled back, running my hands down his broad shoulders so that I could give him a skeptical raised eyebrow. "Try it, and I might go running back to Greyson."

He let out a groan of disappointment just hearing Greyson's name. "Unless he's changed–and Greyson never changes–he's a much kinkier, more sadistic bastard than I am. Now, get his name out of your mouth. I only want to hear you say my name."

He grabbed my thighs and boosted me onto the edge of the island in one smooth motion. I laughed, my hands clutching his powerful shoulders and my thighs automatically clutching his lean waist as I settled myself.

"How did you know my favorite color's red, anyway?" I teased him.

"I wanted to see you dressed in the Devils colors. Like one of the hockey wives." He stroked his hands down my thighs, looking down at me dreamily. "You are so fucking beautiful.

It's a dream, waking up, knowing you're here in the house with us."

He said it as if he wouldn't mind if I stayed. But obviously, I couldn't do that. As much as I felt an attachment to these men, I couldn't just move into their house when I barely knew them. Hell, I barely knew *me*.

But for now, I just grabbed the front of his shirt and tugged him down to kiss me. His lips met mine in a long, passionate kiss. When he finally pulled away, he gazed down at me with soft, bedroom eyes.

I talked to the front of his shirt. "Why are you wearing a shirt, anyway?"

"Why are you?" he teased me, before pulling his shirt over his head, slowly and deliberately, the movement sexy as his muscles rippled through his powerful shoulders and abs.

I feasted my eyes on his gorgeous body.

"Now you," he murmured hungrily. "You don't need to wear clothes at our house. It'll save on laundry."

"Always so practical," I said with a laugh, but then my laugh was cut off as he tugged my shirt over my head. Too late, I raised my arms so that he could tug it the rest of the way off, but he stopped there, the shirt covering my face so I couldn't see, while he bowed his head and began to use his tongue over my nipples before drawing them into his mouth and suckling on them.

I let out a moan, my thighs locking around his waist, using my legs to tug him in toward me. My heels hooked behind his back, feeling the way his muscles flexed against my calves.

Finally, I fought my way out of the shirt, and as soon as I was free of it, his lips captured mine in another wild kiss.

"Could you two refrain from fucking on the island?" Jack drawled as he walked into the kitchen. "And if you must make the kitchen unsanitary, the least you can do is share."

Jack leaned over the other side of the island, grabbing my shoulders and tugging me down so my bare back was pressed to the cool surface, and I let out a giggle over it before his lips met mine. He kissed me, and I slid my hand through his hair, savoring having the two of them here with me.

The next thing I knew, Sebastian was drawing my panties down my thighs. "You don't really need these either."

"Hey," I protested.

He stuffed them into his pocket with an unrepentant grin that told me I was never getting those back.

"Be a good girl and listen to Sebastian," Jack murmured, his big hands gathering my wrists and bracing them up by my head as his lips captured mine again.

To Sebastian, he added, "You can have her sweet pussy as long as I can have her mouth."

"I don't recall inviting you to my party," Sebastian said, but without rancor.

Then Sebastian leaned down over my thighs, a mischievous gleam in his eyes, right before he darted out his tongue and licked slowly all the way up my seam. My hips bucked, and he put his hands on my thighs, spreading them out before him.

"Breakfast of champions," Sebastian quipped before he settled down, his tongue lapping through my folds, then settling inside me as his mouth began to work against my clit.

I let out a moan. This had to be the best way to wake up, even better than pancakes and chai. Jack covered my mouth, letting out a little groan himself as if he was overwhelmed by the sounds I was making.

I tried to writhe away from them as sensations started to overcome me, but the two of them had me pinned firmly to the table, making it impossible for me to escape Sebastian's incredible tongue as he drove me further and further into my orgasm.

As I cried out as the powerful orgasm ripped through me,

Jack moved to kiss the sides of my throat in the way that drove me crazy, releasing one hand so that he could slide it down my body and caress and tweak my nipples.

Having two big, powerful men work my body like this, to incredible ecstasies of pleasure, was amazing.

But even as I was clenching around Sebastian's incredible tongue, I couldn't help but think, why not four? How incredible would four men be?

"You all are degenerates," Carter said, sounding amused as he leaned in the doorway.

Sebastian caught my wrists and pulled me up to sit. The world swam, as if I were lightheaded from the power of that orgasm, but it didn't matter, because he gathered me up into his arms as if I weighed nothing. He lifted me against his body, my throbbing clit pressed against his bony hip through his gray sweatpants, and he carried me with him as he went to get a cup of coffee. "You're just mad you slept through all the fun."

Carter's gaze sparkled. "Not all the fun. We're not done."

"She needs to eat first. Get ready for the game," Sebastian said. "You're going to watch, right?"

"I can't," I said. "I'll be working."

The three of them all stopped as if I'd said I were going to go to the game naked. Actually, they probably would have reacted better to that.

"Why?" Jack asked. "I get it, you're independent. But you just lost your apartment. Life's been busy lately. You're trying to recover your memories...You should take some time to rest and recover. We can make sure you have everything you need."

"I have to work, and of course I'm going to watch your game as much as I can, but I also need to find time to do some apartment hunting soon. I'm gonna have to get a new place."

"No, you aren't." Sebastian set me back down on the edge of the island, but this time when his big arms were braced on either side of me, I felt like he was using his massive size to dominate me. "You can live with us."

"I can't just live with you," I said in exasperation. "Look, possessive-and-protective can be a cute look, but not if you take it too far."

I wished I wasn't having this conversation naked. I tried to escape Sebastian's thick arms, but it was like a bunny trying to escape an iron cage.

"Let her go," Jack urged. Always the reasonable one. Then he added, "If you want your own place, we'll help you get one. It just...needs to be safe.

"And nice enough for us to sleep over," Carter muttered.

"My old apartment was safe," I said. "Nothing bad ever happened to me there in five years. Except for the fire."

Jack and Sebastian exchanged a look. "Exactly, except for the fire," Sebastian said smoothly. "Kennedy, we just want to take care of you. Why is that so terrible? It doesn't seem like anyone's taken care of you for a long time. Why not let us do it?"

"It's not terrible," I protested. "I appreciate it. But you can't pretend that your care doesn't come with some strings. Like, I don't think I'm exactly going to be invited to bring Greyson over to watch a movie."

They all stiffened. Sebastian bristled at my second mention of Greyson.

I mean I bristled at the mention of Greyson—I was still confused and upset about what had happened the other night...

But it just didn't feel right not to be with all four of them.

Which was interesting, when the four of them used to be so close.

"Why did he give up hockey, anyway?" I asked.

"Maybe because Greyson was always a better gangster than he was a wing?" Carter said, his voice harsh.

Carter was captain of the Devils, but from the articles I'd found, Greyson had been captain of their high school team. And he had led them to a state victory.

"Then why was he captain of your team in high school?"

A look of frustration came over Carter's face. "I can't talk about this before a game. I need to focus."

He started to walk away, then turned back and threw back at Sebastian and Jack, "Let me know when you're all ready to really talk."

I glanced between Jack and Sebastian. Sebastian had that stern look on his face that always made me want to make him melt. Jack looked frustrated, almost upset, as if he couldn't stand when we all fought.

"What does he mean? When we're ready to really talk?" I demanded. "I'm *ready* to really talk."

"Just take the day off and come watch our game, OK? Please?" Jack pleaded. "We have a big game today and I need to focus. I'm not going to do that knowing that some guy might be drooling all over you or pinching your ass when you're trying to work. I don't like you working at the bar."

"And I don't like you all being controlling, but here we are," I returned.

Sebastian looked exasperated. I had the feeling he was about to unleash on me, but Jack grabbed his arm and tugged him back.

"It's alright," Jack told us both. "Kennedy, go ahead and get ready. It looks like your Civic got torched. It was parked too close to the apartment. So you can ride with us."

I could have sworn Jack and Sebastian exchanged another look. Like they weren't sad that my precious, ugly, little car was no longer with us.

But when I got to work, my manager insisted that I call off for the day. "Just relax, Kennedy," he told me. "You've been through a lot lately. And I owe you extra hours for working that charity auction. That was a huge favor."

Why did I have the feeling the guys were behind this somehow?

I was waiting outside their locker room when Jack came out. His face brightened when he saw me, his eyes crinkling at the corners. It was a look that made a rush of joy rise up in my chest. "I know you're annoyed by us," he murmured, kissing my cheek. "I'm sorry, you're our little good luck charm and we get distracted if we don't know you're safe. Will you please just humor us?"

"Fine," I agreed. "I'll be up in your box."

His answering grin was like the sun coming out. It was so warm I could bask in it.

"Good girl," he murmured, before he caged me against the wall and kissed me until one of his teammates came to pull him away for the game.

I was walking through the lobby towards concessions when a familiar figure passed through the front entrance.

Greyson grinned at me like he couldn't believe his luck in finding me there.

Joy surged through me, and I was amazed by the realization of how much I had missed him—until I remembered everything he'd done the other day.

Fucking asshole.

I thought about turning around, but then I decided it wasn't worth the energy, because he'd just track me down.

He walked towards me, and I did my best not to drool. All the versions of Greyson I'd experienced were hot—if psycho—but Greyson in a fitted tee and tight jeans?

Another level.

I tried to hide how happy I was to see him, but his grin told me he could see right through me. I popped my hands onto my hips. "Tell me you didn't burn my apartment down."

"I promise you, I did not," Greyson said. "And if I did, it sure as hell would have backfired, given that you've moved in with those three jackasses."

"You say it like you thought about it," I said with a lifted eyebrow. I tried to be strong for a whole second, but then he hugged me so hard he lifted me off my feet, and I found myself fucking hugging him back–like he'd really succeeded in rewiring my brain...and my body.

He eventually set me back down and pressed a hard kiss to my lips. He kissed me like he was trying to claim me for his own.

"And anyway," I said, slightly breathless. "I'm not living with them. I'm just staying there for a few days while I figure out a new place to live."

"Is that so?" he murmured. "Interesting."

"But that doesn't mean I'm moving in with you."

"I bet I could change your mind."

"Not possible. Because I still hate you," I whispered, so confused about how I was feeling.

He nuzzled against the top of my head.

"I still don't believe you."

For the first time, I noticed that he was carrying a bag. "What's that?"

"A little gift for you," he said, handing it over to me.

I opened the gift bag to find a high school jersey. As I pulled it out, the green and black colors struck me with a wave of nostalgia. I'd learned to recognize the feeling, even if I couldn't access the memories behind the emotion.

"Your old jersey?"

He nodded. I turned around to see his name written across the back.

"Are you sure that you want to give this to me?" I asked. "It must have so many memories attached to it..."

"That's exactly why I want to give it to you," he told me. "Because those memories belong to you, Kennedy."

I stared at him, feeling lost for words as hope blossomed inside me.

"So, you *do* know who I am?"

"I do."

"Why haven't you told me?" I cried out, feeling lost and overwhelmed.

"Let me explain." He glanced toward the arena, where there were noises like the game had just started. "You want to go in? I know they won't be able to concentrate without you."

"They know who I am too?"

Greyson nodded.

Abruptly, I shook his jersey out and pulled it over my head. I mean he deserved a reward for finally giving me...something.

A look of sheer joy came over Greyson's face. "That looks good on you. I haven't seen you wearing my jersey in so long. It's going to make them crazy, you know..."

"I know." It wasn't quite a memory, teasing at my conscious mind. Just something I knew about these guys. "They deserve it."

* * *

A few minutes later, Greyson and I were sitting right behind the penalty box, despite the fact that I'd told him I wasn't going to sit by him.

"I wish I could've seen you play in high school," I said, toying with my name necklace, which I'd always had a habit of fidgeting with. "I would've been your number one fan. Or...was I?"

"You were the best fan," he told me, his gaze fond. "The only one I ever cared about."

"Greyson... please...talk to me." Tears tinged my voice, surprising us both. I wiped them away, and he tried to pull me into his lap, but I pushed him away.

"Kennedy." He got down on his knees in front of me, tugging my hands away from his eyes so I was forced to make eye contact with him. "Listen. Don't hate me for not telling you...hate those motherfuckers if you want, but don't hate them for that. We had good reason."

"What's that?"

"I did my research on amnesia," he told me. "I talked to some of the best doctors in the country trying to figure out how to help you. If anyone just tells you about your past, you might never recover the memories for yourself. You'll just have the version of whatever they tell you, but not your memories. And I need you to remember, Kennedy. I need you to remember us."

I stared down at him. "So this has all been some elaborate plot..."

"You need to work through your amnesia yourself," he told me firmly. "As things jog your memory, as you dream about the past, your brain is trying to reconnect those synapses. There's no shortcut here, though, Kennedy. If we tell you about your past...we destroy your chance of ever recovering it yourself."

"So why not tell me that?" I demanded. "Why play these stupid games?"

"Because these stupid games might help you connect with your memories," he said. "When you come close to reliving something from your past...do you ever feel like you're remembering?"

"Sometimes," I whispered. "But what if I never get my memories back?"

"Then I'll tell you everything I know about your past," he whispered to me. "But it won't be quite the way you remembered it... because through my eyes, you've always just been perfect."

I let out a shaky laugh. "I'm definitely not perfect—"

There was a commotion on the ice.

I looked up to find Jack bashing the shit out of another hockey player. But even as he clocked him, his gaze found mine.

"That would be you making them crazy," Greyson muttered.

Jack was in the penalty box a moment later, clearing the wall as if it were nothing but a curb. One of the coaches leaned over the side of the box to talk to him, and Jack leaned in and whispered something to him urgently. The coach pulled back with a *what the fuck* expression on his face, but Jack was already turning to me.

Jack's gaze locked on mine. "What are you doing?"

"I'm watching your game, like you wanted."

Jack's jaw was tight, his eyes dark with fury as they roamed over my jersey. "Take it off."

Greyson said helpfully, "It's my old jersey."

"I guessed that," Jack snarled. His furious gaze met mine again. "Kennedy. I'm not going to ask again. Take. It. Off."

"Or what?" I demanded. I understood Greyson's argument about why they had kept our past from me, but I hated the thought of them making decisions like that behind my back, on my behalf.

It was haunting to think they all had these memories of me and I had nothing. It made me feel so vulnerable.

"Kennedy," Jack's voice was low and demanding, and it

264

sent a shiver of tension up my spine... kind of a good shiver, actually. I hadn't seen this dominating, dark side of Jack before. "If you wear any fucking jersey but mine, I will tear it off you. You're mine."

And it was fucked up, but it turned me on.

Greyson was on his feet. "Fucking try it, Jack. You aren't fucking touching her in front of me unless she wants it...and even then."

Malice hung in the air.

I hated seeing the two of them fight.

The coach came back, carrying something that he tossed to Jack. Jack caught it easily out of the air without even looking and shook it out in front of me.

It was a Devils jersey. Jack's name was across the back.

"Hockey wives wear the team colors," he told me. "That green and black is from the past. You need to wear Devils colors."

"I'm not a hockey wife," I reminded him.

"You will be," Jack said with complete confidence. "Now put it on."

He handed me the jersey.

Greyson reached to knock it away. "Get back out on the ice, Jack. You're letting down your team...just like you always let her down."

"I'll fucking kill you," Jack snarled at him, and right now, I didn't doubt he would.

Seeing the two of them fight tore at my heart.

I grabbed the jersey from Jack. A satisfied look came over his face, but that wasn't good enough.

"Have I ever worn your jersey before, Jack?" I demanded.

He hesitated, then looked away.

The crowd roared, muffling my voice so Jack couldn't hear me.

"I'm not wearing any of your jerseys when you're fighting," I told Greyson. "If I need you to unlock my memories...if I need to experience what I felt in the past... then I need all four of you. Don't I?"

Greyson shook his head.

I dropped it at my feet. Then I pulled off Greyson's jersey. The green-and-black joined the red and black colors of the Devils.

"If you want me to wear your jersey, earn it," I told them both. "But I'm not just yours because you want me to be."

Jack stared at me, his jaw flexing. Greyson looked as if he might jump over into the penalty box to knock Jack out.

Jack was getting called out of the penalty box and back onto the ice.

One of the coaches abruptly climbed into the penalty box. "You're causing a scene," he told Jack. "Get on the ice."

"Not like the scene I'm going to cause later," Jack warned us, and even as I felt a prickle of anxiety to protect these guys from tearing each other apart, I also felt a sudden surge of lust.

This was a dark, dominating side of Jack, and I fucking loved that too.

Just like I loved watching him kick ass on the ice.

"Earn it," I told him again.

Abruptly, he turned and leapt out of the penalty box. He skated back into the fray.

Sebastian clapped his shoulder and looked at Greyson and me. The look on his face was that stern, unreadable look, but his eyes blazed with fire when he saw Greyson.

The crowd roared with excitement as play continued, and I leaned forward, on the edge of my seat. A good fight always seemed to get the Devils' fans even more whipped up.

And right now, Jack was a force of sheer violence. He slammed into one of his opponents, knocking them onto their ass, taking control of the puck without a backward glance and skating hard down the ice with it.

"Take the shot," I urged silently, knowing he was so far away from the goal that most players could never make that shot.

But Jack could. I knew it.

With his usual ability to move fast and unpredictably, never telegraphing, he suddenly whipped around and launched the puck down the rink. The goalie moved to intercept, but the puck slammed into the top left corner of the net. The crowd screamed. It was a one in a million shot but then, Jack was a one in a million player.

The buzzing energy in the rink seemed to emanate from Jack himself as he scored goal after goal. He was a force of nature tonight, his eyes locked on the prize, each stride across the ice even more determined than the last.

"Keep your stick down, Jack!" I muttered. Greyson glanced over at me, a smile playing on his lips.

And as if he could hear me, Jack's stick lowered just in time to intercept a pass and send the puck sailing into the net. A grin stretched across my face.

Just then, the other team's offense made a bold move, going straight for Carter, our goalie.

"Watch the crease!" I yelled, but my voice was drowned out by the relentless noise.

Sebastian seemed to sense the danger and skated in, guarding Carter. His quick decision making and loyalty never ceased to amaze me. In a split second, Sebastian's agile stick work wrested control of the puck away from the opposing team.

With a swift motion, he sent it flying towards Jack.

"Go, Jack!" I whispered, leaning forward. My heart raced as I watched him catch Sebastian's pass.

Jack propelled himself forward with superhuman speed, weaving through defenders with the grace of a dancer.

"Finish it, Jack," I urged him silently, praying that somehow my thoughts would reach him. As if on cue, Jack wound up and fired a one-timer straight into the net, the puck whizzing past the flailing goaltender. The crowd erupted in a deafening cheer.

"Yes!" I whispered, a grin breaking across my face.

Greyson told me, "I love watching you watch hockey."

There was a wistful expression on his face, as if he missed playing for me.

"Why did you give it up?" I asked him.

"I had to focus on taking care of my sisters. Protecting them. I was afraid I'd lose them like..." He stopped himself, shaking his head. "I got mixed up in such a dangerous business. I wasn't content following orders... so I had to prove I could lead the Jackals. Become the Jackal."

I took his hand, squeezing it in mine. It was obvious he had lost so much.

Jack was dominating the ice. He was like a god in the rink tonight, and the other team didn't stand a chance.

"He's always been good, really good," Greyson admitted, and I was surprised to hear him compliment Jack, but it also made me feel good. Greyson had a good hearted side. "But when he's playing for you, he's incredible."

"He's not playing for me," I demurred. "He wants the Devils to win for himself."

Greyson gave me a disbelieving look. "Kennedy... he is playing for you."

"Too bad I don't give a shit about hockey," I said.

Greyson let out a little chuckle. "All right. You've always been the sweet, innocent, honest one... don't start lying to yourself now."

Jack scored yet again, practically single handedly. The buzzer went off and the team gathered around him, celebrating the victory...and Jack's incredible performance.

"Come on, we'd better get out of here," Greyson said. He offered me his hand. "You know those guys are going to come right for us...trying to kill me and fuck you."

"And where are we going?" I teased him. "Do you promise not to kidnap me?"

"No," he said shortly. "I'm never going to promise that."

Before he could say anything else, there was a bang on the glass and I jumped. Jack was standing there, a sweat-soaked, hot mess.

"Drama queen," Greyson drawled, shaking his head. He studied Jack, biting down on his lip.

Jack made a slicing motion across his neck with the hockey stick.

"To think he used to be the sweet one."

"He was the sweet one?"

Greyson opened his mouth to respond, but then his pocket started buzzing. He pulled his phone out, scowling from whatever he'd read on it.

"Unfortunately, I'm going to have to leave you with Twiddle Dee over there after all. I have some–business to attend to."

"Business. Right," I said, adding another check mark in the column of why Greyson was bad news.

The only problem was that with every red flag I found...I started to like him more.

He drew me in for a kiss that left me breathless before saluting Jack, who looked ready to kill him.

"See you soon, baby," he said before hustling back up the stairs.

"Meet me outside the locker room," Jack growled before skating away.

"Sir, yes, sir," I murmured, bending down to pick up the jerseys I'd abandoned on the floor.

But despite the fact that I was annoyed at his attitude...I found myself hovering outside the locker room a few minutes later.

Jack came out almost immediately, his hair wet from what must have been the quickest shower in history.

He looked out of sorts though, kind of crazy. I was used to that from Greyson...but I didn't know what to do with that from Jack.

"Do you have the jersey?" he growled.

"Yes, Mr. Growly. I have the jersey."

"Good," he said, taking my hand and dragging me down the hall, and then another. He didn't stop until he got to the practice rink connected to the arena.

"What are we doing?" I asked, but he just grunted, pushing the boards door open and leading me out onto the ice. I stared around the rink. There was no one else here despite the fact that the rest of the building had been teeming with lingering fans.

Jack ripped the jersey from my hand, and then took a deep breath.

"If I don't fuck you in my jersey...I'm pretty sure I'm going to die," he finally said.

I huffed out a laugh. "What?"

"I'm serious," he said, rubbing a hand down his face. "I'm afraid I might die if I don't get to do this with you. I need this. I need your sweet cunt. Please," he begged, and there was in fact an edge of desperation in his words.

I blinked several times, wondering when my life had gotten so freaking weird.

And hot.

I mean, wanting to fuck me in his jersey was definitely some hot, fetish shit that...sounded pretty good to me.

"Strip for me, Kennedy," he commanded gently, his eyes never leaving mine.

I thought about it for one more second, and then I slowly unbuttoned my white dress shirt. He watched me hungrily, his gaze intent like I wasn't wearing my work uniform. I pulled the crisp fabric down off my shoulders, exposing the simple lines of my plain white bra.

Then, meeting his gaze, I slipped one bra strap off my shoulders, then the other. I released the latch and let the bra fall from my body onto the ice, enjoying the way his eyes lit on my breasts, watching me greedily. I shivered as the cold air hit my nipples. Jack's cock strained at the front of his sweatpants he'd thrown on after his shower.

"Now your pants," Jack ordered.

I toed my shoes off and then slid my pants slowly over my hips before stepping out of them. As I stood there in my under-wear...and socks, feeling exposed and vulnerable, completely conscious of every curve, Jack stared at me as if I were the most beautiful thing he'd ever seen.

"Don't you ever drop my jersey again," Jack chided me as he stepped forward. "You're mine, Kennedy. You're going to learn that."

Man, these men with their "mine" comments.

Except, I found that I didn't hate it. Not really.

Because before I'd met them, I'd been a girl that didn't belong to anyone. And now I suddenly belonged to four of them.

Well, *they* wanted me to belong to them.

I happened to still be very much on the fence about it all.

Or at least I was telling myself that.

271

"Yes, sir," I said saucily, mostly because I had a feeling I knew how he would respond. Heat flared in his eyes as if he had loved the sound of that.

Jack draped the jersey over my body. The familiar scent of him enveloped me, and I let out a sigh of pleasure.

"Beautiful," he murmured, drinking me in. Then he knelt at my feet onto the ice, his hands trailing up my legs. I shivered again, but this time it wasn't from the cold, it was because of the lust coursing through me as I stared down at the gorgeous god-like specimen on his knees...for me.

"Almost perfect," he whispered. He reached up and hooked his fingers into the waistband of my underwear, peeling my panties off so I was wearing nothing but his jersey. The air felt cool against my bare skin, but the heat in Jack's gaze warmed me from the inside out. Jack slid his fingers through my sopping wet slit for a second, smiling when I shivered. Then he gracefully stood up.

"Come here," he said, pulling me close to him. It was freezing cold in here, but frostbite didn't seem so bad at the moment—not while he was holding me.

"So, in this fantasy of yours...did I reward you for a good game?" I teased him, my confidence returning as I slid from his arms and unbuckled his pants.

"You did," he said breathlessly.

Kneeling in front of him—tucking the jersey under my knees so it wasn't quite as ridiculously cold against my skin—I began to give him a blow job, feeling the thrill of power as he moaned softly. His fingers tangled in my hair, guiding me as I pleasured him. He urged me to take him deeper, and I let my throat open, relaxing my jaw, letting him fuck my mouth. He let out a groan.

"God, Kennedy," he whimpered, his voice heavy with desire. "You're incredible."

As I continued to pleasure Jack, a sudden flash of memory struck me—I had done this before, but there was someone else in the room. The realization sent a shiver down my spine, and I desperately tried to recall who it could have been. However, my amnesia reared its ugly head, leaving me feeling unmoored and vulnerable.

"Kennedy," Jack panted, his grip on my hair tightening slightly. "You...feel so good."

His words snapped me back to the present. The cold seeping through the jersey into my skin, the scent of Jack's cologne mixed with our arousal, and the weight of his hockey jersey hanging off my shoulders. Despite the confusion swirling in my mind, I found comfort in being with him, sucking his perfect cock.

"Ah, fuck, Kennedy, I'm close," he moaned, his fingers massaging my scalp. His praise, both tender and erotic, spurred me on. I ran my tongue along his shaft, my fingers wrapping his balls and squeezing hard—suddenly sure that he liked that.

He thrust into my mouth one more time than froze, his fingers tangled in my hair as he came hard into my mouth.

"Show me," he commanded, pulling my hair to urge my head back.

I looked up at him, not understanding at first, then it struck me as if I had done this before. I stuck out my tongue, showing him his cum on my pink tongue.

"That's my girl," he said. "Taking in all my cum. Swallow it."

I did, seeing the pleasure gleam in his eyes, knowing that his cum was inside my body.

"Come here," Jack commanded softly as he pulled me up by my arms, pressing a passionate kiss to my lips, not seeming to care he could probably taste himself. "You're incredible, Kennedy. Absolutely breathtaking."

"Thank you," I whispered against his mouth.

He led me over to the bench and I glanced around, relieved there still didn't seem to be anyone in here—I'd kind of forgotten this was usually a public place when I'd sucked his dick. Jack sat down on the bench and pulled me onto his lap, guiding me to straddle him. Our eyes locked as he teased his cock through my wet folds.

"You're so wet," he murmured. "It turns you on, doing that for me, doesn't it?"

"Always," I whispered, sure that it was true.

Jack held my hips firmly, guiding me down onto his cock. I gasped at the sensation of him filling me. He was so big.

His gaze roamed my face as I rode him, each thrust sending waves of ecstasy through my body. In the heat of the moment, all doubts about my fragmented memories were temporarily erased, replaced by the all-consuming desire that coursed through me.

"Jack!" I cried out, my body trembling around his cock.

He groaned. "You take me so good, baby," he murmured as he grabbed my hips and dragged me down, rolling his hips up in a way that hit my g-spot perfectly, driving me into a second orgasm. The two of us came together, and he spurted into me before I collapsed forward into his arms.

Exhausted and sated, I curled up on Jack's lap, feeling the sticky evidence of our passion leaking across my thighs, clinging to my skin. His strong arms wrapped around me, cradling me tenderly.

A shadowy, incomplete memory flickered at the edge of my consciousness. I remembered being cozy and content with him like this, but then someone tried to pull me away from him, their harsh voice calling me a slut. The face remained blurred, unrecognizable. Was it one of the other guys? Or one of my parents?

"You look like you're in another world, baby," Jack whispered.

"A memory,' I whispered back.

He froze, but recovered a second later, rubbing a soothing hand down my back.

"Tell me what you remember," Jack urged softly, his breath warm against my ear.

I hesitated for a moment, then told him, "There was someone else there...trying to separate us. They called me a slut, but I can't remember who it was."

Jack's jaw tightened. "We'd better find the guys and get going," he said.

Frustration coursed through me. "Okay," I whispered.

He was tender with me as ever, walking onto the ice to grab my discarded clothes, and then kneeling to help me dress in my panties and pants.

But something felt different between us now.

The ride across the city to the penthouse felt cold and wrong.

Falling asleep in his bed however...in his arms...did not.

Something woke me up in the middle of the night.

I stared around the inky blackness, my eyes finally coming to rest on the shadow of a man sitting in a chair just a few feet away from me.

Before I could scream, Greyson was in front of me, covering up my mouth. "Shhh, sweetheart. It's just me."

I glanced back at Jack, but he was still sound asleep, his breaths coming out slow and even.

"What are you doing here?" I hissed.

"I couldn't stay away. I never could."

I fell silent at that little pronouncement, staring at him sleepily.

But I still wanted some answers.

"My past...it wasn't happy, was it?" I whispered, desperate for answers, feeling a knot of sadness forming in my chest.

He sighed and then shook his head. "No, not always."

"Is it even worth remembering?"

"It made you who you are today."

I huffed.

"Fucking incredible," he continued.

"I'm getting a little closer to remembering all the time," I whispered to him, ignoring his cheesiness. I wasn't entirely sure if it was true or if it was just what I wanted to believe.

"I'm always here for anything you need," he told me.

"I know." I chewed my lower lip. "And that's why I hate to ask you to..."

His brows arched. I'd trailed off, and he prompted, "Say it, Kennedy."

"I–I want them too," I said in a rush.

"I can be enough for you," he told me, anguish breaking through his stern tone.

"Of course you are enough," I told him. "You're amazing, Greyson. But I need all of you for my memories. If you have a piece of my past that you can help me remember...they have pieces too."

"That's not the only reason. You've always wanted them. Let me show you that I'm enough on my own now."

"You are enough, Greyson. I just...I loved them too, didn't I?"

He nodded. "Yes," he admitted. "You loved them too."

He stood up from the chair, and I couldn't help feeling as if I might never see him again.

"I'll see you again?"

"Of course," he frowned, then said, "Do you think anything could make me stay away from you?"

"Don't give up on me," I whispered.

"Never," he said, leaning over me on the bed. His lips brushed mine in a tender kiss, then he deepened it, his hand cradling my cheek, kissing me as if he would never stop.

I was breathless when he released me. His icy blue eyes studied mine as he promised.

And somehow Jack continued to sleep.

"I'm not like them... I've never given up on you and I never will. Someday, you'll see I'm the only one you need."

I watched as he left, a flicker of unease in my stomach...for no apparent reason at all.

18

Kennedy

Once Carter, Sebastian, and Jack left for practice the next day, I slipped out of their luxurious condo building myself, my heart pounding. I couldn't help but feel like one of them—or Greyson—would be watching over me.

The warmth of their home left me as soon as I stepped from the sumptuous lobby into the wind-whipped street.

The city outside seemed grimier than usual, a stark contrast to the opulent lobby with the doorman and the lavish penthouse. I pulled my coat tighter around me, but the wind seemed to bite right through my coat. My lips felt as if they were growing dry and chapped, and I stuffed my cold hands into my pockets.

As I walked back by the hospital where I had once lived and then further into the part of the city where I could afford to rent an apartment, I felt a sense of unease. I stayed far away from Wakefield Street and the burnt ruins of my old apartment building. Sebastian must have sensed what I would worry about most, because he had been sure to tell me there had been no deaths or real injuries from the fire.

The streets were littered with trash, and some of the buildings were marked with graffiti. I almost walked right by the squat yellow brick apartment building, then turned around and went in. I'd made an appointment to tour the building, and I didn't want to be rude.

"Ah, you must be Kennedy," said the tired but friendly apartment manager when I buzzed into the office. His eyes bore the weight of years of managing less-than-ideal living situations, but his smile held genuine warmth. "Let's take a look at the one bedroom we have for you, shall we?"

"Thank you," I replied softly, trying to put on a brave face as we entered the dimly lit hallway. As we made our way through the small, cheap apartment, we exchanged polite small talk about the weather and the latest happenings in the city.

"Sorry about the state of the place," he apologized, scratching his head. "But it's all we have available right now."

I forced a smile, trying not to think about the discolored walls and cracked tiles. "It's fine. I understand."

I'd made a sad little apartment like this into a cozy home.

But would any place really feel like home now?

All I could think about as I looked around was how much I'd rather be with Jack, Carter, Sebastian, and Greyson.

I'd felt so safe with each of them, despite their psycho sides. Having their strong arms wrapped around me was the most comfortable, cozy place in the world. Making them laugh filled me with so much joy that when I pictured their handsome, laughing faces, I smiled myself.

But when they fought, I felt like I was being ripped apart.

If someday, I could feel safe with all of them...

I could be home.

"Is something wrong?" the manager asked, noticing my distant expression.

"Um, no," I lied, shaking my head. "Just thinking."

"Take your time, Kennedy," he reassured me. He looked down at his phone as a text came in. "I've got to get back to the office. You can see yourself out, yes? Email me if you decide to put in an application."

"Thank you."

As I stood there in the cold, empty apartment, the enormity of what I was about to do hit me like a ton of bricks. Was I really ready to leave them behind? Moving out to my own apartment...it seemed like it would be lonely now that I had found them. I couldn't imagine myself coming here each night when I could be with them.

Except...I couldn't be with all of them. Greyson seemed to be mortal enemies with Carter, Sebastian, and Jack now. Why did it have to be like that? Especially when I felt like I could never recover my memories until we were all together?

If I couldn't have all of them...I closed my eyes against a sudden wash of pain. It felt like I would never be whole without all of them. As if they were tearing me apart.

"Maybe this place isn't so bad after all," I whispered to myself, clutching my coat even tighter as I stepped out onto the street. The door banged shut behind me, the lock clicking as I stepped out onto the sidewalk. "Maybe...maybe I can make this work."

Leaving the apartment building behind, I started to walk back toward their condo. The city seemed even grimier than before.

A cold shiver ran down my spine as I noticed a van driving slowly down the road, keeping pace just behind me. I turned onto the street that would lead me back home, and felt suddenly dismayed as I realized how empty it seemed. Like a ghost town.

The van was an incongruous sight in this part of town, sleek and black with tinted windows. My gut told me something wasn't right.

"Keep it together, Kennedy," I muttered under my breath.

But my instincts screamed at me to run.

And I did.

As soon as my feet picked up speed, the van burst into motion, accelerating alongside me. Panic rose in my chest like bile, burning through any rational thought.

"Hey!" I shouted, hoping someone would hear me. But the streets were strangely empty, as if everyone had sensed the danger and disappeared. "Help!"

The doors to the van slid open, and two masked men jumped out. I heard their boots hit the street and dared a glance back as they raced after me. Their eyes were emotionless, predatory.

I knew I couldn't outrun them, but I had to try. My heart pounded against my ribcage as adrenaline coursed through my veins.

"Leave me alone!" I screamed, but my voice sounded weak. They didn't respond; they were gaining on me.

The van pulled abreast of me. The door swung open, moving back and forth with the motion of the van, and one of the goons jumped out—right in front of me.

I put on a burst of speed and lowered my shoulder. I caught a glimpse of his surprised eyes behind the mask as I slammed into him. He tried to grab me, and I lashed out, hitting him across the face as hard as I could. My knuckles burst open, pain spiking up my arm, but he stumbled backward, momentarily stunned by the unexpected resistance.

Then I bolted down the street, running for my life. The

men were right on my heels. My breathing was loud and desperate as I tried to escape.

Suddenly, a man came running toward me. "Go!" he shouted at me, drawing a gun from his jacket.

He stepped between me and the men who were chasing me and squeezed off a round.

Relief rushed through me. I wasn't alone. I didn't understand where he had come from, but I was so thankful he was there.

The crack of gunfire exploded just behind me, so loud it blew out my eardrums.

And then there were more shots. I wove into an alleyway, trying to get out of the line of fire, as bullets sprayed above my head.

I glanced back over my shoulder and saw the man who had intervened slam into the sidewalk, bullet wounds blossoming bloody across his chest.

One of the masked men was on the ground too. The other two were running for the van, but one of them clutched his gut, blood spilling out onto his hand, his posture telegraphing shock. I reached the end of the alley and cut left, the streets a desperate blur, barely able to figure out where I was and which way to run.

To get back to the ice arena.

The van hurtled down the alley, and I heard it clip one of the dumpsters, slamming it into the brick wall. I ran frantically, cutting around another corner, hoping I could lose them on the streets.

As I sprinted through the city, all I could think about was getting back to Carter, Sebastian, and Jack. I felt like I would be safe if I could just get to the ice rink.

Even though I knew they had practice today, as I turned through the streets nearing the arena, I couldn't escape this fear that I would get there and find locked doors. That these men would corner me. The world was a wild, terrified blur around me as I raced along.

I just had to get to my men.

But...Was this why they had been so determined to protect me?

Had they known this would happen?

Was this another secret they had kept from me?

"Almost there," I panted, my legs aching as I pushed myself to keep going. The van's engine roared behind me, echoing through the deserted streets like a predator closing in on its prey. But even though my limbs were growing weak like a hunted animal, I couldn't give up.

The hockey arena loomed ahead, towering above the street like a beacon of hope.

Carter, Sebastian, and Jack were so close.

My men. My safety.

"Come on, come on," I muttered under my breath, willing my legs to carry me faster. The sound of the van's tires screeching as it took corners echoed ominously through the air, fueling my desperation. My lungs screamed for air, but there was no time to stop. I had to keep moving.

As I turned another corner, the hockey arena finally came into full view. I could see the doors leading inside, so tantalizingly close. Relief surged through me, momentarily dulling the ache in my limbs. I pushed harder, determined not to let the men in the van catch up.

"Help!" I cried out as I burst through the doors, the cold air of the arena hitting me like a wall. The van skidded onto the sidewalk outside, its engine still roaring menacingly.

The lobby was empty. It was terrifying.

I looked back, wondering if the men were running up the

steps, ready to jump me and drag me out when I was so close to safety.

I sprinted through the lobby, the fear clawing at my insides refusing to let go.

"Kennedy? What the hell?" someone shouted as I barreled into the locker room. The players scattered, their faces a mixture of shock and confusion at the sudden intrusion. But all I saw was Carter, his eyes wide with concern as he took in my disheveled appearance.

"Please," I gasped, the words barely making it past my lips before Carter's strong arms enveloped me, pulling me against his chest. His familiar scent calmed my racing thoughts as he folded me into a tight hug. I couldn't see anything but his broad chest as he hugged me, but I could hear Jack and Sebastian moving closer.

"Whoa, what happened to you?" Carter demanded, his voice tense as he held me close.

"Chased...van...men," I managed to choke out between ragged breaths, my lungs craving oxygen. "I fought them off, but they kept coming."

"Men followed you here?" Sebastian demanded. He touched my shoulder protectively. "Jack and I will check it out, Kennedy. Carter, protect her."

"They might still be out there," I gasped out. "You have to call the police."

Grimly, Jack grabbed a hockey stick. "I *hope* they're still out there."

Sebastian and Jack exchanged a determined glance before bolting from the room.

My chest tightened as I struggled to breathe, trying to piece together the words that would explain the terror I had just experienced.

Carter held me tightly, his voice soft but firm. "I promise, we'll protect you. No one's going to hurt you."

"Thank you," I whispered, relief washing over me in waves. I had never felt so vulnerable, but with Carter by my side, I knew I was safe.

When Sebastian and Jack returned, their faces grim, they announced they had taken the day off practice. They escorted me out of the arena and into their car, ensuring I was safely tucked between them. As we drove towards their penthouse, the city outside seemed muted, as if the world was holding its breath along with me.

"Can you call Greyson?" I asked, my voice barely audible.

I needed all four of them to truly feel secure, and his absence only heightened my anxiety.

"No," Carter replied, his hand on my knee reassuringly. "We can handle this. We'll protect you."

"Shouldn't we call the police?"

Jack's eyes darkened, his grip on the steering wheel tightening.

"Trust us," he said grimly. "We can protect you better than the police."

As much as I wanted to believe in their ability to protect me, doubt gnawed at me. I'd been alone on those streets today, running for my life.

Except for the man who had run in to rescue me...

"Did you have someone following me?" I asked in a whisper.

"No, baby," Carter said, giving Jack a glance as if maybe they should have.

Then had Greyson sent one of his goons to follow me?

If so...I was suddenly feeling very grateful for Greyson's psycho protective side.

As I leaned into Carter's arms, relaxing against his

powerful chest, the memory of the bone-chilling fear I had felt while running for my life lingered, casting a dark shadow that it felt like I could never escape.

Not while I was in this dark, terrible city.

Not much later, the softness of the couch enveloped me as I curled up with Carter, Sebastian, and Jack. Carter held me protectively in his lap, his arm wrapped around my shoulders, his chin nuzzling the top of my head. Jack had my feet in his lap, gently massaging the balls of my feet, my aching calves and thighs. His touch was magnetic, healing the pain of my aching muscles from running...If I hadn't felt so drained from my frantic escape, his touch would've turned me on.

Sebastian paced behind us. He couldn't seem to settle down, as if he wouldn't be able to relax until he knew whoever had hunted me was dead.

"Sebastian, sit down," Jack scolded him. "We'll figure it out. She's safe for now. But you are miserable to watch a movie with."

I could tell they loved me, because they'd voluntarily put on a cheesy Hallmark holiday romance movie.

The room was dimly lit, casting a warm glow that made their faces appear softer, more welcoming. But, despite finding comfort in their presence, I couldn't shake the feeling that something was missing.

Greyson.

"Guys," I began hesitantly, "I need to know. Was I ever in danger because of... because we were together...before?" All three of them flinched and stared at me with various looks of shock.

My heart pounded as I awaited their answer, my fingers nervously tracing the outline of the name necklace I always wore. That one little piece of my past was so precious to me.

Sebastian sighed, his eyes filled with pain and guilt. His

gaze seemed to catch on the way I was worrying the necklace. "Greyson told you, didn't he?" He sounded more resigned than anything else, like he'd been preparing himself for this moment.

"He did. The question is why didn't you?"

The heat of anger flushed over me, fueled by the fear and confusion of the day. I also suddenly couldn't stop thinking about the fact that they'd known me, and then they'd left me all these years–alone.

"What did Greyson tell you?" Carter asked, of course not answering my question.

"He told me that you all knew me. But I'd basically figured that out on my own."

"When you were in your coma, we didn't claim you because we wanted to protect you. We erased you from the public eye, made sure there were no records of you," murmured Jack, looking absolutely devastated that we were having this conversation.

Sebastian leaned over the couch, and his fingers gently brushed the necklace and my decolletage, a sad smile playing on his lips. "I gave this to you, but I tried to take it away too. It hurt me, but I thought it would be worth anything to protect you."

I pulled my legs away from Jack, then got to my feet. I couldn't stand to have them touching me anymore. "What if it wasn't worth it to me? Losing you? Not even knowing I was in danger to protect myself?"

They exchanged glances before Carter spoke, his voice soothing yet firm. "We'll always protect you, Kennedy."

"You weren't there today!" I spat out, my chest heaving with emotion. "I have to be able to take care of myself, not depend on you all the time."

They stared at each other, and I couldn't read their faces.

They'd been friends for so long; it seemed like they didn't need to speak to each other to communicate.

But I was left out in the cold.

"You have to let me see Greyson too," I whispered. "I need all of you. I need to get my memories back. So I can protect myself from whoever it was...You have to stop fighting."

"Kennedy," Jack whispered, his eyes filled with concern. "We understand. We don't want you to feel trapped by us. We just want to protect you."

"Let's work together then," I offered, my voice barely above a whisper. "I need you guys, but also...I need Greyson."

I was sure he was the reason I was alive now...the one who had sent a protector to watch over me.

A protector who was dead now.

That was probably the only reason Greyson hadn't reached me already...because the man who had kept me alive had died without being able to tell him what happened.

"Why?" Carter exploded. "You don't need him!"

The words sent me over the edge, and the next thing I knew, tears were pouring down my cheeks.

"Jesus Christ, Carter!" Jack shouted at him, then pulled me into his arms, in a tight hug. "It's alright," Jack told me soothingly. "Everything's going to be okay."

Tears blurred my vision as they each tried to comfort me, their voices soft and apologetic. But in the end, I couldn't find solace in their words or their touch, not when my heart felt like it was being torn apart.

"Please," I whispered, choked by emotion. "I just want to go to bed. I need some space."

"Of course," Carter murmured, his voice filled with concern. He led me to the guest room, the others following silently behind us. They helped me into the plush bed, tucking the blankets snugly around me, trying their best to make me feel safe and secure.

"I'm sorry, Kennedy," Carter said, pressing a tender kiss to my forehead, his eyes glistening with unshed tears. "I didn't mean to be such a dick. I just..."

He shook his head, and when he blinked, the sheen of tears was gone, and I wasn't sure if I'd just imagined it. He turned and paced out of the room.

There was a darkness hanging over him that I didn't know if he could escape...if he could ever love me and let me love Greyson.

"We'll be here for you," Jack promised, his lips brushing against my cheek. "No matter what."

"Sleep well," Sebastian murmured, planting a gentle kiss on my other cheek before leaving the room, the door closing softly behind them.

I lay there in the darkened room, feeling the softness of the sheets and the warmth of the blanket enveloping me. But despite their efforts to comfort me, I couldn't shake this feeling of unease.

Of course, I couldn't actually sleep. I'd just needed some space. It bothered me that Greyson would be going crazy, knowing something had happened, and the guys wanted to keep it secret from him.

I wanted all four of my men. It felt impossible, and that hurt so much that it felt as if I were cold and lonely even in the guest room of their lavish penthouse.

I shivered, wondering if it was just me convincing myself that I was cold without Greyson in my life. Or maybe it was the incredibly high ceilings and floor-to-ceiling windows every-where that made the penthouse chilly, at least when I didn't have a tall, powerfully muscled, warm hockey player to wrap myself around.

Since I was currently frustrated with all the tall-and-muscled smirking men in my life, I decided to find an extra blanket. I climbed out of bed and pulled open the door to the walk in closet. It took me a second to find the light switch, and when I did, I was surprised to see the closet was full, with a series of totes lining the wall. On the shelf above the totes were a few thick, snuggly soft blankets and extra fluffy pillows, and I pulled down a soft, cozy fleece blanket and cuddled it to my chest.

I almost went back to the room without seeing anything else about the totes.

But then neat handwriting—Jack's, almost certainly—in Sharpie on masking tape across one tote caught my eye.

Kennedy.

A wave of confusion washed over me as I reached for the nearest tote. I cast a glance at the door. What the hell else were these guys keeping from me?

I carefully lifted the lid and peered inside. There were photo albums, an old hoodie, several Barbie dolls who had seen better days. My hands trembled as I picked up a small, worn teddy bear, its fur matted with age.

"Happy birthday, sweetheart," my mother beamed, her eyes sparkling. She walked the bear across the pile of shiny wrapped presents on the kitchen table. "Presents first? Then chocolate cake for breakfast?"

The memory jolted through me like an electric shock. I could barely breathe. When I tried to focus, tried to sharpen the memory, it faded away.

I'd glimpsed my mother's face for a split second, but now I couldn't remember it—just the outline of her, the sense of dark hair that fell in long, loose waves. Hair like mine.

My eyes were suddenly wet and blurry. I wiped tears away, feeling like I wiped dust into my eyes at the same time. Why did the guys have this stuff? Had they kept it for me in case I recovered my memories?

Why the hell hadn't they told me?

It was one thing to wait for my memories to come back on my own instead of telling me...

But these objects helped reawaken my memories.

I pulled out the tie-dye hoodie. It said *Ocean City* across the front, and it was too small to fit me now.

We'd walked along the boardwalk, seagulls following us while we ate the best French fries in Maryland. There were rows of little shops, and I'd pointed at the hoodies, knowing how much my mother loved tie-dye.

Tears welled up in my eyes as I opened a photo album to a random page. I beamed out of the photos in this book, missing my two front teeth. My mother looked at me like she adored me.

Then I turned a page, and now there was a man in the photos too, and my mother kept looking at him. Not me. Not anymore. My stomach curdled.

Something had gone very wrong in my childhood. But it hadn't all been bad.

It was worth remembering.

I flipped back in the album and traced my fingers over the photo where my mother held me in her arms, grinning down at me. We were sitting on the porch steps in front of a farmhouse. Eagerly, I flipped back through the photos, hoping I would see more of it.

If objects triggered my memories...maybe the house where I'd grown up would too.

Maybe this was my grandparent's house, or a house where my father still lived. Maybe there was someone out there who knew me.

In one photo, I spotted the house number: 536. I mouthed

the numbers over and over to myself, afraid to lose them. Maybe, just maybe, I could go there and unlock more memories.

Raised voices were muffled, given how expansive the penthouse was, but I still heard them.

I even heard Jack curse at the other two, telling them to quiet down before they woke me.

But I wasn't asleep at all. I put the top back on the tote hurriedly and opened the door to the room so I could hear better.

"Greyson claims he's going to shoot the doorman if we don't let him up," Carter said.

"Hmm," Sebastian said. "Is it the one we like, or the one who talks so much about the weather—"

"It's not a joke!" Carter said. "We have to figure out what we're going to do. If we're going to let him see Kennedy—"

I mouthed the words to myself in disbelief. Were they going to *let* me see Greyson?

I loved these men, but they were morons.

"We could use Greyson's help dealing with this," Jack said.

"No," Carter disagreed. "He would have something to hold over us for the rest of our lives—"

"He's going to *want* Kennedy for the rest of our lives!"

"Jack, he's not here to help," Sebastian interjected, his tone uncharacteristically sharp. "He's dangerous, and you know it."

"I don't want to risk losing her either," Carter said. "But if Greyson can help us protect her—"

"We're not letting Greyson anywhere near her," Sebastian disagreed. "He's the reason she was almost killed in the first place."

"Do we know that?" Jack demanded. "We still don't know who was trying to take her... then or now. We need him."

"No, we don't!"

293

I headed for the living room. The three of them turned when I walked in, looking like a dream as always; even when I was pissed, there was a part of me that reacted to them. They exchanged a look.

"I want to see Greyson." My voice was firm, leaving no room for argument.

"Kennedy, I'm sorry," Jack said, crossing the shadowy living room to wrap me up in his arms.

I let him wrap his big, muscular arms around me, leaning against his powerful chest—even though I wasn't sure how much I could trust him right now. There was a fire crackling in the fireplace, casting Sebastian and Carter's gorgeous faces in flickering shadows.

I'd trust the three of them with my life. But I loved and needed Greyson too, and right now, I felt like I couldn't trust any of them with my heart.

"He did kidnap you before," Sebastian said dryly, defending himself. "And I'm pretty sure he'll feel more protective than ever right now."

"I'm pretty sure I would be dead if he weren't a possessive psychopath," I reminded them.

Sebastian's jaw worked in irritation. But after a second, he nodded. "I'm glad for that. But I don't want him to try to take you away from us."

A fierce edge had entered his tone. As if Greyson might try...but it would end badly.

Jack's arms tightened around me, as if he'd heard the threat too and he wanted to protect me from the pain if these men continued to fight. Jack dropped a kiss in my hair. "Everything's going to be alright."

The memory of all those boxes piled up with pieces of my life they'd kept from me rose in my mind. Greyson had given me a reason: if they interfered, I might never regain my true memories for myself.

But it still felt wrong. The men who loved me shouldn't keep so many secrets from me. Anger pulsed through me. They were so controlling.

"I'm going down to the lobby to talk to Greyson," I told them. "And if you won't let me go—"

"We're not kidnapping you, Christ," Jack said as if it were insane.

But Sebastian and Carter glanced at each other as if it weren't out of the question.

Still, the guys agreed, reluctantly, and the four of us climbed into the elevator. It was a tense, silent ride down to the first floor.

The doors slid open, and a certain dark haired man was pacing away from me, his lean body tensely coiled in his dark suit as if he were on the verge of killing someone. I was surprised he'd been so patient.

"Greyson!" I called, rushing toward him.

He turned, his face lighting up.

Then I was in his arms, and he wrapped his arms tightly around me. His embrace was suffocating, yet comforting. "I was so worried about you."

"I'm okay," I assured him, trying to mask the uncertainty in my voice.

Was I okay?

Seeing the photo albums upstairs had made me feel so close to my past...and so shaky and unsettled. As if I were on the verge of something important and something easily lost.

As if these men had stolen something from me.

"Did you have someone following me?" I whispered.

Greyson nodded, some of the light dimming from his face.

The memory of the man sprawled across the pavement haunted me.

"He died." My voice came out in a whisper. "Didn't he?"

"Don't waste a second thinking about that, baby," Greyson told me. "Don't be sad. There was nothing you could do. It took me so long to find out what happened, though...why didn't you call me?"

That question was asked in a louder, clearer voice than before. It wasn't a question that was just for me.

"You don't have a habit of making things better, Greyson," Carter told him.

"Or keeping her safer," Sebastian said under his breath.

Greyson pulled away from me. "Last time I checked, she was under your protection, and has been every time she's gotten hurt. But I guess you can't send a boy to do a man's job."

"Really?" Sebastian gave him a dismissive look. "That's your best insult?"

Carter crossed his arms defensively. "Can we focus? We have things to discuss."

"Like how you plan on keeping her safe?" Greyson shot back, a mocking edge to his tone. "Since you're so desperate to keep her away from me? Are you planning on abandoning her again like you did before?"

"Watch your mouth," Sebastian growled, stepping forward. "We will never give her up again. We're going to keep her safe.."

"Is that right?" Greyson smirked, unfazed by Sebastian's aggression. "Because from where I'm standing, it seems like I'm the only one who's been there for her all these years."

The four of them erupted into an argument. It felt like they barely noticed I was there.

No one had been there for me. Greyson had apparently searched for me. But I'd been on my own.

And for five years, until I stumbled across the four of them, I'd been safe.

Safe. Hidden. And lost, a stranger to my own life.

These men were the key to getting my past back, if only they would stop fighting and work together. If they would choose me over their pride, their arguments, and the challenges of a future where we didn't all fit together.

"Please," I whispered, tears welling in my eyes.

To my surprise, they heard me over the sounds of their own bullshit. All four of them turned toward me, their brows crinkling. Greyson reached for me, and Carter did at the same time.

"Don't fight over me," I said softly, holding my hands up to keep the two of them from touching me. I wanted their comfort...but I needed them to listen.

"Listen to me," I pleaded, choking on the emotions that threatened to overwhelm me. "I need all four of you to help me unlock my memories. You were all a part of my life before, and I loved each and every one of you."

My voice trembled as I continued. "Pieces of my memories...I think they're bound up with all four of you. I *need* all four of you. And some of those memories...they're of the five of us together, right? If you can be..."

Sebastian sighed, rubbing a hand over his face. "Kennedy, we want to make you happy. We want to help...But our friendships...they're too fractured to ever fix. And Greyson—" He broke off, glaring at the man in question.

"Greyson may not be the man I grew up with at all," Jack admitted, his eyes locked on mine. "But if Kennedy thinks that us working together will make things right...we should try, shouldn't we?"

"Thank you," I whispered.

I still felt so confused and upset. But at least it was a little bit of hope.

Jack gave me a small smile.

"That sounds great," Carter said. "How's that really going

to work? Greyson, you want to move in and sleep on the couch?"

"My house actually has enough guest rooms for you all," Greyson said coolly. "If you can be trusted."

Sebastian scoffed. "I'm not the one with the history of—"

"No, you're just the one with the history of setting fires," Greyson returned. "I'd hate for my home to go up in flames when you get peevish, pyro."

Horror clutched my chest.

Sebastian had set the fire that terrified me so much?

As the four of them argued between themselves, loneliness fell over me like a heavy, chilly fog. They were so consumed by their own bitterness and darkness that they seemed to have forgotten about me entirely.

And they would hurt me in order to win. I'd thought Sebastian was my hero, carrying me out of the fire, rescuing me from my nightmare...but he was the one who had started it all.

I wrapped my arms around myself, trying to ward off the cold emptiness that had settled in my chest. Usually, one of the guys would've noticed and moved to wrap me up in their warmth, but right now they were too busy with their fight.

They wanted to help me, but they were all cocky alpha types who had a hard time letting anyone else in. I wondered what it had looked like in our past. The five of us had all loved each other then, hadn't we?

And as much as I loved them, I couldn't shake the feeling that I needed to find the answers to my past on my own.

Because I couldn't really trust any of them.

Fury shot through me.

I couldn't be stupid. Someone had attacked me once and would again, and these guys did have the ability to protect me.

But my only option was to go further back in my past and unlock my memories myself. I couldn't count on them to help me connect with my past. They'd kept so much from me. I needed to find answers, to understand who I really was before all of this mess began.

I needed to go back to the house where I grew up.

"Excuse me," I murmured.

Let them think I was making my way to the bathroom. Carter and Greyson were straining toward each other as if they were about to come to blows. Carter was still pissed, I knew, about how Greyson had purposely activated an old injury. The concussion and ruined date weren't helping either.

Maybe it was impossible to ever bring these four men back together.

My heart raced as I made my way across the lobby. They would notice I'd stepped away soon, but it stung that they even let me get this far. As soon as I stepped outside and let the door close behind me, the silence enveloped me like a blanket. The city was quiet outside, the moonlight diffused by the clouds and the soft rain falling across the empty street.

I had to be careful. Someone wanted to use me to hurt them. I wasn't going to do anything stupid.

I pulled out my cell phone and texted Carrie. *I need help...*

Carrie and I could figure out a way for me to get back to my old house without putting myself in needless danger...or her. There was no way I was letting Carrie get mixed up with whatever was happening. But Keith, as big of a dork as he was in some ways, had a background in the Special Forces, and he had friends who could help.

I wasn't going to run away from these guys without a plan. But God, did I ever need a break from them all.

And I had memories from before I met Carter, Sebastian, Jack, and Greyson. And just like these men helped me unlock some of my memories...if I ever wanted to remember my mother's face, I needed to go back.

C.R. Jane & May Dawson

I stepped out onto the sidewalk, into the cold.

Suddenly, out of the corner of my eye, headlights gleamed brightly. A car raced toward me. It shouldn't matter, I was on the sidewalk. But old fear still gripped my chest.

I tried to take a step backward, but I couldn't move.

The memory gripped me like a vice, pulling me back into the past. I was once again standing on a different street, my heart pounding as I watched a car barrel toward me. That night had been dark and stormy, rain blurring the headlights. I'd thought that I was seeing things wrong. Sebastian's urgent voice echoed... through the past? The present? I didn't know where I was anymore.

I'd turned and run, and I ran now. My breathing was loud in the night air, rain splattering across my face. It was instinctual panic that made no sense.

I glanced over my shoulder as I careened wildly for the building, trying to get someplace the car couldn't leap the curb and hit me.

Time seemed to slow down as the engine revved.

The car jumped the curb. It was mere feet away from me, its headlights casting an eerie glow across the rain-soaked pavement.

Realization hit me like a punch to the gut.

This time I'm going to die.

A one, two punch.

The next thought was:

My name is Kennedy O'Shannon. I know how to get home.

The driver was wearing a mask. Our eyes connected that last second, when there wasn't another chance to escape.

I felt a sharp jolt of pain, and everything went black.

Finish Kennedy's story in Our Pucking Way. Get it here.

The Rich Demons of Hockey Prequel

Want more of Kennedy and the guys? Sign up for our newsletter and get the first chapter free here HERE.

Our Pucking Way

Order Our Pucking Way, the conclusion to the Rich Demons of Hockey duet here.

Sneak Preview

Want to read about some other Rich Demons? Keep reading for the complete, dark, enemies to lovers, college romance, Make Me Lie. Available on Amazon and KU HERE.

Make Me Lie

The world knows me as the Demon's Daughter.

He's a famous serial killer. And I may have been his accomplice.

But no one knows for sure except for me.

The dangerous, cruel men of the Sphinx secret society intend to uncover my secrets...and break me.

Stellan, my childhood crush who lost his sister to the Demon.

Cain, the boy with the face of an angel to who manipulation comes as easy as breathing;

Remington, the playboy soccer star full of secrets.

Pax, the dark psycho who hides behind his fists.

I hoped for a second chance at Darkwood University, only to have my dream ripped away the first time I kissed one of the handsome bastards.

They know who I am.

And they're determined to make me pay.

They should have thought twice about who they were playing with.

Because I am the demon's daughter. And just because they have the power, the connections, the faces and bodies of gods... do they really think they'll win?

I wanted a new life, not a war.

But if they insist, we'll see who ends up playing.

Prologue

GABRIELA

DELILAH

AURORA

The world ended for me, then started again in technicolor, on a Tuesday afternoon in fourth grade.

    I gripped the doorknob of the back door to steady myself as I unlaced and pulled off my Converse. My adoptive mother hated when I wore my shoes into the house, but these high tops took so long to get on and off, and that made it hard when I was so desperate to get through the house to my room before my "brother" Lucas caught me.

The door abruptly jerked open, and I tumbled into the kitchen, landing on the pristine white tile.

Lucas leered down at me. "What are you doing out there? Come inside, Gabriela. We've got our chores to do."

"I'll do them when Mom gets home," I said. It was safer to wait until she was home so I didn't have to be around Lucas, even though sometimes she'd get mad at me for waiting. If I made it to my room and locked the door, I could do my homework and read my books in peace. Even Lucas wasn't going to risk banging up the door to get to me when Mom's house was her most precious thing—more precious than either of us. Definitely more precious than me.

I edged sideways trying to get away from Lucas, but he pinned me to the wall. "Mom is going to be so mad at you. She told us both that if we didn't do our chores, she was gonna be mad, and you know what that means."

My stomach churned. "I'll get them done."

I tried to get away from him, but he grabbed my pony tail and reeled me against his body. Lucas was seventeen, and he stank of body odor as he pulled me close. I tried to wriggle free.

"Mom said I could spank you if you didn't listen to me."

"No, she didn't." I kicked against one of the cabinet doors, trying to get loose.

"She did, and you're gonna get it from her too if you don't listen." He tried to wrench me with him, and I struggled to get free.

The two of us slipped. I kicked out, trying to get away from him. I managed to land on my feet while he landed hard on his knee and let out a grunt of pain. I ran desperately for my room with no plan but to get the hell away from Lucas while he was so furious at me.

The two of us raced through the hall. He was right behind

me as I reached my room. I swung the door shut, but he threw his shoulder into it, and it banged open, knocking me back.

I fell back and slammed my head into the drywall so hard that I couldn't breathe for a second. The world spun darkly around me.

"Oh shit," Lucas said, and now even he sounded scared.

I got to my feet and saw the crack running down the drywall. There was no way Mom wouldn't see that.

"You are so screwed," Lucas said, starting to grin. "Do you want me to tell her that it was an accident? That you tripped? Or that you had a temper tantrum and did it on purpose?"

None of those were the truth.

"Lucas," I said, stunned.

He shrugged. "Up to you, Gabriela."

He always said my name like it was a joke, but everything about my existence seemed like a joke to him.

"What do you want?" I asked.

"Nothing. Let's just get our chores done so she's not mad about that too." He slung his arm around my neck and squeezed, the sour odor of his body washing over me. The affection was confusing. "We've got to have each other's backs, little sister."

I hurried to do my chores, putting away the dishes from the dishwasher that had run while we were at school, vacuuming again, making sure the house was spotless. Lucas had less to do since he pretty much took the trash out and did chores around the outside of the house, but he came over and helped me finish cleaning the kitchen which was nice and unexpected.

When we were done, he pulled out a bag of chips and said, "Come on. It'll be worth vacuuming again before Mom gets home."

She hated for us to have snacks outside of meals, but he

rustled the bag with my favorite kind of chips, and my mouth watered. "Where did you get those?"

"I picked them up from 7-11 on my way home. Lunch at the high school sucks. I've been starving all day."

"They're not from Mom's secret stash?"

He grinned. "Nope. But she really needs to get over being so weird about *us* having junk food when she's keeping Hostess cupcakes in her underwear drawer. Come on."

It was unusually nice of Lucas. The two of us ended up sitting on the couch, watching a television show and sharing chips from the bag. When the bag was empty, I ran and buried it under some trash in the kitchen to make sure Mom wouldn't find it. I sat back down to watch the rest of the show.

Lucas rested his arm around my shoulders, and I leaned into him. It felt awkward but even though he smelled bad, it was kind of nice to be close to someone, even if it was Lucas. Maybe things would be different from now on. Sometimes it seemed like he'd hated me since I moved in four years ago, when I'd been taken away from my first mom. Back then I'd cried all the time, but I'd grown up since.

Then Lucas slid his other hand down my leg. It felt like he was just petting me absently, but I froze, pretending not to notice. It wasn't absent at all. His attention was just as razor-focused on me, on waiting for my reaction.

"Lucas..." I tried to squirm away, and he grabbed my thigh, his fingers sinking painfully into my skin.

"Come on, Gabriela. Remember what I said about how we've got to watch each other's backs?"

"Lucas, please..." I didn't even know what I was begging for, but something about the way he was touching me felt so wrong.

I didn't want him to tell Mom that I'd had a temper tantrum and broken the wall. I didn't know how to fix the wall or hide it from her, even though I'd been racking my brain trying to find a way out ever since it happened. I was going to be in so much trouble, and my stomach ached every time I thought about it. Maybe if she believed it really was an accident though, she wouldn't be mad. Sometimes she could be really nice... just like Lucas.

He pushed up the bottom of my t-shirt and slid his hand into my leggings. Just rested it there, against my bare skin just under the waistband of my panties. I closed my eyes because hot tears were building, threatening to spill over. I'd been lying to myself when I thought I was grown up and didn't cry anymore. I felt small and helpless.

"Shh, Gabriela, it's all right," Lucas said, but I knew it wasn't all right. It wasn't going to be all right. He was just touching me lightly for now, but somehow, I knew it was just going to keep getting worse and worse.

There was the rumble of the garage door, and the two of us jumped apart. I pulled the hem of my t-shirt down, pulling it taut against my body. Lucas knelt next to the couch, trying to sweep up crumbs from the chips that I hadn't noticed when I got up before; they must have been hidden under his leg.

"Shit," he grumbled. "You better hope she doesn't notice any more crumbs."

I turned and ran to my room, afraid of being caught in the living room while he fumbled with the remote.

A few minutes later, as I was turning the pages of my Nancy Drew book and trying to pay attention, I heard a familiar shrill scream. "Gabriela!"

"Coming!" I shouted back, throwing my book down without even remembering to put a bookmark in. I raced down the hall to the kitchen, where my mom was livid with rage, holding the empty chip bag.

"Did you try to hide this from me?" Her voice was the kind of white-hot that meant I was in deathly trouble.

"It's Lucas's," I whispered.

"Right, because they are *his* favorite chips that he always gets for his birthday," she said, tossing them into the trash again. "Where'd you get the money? Or did you steal them?"

"I didn't," I said. "I came right home after school."

"I told her she shouldn't have them," Lucas said from the doorway, and Mom's irritated gaze snapped to him. Before she could bite his head off, he added, "And you should see what she did to her room when I tried to take them from her."

"No, no, no," I begged as Mom towed me by the arm down the hall to my room. Her face went white with rage when she saw the crack in the wall.

She slapped me across the face so hard my vision went red. "Really, Gabriela, is there *anything* you didn't do today? Lying, stealing, destroying our house?"

"I didn't," I whimpered, but I knew she wasn't going to stop as she dragged me across the carpet to my closet door.

She rummaged through the closet, knocking one of my dresses to the ground as she pulled out a wire hanger.

I caught a glimpse of Lucas in the door, grinning, before I couldn't pay attention to anything but the pain.

That night, I lay in bed, trying to sleep despite the terrible pain. My Nancy Drew book was still lying with its spine open on the floor where it had fallen, and its pages were probably getting creased. I finally managed to get out of bed and pick it up, trying to read by the street light that came in through the window because I didn't dare get caught with my light on. Every once in a while, a car would come down the street and my page would get brighter for a moment with their headlights; I'd read frantically, skimming the page as fast as I could. I put the book under the pillow next to me, raising it just enough to hold the page up so I could drop it and hide the book at a moment's notice.

It was only because I was still awake that I heard the door creak open. I went still, letting the pillow fall, pretending to be asleep.

Lucas came to the side of my bed. He peeled back the blanket and the sheets, and I froze, pretending I was still asleep.

How many times had he come into my room like this?

He didn't touch me again, just touched the front of his pants, then pulled his manhood out. I kept my eyes closed, wanting to scream as he jerked his hand up and down along his pale thing.

Then suddenly, he made a short, desperate sound.

I opened my eyes to see him frozen, one hand still gripping himself, his eyes and mouth wide with horror.

A bright red smile had been cut across his throat, and the man with the knife was standing right behind him. The man touched the knife to his lips, warning me not to make a sound.

Gently, he eased Lucas's dying body onto the bed beside me.

I scrambled back and off the bed, staring at the stranger.

"It's all right," the man whispered. "I'm sorry it took me so long to find you. But nobody's ever going to get the chance to hurt you again."

He reached out his hand to me. I wasn't sure what to do, but his eyes were kind.

"Who are you?" I whispered.

"They call me The Demon," he whispered back. "But you can call me Dad, if you want."

"Where are we going?"

A grin spread across his face. "That's my girl. Wherever you want, darling, that's where we're going. But first, we have to make one more stop..."

I took his hand. He frowned at the sight of the bruises on

my body and said, "Why don't you pack a bag while I go have a talk with that woman who pretended to be your mom?"

"Okay," I answered in a trembling, but hope filled voice.

I was putting my books into my suitcase when I heard the faintest start of a scream, so quiet that I didn't think it reached outside the house. I froze for a second, then went on, getting my favorite t-shirts.

He came back in for me, and took my suitcase out to the car while I got dressed in real clothes instead of my pajamas. Then he picked me up, as if I were a little doll, and carried me out into the hallway.

"Don't look," he whispered to me. "Close your eyes."

But I didn't want to keep my eyes closed anymore, and I shook my head, wondering if he would hurt me like everyone else had if I didn't obey him.

But he just smiled.

He carried me into the hallway, where my mother lay half-in and half-out of her bedroom, the carpet stained dark with blood in the dim light.

"You were always only pretending to be sweet and helpless, Gabriela," he whispered in my ear.

"I was?"

"You forgot who you really were, sweet child, because you had to forget. That was the only way for us to keep you safe. But you've always been something more than anyone could realize. You've always been fierce."

I tried to understand what he was saying. Had I always known deep down that I was his daughter, that someday he would come back and claim me? That I was never really help-less, no matter how I felt?

I could leave behind Gabriela, the scared little girl who was locked in closets and beaten with anything handy. She was nothing but a ghost in the house that I was leaving behind, along with the bodies. She wasn't ever real.

The real me could never be hurt, broken...destroyed.

Especially not when I was with my daddy, and my daddy was the devil himself. I smiled up at him, and a slow smile spread across his face, as if he understood what I was thinking. He looked so handsome and strong when he smiled. He pressed a kiss to my forehead.

"My darling, precious, blade of a daughter," he murmured. "The only way anyone will ever see you as a victim again is if you want them to. And at any time, you can pull the blindfold from their eyes and show them you're always the one with the knife."

Chapter 1
Aurora

I rehearsed my cover story as I drove to college.

I'd had a cover story all my life, ever since The Demon rescued me. But this time was different. My heart sped as I turned the corner and the stone buildings and green hills of Darkwood College rose in front of me.

I had to come to a stop as I joined a long line of cars waiting to turn into the campus circle in front of the dorms. As I waited, I pulled my sunglasses off and checked my face in the rearview mirror.

I'd been getting worried the swelling and bruising from surgery wouldn't go down in time. But it finally had; there was just the faintest puffiness that I couldn't quite cover with makeup. I mentally amended my cover story: I'd been partying hard the night before, enjoying one last night with my dear friends.

I'd spun my cover story out of a fantasy I'd had when I was a kid, imagining I had half-a-dozen close-as-hell girlfriends who were my absolute ride-or-die besties. Now I was bringing my imaginary friends back, pretending that I'd left them in my hometown, where we'd played lacrosse together. I even had photos starring me and a couple of deep fakes, sitting on the front porch of a house I'd never been to, or standing pink-cheeked with our arms around each other's shoulders and red Solo cups in hand.

The face staring back at me in the mirror was pretty: high cheekbones, delicate nose, large, hooded eyes that were a startling shade of violet. I'd picked my new face out carefully. But I couldn't quite bring myself to put contact lenses over my irises, even though I knew I really should. They were the one connection I had with my birth mother, and I owed her some kind of debt.

It wasn't like me to be so emotional. "You're going to get yourself hurt being stupid," I mouthed at myself, watching my bright pink lips move, before I slipped my sunglasses back on to hide the swelling.

I didn't know then how right I was.

Half an hour later, the line of cars had finally crept forward until I was parked in front of the dorm. I checked in, then popped the trunk of my car and slung my duffel bag over my shoulder. I didn't own much, but I'd definitely have to make more trips.

The sun was shining and the campus was beautiful. The students streaming around me while unpacking their cars with their parents all seemed so happy. It made me feel like an outsider, because I was alone. I wouldn't have wanted to bring my father. Just imagining him in this scene was like imagining the beautiful setting slowly being infested by a dark poisonous blot.

"Let me help you." The voice was deep and sexy, and I spun to find myself facing a tall, good-looking guy with broad shoulders and a powerful body.

Chapter 1

He flashed me a boyish smile. "It's a service our frat offers everyone. Whether or not they're a pretty girl."

He'd towed over a bright yellow rolling caddy. Behind him, another guy was pushing a caddy into the dorm while a girl and her parents walked behind him.

"I might not be a pretty girl, but I'll take the help," I said.

He grinned at me like he knew I knew better, then began to unload the boxes in the trunk into the cart. I stood back and watched him. There was no reason he'd open the tire well and see the weapons hidden inside, but I couldn't help feeling wary.

"What's your room number?" he asked.

I normally wouldn't volunteer any additional information about myself to strangers. In my experience, being casual with your personal information was a great way to end up locked in a wooden box.

Be normal, Delilah...Aurora. Shit.

"Four-twelve," I said, giving him a smile.

When we reached my new room, it already seemed full. A girl with long blonde hair, her parents, and a surprising number of small children seemed to fill the room.

"Oh! Get out of the way, Patrick," the blonde girl said, tugging one of the people out of the way of the frat boy and his caddy. She smiled at me, her eyes crinkling at the corners. "You must be Aurora!"

"You must be Jenna!"

"It's so nice to meet you!" She hugged me.

I'd exchanged a few emails with my new roommate. We weren't really on hugging terms but I was good at adapting to what other people wanted from me. So I hugged her back and smiled. She seemed genuinely warm and sweet just within a few seconds of meeting her, although that could always be an act.

She quickly introduced me to her parents, and to her three

younger siblings who had all come along to help her settle into her new dorm.

"Let me get the circus out of here while you unpack," she said, trying to shoo her family out. "Do you have family?"

Here. She meant here.

But I would've said no anyway. I shook my head.

"Okay! Then once I get them to give me some space, we'll go to dinner tonight. Six?" She called over her shoulder as she gently shoved her father out the door.

"Six is good," I answered.

The room felt quiet after they left. I sat down on the mattress, feeling exhausted after only a few moments of being Aurora. My whole life had been a cover story; why was this so tiring now?

Maybe I just wanted to be myself.

Then I thought about what kind of results would come up if I googled *Delilah Kane,* and I knew, no, that wasn't what I wanted.

I just wished I could genuinely *be* someone else.

* * *

By six o'clock, I'd unpacked my belongings into my room. I was glad that Jenna wasn't here to see me pull the tags from some of my clothing and hastily discard them, covering them up with crumpled paper at the bottom of the trash bin. I'd had to buy everything new, enough to make it look like I had a real past. I'd scuffed up my shoes in a hotel room, washed some of my new clothes and run them through several dryer cycles on hot, but I hadn't had the chance to do that to all of them.

By six fifteen, I thought Jenna wasn't coming back after all, and I was relieved. This would be so much easier if my room-mate wasn't nice.

Then the door swung open and she rushed in. "Oh good, you're still here! I'm sorry I'm late!"

"No problem," I said, feeling a sudden sense of dread about heading down to the dining room. "I knew you wouldn't abandon me."

She laughed. "No, freshmen have to stick together. Especially around here!"

I wanted to know why, but she was already kicking the rubber wedge that held the door open, holding it for me to go with her.

As we headed down to the dining hall, she prattled on, "I wouldn't miss dinner tonight anyway. The frat that helped our dorm move in will be eating with us tonight, and I want eye candy as much as I want some chicken tendies."

I had to smile. "How do you know everything that's going on around here? I'm pretty sure that *eye candy* wasn't in the schedule *I* got from the school."

"Oh, I'm a legacy," she said lightly. "My parents met here and fell in love here! My mom didn't just get her Mrs. degree though, she also did pre-med here."

"She's a doctor?"

She nodded. "And my dad's a mechanical engineer. Don't even get him started talking about gardening—he's engineered all these automatic watering systems and grow lights. If you walk past our basement windows in the spring and see the glow, you'd think he was growing something besides tomato plants."

"What are you going to major in?"

"Pre-med. Not because of my mom," she added quickly. "I want to be a completely different kind of doctor. She's a dermatologist. I am not devoting my life to other people's acne!"

Jenna was easy to talk to, especially since she did most of the talking anyway. The two of us separated in the busy, noisy cafeteria, and by the time I'd begun to load up my tray, I felt a little lost and alone.

But then Jenna waved at me manically from across the cafeteria. She clearly didn't care if anyone side-eyed her nonstop enthusiasm. It was refreshing.

And dangerous.

No, just refreshing, I reminded myself. Just because I knew how dark the world could be, I couldn't stop trying to believe in the happier, brighter version that co-existed right alongside it.

I walked over to Jenna and let her chatter wash over me as I took in the students around us. People were already forming into groups...or trying to. We were such pack animals.

There was a change in the air, a sudden tension, a bit of a hush. I looked up, curious about what had driven the change.

Four of the most good-looking guys I'd ever seen had just walked into the room. But what was fascinating to me wasn't the perfectly styled hair above handsome faces or the broad shoulders and athletic bodies.

It was the way they commanded a room, the way everyone had stopped for a second when they saw them. My heart suddenly beat a warning. They seemed to be in a good mood, getting food, making small talk.

But they bled a sense of power and certainty that I knew. These guys were predators.

"See what I mean about eye candy?" Jenna said, because that girl was oblivious to danger.

"Who are they?" I asked.

"Cain, Remington, Pax, and Stellan." She pointed at each of them in turn, and I sighed under my breath. She was going to draw their attention to us. "Four stars of the school."

"Really? We're not in high school anymore."

"Cain is an amazing quarterback," she gushed.

Maybe we were still in high school. Maybe high school never really ends.

What a depressing thought.

"Pax and Remington kill it on the soccer field together," she said. "And Stellan is the captain of the hockey team."

"Jocks," I said. "Oh, fantastic. I love jocks."

I glanced over my shoulder at them again. They were surrounded by girls.

"Everyone loves them," Jenna added.

"Probably not as much as they love themselves."

Jenna laughed, but I meant it.

I couldn't help keeping a wary eye on them as I continued to get my food.

I hadn't met many men like them in my life, but all the ones I had known?

They were trouble.

Read the rest of the book here.

Sneak Preview

Want to read about some other hockey psychos in the same world as No Pucking Way? Keep reading for the standalone hockey romance, The Pucking Wrong Number. Available on Amazon and KU HERE.

The Pucking Wrong Number by C. R. Jane

Copyright © 2023 by C. R. Jane

All rights reserved.

For permissions contact:

crjaneauthor@gmail.com

This book is a work of fiction. Names, characters, businesses, places, events, locales, and incidents are either the products of the author's imagination or used in a fictitious manner. Any resemblance to actual persons, living or dead, or actual events is purely coincidental.

Cover Design: Cassie Chapman/Opulent Designs

Photographer: Cadwallader Photography

Editing: Jasmine J.

Prologue
Monroe

"Monroe. My pretty little girl," Mama slurs from the couch. She's staring up at the ceiling, and even though she's saying my name, I know she's not talking to me. Or at least the me that's standing right here, scrubbing at the vomit stain she left on the floor. She's talking to the me from the past, or wherever it is her brain takes her when she's high as a kite.

There's a knock on the door, and I glance at it fearfully, dread churning through my insides. Because I know who it is. One of her "customers" as Mama calls them.

The door opens without either of us saying anything. I'm not sure Mama even heard the knock. In steps a sweaty, pale-faced man that I've seen once or twice before. He has rosy cheeks and a belly that protrudes over his jeans. Like a perverse Santa Claus. Not that I believe in that guy anymore. He's certainly never come to our place on Christmas Eve.

The man's eyes gleam as he stares at me, but then Mama groans in a weird way, and his attention goes to her.

"Roxanne," he says in a sing-song voice as he makes his way over there.

I want to say something. Anything. Tell him that Mama's in no shape for company, but I know it's no use. Besides, Mama would be furious with me later on if she missed out on the money she needs to get her fix.

I leave the room and lock myself in the one bedroom we have in this place. Mama and I share the room, but more often than not, she can't make it any further than the couch.

The disgusting noises I've learned to hate start, so I turn on the radio, trying to drown them out. I fall into a fitful sleep, and my dreams are haunted by the image of a healthy mother that cares more about me than she does about escaping the life she created.

I wake with a start, panic blurring the edges of the room until I can convince my brain that everything's fine.

Except everything doesn't feel fine. It's so quiet. Way too quiet.

I creep towards the door, pressing my ear against it to see if I can hear anything.

But there's nothing.

I slowly open the door and peek out into the room. There's no sign of the man, or my mother. Thinking the coast is clear, I make my way out of my room, only to come to a screeching halt when I see my mother on the ground by the front door, a pile of green liquid by her face.

I sigh, thinking of the clean-up ahead. Again. I hate these men. Every time they come here, they take a piece of her, while leaving her with nothing. It's always like this after they're done with her.

When I walk over with a rag and bucket, I see Mama is shaking, tears streaming down her face. She's a scary gray color I don't think I've ever seen before.

"Mama," I whisper, reaching down to touch her face, only to flinch at how icy cold her skin is. Her eyes suddenly shoot open, causing me to jump. They're even more bloodshot than normal. Her bony hand claws at my shirt, and she frantically pulls me closer to her. Her lip is bruised and bloody. The bastard must've gotten rough.

"Don't let 'em taze your heart," she slurs, incomprehensibly.

"Mama?" I ask, worry thick in my voice.

"Don't...let a man...take your heart," she spits out. "Don't let him..." Her words fade away and her chest rises with one big inhale...before she goes perfectly still.

"Mama!" I whimper, shaking her over and over again.

But she never says another word. She's just gone, like a flame extinguished in a dark room.

And I'm all alone, with her last words forever ringing in my ears.

Chapter 1

Monroe

I sat on the edge of my bed, staring out the window into the dark, seemingly starless sky. Freedom was so close I could taste it.

18.

It felt like I'd been waiting my whole life for this moment. For this specific birthday. The thought of finally being able to leave this place, to start my life, on my own terms...it helped get me through each day.

I knew it would be difficult when I left. I only had my scrimpy savings from my after school job at the grocery store to start my life. But I'd do whatever it took to make something of myself.

Something more than the empty shell my mother had left me that day.

I'd been in the foster system since I was ten years old, the day after that fateful night where I'd lost her. Everyone wanted to adopt a baby, and a baby I had not been. I'd gone through what seemed like a hundred different homes at this point, but my current home was where I'd managed to stay the longest.

Chapter 1

Unfortunately.

My foster parents, Mr. and Mrs. Detweiler, and their son Ripley, seemed like nice people at first, but over time, things had changed. They were different now.

Mrs. Detweiler, Marie, had come to think of me as her live-in maid. I was all for helping out around the house, but when they got up as a collective group after every meal and left everything to me to clean up—as well as every other chore around the house—it was too much.

Someday, hopefully in the near future, I would never clean someone else's toilet again.

While I could deal with manual labor for another month, it was Mr. Detweiler, Todd, who had become a major problem. His actions had grown increasingly creepy, his longing stares and lingering glances making me sick. Everything he said to me had an underlying meaning...was an innuendo. He'd started talking about my birthday more, like he wanted to remind me of it for reasons far different than the promise of freedom it represented to me. I'm not sure it had even occurred to any of them yet that I was actually allowed to leave after that day. Both my birthday and high school graduation were the same week. Perfect timing. I just hoped he could control himself and keep his hands off me long enough to get to that point. Some people might not think a high school graduation was anything special, but to me, it represented *everything*.

Ripley was fine, I guess. He was more like a potato than a person, which was better than other things he could be. His eyes skipped over me when we were in the same room, like I didn't actually exist. And maybe I didn't exist to him. As long as his bed was made every day, and he had food on the table, and toilet paper stocked to wipe his ass, he could care less. He was much too involved in his video games to care about the world around him.

I glanced at the clock. It was 4:55pm, time to get dinner started before Mr. Detweiler got home from work. Sighing, I absentmindedly smoothed my faded quilt that Mrs. Detweiler had brought home from who knows where, and headed out to the hallway and down to the kitchen. The house was a three bedroom rambler in an okay part of town. It was nicer than other places I'd stayed, but I'd found that didn't matter all that much. The hearts beating inside the home held a much greater significance than how nice, or not nice, the house actually was.

I'm sure I could have been perfectly happy in the hovel I'd started life in with my mother...if only she'd been different.

I came to a screeching halt, and panic laced my insides, when I walked into the kitchen and saw Mr. Detweiler leaning against the laminate counter. How had I missed him coming into the house? I couldn't recall hearing the garage door opening.

He was nursing his favorite bottle of beer, which was actually the fanciest thing in the kitchen, costing far more than any of the other food they bought. Todd Detweiler was still dressed in the baggy suit he wore to the accounting office he worked at. He had a receding hairline that rivaled any I'd seen, so he brushed all the hair forward, carefully styling it to a point on his forehead right above his watery blue eyes.

He raised an eyebrow at the fact I was still frozen in place. But he usually didn't get home until 6:30, long enough for me to get dinner on the table and hide away until they were done.

"Well, hello there, Monroe," he drawled, my name sounding dirty coming from his lips.

I schooled my face and steeled my insides, taking methodical steps towards the fridge like his presence hadn't disarmed me.

"Hello," I answered pleasantly, hating the way I could feel

his gaze stroking across my skin. Like I was an object to be coveted rather than a person.

I knew I was pretty. The spitting image of my mother when she was young. But just like with her, my looks had only been a curse, forever designed to attract assholes whose only goal was to use and abuse me.

I reached into the fridge to grab the bowl of chicken I'd put in there earlier to defrost...when suddenly he was behind me. Close enough that if I moved, he'd be pressed against me.

"Is there something you need?" I asked, trying to keep the edge of hysteria out of my voice. His hand settled on my hip and I squeezed my eyes shut, cursing the universe.

He leaned close, his breath a whisper against my skin. "You've been thinking about it, haven't you?" Todd's breath stunk of beer, a smell that would prevent me from ever trying it, no matter how expensive and nice it was supposed to be.

"I—I'm not sure what you're talking about, sir." I grabbed the chicken and tried to stand , hoping he would back away. But the only thing he did was straighten up, so our bodies were against each other. I tried to move away, but his hand squeezed against my hip. Hard.

"I need to get this chicken on the stove," I said pleasantly, like I wasn't dying inside at the feel of his touch.

"Such a tease," he murmured with a small chuckle. "I love how you like to play games. Just going to make it so much better when we stop." There was a bulge growing harder against my lower back, and I bit down on my lip hard enough that the salty tang of blood flooded my taste buds.

My hands were shaking, the water sloshing around in the bowl. An idiot could figure out what he was talking about.

"Have you noticed how much I love to collect things?" he asked randomly, finally releasing my hip and stepping back.

I moved quickly towards the sink, setting the bowl inside

and going to grab the breadcrumbs I needed to coat the chicken breasts with for dinner.

"I have noticed that," I finally responded, after he'd taken a step towards me when I didn't answer fast enough.

How could anyone miss it? Todd collected...beer bottles. Both walls of the garage had various cans and bottles lined up neatly on shelves. There were so many of them that you could barely see the wall—not sure how social services never seemed concerned he might have a drinking problem with that amount of empties. But Todd was never worried about that. He added at least five to the wall every day.

"Virgins happen to be my favorite thing to collect."

I'd been holding a carton of eggs, and I dropped them, shocked that he'd outright said that, shells and yolk ricocheting everywhere.

Just then, Mrs. Detweiler ambled in, her gaze flicking between her husband and me suspiciously. "What's going on in here?" she asked, her eyes stopping on the ruined eggs all over the floor.

Marie had once been a pretty woman, but like her husband, her attempt to hold onto youth was a miserable failure. Right now, she was wearing a too tight flowered dress that resembled a couch from the eighties. It accented every roll, and there was a fine sheen of sweat across her heavily made up face, probably from the effort she'd had to make to get out of her armchair and storm in here. Her hair was a harsh, bottle-black color, and though she attempted to curl and keep it nice, it was thin and limp and I'm sure disappointing for her.

I usually didn't pay attention to looks; I knew better than most they could be deceiving, but Todd and Marie Detweiler's appearances were too in your face to ignore.

"Just an accident, honey," he drawled, walking towards her and pulling her into a soul sickening kiss that made me want to puke considering Marie most likely had no idea where else that mouth had been.

They walked out of the kitchen without a backward glance, leaving me a shaking, miserable mess as I cleaned up the eggs and tried to make dinner.

If that interaction hadn't sealed the deal that waiting for my birthday to leave wasn't an option...the next night would.

I was in bed, tossing and turning as I did every night. When your mind was as haunted as mine was, sleep was elusive, a fervent goal I would never successfully master. I'd never had a night where I could relax, where the memories of the past didn't creep in and plague my thoughts.

It was 3 am, and I was on the verge of giving up if I couldn't fall back asleep soon.

Light footsteps sounded down the hallway by my door. I frowned, as everyone had gone to bed long ago. I knew their habits like they were my own at this point.

Was someone in the house? Someone who didn't belong?

The footsteps stopped outside my door, and shivers crept up my spine.

"Hello?" I whisper squeaked, feeling like a fool for speaking at all when the doorknob tried to turn, getting caught on the lock I was lucky enough to have.

I felt like the would-be victim in a horror movie as I slid out of bed and yanked my lamp from the nightstand, prepared to use it as a weapon if need be.

The person outside fiddled with the lock and it clicked, signaling it had been disengaged.

There was a long pause as I stared breathlessly at the door, waiting for the inevitable.

The door creaked open and a hairy hand—that I recognized —appeared.

It was Mr. Detweiler's.

Chapter 1

I didn't think, I just started screaming, knowing I had one chance to get him away from my room.

I needed to wake up his wife. With their bedroom right down the hall, I just needed to be loud enough.

Sure enough, a second after I started screaming, the door banged shut, and footsteps dashed away. A moment later, I heard the Detweilers' bedroom door fly open, and then a moment after that, my door cracked against the wall and Marie's harried form was there. Her chest was heaving, pushing against the two sizes too small negligee she was wearing–that made me want to burn my eyes–and her gaze was crazed as they dashed around the room, finally falling to me standing there in the middle of it, a lamp clutched to my chest.

A red mottled rash spread across her chest and up to her cheeks as anger flooded her features.

"What the fuck is wrong with you?"

"Someone was trying to get into my room. Someone unlocked the door."

I didn't say it was her husband, because that would give me even more problems.

A moment later, Todd was there, faking a yawn with a glass of water in his hand. "What's going on?" he asked casually. Our eyes locked, and in that moment, he knew I knew it was him. His features were taunting, daring me to say something, like his wife would ever believe anything that came out of my mouth when it came to him.

"The girl's saying someone was breaking into her room," Marie scoffed before pausing for a second and examining her husband. "Why were you up?"

The way her lips were pursed, the way her flush deepened —it told me a lot. Apparently, Marie wasn't so unaware of her husband's true nature after all.

Not that she would ever do anything about it.

"I was getting some water when I heard Monroe scream. But I didn't hear anyone else in the house." His gaze feigned concern. "Are you sure you didn't just have a nightmare?"

I stared at him for a long, tense moment before I took a breath. "Maybe that's all it was," I finally whispered, eliciting a loud huff from Marie.

"Get yourself under control, you brat. The rest of us need our sleep!" she snapped, whirling away and leaving, curses streaming from her mouth as she walked back to her room.

Todd lingered, a smug grin curling across his pathetic lips. "Sleep well, Monroe," he purred, a firm promise in his eyes that he would be back.

And that he would finish what he started.

I fell to my knees as soon as the door closed, sobs wracking through my body.

I'd never felt so alone.

He had ruined everything. A month away from a high school diploma, and he'd just torn it from my grasp.

If Todd got his hands on me, he would break me. And I wasn't talking about my body—I was talking about my soul.

The image of my mother's desolate, destroyed features flashed through my mind.

That couldn't be my story. It couldn't.

I had to leave. Tomorrow. I had no other option.

* * *

The Detweilers lived in a small town right outside Houston. I decided Dallas would be my destination, about four hours away. I'd never been there before, but the ticket price wasn't too bad, and it was big. Just what I needed to hopefully disappear. Surely the Detweilers wouldn't try and go that far, not with only a month left of state support on the line. I bet they wouldn't even tell anyone I was gone. They'd want that last check.

I didn't let myself think about what my virginity would be worth to Todd. Hopefully, "easy" was one of his requisites, and he would forget me as soon as I disappeared.

I went to school, my heart hurting the whole day. I'd never been one to make close friends—when you never knew when you'd be moving on, it was best not to make any close connections—but I found myself wishing I had longer with the acquaintances I did have. I walked the familiar hallways, wondering if it would have been hard to say goodbye at graduation, or if I was simply feeling the loss of my dream.

Mama had never graduated from high school. In her lucid moments, though, even when I was little, she would sometimes talk about her dreams for me. Dreams of walking across that stage.

I'd just have to walk across a college stage, I told myself firmly, promising myself I'd get a GED and make that possible.

After school, I went to the H.E.B. grocery store where I worked, putting even more hustle in than usual since I'd be a disappearing act after this shift. The timing worked out, because it was payday, and I was able to get one more check to take with me. Every penny would count.

After my shift, I bought a prepaid phone since I didn't want to take my Detweiler phone with me. Knowing them, they'd probably try and get the police to bring me back by saying I'd stolen their property. A part of me was a little afraid they could track me with it too. I knew I wasn't living in a spy thriller...but still, better to be safe than sorry.

Once I got home, I packed a small bag with some clothes, my new phone, and the cash I'd saved up. And then I sat on my bed, hands squeezing together with anxiety.

I didn't have a good plan. For as much as I'd been dreaming

of getting away, my plans were more fluid than concrete. And all of them had depended on me having a high school diploma so I could get a better job, as well as not having to look over my shoulder every second for fear the Detweilers were after me. The state also had a support system for kids coming out of foster care, and I'd been hopeful I'd have that to lean on.

But I could do this.

I cleaned up after dinner. Marie had ordered pizza, so it didn't take as much effort as usual. And then I sat in the corner of the living room, biding my time until I could say goodnight. It was a tricky thing. I had to escape tonight–late enough that they'd gone to bed, but not so late that Todd decided to give me another late night visit.

My departure was the definition of anticlimactic. My mind had conjured this image of the Detweilers running after me as I escaped with my bag out the window, the sound of a siren haunting the air as I ducked in and out of the bushes, trying to avoid the police.

But what really happened was that I slipped out the window, and everyone stayed asleep. I walked for an hour until I got to the Greyhound station, and no one came after me. The exhausted-looking attendant didn't even blink when I bought a ticket to Dallas.

It was nice for something to go my way every once in a blue moon.

The bus ride took twice as long as a car would have. And although I tried to catch a few hours of rest, I kept worrying I'd somehow miss my stop, so I never could slip into a deep sleep. My mind also couldn't help but race with thoughts of what my future held. Would I be able to make it on my own?

Despite my worries, a sense of relief flickered in my chest as the distance between Todd and me grew with each mile that passed.

Chapter 1

At least I could cross keeping my virginity safe off my list of to-do's.

When we finally arrived in Dallas, the morning sun was just peeking over the horizon. Even with the dilapidated buildings that surrounded the Greyhound station, I couldn't help but feel excitement. I was here. I'd made it. I may have never been to Dallas before, and I may not have known a single soul here, but I was determined to make a new life for myself.

This was my new beginning.

* * *

It took about twelve hours for the afterglow of my arrival to fade and for me to find myself on a park bench, debating whether I could actually fall asleep if I were to try. Or if it was even safe to attempt such a thing.

I'd gotten off the bus and was in the process of calling for a cab to take me to the teen shelter I'd found online. And then I'd been fucking pick pocketed while I looked the address up. They'd taken all the cash in my pocket that I'd pulled out for the cab, and swiped my phone right out of my hand.

You can bet I ran after them like a madwoman. But with a backpack containing all my earthly possessions weighing me down, the group of boys easily outran me.

I hadn't dared to spend any of the rest of the cash I had left, except to get a bag of chips from a gas station that had seen better days.

I'd walked all over for the rest of the day, trying to find the shelter, scared to ask for directions in case anyone got suspicious and reported to the authorities that I looked like a runaway teen.

Obviously, I never found the place, because there I was, on the park bench. Cold, hungry, and pissed off.

Chapter 1

And exhausted.

Apparently, when you hadn't slept for close to forty-eight hours, you could fall asleep anywhere, because eventually... that's exactly what I did.

* * *

I woke with a start, the feeling of someone watching me thick in my throat. Night had fallen, and a deep blue hue had settled over the park. The trees and bushes were indistinct shadows against the darkened sky. The street lamps had flickered to life, casting a warm glow on the path and the nearby benches. The light danced and swayed with the gentle breeze, casting long shadows on the ground. You could hear the rustling of leaves and the chirping of crickets.

I yelped when I saw a grizzled old man sitting next to me on the bench, a wildness in his gaze that matched the tattered clothing on his body. There was the scent of dirt and body odor wafting off him, and when he smiled at me, it was only with a few teeth.

"Oy. I've been a watchin'. Making sure you could sleep, my lady," he said in what was clearly an affected British accent.

I flinched at his words, even though they were perfectly friendly and kind, and scooted away from him.

"Oh, don't be afraid of Ole Bill. I'll watch out for ye."

I moved to jump off the bench and run away...but I also had a moment of hesitation. There was something so...wholesome about him. Once you got past his looks and his smell, obviously.

"This park's mine, but I can share. You go back to sleep, and I'll keep watch. Make sure the ruffians stay away," he continued. Even though I had yet to say anything to him.

I opened my mouth to reject his offer, but then he pulled a clean, brand new blanket with tags out of his grocery sack.

When he offered it to me...instead of talking...I found myself crying.

I sobbed and sobbed while he watched me frantically, throwing the blanket at me like it had the power to quell hysterical women's tears. When I still didn't stop crying, overwhelmed by the events of the past few days...and his kindness, he finally started to sing what I think was the worst rendition of "Eleanor Rigby" that I'd ever heard. Actually, it was the worst rendition of *any* song I'd ever heard.

But it worked, and I stopped crying.

"There, there, little duck. Go to sleep. Ole Bill will watch out for ya," he said soothingly after he'd finished the song—the last few lyrics definitely made up.

I was a smarter girl than that, I really was. But I was so freaking tired. And everything inside of me really wanted to trust him. After all, he had called me "little duck." Serial killers didn't have cute pet names for their victims, right?

"Just a couple of minutes," I murmured, and he nodded, smiling softly again with his crooked grin that I was quite fond of at that moment.

I drifted off into a fitful sleep, shivering from stress and exhaustion, and dreaming of better days.

When I woke up, it was far later than ten minutes. It was the rest of the night, actually.

Bill was still there, watching over me, and whistling softly to himself, like he hadn't just stayed up all night. My backpack was still under my head, the cash still in it, and at least I didn't *feel* like anyone had touched me.

Fuck, I'd gotten desperate, hadn't I?

"Do you have a place to stay, lassie?" he asked softly. I shook my head, biting down on my lip as I thought about spending another night on this bench.

"Ole Bill will take you to a good place. It's not as nice as my castle, but it will do," he said, gesturing to the park proudly as if it was in fact an English castle complete with a moat, and he was its ruler.

Despite the fact that he'd at least proven trustworthy enough not to do anything to me after a few hours, it was still pure desperation that had me following him to what I was hoping wasn't a trafficking ring, or something else equally heinous.

I relaxed a little as he took me to a slightly better part of town than where I'd been walking the day before. He chattered my ear off, all in that fake British accent, regaling me with stories about places I was sure he'd never visited.

Before I knew it, we were standing in front of the entrance to what appeared to be a fairly new shelter. The sign read that it was a women's shelter, and the sight made me want to cry once again.

"When you get in there, tell 'em Ole Bill sent you...they'll give you the royal treatment," he chortled, and tears filled my eyes for what seemed like the hundredth time—causing him to take a step away–probably fearing I would burst into hysterics again.

I hesitated for another moment before I finally ascended the steps that led to the shelter doors. Stopping halfway, I glanced back at Bill, who gave me another charmingly snaggle-toothed grin. "I see great things for you, little duck," he called after me when I continued to walk.

I knew I'd never forget him. He may have been homeless and slightly crazy, but he was also one of the kindest people I had ever met. He'd watched over me, a stranger, and helped me when I needed it the most.

As I walked inside, exhaustion still stretched across my shoulders, I strangely felt at peace right then that everything was going to work out.

Chapter 1

"Welcome to Haven," a kind woman murmured as I approached the front desk.

Haven indeed.

I could only hope.

Keep reading The Pucking Wrong Number here.

Acknowledgments

I've been having so much writing red flag hockey boyfriends that May and I decided that we needed to write one together. Getting back to my roots, RH, was just what the doctor ordered! Writing sweet psychos is a special kind of fun that I don't think I'll be getting tired of anytime soon. We can't wait to show you what else is in store for Kennedy and her men.

A few thank you's...

To our beta readers, Crystal, Blair, Mona, Janie, Patti, Janet, and Tanya, thank you for stepping in and helping us make our baby shine. We're so grateful that you take time out of your busy lives to read our words.

To Jasmine, our editor, thank you for always showing up for me. Thank you.

To Caitlin, thanks for supporting us in this crazy career.

And to you, the readers who make all our dreams come true. Thanks for embracing our crazy book boyfriends and allowing us to have fun for a living.

About C.R. Jane

A Texas girl living in Utah now, I'm a wife, mother, lawyer, and now author. My stories have been floating around in my head for years, and it has been a relief to finally get them down on paper. I'm a huge Dallas Cowboys fan and I primarily listen to Taylor Swift and hip hop...don't lie and say you don't too.

My love of reading started probably when I was three and it only made sense that I would start to create my own worlds since I was always getting lost in others'.

I like heroines who have to grow in order to become badasses, happy endings, and swoon-worthy, devoted, (and hot) male characters. If this sounds like you, I'm pretty sure we'll be friends.

I'm so glad to have you here...check out the links below for ways to hang out with me and more of my books you can read!

Visit my **Facebook** page to get updates.

Visit my Website.

Sign up for my newsletter to stay updated on new releases, find out random facts about me, and get access to different points of view from my characters.

Books by C.R. Jane

www.crjanebooks.com

The Sounds of Us Contemporary Series (complete series)

Remember Us This Way

Remember You This Way

Remember Me This Way

Broken Hearts Academy Series: A Bully Romance (complete duet)

Heartbreak Prince

Heartbreak Lover

Ruining Dahlia (Contemporary Mafia Standalone)

Ruining Dahlia

The Pucking Wrong Series (Hockey Romance Standalones)

The Pucking Wrong Number

The Pucking Wrong Guy

The Pucking Wrong Date

The Fated Wings Series (Paranormal series)

First Impressions

Forgotten Specters

The Fallen One (a Fated Wings Novella)

Forbidden Queens

Frightful Beginnings (a Fated Wings Short Story)

Faded Realms

Faithless Dreams

Fabled Kingdoms

Forever Hearts

The Darkest Curse Series

Forget Me

Lost Passions

Hades Redemption Series

The Darkest Lover

The Darkest Kingdom

Monster & Me Duet Co-write with Mila Young

Monster's Temptation

Monster's Obsession

Academy of Souls Co-write with Mila Young (complete series)

School of Broken Souls

School of Broken Hearts

School of Broken Dreams

School of Broken Wings

Fallen World Series Co-write with Mila Young (complete series)

Bound

Broken

Betrayed

<u>Belong</u>

Thief of Hearts Co-write with Mila Young (complete series)

Darkest Destiny

Stolen Destiny

Broken Destiny

Sweet Destiny

Kingdom of Wolves Co-write with Mila Young

Wild Moon

Wild Heart

Wild Girl

Wild Love

Wild Soul

Wild Kiss

Stupid Boys Series Co-write with Rebecca Royce

Stupid Boys

Dumb Girl

Crazy Love

Breathe Me Duet Co-write with Ivy Fox (complete)

Breathe Me

Breathe You

Breathe Me Duet

Love & Hate Co-write with Ivy Fox

The Boy I Once Hated

The Girl I Once Loved

Rich Demons of Darkwood Series Co-write with May Dawson (complete series)

Make Me Lie

Make Me Beg

Make Me Wild

Make Me Burn

Make Me Queen

Books By May Dawson

May Dawson's Website

The Lost Fae Series

Wandering Queen

Fallen Queen

Rebel Queen

Lost Queen

Their Shifter Princess Series

Their Shifter Princess

Their Shifter Princess 2: Pack War

Their Shifter Princess 3: Coven's Revenge

Their Shifter Academy Series

A Prequel Novella

Unwanted

Unclaimed

Undone

Unforgivable

Unstoppable

The Wild Angels & Hunters Series:

Wild Angels

Fierce Angels

Dirty Angels

Chosen Angels

Academy of the Supernatural

Her Kind of Magic

His Dangerous Ways

Their Dark Imaginings

Ashley Landon, Bad Medium

Dead Girls Club

The True and the Crown Series

One Kind of Wicked

Two Kinds of Damned

Three Kinds of Lost

Four Kinds of Cursed

Five Kinds of Love

Rich Demons of Darkwood Series Co-write with C.R. Jane

Make Me Lie

Make Me Beg

* * *

Subscribe to May Dawson's Newsletter to receive exclusive content, latest updates, and giveaways.

Join Here

About May Dawson

May Dawson lives in Virginia with her husband and two red-headed wild babies. Before her second career as an author, she spent eight years in the Marine Corps and visited forty-two countries and all seven continents (including a research station in the Antarctic). You can always find her on Facebook in <u>May Dawson's Wild Angels</u> or on the internet at MayDawson.com

Printed in Great Britain
by Amazon

41008536R00208